Praise for

The Crescent Moon Tearoom

"Sivinski's novel is positively delightful... The result is a tale of family, love, and the things that make a house a home. A delightfully sweet and cozy novel that's as comforting as a warm cup of tea."
—*Kirkus Reviews* (starred review)

"This cozy fantasy leads the sisters and readers down a primrose path of fear and foreboding—revealing villains around every corner—only to turn delightfully on its heel and magically change into a story of love and hope and a sisterhood that will endure as fate takes the hand it was meant to in each of their paths."
—*Library Journal*, starred review, Fall Fiction Preview Reviews Director Pick, and Debut of the Month

"Sivinski's droll telling details the lovable Quigleys with all their quirks and charm, each with their own moving emotional arc... With its sweetness, realistic challenges, and satisfying resolution, *The Crescent Moon Tearoom* is a rare pleasure. Readers will miss the Quigley sisters at this novel's end."
—*Shelf Awareness*

"Sivinksi's debut takes place in a deftly built but lightly fantastical world in which those with magical powers exist in the shadows of the non-magical world. Exploring themes of family, destiny, and secrets, this cozy historical fantasy will appeal to relationship fiction readers as much as it will to genre fans."

—*Booklist*

"Charming... the fierce love between the protagonists rings true, and the rich, cozy setting will make readers wish they had their own warm cup of tea."

—*Publishers Weekly*

"With a dash of fate and a sprinkle of fortune-telling, Stacy Sivinski has given readers an impossibly endearing tale about three tea-reading witches lured their separate ways. Steeped in magic and sisterhood, *The Crescent Moon Tearoom* will enchant and delight readers with its whimsical charm. Like brewing a favorite tea in a treasured mug, there's something uniquely inviting about this book. It's sure to be a reader favorite!"

—Sarah Penner, *New York Times* bestselling author of *The Lost Apothecary*

"Charming, uplifting, and utterly enchanting. The Quigley sisters—what's more magical than witchy triplets?—and their lovely, cozy stories will steal your heart."

—Lana Harper, *New York Times* bestselling author of the Witches of Thistle Grove series

"Stacy Sivinski's *The Crescent Moon Tearoom* is a decadent tale that wraps you up in its enchanting world like a warm embrace. The magic system is flawlessly executed and the characters are so real that you long to share a cup of tea with them. An exquisitely crafted story about the threads of fate that bind us even when it seems they're pushing us apart and how, as we grow into ourselves, we also grow into our power. I may not be a fortune teller, but I don't need to be able to decipher tea leaves to know that readers will fall deeply in love with this charming novel and all the emotions that come with it."

—Breanne Randall, *New York Times* bestselling author of *The Unfortunate Side Effects of Heartbreak and Magic*

"Make your appointment for *The Crescent Moon Tearoom*. It's warm and cozy as a cup of tea on a chilly evening. You won't regret meeting the magical Quigley Sisters."

—Meg Shaffer, *USA Today* bestselling author of *The Wishing Game*

"*The Crescent Moon Tearoom* is a truly lovely book—beautifully written and infused with lushly warm, delicious imagery that makes reading it a wonderfully cozy experience. Your tastebuds—along with your imagination—will delight at so many of the descriptions! The three Quigley sisters are each lovable in their own way and the magic of their world is fascinating, weaving through the story like a dream. This is the sort of book you'll want to tuck yourself into, and are sure to return to whenever in need of some literary comfort."

—India Holton, international bestselling author of *The Ornithologist's Field Guide to Love*

"In this enchanting tale of sisterhood, the Quigleys will have you believing in magic as they navigate the delicate balance between destiny and self-discovery. *The Crescent Moon Tearoom* is a captivating story that brews a spellbinding blend of fate, love, and the power of family. Stacy Sivinski has created three sisters whose wisdom and kindness will be remembered long after the last page is turned. Please serve with a warm cup of your favorite tea."

—Susan Wiggs, bestselling author of
The Lost and Found Bookshop

"Prepare to fall in love with the singular Quigley sisters in this heart-warming tale whose every page will make you feel as though you're basking in the glow of a cozy fire. As lovely and surprising as life itself, *The Crescent Moon Tearoom* will delight and entertain even as it challenges you to reflect on where sisterhood ends and selfhood begins."

—Bianca Marais, international bestselling author of
The Witches of Moonshyne Manor

"Charming, heartwarming and enchanting, Stacy Sivinski's *The Crescent Moon Tearoom* is a delight! Themes of sisterhood, agency, and fate are brewed together with witchy hijinks and plenty of coziness, all of which creates a captivating read. I loved spending time with the Quigley sisters—this book has me under its spell."

—Karma Brown, bestselling author of
What Wild Women Do

"*The Crescent Moon Tearoom* is a wonderfully imaginative and bewitching novel about the bonds of sisterhood and the unpredictability of fate. If you've ever peeked into a teacup, hoping to see your future, you'll enjoy Stacy Sivinski's whimsical story about a family of witches seeking to find their true paths against mysterious odds. This novel shows readers through spellbinding prose and charming characters that we can rely on the power of memories and love to bring us home."

—Celestine Martin, author of
Witchful Thinking

ALSO BY STACY SIVINSKI

The Crescent Moon Tearoom

The Witching Moon Manor

~ a novel ~

Stacy Sivinski

ATRIA PAPERBACK

New York • Amsterdam/Antwerp • London • Toronto • Sydney/Melbourne • New Delhi

An Imprint of Simon & Schuster, LLC
1230 Avenue of the Americas
New York, NY 10020

For more than 100 years, Simon & Schuster has championed authors and the stories they create. By respecting the copyright of an author's intellectual property, you enable Simon & Schuster and the author to continue publishing exceptional books for years to come. We thank you for supporting the author's copyright by purchasing an authorized edition of this book.

No amount of this book may be reproduced or stored in any format, nor may it be uploaded to any website, database, language-learning model, or other repository, retrieval, or artificial intelligence system without express permission. All rights reserved. Inquiries may be directed to Simon & Schuster, 1230 Avenue of the Americas, New York, NY 10020 or permissions@simonandschuster.com.

This book is a work of fiction. Any references to historical events, real people, or real places are used fictitiously. Other names, characters, places, and events are products of the author's imagination, and any resemblance to actual events or places or persons, living or dead, is entirely coincidental.

Copyright © 2025 by Stacy Sivinski

All rights reserved, including the right to reproduce this book or portions thereof in any form whatsoever. For information, address Atria Books Subsidiary Rights Department, 1230 Avenue of the Americas, New York, NY 10020.

First Atria Paperback edition October 2025

ATRIA PAPERBACK and colophon are trademarks of Simon & Schuster, LLC

Simon & Schuster strongly believes in freedom of expression and stands against censorship in all its forms. For more information, visit BooksBelong.com.

For information about special discounts for bulk purchases, please contact Simon & Schuster Special Sales at 1-866-506-1949 or business@simonandschuster.com.

The Simon & Schuster Speakers Bureau can bring authors to your live event. For more information or to book an event, contact the Simon & Schuster Speakers Bureau at 1-866-248-3049 or visit our website at www.simonspeakers.com.

Manufactured in the United States of America

1 3 5 7 9 10 8 6 4 2

Library of Congress Contol Number: 2024055248

ISBN 978-1-6680-5841-1
ISBN 978-1-6680-5842-8 (ebook)

For Jamie and Daniel

PROLOGUE

A Bell

*Appears just before something
is about to awaken.*

It was a well-known secret that something was not quite right about the house tucked at the very center of the street.

For one, strange silhouettes always stretched across the vast marble facade whenever the sun began to set and the gas lamps flickered to life. Anyone who lingered on the sidewalk and turned their face toward the darkened windows would see shadows twisting there that sometimes took the shape of people, though there wasn't another soul to be found along the road.

For another, whenever the windows were left open, whispers drifted into the neighbors' homes, carrying with them notes of longing and a desire to be heard. They snuck through the cracks in the plaster and sank into silences, causing gooseflesh to rise along the necks of those who came across the sound. And on nights when the light of a full moon flickered against the manor, the murmurs grew louder, the soft hushes sharpening into something that sounded like secrets slipping through a keyhole.

But because these oddities were too fantastical to put into words, no one spoke of them aloud. After catching sight of the dancing shadows in the corners of their eyes, the neighbors simply shifted their gaze to the more practical-looking brick homes on the other side of the street. And when those hushed whispers emerged between the regular rhythm of chores, whoever heard them turned their focus to the clicking of their knitting needles, muttering to themselves that nothing good ever came from giving way to flights of fancy.

For it is easier to brush aside the mere possibility of magic than to consider that it might be resting beneath the familiar comfort of the everyday.

In fact, the only outward sign that the neighbors suspected something was amiss was the way they let their pace quicken as they shuffled past the house. It was an arrangement that suited everyone perfectly well, and so these peculiarities remained an open secret to the mutual contentment of all.

The problem now, though, was that the house had gone entirely silent.

Though shadows could still be seen on the other side of the windows, they didn't reach beneath the panes and trickle onto the sidewalks. And even when the neighbors grew still and strained to hear the raspy voices that had always been waiting for a chance to speak before, they couldn't hear anything but the creaking of their floorboards.

It was one thing to have known about these oddities and brushed them aside, but to recognize that they were gone now meant acknowledging that they'd existed in the first place. And so, everyone grew warier, peeking between the gaps in their curtains to see if anything else was changing about the marble manor.

And one night, they did manage to catch a glimpse of something curious.

It happened just after the sun had well and truly set, when the man who lit the gas lamps had turned the corner and everyone was beginning to let the fires flickering in the grate ease the tensions of a busy day.

As a stillness settled along the street, they heard it: the barest of whispers creeping into the silent pause.

More than one inquisitive neighbor had risen from their chair then and gone to the window, where they parted the curtains just an inch so that they could peer outside.

At first, they couldn't find anything to be remarked upon about the house. Things were just as they had been when they'd passed by it on their way home only an hour or two before. After a moment, they wondered if they'd only imagined the sound and considered abandoning their posts by the glass panes.

But something kept them from moving back toward the familiar comfort of their hearths, and soon, their patience was rewarded.

A figure suddenly emerged at the bottom of the stoop, and everyone looking on gasped in surprise, wondering how the stranger had managed to slip out of thin air.

But after a moment, they realized that the visitor was merely wearing black, giving the illusion that he'd suddenly risen from the shadows of the sidewalk. When he pulled away his hat, though, they could see him easily enough, for his hair was shockingly white, nearly the same shade as the marble that all but glimmered in the light of the gas lamps.

The stranger stared up at the house then, and as his foot landed on the first step, the pulse of those gazing on from the other side of the windowpanes began to beat faster and faster, though they didn't understand why.

As the man came closer to the front door, the shadows started to slip beneath the sills, trailing toward him like they were trying to curl around his coattails and usher him inside.

When he came to rest at the threshold and reached toward the handle, the neighbors realized that they were all holding their breath, not daring to make a single sound as they waited to see what happened next.

For some reason, they half expected him to find the door locked, that he would turn around in disappointment and slip back into the darkness once more.

But something else happened that felt ordinary and spectacular all at once.

The door opened, and all the whispers that had faded from the silence of the everyday returned, quieter now but still noticeable to anyone who had heard them before.

As the neighbors listened to the soft murmurs creep through the floorboards, they saw the stranger hesitate before the threshold, as if he was just as surprised that the door had clicked open when his fingers touched the handle. And though his hand remained still, he took the barest step backward, the stiff rise of his shoulders hinting that a new burden had come to rest there.

But when he turned his face upward to peer at the shadows dancing through the panes, everyone pressed their cheeks a bit closer to their own windows and watched as the worry lines that marked his brow gave way to an unmistakable expression of determination.

Before they could guess what had brought about this sudden change, the man slipped into the house, snapping the door shut behind him.

And though the neighbors let out a sigh of relief as they returned to the warm chairs before their hearths, they couldn't help but think that the silence of the street had been replaced by something much more troublesome: questions so extraordinary that they might slip beyond the safe confines of their imagination.

CHAPTER 1

Rosemary
Symbolizes remembrance.

As the bells dangling from the front door chimed on the first day of the new year, the Crescent Moon was busy filling the shop with reminders instead of resolutions.

Though it knew that the customers who crossed the threshold were thinking of changes to come, the shop also understood that now wasn't the time to turn away from the past. Spring was the season for sweeping aside cobwebs and sorting through what should be packed away, not the height of winter, when the days were dark and the bitter bite of the wind made you want to cling to the things that were worth keeping.

And so, when most people were pulling down their wreaths and shaking their heads at the shadows left behind, the house was doing its best to infuse the tearoom with warm recollections, ones that made you sink deeper into homespun quilts and shift through the afternoon at a slower pace.

Like a man twirling his mustache, it spun fresh garland around all the banisters, tucking sticks of cedar and spools of oranges that had dried alongside nutmeg and cardamon among the greenery. Snippets of holly with bright red berries were scattered across the surface of burgundy tablecloths embroidered with miniature rows of shops similar to the ones that rested on either side of the Crescent Moon, their brick fronts covered in tiny snowflake stitches. And the sunlight spilling in from the frosted windows was softened so that the flames flickering atop the candlesticks took on the hue of stars waiting to be wished upon.

This particular mix of cloves and velvet brought the house back to years when little hands had grasped on to its window ledges in the hopes of peering at the street outside, still unconvinced that what awaited them beyond the cold glass was in any way more magical than the world within the shop.

The house had welcomed most of the changes of the last year, especially the ones that involved a bit of redecoration. It had drawn in a deep breath, stretched its beams and rafters, and settled into the enjoyable task of rearranging the front parlor and, if it was being honest, a few other nooks and crannies when its sole remaining occupant turned her head away. But that was long before Chicago's chill had set into its bones, and now it was determined to sit back and spend a bit of time burrowing into the warm memories that had been tucked to the side during the rush that always consumed the shop toward the end of each year.

If only its keeper could be convinced to feel the same way. . . .

"Don't worry, I'm going to find you a table," Anne Quigley insisted as she tried to usher her companions, Katherine and Celeste, through the quickly growing crowd. Long ago, the two women had been friends of Anne's mother, Clara, but if the way they beamed at their young hostess as she pulled them through the chaotic parlor was any indication, they'd grown equally close with her.

Though most businesses remained closed for the new year, it had seemed cruel to Anne to shut the front door on a day when so many were searching for the barest glimpse of the future. They needed a shred of certainty to steady themselves while flipping through the blank expanse of their calendars and wondering what those days might hold.

But now that the shop was overflowing with skirt trains and thick woolen cloaks, Anne was beginning to question her choice.

"I'm starting to think that adding a second floor wasn't enough," she heard Katherine murmur, her voice nearly lost among the sound of tinkling porcelain as she linked her arm through Anne's to avoid being trampled by a tea cart that seemed to be moving at the pace of a racehorse.

Anne felt the floorboards vibrate under her boots in anticipation and sighed.

"Don't give it any ideas," Anne whispered as she grasped Celeste with her other hand and pulled them both toward the spiral staircase tucked in the back of the room. "I caught it trying to build a solarium the other day."

As the three women twirled up the steps, Anne wished, not for the first time, that the house had chosen a more practical structure to lead up to the new addition. Though their customers seemed enchanted by it, the circular movement always left Anne feeling a bit disoriented whenever she reached the top, which she suspected was a strategic move on the part of the house, though it was going to take more than a dash of dizziness to distract Anne from the sweeping alterations it had made to the front parlor.

Last year, after Celeste lost her powers and Anne took over her place on the Council of Witches, it had been clear as crystal that the shop would need to change. Each of the Council members had different magical abilities and played an important part in keeping the coven safe by ensuring the threads of destiny remained intact, but Anne's role carried a special weight. As the city's Diviner, she looked toward the future, discovering problems and finding solutions before any trouble could snag the delicate fabric of their existence. Her new position would no doubt draw in an even greater crowd of witches eager to ensure they met a fortunate Fate, and that meant the Crescent Moon, like many other parts of Anne's life, needed to grow.

But even she hadn't predicted just how quickly the house would take matters into its own hands.

When Anne had sat down in the kitchen to calmly explain that they needed to make some improvements to the shop, she did her best to convince the house that the alterations should be as simple as possible. As soon as the words left her lips, though, all the walls had flashed a bright daisy yellow before the house cracked open the very center of the foundation, where it quickly got to work making so much noise that Anne's warnings were lost among bits of falling plaster.

The result was an additional floor with vaulted ceilings, towering stained-glass windows depicting the different phases of the moon, and a hearth large enough to hold a boiling copper cauldron that infused the entire room with notes of cloves and cardamon, which always grew richer as morning passed into the afternoon. The grandness of the ceiling was offset somewhat by the soft textures of the velvet armchairs that wrapped around each of the oaken tables and the warm burgundy hues of the rugs. Altogether, the scene made you want to slip away from the worries that waited outside the front door and lose yourself in a second or third pot of tea. The only problem was that the windows within the shop didn't match the ones you saw from the street, though the customers who wandered up to the second floor always seemed to forget that fact by the time their feet left the bottom step of the spiral staircase.

"Here we are," Anne said, a note of victory lacing her tone as she led her guests to a table nearest the cauldron, where the fragrance of cinnamon sticks and citrus was the strongest.

"Won't you join us?" Katherine asked as she settled into her seat and let her knit shawl fall from her shoulder, the movement unveiling some of her hex magic. It looked like dust that had struck the light at just the right angle, casting a shimmering glow against her skin and clothes for the barest instant before being tucked away again beneath the wool cloth. She'd been kept quite busy over the winter social season, when the plethora of balls and holiday events put blessings and curses in high demand. But, judging by the new laugh lines around her eyes, Katherine had enjoyed every moment of it.

"I don't know that there's time . . . ," Anne began, only to be interrupted by the metallic click of a tea cart's wheels.

"She has a few minutes," Peggy said with a smile as she placed a pot of steeping tea on the table alongside a tray brimming over with spicy ginger biscuits that begged to be snapped in two.

When Anne opened her mouth to protest, Peggy merely gave her a wink and quickly pushed the cart away.

"I can't believe this is the first time we've visited since the expansion," Katherine remarked as her eyes continued to wander across the room, stopping here and there when they seemed to be caught by the details of a nightscape painting or the way the light of the flames looked as they danced against curved gas lamps.

"Well, becoming the Diviner kept me occupied in the spring," Anne replied as she poured them each a cup of tea that smelled of refuge on a cold and snowy night. "Then I had to make the house wait until autumn to unveil the changes so that the customers weren't wondering how a second floor sprang up overnight. And by the winter, there was the matter of . . ."

Anne fell silent, the words waiting to be shared too heavy to carry into the conversation. Instead, she looked down at the signet ring that wrapped around her thumb and tapped the hourglass etching ever so carefully against the side of her teacup so that the small grains of sand floated from one end to the other.

"Yes," Celeste said with a sigh. "There was the matter of our Mr. Crowley."

As soon as Celeste spoke the words, Anne was pulled back into memories of her old friend.

The first time that she met Mr. Crowley, Anne had known he was dangerously close to passing on without completing his Task.

All witches carried a purpose, a reason for their existence that contributed in some essential way to the wider web of destiny. If someone failed to finish their Task before they passed on, they were doomed to become a ghost stuck aimlessly between this life and the next. And the delicate balance of magic in the world they'd left behind would be disrupted, the severity of the consequences dependent on how much power a witch possessed.

At the request of the Council, she'd spent months trying to help Mr. Crowley discover his Task, only to realize that he'd known what he needed to do all along. It had taken some time, but Mr. Crowley eventually revealed why he intended to leave such an important errand undone: he wanted to be reunited with the person he'd loved the most, a man named Philip who was still lingering on as a spirit.

Anne of all people knew what it felt like to try and gain control of destiny and had decided to let the matter rest, welcoming Mr. Crowley into the warmth of the tearoom so that he could enjoy the comforts of this life in the time he had left. The other members of the Council chose to leave Mr. Crowley to his fate as well, assured that his unfinished Task would cause only the barest ripple of disruption since he'd displayed middling magical abilities.

And he had remained with them longer than anyone had predicted, nearly a year beyond what the Council initially expected. Every Sunday since the first snowfall, Mr. Crowley had joined Katherine and Celeste at the same table in the Crescent Moon, filling the shop with a chorus of laughter until Anne had to remind them that the house was about to lock the door for the evening and settle in for the night.

But though Death had been patient, she hadn't forgotten.

Before another frost settled on the sidewalks, Mr. Crowley had said his goodbyes, grateful for the friendships he hadn't expected to find but welcoming of a new chapter, one that he'd been waiting to turn to for quite some time.

And Anne had been caught up in the current of her own fresh beginning ever since, the gentle rhythm of the shop quickening to a faster pace even as her new responsibilities continued to pull her beyond the threshold.

"It seems that the new year hasn't brought you much rest," Katherine murmured as her gaze swept across the parlor, taking in the colorful array of hats that were bouncing atop the excited heads of the customers.

Anne nodded as her attention shifted beyond the table and outward, the tendrils of her magic catching against the strands of all the other witches who now filled the shop.

When the news that Anne had replaced Celeste on the Council had gotten out, they'd arrived at the door quicker than a wick catching flame. At first, they merely seemed curious about why she had been chosen, but it didn't take more than a brush with Anne to know that she possessed a rare power. Anne heard them murmuring whenever she passed by and knew that they'd never encountered a Diviner who could so clearly touch the threads of destiny, and alongside their amazement came something much more potent: hope. Where they would have once let whispers of their troubles drift to the ears of the Council, the witches of Chicago were now coming to Anne directly, emboldened by the certainty that someone who could see the future with such precision would be able to bring things to a happy end.

As Anne followed Katherine's gaze about the shop and caught

more than one pair of cheerful eyes peering at her over the rims of porcelain teacups, she felt a sense of comfort knowing that she'd finally found her place among her mother's people.

But her gentle smile wasn't enough to distract the house from the shadows that were starting to pool beneath those blue eyes. Even if Anne didn't seem to mind, the walls were growing troubled by the list of concerns that the other witches were always bringing her, most of which had turned out to be nothing beyond what was to be expected for a community where magic beat at its heart.

"Don't be afraid to share the burden," Celeste said, reaching forward to place one of her delicate hands across Anne's shoulder. "Being on the Council can feel isolating, like you're afraid to speak for fear that the secrets you carry might come tumbling out. But it doesn't have to be that way."

Anne returned Celeste's grasp and nodded, thankful that the former Diviner had stepped into her life at just the right moment. She'd made all the transitions of the past year much smoother, and it had been a welcoming experience to have someone to reach out to for advice once more. Though the lessons that Celeste passed along weren't coated in the same sugar and spice that her mother's wisdom had carried, Anne was at a point in her life when she was beginning to appreciate more subtle flavors. And as she delved deeper into the intricate social networks of the Chicago coven, Anne had been especially grateful for Celeste's stark yet sage guidance.

Even as Anne nodded her head in agreement, though, an unwelcomed thought twisted its way into her mind.

Something strange had been lurking at the corners of her dreams lately, a shadowy presence that carried the texture of the past. And a familiar scent that made her temples tingle always lingered in the room whenever she slipped from sleep to reality, vanishing just before Anne could place the fragrant notes.

But she hadn't been getting enough rest to step deeper into her visions and see what might be hiding beneath her conscious thoughts. There seemed to be quite enough to focus on during her waking hours, and so, Anne had been forced to push these odd occurrences to the side.

Anne was tempted to mention them to Celeste now, but it seemed silly to bring up something that she couldn't even find the words to describe, not when she'd already confronted much more tangible dangers as the city's Diviner.

So, instead of keeping her hand atop Celeste's and turning their conversation toward the odd sensations that had started to slip into her awareness, Anne pulled away and took a sip from her tea instead.

"I appreciate the reminder," Anne said with a smile. "But the shop keeps me from lingering too long in my worries."

The fire in the grate crackled then, as if the house was trying to chase away the chill that caught on the edges of her thoughts by stoking the logs. It was persistent about getting Anne to slip into a slower rhythm, but no amount of lavender tucked between her pillows seemed to be able to taper her pace.

"Yes, let's focus on other matters," Katherine murmured, leaning forward on her elbows in anticipation. "What news do you have to share with us about Beatrix and Violet?"

Anne's smile finally managed to reach her eyes at the sound of her sisters' names. They were three parts of a matching set, triplets so identical that the only way most people were able to tell them apart was by taking note of the different shades of their eyes: light blue for Anne, deep brown for Beatrix, and a shocking shade of purple for Violet.

Though inseparable since birth, the sisters had recently been pulled down diverging paths. They'd said their goodbyes shortly after Anne accepted the position of Diviner, with Beatrix taking the train toward the East Coast to pursue a promising career as a novelist and Violet waving farewell from the back of a wagon as she followed the circus and her husband, Emil, to places where the sharp whip of the wind softened beneath warm sunshine.

"They're caught up in their own adventures," Anne replied, her hand moving toward a pair of letters that rested in the pocket of her dress. She always kept the most recent news there, where it remained within easy reach whenever she thought of them and her chest grew just a bit tighter.

"Last time, you told us that Beatrix was in New York finalizing the edits for her second book," Celeste said. "Is she still there?"

"She's in Boston now, actually," Anne replied. "Another lecture opportunity that her publisher said was too important to overlook."

"But she was supposed to be back in Chicago months ago," Celeste said, clearly disappointed. "And Violet too for your birthday."

Anne sighed and leaned a bit deeper into her chair.

The realization that, for the very first time in their lives, the three sisters wouldn't be together for their birthday had been difficult to accept. But the week before the first snow hit the sidewalk, Anne had glanced into her cup and seen a full moon rising on the rim, a sign that their plans would be disrupted. And sure enough, the day that her sisters were set to travel, an unexpected storm had kept them back.

As Anne had predicted, when the first snowflake fluttered down and touched her upturned cheeks, she'd been standing on the sidewalk alone instead of within the warm embrace of her sisters.

Once again, it seemed that Fate had other plans in mind for the Quigley sisters.

"Yes, but the time wasn't right," Anne said.

Since her ability to peer into the future had grown stronger, Anne had become more patient about allowing a thread of destiny to reveal where it might lead her. Where she once would have wrapped her wrist around the barest hint of a suggestion and tugged, Anne now let her fingers rest against the strings and allowed them to pull her along the path of fortune.

But that certainly didn't mean she had to be exuberant about the unexpected turn of events.

Knowing that she and her sisters would come together again didn't quite ease the sense of loneliness that crept up on her whenever she sat in the family parlor and the sight of the empty settee, still indented from years of Violet and Beatrix's steady presence, caught her by surprise.

"Well, I commend your patience," Katherine replied with a laugh. "But I'd like to see them both here sooner rather than later."

Anne grinned then and met her friend's gaze over her teacup, considering whether or not to share a secret.

"Whenever I pour cream into my morning tea, I see a bow coming together on the surface," Anne finally said. "It grows stronger by the day."

Katherine and Celeste's smiles broadened as the underlying meaning of Anne's words took shape: a reunion to come.

"Then we do have something to look forward to after all!" Katherine cried as she took a bite of the sugarplum scone that Peggy had placed closest to her on the tray.

"And you don't think that there's just the slightest chance Beatrix might be able to give us an advance copy of her new book?" Celeste whispered. "We promise we wouldn't share it with anyone, of course."

Anne knew that, like everyone else who'd encountered her sister's writing, Celeste was waiting with bated breath for the moment her latest story hit the shelves. After all, Beatrix was a word weaver, a witch who's magic rested in spinning stories that ensnared the heart of readers and refused to let them go until the final page.

"If only," Anne replied with a laugh. "Her publisher has all the copies under lock and key after someone tried to break in and take one. As you know, her writing is rather . . . compelling."

Celeste nodded in agreement, though a look of disappointment still settled between her brows.

"It will be a consolation if Violet decides to bring that handsome husband of hers along," Katherine said, beaming from ear to ear.

Celeste playfully batted Katherine on the shoulder, as if she couldn't quite bring herself to reprimand her friend for a thought that had passed through her mind a time or two as well.

"I'll leave you both to consider Emil's finer qualities alone," Anne said as she rose from the table and brushed the crumbs off her skirt. "I need to start my next set of rounds with the customers."

A few of the witches sitting nearest to their table straightened in their seats. They tried to hide the fact that they'd overheard Anne's last remark, but the way they played with the corners of their cloth napkins gave away their excitement.

"Promise us that you'll take a moment for yourself later this evening," Katherine said as she grasped Anne's hand in her own and gave it a gentle squeeze. "You may have an iron will, but even metal will bend under enough pressure."

"I promise," Anne said as she gave her friend a kiss on the cheek before slipping into the quick and chaotic rhythm of the shop.

But in the swirl of carnations and caravans that rested at the bottom of her customers' cups, Anne forgot to glance up from the future and take stock of what was beginning to emerge in the present.

Which was a shame, because if she had, Anne might have noticed the sensation of icy fingers tapping ever so gently along the base of her back, warning about troubles that were on the cusp of taking shape.

CHAPTER 2

A Train

*Indicates that someone
unexpected is about to arrive.*

Beatrix Quigley had come to discover that being on a train did something strange to time.

As soon as her luggage was stowed away and the sound of the wheels grinding against the rails tangled with the scratches of her pen marking the paper, she shifted into a place where the moment seemed to stretch and shrink all at once.

One instant, she was entirely lost in a world of her own making, where her characters were more tangible than the details of her compartment, and the next, a sudden stillness would abruptly pull her from a paragraph, alerting her to the fact that they'd reached the end of the line.

It was a place that seemed to move beyond the steady clicking of a clock, where minutes took on the texture of molasses in the most satisfying ways and daydreams could be captured on the page.

At least, that's how the everyday magic of the train car had felt before this particular trip.

Instead of staring down at her notebook, which was packed in the very bottom of her traveling case, Beatrix's gaze was fixed out the window, where she saw a ghost of her pensive reflection blinking at her from the snow-covered fields that passed by in the background. Her fingers, normally wrapped firmly around a pen, were touching a marigold pendant that rested just above her heart.

"I've found us a pot of tea," a familiar voice suddenly echoed through the train car, its cheerful hue instantly easing the furrow that had taken root between Beatrix's brows.

Turning away from the window, Beatrix smiled as she watched her publisher's assistant try to carry a tray with a silver teapot and a pair of cups through the door of their private compartment, which kept sliding back and forth, making the task nearly impossible.

As Jennings took another step forward, Beatrix noticed a single carnation teetering in a crystal vase next to the tea spout, the sight of the cheerful red petals instantly turning up the corners of her lips. She wondered, not for the first time, how he had known exactly what would bring a smile to her face just when she needed one the most.

"Don't ask what I had to do to get it," Jennings said with a chuckle, his own grin broadening as he glanced down at the flower and tried to get a firmer hold on the tray.

"Let me help you, Jennings," Beatrix insisted as she moved to rise from her seat, only to be thrown backward by a sudden turn of the train.

Unfortunately, the movement also sent Beatrix's companion tumbling forward, and he just barely managed to grasp the handle of the teapot before the rest of the tray's contents spilled to the floor.

"Well, at least I've saved the tea," Jennings laughed as he carefully reached down to collect the cups, which, by some stroke of luck, were no worse for wear. He even managed to return the carnation to its vase, though the petals were somewhat tattered about the edges now.

"Thank goodness for that," Beatrix said with a grin as she reached for one of the saucers and let Jennings fill her cup, trying her best to keep it still as the train continued to rattle back and forth.

As much as her life had changed, the sense of steadiness that Beatrix felt whenever she took her first sip of tea hadn't altered a bit.

"And I did manage to bring you these," Jennings continued as he reached into his jacket pocket and dropped two sugar cubes into Beatrix's cup. Though she wouldn't have dared complain, he knew that she preferred something to take the bite from the strong, bitter tea that they tended to serve in most dining cars.

Throughout the past year of her tour, Jennings had managed to slip effortlessly into the fabric of Beatrix's life with gestures like these, ones that told her he was paying attention to details that even she had a habit of overlooking. When Mr. Stuart first passed along a tumbling list of author engagements, Beatrix had grown weary by the sheer number of dates and particulars that she'd need to keep track of all on her own. But her hesitation had quickly shifted to relief when Jennings appeared at the train station with the news that Mr. Stuart had sent him along to help ensure their bestselling writer had a smooth journey. And after months of dizzying train connections and crowded lectures, Beatrix was more grateful than ever that he could be spared from his desk at Donohoe & Company. Whether it be with just a few soft-spoken words or a gentle nudge that told her which platform to step onto, Jennings always managed to find a way to make her feel grounded, even when the two of them were rolling across the country.

"I'd say we both need a cup of something warm given how chilly it is in here," Jennings said, shivering so that a few strands of his disheveled brown hair fell across his forehead. "It figures that Mr. Stuart would finally decide to let you go home when traveling by rail could lead to frostbite."

Beatrix suspected that the sudden change in her schedule had less to do with her publisher than Jennings thought.

Though her ability to see the future had faded as her word weaving magic grew stronger, Beatrix still occasionally caught the barest whisper of what was to come. These moments were few and far between these days, but sometimes, when she was glancing just so at the clouds above or washing out the remains of her cup, for the barest second, she'd catch a sign out of the corner of her eye.

And yesterday morning, as Jennings had raced into her hotel room with a telegram from Mr. Stuart, she'd seen a bow waiting patiently on the rim of her cup, so close to the handle that she nearly smudged it with her thumb.

Before Jennings could give her the news, she'd already realized that they were going home.

Home.

The word conjured the scent of honey cake and freshly risen cinnamon bread, ready to be torn apart while steam was still spilling in tendrils from the tin. The warmth of the fire nipping at her toes and the murmur of chattering voices in the front parlor. And strongest of all was the memory of her sisters' arms wrapped tightly around her own in an embrace that always let her know where her heart remained.

Jennings caught sight of the grin that had caused the dimples in Beatrix's cheeks to make an appearance and smiled himself.

"What are you thinking about?" he asked, his eyes twinkling in the way they always did when Beatrix knew he was curious about what she would say next.

"The tea shop," Beatrix replied as she leaned back into the cushions and released a deep breath, anticipating how it would feel when she finally stepped back over the threshold. "And my sisters."

The past year had flown by in a rush of author events, train stations, and luggage. Beatrix would sometimes wake in the middle of the night and need to glance at her calendar book to remember what city she was sleeping in. Then there were the lines of readers who waited for hours just to get the chance to have her sign their copies and ask a question or two about her next project, their eyes gleaming in anticipation when she said, "Yes, I am working on another story."

She'd loved every moment of it. Loved realizing that she could step beyond the confines of the tea shop and find pieces of herself waiting to be discovered in every new city, where the towering buildings reminded her just how far people were willing to climb to reach their dreams. Loved learning that she could stand in front of a crowd and find the sense of confidence that she needed to speak about her beloved characters when just a year before, she'd shuddered at the thought of stepping into the front parlor and talking with a handful of regular customers. Loved realizing that she didn't need to split a tarot deck to know the best was yet to come.

It hadn't been until very recently that Beatrix had begun to long for the Crescent Moon in ways that were causing her to slip back into her former self, the quiet shadow that shifted in the corners of the shop hoping that no one would notice her.

"Well, I'm sure it will be the perfect place to work on your next book," Jennings said, stretching his legs out as best he could. They were so long that he needed to bend his knees to get them to fit between the benches of the train compartment.

Beatrix suddenly shifted awkwardly in her seat, moving her hand to pull nervously at the chain attached to her spectacles and knocking her cup of tea off the saucer and onto the floor in the process.

"Oh dear!" she cried, just as Jennings shouted, "I'll get it!"

They both jumped forward at the same moment the train decided to take another sharp turn, sending them tumbling onto the tea-stained carpet and into each other's arms.

Beatrix was on top of Jennings now, so close that she could smell the aroma of black coffee and freshly pressed paper that somehow always clung to his clothes, no matter how long he'd been away from the halls of Donohoe & Company.

A blush quickly spread across Beatrix's fair skin as she tried to pull herself away before Jennings could realize that she'd leaned into his lapel when she first caught his familiar scent. But the chain of her spectacles was tangled in the buttons of his vest, snapping her back so that her face was so close to his that one of her copper curls touched his cheek.

Jennings gently wrapped a finger around the strand and carefully put it back in place behind her ear. His lips pressed together and then parted, as if he'd decided to say something important.

"Next stop's Chicago!" a harsh voice cried.

Beatrix glanced up as a man in an official blue uniform poked his head into their compartment, his eyebrows twisting together in confusion when he didn't see anyone on the seats and then rising to his forehead as he looked down and saw them tangled together on the floor.

"We fell!" Jennings exclaimed as he freed Beatrix's spectacles from his vest and helped her sit upright.

"Then you'd better get up again," the train attendant said calmly, as if he'd seen stranger things in his time on the rails. "Chicago's the end of the line, and you'll need to stay there unless you're planning to turn right around and head back to Boston."

"I don't think I'd mind at all," Beatrix heard Jennings murmur to himself, so softly that she nearly didn't catch the words.

After they'd settled back onto their seats—the teapot and cups stacked on the tray as neatly as they could be, given the circumstances—Beatrix let a few moments pass as she worked up the courage to turn to Jennings and ask a question.

"I hope that you aren't disappointed to be returning with me to Chicago," she said in a rush, the words spilling out so quickly that she worried he'd ask her to repeat them.

"Not at all," Jennings replied, his own voice rising in surprise. "I'm happy to be going back."

"Are you sure?" Beatrix asked. "You seemed so pleased when we were traveling along the East Coast. I'd hate to think that Mr. Stuart calling me back has spoiled any of your plans."

"Let me assure you," Jennings said, his words nearly as fast as Beatrix's had been. "There's nowhere else I'd rather be."

"Really?" Beatrix asked, still unconvinced.

"Yes," Jennings replied. "It's only that you'll be entirely focused on writing the next book now. Mr. Stuart's given me my agenda, and it's centered around getting the last manuscript ready for publication while you're working on the new story. I'll miss hearing you speak to readers and exploring new cities together and—"

Jennings stopped himself there and nervously brushed at the front of his vest, though Beatrix had thought he'd managed to get all the dust from the carpet off already.

"And the excitement of it, you understand," Jennings finally managed to continue. "It won't be quite the same when we return to Chicago."

"No," Beatrix murmured, stiffening a bit as she thought of the notebook buried in the bottom of her suitcase. "I don't suppose it will be."

"But once you reach your next deadline, Mr. Stuart will be sending us out on the road again, I'm sure," Jennings said cheerfully.

Beatrix felt her heartbeat begin to race at that, quicker than it had in the moments just before she'd stepped behind a podium to speak in front of a crowd of strangers for the first time.

An expression that Jennings must have mistaken for disappointment flashed across her face, because he suddenly looked alarmed.

"But there'll be plenty of time for you to see your sisters, of course," Jennings said. "I know you've missed them."

"I have," Beatrix replied, reaching for the marigold pendant, which somehow remained warm though frost crept along the sides of the compartment's window.

Beatrix wanted to tell Jennings that she'd miss him, too, and was looking forward to when they'd be boarding the train together again after she met her deadline. But the final word of that thought made her throat so dry that she couldn't manage to speak.

Instead, she simply picked up the carnation that had fallen into the corner of the seat and carefully placed it in the buttonhole of his jacket.

A blush as red as the flower began to spread across Jennings' cheekbones as he clumsily opened the journal where he kept track of all the tasks that waited to be neatly checked off and started talking about production schedules and galley prints.

After a few minutes, Beatrix let herself relax into the easy rhythm of his voice and the train swaying against the tracks, her attention riveted on the feeling of the rails rumbling beneath her feet and the scent of sugar and spilled tea. Drawing in a deep breath, she tried to bottle up all these sensations before they reached the station, where they would say their goodbyes.

Because if her sisters couldn't help her sort through the mess that waited at the bottom of her suitcase, Beatrix very much doubted that she and Jennings would share a moment like this one ever again.

CHAPTER 3

A Buttonhook
*Represents friendships
slipping back into place.*

As Violet Quigley's hand stilled on the garden gate, she began to wonder what she was more afraid of: that everything had changed or nothing at all.

Over the past few months, she'd found herself slipping away from the regular rhythm of the day and into delicately crafted fantasies that took on the texture of tea biscuits and cinnamon scones. Like the dough that she used to knead every evening, she'd folded memories of the shop into her daydreams and let them grow to the point where she suspected they'd begun to stretch beyond reasonable possibility.

What if she walked through the door and realized her recollections were too laced with nostalgia to have ever been real in the first place?

Worse yet, there was the chance that everything was just as Violet remembered, but she'd changed too much to fit back into the steady heartbeat of the shop.

The previous year, she'd stood on the other side of this very gate with her valise dangling in one hand and the iron handle grasped in the other. She'd even been wearing the same woolen coat to ward off the harsh Chicago winds, the one that Emil had given her when they'd realized that autumn had shifted into winter while they were tucked away in his wagon. Though the scene looked nearly identical to the one that had unfolded before, Violet's chest tightened at just how different she felt from the woman who'd closed the garden gate behind her, ready to walk toward her dreams instead of away from them.

But that thought brought along a fragile daisy chain of other concerns that she'd done her best to stay one step ahead of during her journey back home, and so, instead of lingering in the alleyway and letting her worries catch up with her, Violet threw open the latch and stepped into the garden, where the scent of witch hazel and winter jasmine instantly melted away the troubles of the present and ushered her into the warmth of the past.

For a few moments, Violet stood on the pebbled pathway with her eyes closed and let herself pull back the decades until she was a little girl again, discovering how near she could step to the alleyway without anyone noticing.

As the scent of freshly turned earth grew stronger, so did the sounds of her childhood. She could almost hear the pages of Beatrix's book turning as the breeze caught the paper, and beyond that the murmur of Anne's voice as she pointed to signs tethered to the comfort of safe havens. And beyond that still, the rustling of the rough apron that her mother had always worn while working in the flower beds, her laughter faint but so familiar that, for a moment, Violet forgot to breathe.

By the time the sunlight had thawed Violet's chilled cheeks, she was ready to open her eyes once more, and the noises that had somehow slipped beyond the careful confines of the past faded away, leaving her firmly in the present.

Drawing in a shaky lavender-laced breath, Violet took a step toward the house, wondering what it would feel like to turn the knob of the back door and discover what awaited her.

But someone else got there first.

"Violet!" Anne cried, her voice carrying through the garden as she embraced her sister with such force that she nearly knocked them both to the ground.

Before they could topple into the nearest bed of primroses, Anne wrapped her arms around Violet's waist and steadied her, her laughter so strong that Violet could feel it echoing against her own chest.

And in that instant, Violet knew that the most important parts of her past had remained exactly as she needed them to be.

Not one to be left out of a celebration, the house threw open all the shutters and began to snap them back and forth, as if it were clapping.

"Shh," Anne hissed as she waved her arms up at the house. "You'll frighten the customers!"

The house heard the smile that cut the edge off her warning, though, and started to bang all the pots and pans, which turned the heads of a few ladies in the front parlor, who wondered what kind of chaos was unfolding in the kitchen.

"Well, this certainly hasn't changed a bit," Violet laughed as she tightened her hold around Anne's waist and grinned at the house.

"Come inside before it brings down the rafters," Anne insisted as she led her sister toward the door. "Or decides to add another room to the third floor."

But when they stepped through the threshold, Violet could already hear the boards groaning above and saw the herb bundles that hung along the wall shake ever so slightly, both telltale signs that the house was trying to stretch beyond its current limits. No doubt, when she and Anne walked up the staircase, they'd find a room that hadn't been there before, with a bouquet of sweet violets resting on a freshly laundered pillow.

Though the house's sense of excitement hadn't ebbed during her absence, as Violet finally started to take stock of her surroundings, she realized that not everything had stayed the same.

"What's happened to my kitchen?!" Violet cried as she turned about the room, her eyes darting from one alteration to the next until they finally settled on a familiar sight, the oak dining table where she and her sisters had spent hours discussing the details of the day to come over steaming cups of English breakfast tea and plates towering with iced buns that smelled of browned butter and nutmeg when you tore them in two. Evidentially, the house had taken one glance at the scratches carved into the wooden surface and realized that some imperfections were worth keeping just the way they were.

"I tried to stop it," Anne sighed, throwing her hands in the air as if she were speaking about a rambunctious border collie who couldn't be kept from jumping on the furniture. "But the house grew overly confident after its work in the front parlor and started adding an inch or two here and there when I wasn't paying attention. Before I knew it, we had this."

Anne swept her hand around the kitchen, which looked like something that had spilled forth from the garden. Wide windows had grown out of the plaster and were thrown open so that tendrils of the plants rooted outside snuck in and wove their way around the tea tins and cookbooks that rested along the shelves. Sprigs of lavender and thyme now dangled just within reach of the stovetop, waiting to be plucked by hurried hands and filling the entire room with the scent of spring fading gracefully into summer. The ceilings were also at least six inches higher, drawing in a sense of openness that shed light on the corners of the room that had once been shadowed and exposing the more practical touches the house had seen fit to make: a double oven that shone with a fresh layer of polish, cabinets that proudly displayed stacks of dishes with the same crescent moon that winked at passersby from the sign outside the shop, and a new basket with a few less scratch marks waiting next to the hearth for Tabitha's arrival, though at the moment, the cat was nowhere to be seen.

"Don't you like it?" Anne asked, a nervous note sneaking into her voice as she realized Violet might have hoped to step into the same home that she'd left behind.

"I do, actually," Violet said, surprised to find that she truly meant it. "It's only fair that the house has its chance to grow as well."

At that, Violet felt the boards beneath her boots rattling with what she could only assume was agreement.

"But how did you know that I'd arrived?" Violet asked, turning to face her sister. "I went through the back just to surprise you."

"While I was talking with a customer in the front parlor, I suddenly smelled honeysuckle with a hint of sandalwood, and I knew you'd come home," Anne replied. "I excused myself and ran straight to the back door."

"Your powers have gotten as strong as that, have they?" Violet asked with a grin. "I think that you've been holding back in your letters. What else have you been keeping to yourself?"

"You'll find out soon enough," Anne replied in a tone that reminded Violet of restless nights and shoulders strained from leaning too deeply into worries.

Violet opened her mouth to ask what the trouble was when something her sister had said finally clicked into place.

"Did you say you smelled sandalwood?" Violet murmured just

before a chorus of greetings slipped under the door that led to the parlor and the pots and pans hanging from the pegs in the kitchen erupted once more.

"It can't be," Violet said, but she was already racing to the front parlor, tossing her valise to the floor as she and Anne tried to squeeze through the door at the exact same time.

When they finally managed to reach the parlor, a cluster of feathered hats and puffed satin sleeves was growing at the very center of the first floor, and sharp cries of surprise had caused more than one person walking by the front windows to peer inside, hoping to discover the source of the noise that spilled onto the street.

Among the commotion, Violet could see a headful of vibrant copper curls pop up now and again from the crowd of lively customers. It was like watching a nervous robin trying to peer over a flock of boisterous macaws.

"Miss Beatrix, I can't tell you how good it is to see you again!"

"Miss Beatrix, you simply won't believe all the changes your sister's made to the shop, and in such a short period of time."

"Miss Beatrix, you must tell us all about the new book you're working on. We won't take no for an answer!"

Deciding it was time to rescue their sister, Violet and Anne pushed forward, gently slipping between satin sleeves and bustle skirts until they each managed to grab hold of Beatrix's gloved hands.

"Is Miss Violet here as well?!" a voice cried out, followed by an echo of gleeful gasps.

A burst of excitement rippled through the parlor then, and it was clear that if someone didn't act soon, the sisters would be well and truly lost among the eager embrace of their regular customers.

"Give me a moment to have them to myself, ladies!" Anne cried above the chorus of protests as she marched toward the entryway, which was now tucked out of view from the rest of the parlor, though that didn't stop more than one curious gaze from following them until their skirt trains disappeared around the corner.

Once they were surrounded by nothing more than a rack full of colorful cloaks and knit wraps, the Quigleys collapsed into one another, laughing as they pressed their foreheads together and reassured themselves that they hadn't slipped into the past or future but were indeed firmly planted in the present.

Unspoken sentences filled the empty space between them: "I've missed you," "It's been too long," "How good it feels to be back."

But, like many of the moments that make life worth living, their reunion couldn't be expressed in words.

So, instead of saying anything at all, Anne, Beatrix, and Violet took a few minutes to let the beat of their hearts fall into the same easy rhythm and relish the sensation of hearing their laughter tangle together again.

The house chuckled alongside them, shaking the chandelier that now hung in the entryway, as it did whenever a soft breeze slipped from the street and tinkled the delicate crystal drops.

"It's not often these days that I get the pleasure of being surprised," Anne finally murmured.

"A good surprise, I hope," Beatrix said with a grin as she pushed back a curl that had escaped Anne's chignon.

"It's the one that I've been eagerly waiting for," Anne replied, tightening her hold around her sisters' waists.

"I don't think we've completely thrown her off guard, Bee," Violet interjected. "It seems she knew we were coming."

"Is that true, Anne?" Beatrix asked, her eyes widening in amazement. "Did you know that we were on our way back?"

"There might have been a few signs," Anne murmured, her gaze dropping shyly toward her boots.

"She's been keeping secrets," Violet chided. "After we've spent so much time writing all those details in our letters, she didn't think to share this one with us!"

But the way Anne's smile faltered as her attention lingered on Violet's face hinted that she didn't need tea leaves or tarot cards to know something more than homesickness had drawn her sister away from the circus and back to the Crescent Moon. Those worry lines and dark circles were waiting to be read as clearly as clouds on the rim of a porcelain cup.

"I'd say we have quite a lot to catch up about," Anne replied before turning toward the busy front parlor and frowning. "If only it were nearer to closing time. Why don't you two let the house settle you in, and once the customers leave for the day, I'll join you upstairs?"

"And leave you to fend for yourself down here? With these ladies and all their questions about our unexpected arrival?" Violet asked, her copper brows flying toward her fringe. "How cruel do you think we've become?"

"Let us help," Beatrix insisted as she slid a hand through the crook of Anne's elbow.

"But you've only just walked through the door!" Anne sputtered. "You must be tired."

"Not too tired to help our sister," Beatrix said with a grin. "You've forgotten we have a bit of experience with this sort of thing."

Anne opened her mouth again to protest, but before she could say anything at all, Violet threaded an arm through her other elbow and marched them into the front room of the shop, where they were instantly met by the cries of their customers, who were eager to lure them to their tables.

The Quigley sisters, it seemed, had finally returned home.

CHAPTER 4

A Cart

Appears just before a change of fortune.

By the time the last skirt train had trailed over the threshold and out the front door, the Crescent Moon was heavy with the scent of lingering perfume and questions waiting to be answered.

Though the ladies in the shop had been eager to capture the Quigleys' attention, the sisters found their thoughts wandering away from the delicate swirls of tea leaves that awaited their interpretation.

One moment, they were trying to decipher the signs, and the next, the familiar sound of their voices entangling in the tea parlor would cause them to pause and seek out one another's smiles over hat rims and happy customers.

But beneath their satisfaction rested a desire to turn the handle of the clock that ticked above the mantle so they could climb the steps to the family parlor and slip back into the reliable comfort of the past.

"It's just the same," Beatrix sighed in relief as she opened the door and took a moment to savor the sight of the crackling fire before sinking into the emerald settee. Her piles of books were still towering on the side table, threatening to topple to the floor if anyone laughed too loudly, and Violet's knitting remained tangled in a basket next to the hearth, though it looked a bit worse for wear. Tufts of black fur clung to the vibrant red and yellow strands, making it clear that Tabitha had claimed the woolen bundles as her own.

"Only if you forget the fact that it's on the third floor now instead of the second," Violet grumbled, treading over the threshold with a heavy tray of tea and steaming cranberry scones in tow. "I don't know how you make the climb up here every evening, Anne. My toes feel like they've been dipped in bronze."

With that, Violet sat the tray atop the table and threw herself beside Beatrix on the settee, groaning in satisfaction as she burrowed her face in the soft cushions. Sharp winds beat against the windows, filling the room with the rattle of glass panes, but the warmth of the parlor had transformed what should have been the worst of winter into a place of refuge.

"That's a fine comment coming from someone who spends most of her time at the top of a circus tent," Anne laughed before moving to sink into the wingback chair.

Knowing that Violet was no doubt threading together a witty retort, Beatrix turned toward the other end of the settee in silent expectation. As she shifted her gaze, though, Beatrix could have sworn she saw the side of Violet's mouth that wasn't hidden in the velvet fabric tighten a fraction. But before she could be certain, her sister's face had settled back into its familiar smile.

"My feet happen to be dangling above the ground and away from the crowd then, I'll have you know," Violet said, turning away from the pillow so that she could stretch herself far enough to nudge Anne with her foot. "Not darting from one table to the next trying to stay out of arm's reach of the most demanding customers."

"I can't believe you left Mrs. Schmitt to me," Beatrix complained as she removed her spectacles and pinched the bridge of her nose. "And when I can't even read the leaves anymore."

"She seemed happy enough trying to whittle out whatever details she could about your latest novel," Violet replied. "If it makes you feel any better, our Miss Katie Meyer went through two pots of oolong this afternoon trying to catch any detail she could about her wedding. I kept telling her that all I could see were clovers and butterflies, but she seemed determined to find an ill omen."

"It has nothing to do with her feelings for the groom, I can assure you," Anne said as she handed Beatrix and Violet some tea before dropping a sugar cube into her own cup. "There's a true match if ever I saw one. No, she simply knows that nothing, no matter how satisfying, can be perfect. There's always a trouble or two to contend with."

An icy chill slipped into the room then, as if the wind had managed to creep beneath the pane, though Beatrix knew the house had sealed it shut for the winter. It caused her to tuck up her collar and reach for one of the worn quilts that rested next to the fireplace, the fabric pleasantly warm from sitting so close to the flames.

"Enough about the customers," Violet said with a wave of her hand as she tucked the corners of her blanket around her skirts. "You've done a marvelous job with the shop, Anne, but I want to talk about our birthday visions before you tell us all the news we've missed."

The sisters had agreed to save the details of what Fate had shown them for an evening when they could tell one another face-to-face rather than through a letter. There was something about the texture of the story that needed to be expressed through speech instead of pen and ink.

"You go first, Vi," Anne insisted. "Since you're the one who asked."

"Very well," Violet said. "On our birthday, I drew in a deep breath and smelled rosemary, the kind that's just been cut from the stalk and makes your temples tingle. It was so potent that I couldn't taste anything else the rest of the day."

"Rosemary," Anne murmured, as if she'd just pieced together a thread of an idea that had refused to be tethered.

"What is it?" Beatrix asked, startled by her sister's reaction.

Anne parted her lips, but she closed them before any confessions could slip into the conversation.

"Nothing that can't be discussed in good time," Anne replied, her voice rising in the way it always did whenever she was trying to sound more cheerful. "It's my turn to share my vision."

Beatrix looked skeptical but was too curious about what her sister was going to say to press the matter further for the time being.

"And what was it?" Violet asked.

"Laughter," Anne replied.

"But that's what we heard last year," Beatrix said, her voice laced with confusion. "The visions never repeat themselves. It's always something new."

"It wasn't the same laughter as before," Anne replied. "The voice belonged to a young girl. I think it was one of us when we were children."

"That's very strange," Violet said. "The visions are always reflections of the future, not echoes of the past."

"I'm afraid that there aren't any firm lines between the past, present, and future for me any longer," Anne explained. "As my powers have grown stronger, the weaker those boundaries have become. I must have caught on to a memory instead of a glimpse of what rests ahead."

The sisters sipped their tea in silent disappointment. Though they'd expected that they'd each be graced with distinct visions, Beatrix knew it hadn't occurred to any of them that their paths might be diverging so much that they'd be pulled toward entirely different periods of time. The thought made her wonder just how far their threads of destiny were being stretched from one another.

"Well, it's a very fine one to return to, at least," Violet finally said with a smile, shifting their conversation away from shadowy possibilities. "And the house was so full of laughter when we were girls that it shouldn't be a surprise some of it slipped into the here and now."

"I'm quite content with the vision in any case," Anne said with a nod before turning to Beatrix. "And what did you find waiting for you on our birthday?"

Beatrix reached for her spectacles and pulled nervously at the chain. The gesture instantly reminded her of the times before she'd found herself in the lines of a half-finished story, when every spoken word had to be wrenched from her chest.

"I felt the touch of paper," she replied, her answer so soft that it was nearly overpowered by the rattling windows.

"But that's hardly a surprise," Violet cooed, sitting up at the sound of her sister's distress. "You're a writer, after all."

"It was the feeling of paper crumbling beneath my fingers, as if I touched a page that had been torn about the edges and caused the whole piece to fall apart," Beatrix said, her hands shaking so fiercely now that she had to set her cup on the table to keep the steaming tea from spilling onto the settee.

"It could mean anything," Anne replied as she grasped her fingers, which Beatrix knew felt icy even through her lace gloves. "We've all learned that what first seems like a curse might become a blessing."

"If the vision was the only ill omen, I might be able to accept that," Beatrix murmured. "But it isn't."

Anne and Violet caught one another's gazes over Beatrix's curls, their eyes widening in silent surprise.

"What's happened?" Anne finally asked, her hold on Beatrix's hand growing firmer.

"I can't . . . ," Beatrix began, needing to pause before saying the words that were always skittering along the sides of her thoughts. " . . . write."

The confession startled the house so much that the parlor walls shrank inward a fraction, as if the Crescent Moon were gasping.

"What do you mean, Bee?" Anne asked when she realized what her sister had said. "Are you having trouble finishing the next book?"

In her letters, Beatrix had already told Anne and Violet that Donohoe & Company had contracted her for a third novel. The first was such a sensation and the second a sure success that they hadn't even waited for her to pitch an idea for a third, let alone show them a completed manuscript. No, Mr. Stuart had simply told her that he wanted a new book and that she had until spring to finish it.

"That's the trouble," Beatrix replied. "I haven't even started."

Anne almost lost the grip on her teacup but managed to catch it before the porcelain could fall to the carpet.

"Medusa's curls," Violet murmured.

"But you've been able to turn out a novel in practically a blink of an eye before," Anne insisted. "You told us that you only needed a few months to finish the last one."

That was true. After embracing her word-weaver abilities, Beatrix had been so swept away by the details of her next story that she'd managed to finish an entire manuscript before the worst of winter had settled in. Mr. Stuart had been so thrilled by the speed at which she wrote that he hadn't even batted an eye at signing the contract for a third book. But that was months ago, and Beatrix hadn't even managed to produce a prologue.

"Something's different now," Beatrix said with a shake of her head. "I think I'm losing my magic."

Anne and Violet leaned closer to their sister, wrapping their arms around her waist and shoulders as they tried to tether her worries to something grounded so that they wouldn't carry her away entirely.

"Why do you think that?" Anne asked, gently turning Beatrix's chin upward so that she could look directly into those brown eyes.

Beatrix remained silent for a moment but then slowly started pulling off her gloves, tugging one finger at a time until her skin lay bare.

"The words are gone," Beatrix explained as she lifted her hands toward the light of the fire.

The elegant dips and curves of Beatrix's handwriting had disappeared, leaving behind smooth, unmarked skin. She couldn't even make out a comma between the grooves of her knuckles or a period along the hollow of her palm. Now there were only lines waiting to be written upon.

"When did this happen?" Violet asked as she took one of Beatrix's hands in her own and gripped it tight.

"After I signed the contract for the third book, I was so busy with the tour that I didn't notice at first," Beatrix murmured. "But by the time I finally sat down to write again, I could tell that the words weren't quite as dense. And then every day I stared at those blank pages, another letter would fade away until I was left with nothing at all."

"That doesn't mean your magic's left you," Anne said. "It's probably just waiting to be drawn out again."

"I'm not so sure that's true," Beatrix sighed. "I can't describe it properly, but sitting down for hours at the desk only to walk away without having written a single sentence has left me hollow. I've not experienced this sense of loss since . . ."

Anne and Violet hugged Beatrix closer, letting her know that they understood without her having to say the words. Though the sting of their parents' deaths had become less biting, it didn't mean that the pain of losing them had faded entirely. The joys in the present and possibilities of the future had just made the memories easier to bear.

"You will write again," Violet insisted, her tone so firm that it sounded like a demand.

"You can't know that," Beatrix replied with a quick shake of her head.

"But I can," Anne said as she reached for the cup of tea that Beatrix had set on the table and stared down at the leaves clinging to the white curves of the porcelain.

"Oh, you mustn't," Beatrix whispered, but before she could pull the tea away, Anne had caught hold of a sign that rested in the middle of the cup, where it dangled so close to the tea's surface that it nearly slipped back into what remained of Beatrix's orange spice blend.

Beatrix waited for Anne to reveal what she'd seen, but before images of snakes and bats could fly to the front of her suspicions, a smile started to tug at the corners of their sister's lips.

"It's a cart," Anne announced, pointing to the leaves as if she were trying to show her sister where she might catch sight of a falling star.

A cart symbolized a dip in the road of fortune, a moment where challenges and doubts needed to be confronted before moving forward. But like all roads, the one that the cart traveled along would eventually become smooth.

"It's a promising sign," Beatrix said with a sigh. "But I still can't be certain."

"Listen to me, Bee," Violet demanded as she grasped her sister's shoulders. "Now that we're back, you're going to write the best novel that readers have ever gotten their hands on. I won't accept anything less."

Beatrix leaned into her sister's embrace then, a bit of the tension fading from her shoulders as she let Violet take some of the weight she'd been carrying.

"Well, if you insist," Beatrix said, the softness of the words cutting through the sorrow that had hardened her voice.

"Precisely," Violet replied as she laid her head on Beatrix's shoulder and closed her eyes, the strain of her long journey home obviously starting to get the best of her as she drifted off to sleep.

The house noticed the way her arms started to loosen and tucked the quilts just a bit tighter about her chin so that none of the troubles threatening to seep through the cracks in the windowpanes would disturb her sleep.

"Why do you think she's come back?" Beatrix whispered as she brushed her fingers along Violet's fringe and let her own head fall against the back of the settee.

"I'm not sure," Anne sighed. "But she'll tell us when she's ready. I'm just happy that we're all home again."

"*Home*," Beatrix murmured, letting the texture of the word start to carry her off into dreams laced with the taste of honey buns and cardamon icing.

Grinning, she fought to keep her eyes open as the sound of Violet's slow, even breathing and Anne's steady voice lulled her to a place beyond worries.

But, eventually, she fell under the spell of the crackling logs and worn cotton quilts, slipping into dreams where something was lurking about the edges, waiting to step out of the shadows of the past now that all three sisters were together in the present.

CHAPTER 5

Snakes
Indicate that trouble is brewing.

Though the Crescent Moon had let out its seams to give itself more room to breathe, the shop was practically bursting the next afternoon. News of the Quigley sisters' reunion had traveled faster than the cable car that carried their customers up Michigan Avenue, and when Anne unlocked the front door to turn around the open sign, she'd been greeted by a line of colorful skirts and thick coats that stretched so far down the sidewalk she hadn't been able to determine where it ended.

Despite the brutal winds that made them grasp at their hats and hoods, the ladies of Chicago had cleared their calendars for the day as soon as they'd heard of Violet and Beatrix's return. The rapidly falling snow might cause them to grit their teeth as they waited on the street for a table to clear, but the excited chatter and scent of cinnamon that slipped onto the sidewalk whenever someone opened the door kept them from turning away.

And once the ladies were ushered inside the shop and their frozen fingers began to melt against the side of a hot teacup, a sense of satisfaction sank deep into their bones, making it impossible not to linger in the chaos of cloves and cardamon that enveloped them.

Luckily, Beatrix and Violet had once again risen to the occasion, tying crisp white aprons around their waists as they ignored Anne's demands that they use the day to rest and recover from their journeys.

Which was quite fortunate indeed because she'd found very little rest after slipping away from the family parlor and into the warmth of her own bed the night before.

Though the soft patchwork quilts and the sound of snow pattering gently against the windowpane had lulled her to sleep quickly enough, as soon as she drifted into a dream, Anne had awoken, pulled away from her slumber by the same scent that Violet had described while talking about her birthday vision. When she'd sat up in the bed, Anne could smell the lingering aroma of rosemary hanging about the room, carrying with it the nagging feeling that something wasn't quite fitting into place the way it should.

Anne had been so distracted by the thought of it that she'd put her boots on the wrong feet and hadn't noticed until Beatrix pointed out her mistake when they met in the hall on their way down to breakfast.

The trouble was that she couldn't put her finger on what, exactly, was wrong, and the sensation of having overlooked something important had continued to nag at her as the day unfolded, slowing her down as she tried to shift from one table to the next. Even the smiles of her sisters, who'd slipped into the busy rhythm of the shop as effortlessly as dancers falling into a familiar waltz, couldn't distract her from the feeling of icy fingers tapping along her spine.

"What could it be?" Anne murmured as she surveyed the

empty parlor, which had finally been cleared of its very last customer, and turned to watch the snow that was starting to fall beyond the smooth panes of the window.

Anne stepped forward and leaned her forehead gently against the icy glass, hoping that the shock of it would give her the sense of clarity she needed to finally understand what was troubling her. But when she released a sigh that had been building within her all day, a flash of white even more startling than the snow piling up along the sidewalks caught her attention.

Anne's eyes snapped upward, just in time to catch the stark black of a man's coat sleeve shifting out of view, as if he'd been standing beside the door all along and abruptly turned the corner when he realized that the shop was closed for the day.

But Anne hadn't so much as heard the brass knob rattle.

If it were any other afternoon, Anne would have brushed aside the odd occurrence, but as her eyes drifted from the door back to where her cheek had touched the pane, she saw something quite unexpected: the distinct silhouette of two frosty snakes, their tails tangled in a knot just where Anne had rested her temple.

There was no pushing it aside any longer; something was amiss that would continue to unfurl the longer she tried to ignore it.

With that thought, Anne stepped away from the window and marched toward the kitchen, taking care to avoid rattling the towering mountains of soiled cups and saucers that Beatrix and Violet were helping Peggy load onto a train of tea carts.

The kitchen, of course, had fared no better than the front parlor with its heaps of batter-stained bowls and overflowing baskets of linen stained with streaks of caramel icing, but Anne paid the mess no heed as she moved with purpose toward the hand mirror hanging from a nail just next to the stovetop.

Only a year before, Violet had used the looking glass to wipe away the worst of the flour that always seemed to make its way to her cheeks and nose, but since Anne had become Diviner, it served an entirely different purpose.

Reaching a finger toward the glass, Anne traced the outline of a balance against the surface, the invisible silhouette darkening the longer her skin touched the mirror.

It wasn't long before the entire surface of the glass shifted and started taking the shape of a face that was much older and worn than Anne's.

"Anne?"

The question was just the barest whisper against the rows of porcelain pots and copper kettles, but Anne already knew with certainty which member of the Council had appeared on the other side of the mirror. That crackling voice could only belong to Hester.

"We need to meet," Anne said, anxious to get to the heart of the matter.

When she'd first become Diviner, Anne had been harried with doubts about how to interact with the other members of the Council, but it hadn't taken long to learn that they expected her to jump quickly into the task of keeping the threads of the city intact. There simply hadn't been time to worry that she was overstepping or failing to follow the proper protocol. The only rule, she'd come to realize, was being responsible for the welfare of her fellow witches, and that meant speaking up as soon as she felt something might be going awry. Anne had waited long enough now to tell them about her worries, and the sooner they could gather to discuss the matter, the better chance she had of figuring out exactly what was wrong.

"What's happened?" Hester asked, her wrinkled eyes fixed intently on Anne's face.

"Something's slipping out of place," Anne tried to explain. "I'm not sure exactly what it is, but I know that it's significant."

Anne expected to see surprise crease the corners of Hester's eyes, but instead, the witch's mouth pinched together in a way that looked more like resolve, as if Anne's concerns merely confirmed a suspicion that she had been considering herself.

But before Anne could press Hester on the matter, the witch's voice filled the kitchen again.

"When would suit you best?" Hester asked.

"As soon as possible," Anne replied, the sense of foreboding that had crept into her chest tightening with every passing moment.

"I'll tell Nathanial and Isaac," Hester murmured, the rough edges of her voice drifting further and further away as she spoke of the other Council members. "We'll be there within the hour."

Quicker than the bat of an eye, the witch's reflection faded from the glass, leaving behind only Anne's bewildered expression.

It wasn't until she felt fur brush against her ankle that Anne turned away from the mirror.

"Strange," Anne murmured as she lifted Tabitha from the floor and thought of the odd spark of realization that she'd seen flash across Hester's face.

The word echoed against the walls and sank into the foundation of the house alongside Anne's worries, settling into the stone and causing the slightest sense of unease to creep into cinnamon-scented hallways.

The walls tried to lean away from it, but eventually, they accepted the sign for what it was: a clear indication that trouble was brewing within the Crescent Moon once more.

❄

By the time the flames in the gas lamps on the street began to flicker against the windows of the shop, the entire house was saturated with the scent of rhododendrons, a fragrance that carried an undernote of caution beneath its soft floral texture.

Though this was certainly not the first time that the Council had gathered at the Crescent Moon in the past year, the strain in Anne's voice set the house on edge, and now all it could think about was the sense of unease that had slipped into the cracks of its plaster after Hester's grim face faded from the looking glass.

The teacups dangling from the hooks in the kitchen were tinkling ever so slightly, and the stairs that led to the second floor kept creaking, though no one had stepped foot on them since the morning.

The Quigleys, of course, felt just as rattled as the poor house.

Though Beatrix and Violet didn't know why Anne was meeting with the other members of the Council in such a hurry, the way they paced around the kitchen looking for something that needed to be tucked in its proper place hinted that they wished their sister could tell them more.

And as Anne waited for them to make their way upstairs with one hand wrapped around the steady ticking of her clock, she found herself wanting the same thing.

Countless times, Anne had lifted her pen when writing to her sisters to share some of the stories that had unfolded in the past year. They were wondrous tales woven with the threads of mystery and magic, but she would always pause just before the ink could touch the page. The ashy flavor of a secret that needed to remain concealed would cut through the taste of her evening tea, and Anne would steer her pen in a safer direction. There was too much at stake to risk the stories taking on a life of their own and spreading outward for all to hear.

So instead of letting some of her secrets slip into the open air, where they wouldn't feel quite so heavy, Anne had thought of her new responsibilities and kept her tales tucked away in the safe confines of her own memories.

Of course, Beatrix and Violet said they understood, but that didn't mean they always remembered to keep their questions to themselves.

"I wonder what it could be," Violet murmured as she tapped her foot against the floorboards, which caused the house to grow so nervous that the sisters could hear the china cabinet shaking in the kitchen.

"We'd better go upstairs and leave Anne to her work," Beatrix insisted as she gently wrapped her hand around Violet's forearm and began to lead her up the staircase.

"I'll join you as soon as I'm able," Anne said, pulling her sisters close before letting them go again.

She stood for a few moments longer at the foot of the stairs, waiting until the sound of their footsteps was all but the barest whisper, and then shifted quietly toward the front door, where she slipped onto the street.

Though she shivered against the sharp evening winds that whipped against her skin, Anne knew that she wouldn't be out long enough to need her coat. After casting a furtive glance from one end of the sidewalk to the other, she reached toward the gas lamp that flickered just above the mailbox and carefully turned the knob to the right. The shadows began to shift then, changing the shape and hue of the front door as the flames started to flutter to a different rhythm.

When Anne moved her hand back to the doorknob, it felt just a bit wider against her palm, and the hinges squeaked in places that they hadn't before.

By the time she stepped over the threshold, the lingering smell of shortbread and sense of a day's work well spent that always settled into the front parlor after a long day had shifted into something else entirely.

"It must be dealt with as swiftly as possible," she heard Nathanial's stern voice echo from the other side of a circular study filled to its rafters with maps and ledgers.

When the Council members first started meeting at the Crescent Moon, the house hadn't quite known where to put them at first. Seeing Nathanial's iron expression among the lace tablecloths and delicate pink peonies had been unsettling, and inviting Hester into the family parlor felt just like hanging a pair of bloomers out one of the front windows. Then there was the problem of Isaac, who had the habit of slipping out of a meeting entirely and wandering up and down the hallways when no one was paying attention.

It didn't help matters that the texture of the Council's conversations took on a different hue than the ones echoing through the rest of the house, carrying with them the weight of secrets that caused shadows to pool in corners that should have been sunny.

The solution, it seemed, was adding a room where the Council's interests could be better contained, and overnight, a circular study had sprouted up for their disposal. Anne wasn't sure where the house kept the room during the daytime, but she suspected it was somewhere next to the attic since the smell of cedar trunks left for safekeeping sometimes overpowered the scent of sage and salt.

As Anne took her final step over the threshold, she could see Nathanial, Hester, and Isaac sitting in their places around a table that held a map of Chicago. It had taken Anne a few days to notice, but the street lines were always stretching ever so slightly, as if trying to catch up with the ever-growing boundaries of the city.

"The trouble has already . . . ," Nathanial continued to say, only to close his mouth with a sharp snap when he realized that Anne had entered the room.

"I haven't kept you waiting too long, I hope," Anne said as she moved toward her spot at the table and reached for the steaming cup of tea that the house had left for her there.

As she stirred the silver spoon and the rich scent of caramel and vanilla began to infuse the room, Anne felt her heart steady and lifted her gaze to meet the other witches.

She didn't like what she found etched into the lines of their faces—an unease that grew from worries waiting to be brought to light. It reminded her of how she'd felt during the Council's very first visit to the Crescent Moon, when fear had caused a fine sheet of frost to settle on the inside of the windows.

"You are right on time," Nathanial said as he shot a pointed glance at the clock on her chest. "As you always are."

Instead of easing back into his chair, though, Nathanial shifted forward and began to tap his foot against the carpet in a hasty tempo.

"What troubles were you speaking of just now?" she asked, the words causing another icy shiver to melt down her spine.

As Nathanial's eyes drifted toward Hester, Anne caught that same expression she'd seen on the other side of the hand mirror, a subtle tightening of the mouth that made her feel like she was about to receive a pressing piece of news instead of the other way around.

"Strange incidents are happening across the city," Nathanial began, his voice growing so serious that the house pulled the curtains on the windows a bit tighter, hoping it might prevent whatever secrets he was about to share from creeping out. "The reports are coming in so quickly now that we fear they won't be easily contained."

"What kind of incidents?" Anne asked.

"Happenings of a magical nature," Nathanial explained. "Trains turning onto a pair of tracks that should carry the car north but somehow pull it south. Icicles in the shape of

Black-eyed Susans blooming along thresholds during a blizzard. Footsteps appearing in the snow a moment before someone sets their boot on the sidewalk."

Anne listened as Nathanial continued to describe the peculiar incidents unfolding across the city, but her attention soon wandered toward the flames flickering in the hearth, where she began to see thin strands of light dancing in the fire. The longer she stared, the more she noticed that the delicate threads were beginning to tangle where they should have fluttered gracefully upward, a sure sign that the web of destiny had been disrupted.

"A Task has been left undone," Anne murmured in understanding.

"That is what we believe," Nathanial said with a nod.

"Whoever the Task belonged to must have been incredibly powerful for it to have such an effect," Anne replied.

Only a witch with a rare aptitude for magic could have caused this number of unusual incidents to occur all at once.

"But no one like that has been brought to our attention," Anne continued, her brow furrowing in confusion. "And I've been keeping an eye out for witches who might be struggling with their Tasks. How could I have not foreseen something like this?"

Again, Nathanial and Hester caught each other's gazes, clearly deciding which of them would speak next.

"You've been looking toward the future," Isaac said. "And turning away from the past."

Anne jumped at the sound of his flat, icy voice, which perfectly matched the absent intensity of his eyes. He'd been so silent the whole meeting that Anne had almost forgotten he was there at all.

"The past?" Anne asked, her words echoing through the stillness of the room.

Unsettled by the pitying expressions that had suddenly appeared on Hester and Nathanial's faces, Anne stared down at the leaves in her cup. And that's when she found the answer to her question waiting for her along the rim—an hourglass formed from the remnants of her cloves.

"Mr. Crowley," Anne gasped as her gaze shifted from the leaves to the ring wrapped around her finger.

"Yes," Hester sighed. "It seems that Mr. Crowley was keeping a good many secrets to himself."

"But you said he was a witch of middling abilities," Anne said in disbelief, remembering the exact phrase that Nathanial had spat when he'd explained that Mr. Crowley was determined to leave his Task unfinished. "That the consequences would be easily dealt with."

"That is what we thought," Hester said. "But we were mistaken."

She said the last word as if it left a bitter flavor in her mouth.

"But how can we be sure that all this has to do with Mr. Crowley and not another witch?" Anne asked, desperate for another possibility that had been overlooked.

"I went to visit his grave this morning," Nathanial said, his voice somber. "And it was so covered in blackthorn that I could no longer see the stone."

Anne stilled. Blackthorn only grew atop the graves of witches who'd held so much magic that it had started to seep into the soil.

"He must have hidden it away," Anne said as she resigned herself to the truth. "To ensure he wouldn't be forced to complete his Task."

"Yes," Nathanial replied. "We believe he got into the practice of hiding his magic at a young age. By the time he came to our attention, Mr. Crowley was so skilled at cloaking his abilities that we failed to notice them."

Anne blinked, and an image of a young Mr. Crowley tugging his coat closer as he ran toward another boy across the street flew to the front of her thoughts. Of course, it all made sense now. Part of the reason Mr. Crowley had been able to strike up a friendship with Philip must have been that his family didn't think he had much magic worth cultivating. If they knew the strength of his potential, he would have been under a much closer watch, and slipping out to see the human boy who lived on the other side of the road would have been impossible.

And then once Mr. Crowley had learned that Philip would become a ghost, he'd tucked his magic even deeper within himself to ensure that they would be together again.

As Anne put the pieces together, her heart began to beat so quickly that she worried it was starting to outpace the steady click of the clock pinned to her chest.

"I'm sorry we kept this from you," Hester said. "But we wanted to be certain that the source of the trouble rested with Crowley before . . ."

Her sentence trailed away then, leaving in its place a silence so thick that the house nearly pushed out the boundaries of the baseboards by an inch or two.

"We must get to work concealing the effects," Anne said, trying to calm herself by making a list that could be neatly checked off. "Until things settle down again."

"That's the trouble, though," Nathanial interrupted. "It's not a minor rip in the fabric of Fate that can be quickly patched together. The whole web will continue to untether until we fix the heart of the problem."

"What exactly are you suggesting?" Anne asked, gooseflesh rising along her arms.

"We have to complete Mr. Crowley's Task for him," Nathanial explained, pointing to the ring that rested on Anne's finger. "It's the only way to ensure these events don't worsen."

"No," Anne insisted as she hid the ring from view, just as

Mr. Crowley had during the session where his Task had come to light. "We can't do that."

If they managed to discover who the ring belonged to and returned it, then Mr. Crowley would no longer be a ghost. He'd pass on to the next phase, leaving Philip behind to struggle on his own. After all the sacrifices that Mr. Crowley had made to ensure they'd be together, it seemed impossible to consider pulling them apart again.

"But we must," Hester said, surprising Anne with an uncharacteristic softness that smoothed out the edges of her crackling voice. "We know what Crowley wished for, but if we don't complete his Task, and soon, our world will continue to unravel. The humans have already started to notice, and though they haven't yet dared put their suspicions into words, it's only a matter of time before they do. And just think of how many other Tasks might be affected by this change of Fate. How many witches might be forced to linger in between, lost and confused about the path they've stumbled onto."

She was right about the consequences, of course. Now that Anne had opened herself to the possibility, she realized the entire fabric of Fate had been snagged. It was why she'd felt so strange these past few weeks, the reason for that sense of having left something behind and not knowing what needed to be retrieved.

But she still wasn't certain that the price of pulling everything back together was worth the cost.

"You must focus on finding out who that ring belongs to," Nathanial said, his steely gaze fixed on Anne. "And soon."

Anne wanted to ask why she had to be the one to shoulder such a heavy load. How could they think to ask it of her when the distinct scent of chrysanthemums that had always followed Mr. Crowley still clung to his favorite seat in the shop?

But, of course, as the city's Diviner, that responsibility must fall on her. Who else would be able to see the threads of destiny and ensure that every strand was put back in its proper place?

"You are powerful and strong enough to bare this burden," Hester murmured, the sound of her voice cutting through the thoughts that were threatening to carry Anne away from the present moment and toward more sinister possibilities that rested in the future. "Our talents will be put to use elsewhere."

"We'll solve the problems that arise while you complete Mr. Crowley's Task," Nathanial added as he rose from his chair and gestured for Hester and Isaac to follow. "As you can imagine, that will keep us quite busy."

The other council members would be running about Chicago from morning to night trying to patch up any hint of magical trouble before it became obvious that something was amiss. As the weeks continued to slip by and the force of Mr. Crowley's remaining Task continued to grow, they'd have to work even harder to keep the worst of their secrets in the dark.

Instead of nodding, though, Anne remained silent, knowing that any agreement she uttered in that moment would carry with it the singed sweetness of a lie.

"I know it is a difficult position, but you must remember your duty," Hester said as she shifted toward the doorway, her words entangled in a brutal gust of wind that blew past the threshold. "For the city's sake."

Anne wrapped her hands around the cold porcelain of her teacup then, her shoulders buckling under an unseen weight, and stared at the hourglass that hovered on the rim while she waited to hear three pairs of footsteps patter on the cobblestones.

But when she realized that she'd only detected the heavy tread of Nathanial's boots and Hester's quick steps, Anne glanced up and saw Isaac waiting near the open door, staring both at and through her all at once.

"You'll find a way," he finally said in the same tone a sleepwalker might when encountered in the hallway.

"A way to do what?" Anne asked, knowing that when it came to Isaac, nothing was quite as it appeared on the surface.

"To trim off the loose ends," he replied. "While keeping the whole intact."

But as Anne listened to Isaac step onto the street and shut the door behind him, she couldn't help but feel like everything was dangling by a thread. And that if she made a single mistake, the entire fabric of her world would unravel in an instant.

CHAPTER 6

A Key

Suggests that help will come during times of difficulty.

As Beatrix and Violet waited for Anne to join them, they tried their best to savor the familiar embrace of the family parlor. After spending so much time away, tucking themselves in the worn quilts and letting the warmth of the hearth stones sink into their toes made it feel like the house had wrapped its arms around their tired shoulders and pulled them in close. It doted on them as if they were girls again, unveiling a box of chocolates that had been hidden away for safekeeping and encouraging them to settle back on the freshly fluffed cushions of the settee so that their eyelids would grow heavy.

But though the Crescent Moon was doing everything it could to convince the sisters that there was no need to leave home again, Beatrix could tell its thoughts were drifting from the parlor.

The embers needed to be stoked, and the curtains that usually covered the windows this time of the night were still tied back on either side of the pane, letting the light from the gas lamps that lined the sidewalk shine freely into the room.

The house wouldn't sit back and enjoy the comfort of the evening, it seemed, until Anne returned to her place in the worn wingback chair and made the parlor feel whole again.

"When do you think she'll join us?" Beatrix asked as she gazed toward the door.

"It's difficult to say," Violet sighed. "Especially since we don't know what these types of meetings entail."

She started to tap her feet against the floorboards but shifted abruptly so that they were trapped beneath her on the settee. Beatrix noticed the odd movement, wondering why Violet seemed to be trying to make herself sit still.

"It's strange knowing she has secrets that we can't share in, isn't it?" Beatrix asked as she turned a careful eye toward her sister. "After all we've been through, it would be nice not to have to worry about which questions to stray away from."

At that, Violet moved again, tucking her legs to her chest so that she could rest her cheek against her knees. The gesture made her look fragile, as if she needed to protect herself against questions that could break her, and Beatrix remembered that Anne wasn't the only one who seemed to be hiding parts of herself from view.

Beatrix set her cup on the side table and placed a hand against Violet's cheek, silently urging her to turn her striking eyes upward.

"Won't you tell me what's troubling you?" Beatrix asked. "I feel the weight you're carrying as if it were settled across my own shoulders."

"You have enough to worry about while writing your next book," Violet replied with a shake of her head, though Beatrix could sense that her resolve was wavering.

"My sisters will never be a burden," Beatrix said as she brushed Violet's fringe to the side so she couldn't hide beneath the short curls. "Please tell me what you're running from."

"Something that I can't escape, it seems," Violet whispered. "No matter how far I go."

Beatrix parted her lips to utter the words that would push Violet forward, but before she could say *Let me help you*, the floorboards in the hallway began to creak, announcing that Anne was about to walk through the door.

As soon as the footsteps neared the threshold, Beatrix felt Violet pull away and knew that the moment where she might have confided in her had passed as abruptly as a coal cracking in the stove.

Turning toward Anne in the hopes that her sister might be able to put everything back on course, Beatrix was startled to find that she looked like someone who'd wandered down the whole of State Street only to learn that the shop they were searching for was on the opposite end of the city. Her cheeks were stained a deep shade of red, and her lips were pinched so tightly together that Beatrix felt an ache beginning to radiate from her own jaw. It was an expression that always appeared on Anne's face just before she displayed a rare show of frustration, and Beatrix instantly wondered what had rattled her eternally composed sister.

"What's happened?" Violet asked as they both watched Anne start to pace in front of the hearth, one hand tucked tightly around her rib cage and the other held up to her lips, as if the movement might help her conjure the words that remained out of grasp.

Anne turned to them then, opening her mouth for just an instant before closing it again.

"She can't tell us," Beatrix whispered, laying a hand on Violet's shoulder in a gentle reminder.

But a sense of fear was starting to flitter across Anne's face, so strange and unfamiliar that it caused a shiver to rake down Beatrix's back. It seemed like the worries brewing within her had grown so strong that they were starting to crack through her calm exterior, working their way into her trembling hands and tired eyes.

"I've overlooked something," Anne finally confessed, turning away from her sisters so that she was staring at their reflections in the gilded mirror above the mantle, as if the distance might help her remember how much she could reveal. "And now I don't know how to put it to rights."

"You can't expect to foresee every problem in time to stop it," Beatrix sighed.

Forgiving others came as easily to Anne as picking up the shards of a saucer that had fallen to the floor. But when judging her own faults, she was as meticulous and unrelenting as a parlor maid scrubbing every last smudge from a silver tea set.

"But I wasn't even keeping my eyes open for the possibility," Anne said. "And now, what hope do I have of fixing it?"

As her voice broke, Anne looked down at the mantle so that her face was hidden beneath her shaking fingers.

But Beatrix and Violet didn't need to see Anne's reflection to know that her thoughts had taken a dark turn. Her shoulders were shuddering in the way they only did when she was trying to hold back some deep emotion that would draw out her vulnerability for all to see, and the sight made them leap from the settee and wrap their arms around her, hoping that the strength of their embrace might give her the foundation she needed to let go.

And, as Anne leaned into the steady rhythm of her sisters' comforting words and finally let the warmth of their bodies chase away the icy fear that had so obviously chilled her to the core, the texture of the parlor began to slowly change.

The scent of peppermint, black tea, and early morning dew infused the room, and the house knew that Anne was drifting away from the present and fading somewhere beyond time.

Her magic vibrated outward as the fragrance grew stronger, causing the delicate hairs along Beatrix and Violet's arms to stand on end while they watched her eyes flitter beneath her closed lids, fixed on impressions that they couldn't fathom.

And gradually, the heady scent of Anne's power was consumed by an even more potent aroma that managed to seep out of her vision and into the parlor: chrysanthemums, rosemary, and the distinct essence of aged paper.

Anne's eyes snapped open then, and as soon as her gaze met the looking glass, the entire surface cracked, as if it had been suddenly cast into the freezing winter's night.

The sisters gasped, but something kept them rooted in their spots before the mantle, and after taking a moment to catch their breaths, they gazed up at the mirror and realized that the breaks formed a pattern.

Hundreds upon hundreds of delicate miniature keys were now imprinted across the looking glass, radiating outward from the Quigleys' shocked reflections. Their mother had taught them that whenever a key appeared on the rim of their teacup, they should look to one another for help.

Beatrix could feel Anne's knees begin to buckle, but she and Violet tightened their hold just in time to keep her standing. Anne may have fallen into the habit of taking on every burden before her sisters had left to pursue their own paths, but they'd returned, ready to lend a hand if Anne was strong enough to ask.

Glancing toward the mirror again, Beatrix watched as something shifted in Anne's expression, a softness settling where there had been only hard lines before.

Still facing the looking glass, Anne gazed at her sisters' reflections and whispered, "I'm going to share something with you that I shouldn't."

She said the words in the same tone that their mother had whenever she tucked the girls into their quilts for the night and was about to tell them a new story, one that promised to keep them from fidgeting or asking if they could stay awake beyond their bedtime.

"But what about the rest of the Council?" Beatrix whispered, the fear that they had all felt every time one of their calling cards arrived still fresh in her mind.

"The others won't know I've told you until after everything's been resolved," Anne said with determination. "You both are meant to help. I can sense it in the depth of my bones."

The strength in her voice reminded Beatrix that Anne was no longer under the watchful eye of the Council but a part of it herself, with all the power and responsibility a witch of that sort possessed. It was still taking some getting used to, the idea that Anne, who'd seemed so rooted to the Crescent Moon, had moved beyond the boundaries of the shop as well, her magic and knowledge of the city growing in ways that were difficult to imagine. But as Beatrix glanced back at the keys etched into the looking glass and noticed the assured set of Anne's shoulders, she understood that her sister's intuition could be trusted.

"Tell us," Beatrix said, ready to help in any way she could.

"There are strange things happening in the city," Anne began to explain as they shifted to the settee. "Beyond what we typically expect to see. Objects going missing when they should be staying put. Time speeding up or slowing down and leaving gaps that people are starting to notice."

"Do you know what's causing it?" Beatrix asked as she turned toward Anne.

"Yes," Anne said, pausing as if considering how to deliver the news. "Someone has failed to complete their Task. A very powerful witch who hid his abilities."

An icy chill filled the room that had nothing to do with the harsh wind rattling the windowpanes. Violet and Beatrix didn't know where this sudden sense of unease had come from at first, but as they grasped the gingham cloth of their quilts and pulled the edges closer, the underlying meaning of Anne's words began to take shape. And they realized the unsettling sensation was coming from suspicions that had been waiting to be drawn out from the past once more.

"You can't mean Mr. Crowley!" Violet cried when she managed to fit the pieces together.

"I'm afraid so," Anne sighed as she reached forward to grasp her sister's hand. "I need to complete his Task to keep the threads of destiny where they're meant to be."

"But you can't," Violet insisted, her thoughts obviously flying to that night in the train station when Mr. Crowley had uttered the name of the one person who'd ever made him feel whole. "It's not what he wanted. If you complete Mr. Crowley's Task, he and Philip will be separated again, this time for good."

The floorboards groaned beneath their feet at that, a clear sign that the house was just as unsettled by this possibility as the Quigley sisters. For though Mr. Crowley could still pass on if another witch was able to complete his Task before everything unraveled, Philip's chances of moving forward were more uncertain. Something was keeping him here, and if that lingering sense of restlessness remained, he would be tethered in between this life and the next forever.

"The longer Mr. Crowley's Task is left undone, the worse these instances are going to become," Anne replied. "And the more likely it is that other witches won't be able to meet their Fate."

Violet fell quiet, apparently silenced by the sheer weight of the situation.

"But what if there's a way to help Mr. Crowley get what he wants while ensuring that everything else remains where it needs to be?" Beatrix murmured, her thoughts slipping away from her sisters and toward an alternative end to their friend's story.

"What do you mean, Bee?" Anne asked while Beatrix continued to sort through all the different possibilities, just as she did when trying to knit together the delicate plotlines that carried her characters in the proper direction.

"Mr. Crowley wanted most of all to be with Philip," Beatrix explained. "It wasn't so much about where he ended up as it was who he was with."

"Yes," Violet agreed hesitantly, her tone indicating that she was unsure where Beatrix's train of thought would lead them. "It wasn't as if he was looking forward to becoming a ghost. All he wanted was to be with Philip."

"That's it!" Anne declared, clearly understanding now what Beatrix was proposing.

"What's it?" Violet asked, but as her gaze flitted from Anne to Beatrix, she appeared to see the path that was slowly unfolding before them.

"We need to figure out what's keeping Philip here so that he'll be free to move forward into the afterlife," Beatrix said with a note of finality, as if she were reading the final card of a tarot spread. "And when we do that, we'll finish Mr. Crowley's Task so they can go together."

The sisters' hearts began to race then, pulled forward by a newfound sense of hope. The shift in their spirits was so strong that the parlor began to feel warmer and more welcoming, drawing them deeper into the corners of the cushions so that they could begin to plan in earnest.

"Everything would have to come together at just the right moment," Beatrix said as she considered all the pieces that needed to fall into place.

Mr. Crowley and Philip had both been lingering in between, and the only way to be certain that they could be together was to make sure they moved forward at the same moment. Neither of them had been grounded in the next phase, and if they failed to cross over together, it was likely that they'd lose one another again before finding their way to what rested beyond this life.

"Time isn't on our side," Anne murmured. "We don't have until the end of the year as we did with the curse. This needs to be sorted out in a matter of weeks, or the situation may slip entirely beyond our control. And we'll need to try and uncover the rightful owner of Mr. Crowley's ring while figuring out what can be done for Philip so we're ready to reunite them when everything falls into place."

"There's the shop to consider too," Beatrix added.

She knew that if Anne neglected the Crescent Moon, the other members of the Council would wonder what was carrying her away from the shop and begin to notice that her focus wasn't entirely on completing Mr. Crowley's Task. Then they might realize what she was up to and take matters into their own hands, demanding the ring and finishing the Task themselves before the Quigleys could be certain that Philip wouldn't be left behind.

"But you have me," Violet said, reaching forward to pull Anne's hand into her own. "I can help uncover clues and keep the shop running smoothly so you can focus your effort on putting things to rights."

"I'm relieved to hear that," Anne replied. "Because I'm not going to be able to do this on my own."

"I can help too," Beatrix added.

Anne drew in a breath then, as if a distinct fragrance had drifted into the room.

"You certainly will," Anne replied as she considered her sister. "But I think that you must also try to write. I have a feeling that you need to stay on your path for us to set Mr. Crowley and Philip on theirs."

"Why do you think that?" Beatrix asked curiously.

"Your birthday vision was the sensation of paper crumbling beneath your fingertips," Anne explained. "And in my vision just now, I could smell aged paper. It must all be connected somehow."

Beatrix wanted to protest, but when she met Anne's eyes and saw the sense of certainty that had grown there, she merely sighed and leaned against the back of the settee.

As much as she would have liked a distraction from her own troubles, if Anne thought that she needed to stay focused on her writing to help their friend find the same sense of peace their mother must have felt when she slipped beyond the worries of this life and into the arms of their father, that was what she would do.

"You're just going to have to trust me," Anne murmured as she reached forward and gripped Beatrix's fingers with her free hand.

"I do," Beatrix replied, returning the pressure. She believed in her sister's intuition, now more than ever.

"Then let's begin," Violet declared as she laced her hand through the crook of Beatrix's arm, drawing the three of them together in a single interconnected knot. "Since we don't have a moment to waste."

With that, the house prodded the fire until the flames were roaring, knowing that the Quigley sisters would remain awake in the family parlor long into the evening hours as they discussed how a bargain might be struck with Fate once more.

CHAPTER 7

A Beetle

*Signifies unrest and a sense of
things moving out of place.*

Hours later, when the sisters had said sleepy goodbyes and stepped out of the family parlor to drift toward their beds and the rest that awaited them there, Violet found herself slipping away from the Crescent Moon and into a dream tinged with the scent of caramel apples and sawdust.

Though she'd done her best to keep herself from falling asleep, knowing what visions lurked there, her eyelids had grown heavy, and eventually she'd succumbed to the sensation of losing touch with the soft flannel sheets beneath her fingertips.

She was no longer in the safe and comfortable confines of the house, but climbing to the very top of a wooden platform on the side of the circus ring. A chaos of sparklers and flames was unfolding beneath her, and though she couldn't see the faces of the onlookers, gasps and cheers of utter delight told her that the rest of the troupe were working their magic on the crowd.

Violet was surprised that she could hear all the excitement in the tent, given how loudly her own heart was beating within her chest. The sound of it seemed to be coming from everywhere, growing louder and louder with every step that she took toward the edge and reverberating against the corners of her dream until the whole scene started to shake.

After a few breaths, Violet realized that she felt just as she always did before allowing her impulses to take over and pull her where they may: nervous about flinging caution to the wind but eager to feel the electric shock that shot straight from the base of her spine all the way to the tips of her fingers whenever she couldn't predict what might happen next.

She was standing on the precipice of the platform now, so close to the edge that her toes wrapped around the boards, ready to launch her away from safety and into the open air.

But before Violet could take that final step toward the unknown, a voice started to cut through the rhythm of her heartbeat, so faint that she wondered if it was just one of the violins in the flock of musicians below drawing out a fresh chord. She almost shook off the noise and the feeling of hesitation that came along with it, but then a calloused hand gripped her own, gently pulling her away from the edge.

"Wildfire, listen to me," Emil was saying. His voice, normally so playful and full of mischief, was rougher now, tinged with the weight of worries straining to be heard.

The scent of fireside smoke slipped into Violet's dream then, causing the tightness in her muscles to relax as she thought of how much stronger the aroma of summer midnight would be if she stepped back and leaned into Emil's arms.

"We're ready," Violet heard herself reply in the same tone she used whenever her mind was already made up. "I know we are!"

Emil shook his head, clearly torn between letting Violet leap off the platform and into the rush of the performance and reminding himself that at least one of them should remain grounded for just a moment longer.

"We haven't practiced the new routine enough," he said, his words vibrating against the edges of the dream and causing the whole scene to ripple. "We can't do it without the net."

Violet took a second to consider what Emil was saying, and as she let his words sink in, she felt the softest tingle along her spine, like the first tap of an icy finger. But before the sensation could rise to the front of her awareness, Violet's attention was quickly caught by the abrupt applause of the crowd.

Instantly, her body began to vibrate in anticipation of soaring across the top of the tent and causing an even stronger reaction to ripple through the stands, one that would make her heart beat faster and propel her from one twist of the bar to the next.

Instead of stepping toward Emil, Violet flashed him a wide grin and flung herself off the side of the platform, daring him to follow her.

She didn't need to look back to know that he was already jumping into the air, just a beat behind as they twirled above the performers in the ring, capturing the gaze of the crowd and pulling everyone's attention upward. Ever since the night they'd first soared above the stands, Violet had known he'd follow her anywhere.

And as she had expected, the gasps of amazement that radiated from the crowd made her feel just like a falling star, burning so bright that nothing could stand in her way.

It wasn't until the middle of the routine that Violet noticed she and Emil hadn't managed to quite match one another's rhythm. She'd leapt toward the first bar a moment before their cue, and Emil seemed to be scrambling to catch up, his movements tinged with a tension that was normally absent from his graceful and seemingly effortless swings between the bars.

Time, which had been moving forward in a rush, slowed to the pace of honey dripping down the jar, as it often does when you reach the part of a dream that you hope to wake up from.

Though Violet couldn't remember exactly what would happen next, she felt the thrill of her performance quickly shift into a sense of unease that made her shudder, as if her body had relived this moment so many times that it didn't matter if her memory couldn't quite find the source of the trouble to come.

And then she saw Emil swinging toward her, his arm extended so that he could grasp her hand and gain just enough momentum to make it to the open bar that dangled a few feet beside her.

But his hand seemed just the barest whisper of an inch farther than it had been when they'd practiced, and though Violet stretched as far as she was able, in the moment they were supposed to lock together, her fingers brushed cold air instead of the warmth of Emil's palm.

As Violet shot awake and gripped the icy sheets beneath her skin, she could still hear the screams of the crowd, so sharp and shrill that it felt like they were going to rip her apart.

The house heard the cry that she managed to stifle just before it became loud enough to wake her sisters. It instantly kindled the fire in the room, frightened by the frost that had managed to coat the inner pane of the window and looking glass of the vanity while Violet tossed and turned in her sleep.

She was shaking uncontrollably now, trying to orient herself in the present so that the tethers of the past wouldn't pull her beneath the weight of her guilt and sorrow, as they always did when she didn't have something else to focus on.

The crazy quilts that had fallen to the edge of the bed shifted closer, tucking Violet within the comforting chaos of their colorful calico patches, and she could smell frankincense infusing the room from a vial of perfume that the house had found in the drawer of the vanity and remembered Clara Quigley pulling out whenever one of the girls awoke from a nightmare.

The fragrance warmed Violet in places that the flames in the hearth could never touch, and gradually, she was able to lean back against the pillow and into the sound of the logs crackling a few feet from the bed.

In an instant, she was a child again, waiting for the next brush of her mother's hand through her curls as she whispered words that were too soft to understand but somehow still had the strength to loosen the strain in her chest.

That's all Violet wanted at the moment, anyway—to drift so far back into the past that she'd forget what it had felt like to realize Emil's hand was going to miss hers.

"He's okay. He's okay. He's okay," she murmured over and over again, trying to make herself remember that Emil had survived the fall. That his body was healing, so quickly that he'd soon be back in the ring. It had only been a few months since the accident, and already he'd started practicing on the bars again, seeing how much of his strength he could depend upon before moving away the ropes and swinging about in the open air once more.

His spirits hadn't been permanently fractured by the fall, either, and when Violet conjured up the last time she'd seen his face, leaning forward to kiss her goodbye before she left on the last train to Chicago, she saw only the steady love that had grown between them since that very first night by the lakeshore.

The trouble was that Violet hadn't found a way to forgive herself.

Suddenly, the frost that had melted along the windowsill began to freeze again as Violet thought about when she'd need to return to the ring.

The circus would move north as soon as the snow that coated the city streets began to melt and the harsh bite of winter gave way to spring. Violet had promised Emil that once the troupe arrived in Chicago, she would join him for his first performance since the fall, giving him the support he needed to fly between the bars again.

But though Emil's trust in Violet hadn't wavered, she couldn't say the same. How could she when it had been her impulses and refusal to look beyond the present moment that had led to disaster?

She had almost lost him.

The thought sent a fresh shock through Violet's body, and the weight that had eased somewhat from her heart began to press down once more, threatening to push her through the bed and into the dark depths of those memories she couldn't manage to leave behind.

Noticing the ice that was starting to creep along the intricate woodwork, the house stoked the fire before Violet could start shaking again, determined to keep her safe from the burdens that were trying to pull her away from the comfort of home.

And eventually, Violet did succumb to the spell of the Crescent Moon, her heartbeat slowing to the rhythm of the smoldering embers in the hearth and into a slumber laced with frankincense that warded off unpleasant dreams.

For now, she could take refuge in the haven that she'd hoped to find when her hand had grasped the garden gate the day before and lose her worries in the spicy scent of citrus and the steady comfort of knowing that she didn't need to move forward, not yet.

CHAPTER 8

Buttons
Appear when someone is overwhelmed by their options and struggling to make a choice.

When Beatrix set about the task of writing the next morning, she discovered that her mind wasn't the only place that had grown cluttered.

Though the Crescent Moon had mastered the art of carving additional space from nothing, over the past year it had needed to trim away at nooks and crannies in forgotten corners to make room for the growing demands of the shop. For houses, like people, need to account for the living parts of themselves as well.

Unfortunately, however, this meant that Beatrix had been welcomed by a less-than-pleasant surprise when she opened the door to what had once been her study.

"Oh dear," Beatrix had sighed as she attempted to fold herself into the wooden chair. Before, she'd been able to lean back and stretch, but now, the dusty records stacked on the bookcase shelves were practically spilling onto the desk.

Beatrix had only managed to sit in her old spot after climbing atop the chair and tucking her legs to her chest, the space beneath the desk bursting with so many books and boxes that her boots didn't have a hope of touching the floorboards.

After she'd managed to pull out her notebook and fill her pen with ink, the ache that she felt in her awkwardly bent knees and elbows had seemed to grow beyond reasonable proportion until all she could think about was how to find a more comfortable position. It hadn't helped matters that the low murmur of their customers' voices and subtle clinks of teacups being set to rights on saucers kept seeping through the floorboards and into the study, where they managed to echo despite the fact that the walls were pressed so closely together.

Before she'd left home, a steam engine running through the center of the hallway couldn't have pulled Beatrix away from a story that needed to be threaded together. But now every discomfort festered into a distraction that kept her from choosing a potential plotline and stretching it onto the page.

"It's no use," Beatrix sighed as she attempted to shove her chair back, forgetting how close the bookshelf was now and dislodging several of the folders, which poured down on her from above in a puff of dust.

Sensing Beatrix's distress, the house tried its best to widen the study and give her enough space to free herself from the chair. But the front parlor was packed, and it couldn't find an extra inch to borrow in time to help Beatrix avoid hitting her shin against the side of the desk as she swatted away the papers.

"It's not your fault," Beatrix murmured as she reached forward and placed her palm against the wainscoting, trying to reassure the house that it wasn't its walls she was worried about crashing in around her but the foundation of her own inner world.

The plaster beneath her hand shook in relief as the house let out a shaky sigh of its own. It so wanted Beatrix to feel at home again, but no amount of freshly laundered sheets and honey buns seemed to be helping her settle in.

Before the house or Beatrix could convey anything more, though, the sound of boots clicking against the floorboards drew their attention away from their worries and toward the hallway.

"Beatrix!" Violet exclaimed as she threw open the door and started to step inside, only to come to a sudden halt when she realized that there wasn't even enough room to sneeze.

"What did you come running in here for?" Beatrix asked as she hastily covered the blank pages that littered the desk.

A spark of delight flashed across Violet's face then that nearly overshadowed the deep circles beneath her eyes.

"There's a *man* out in the parlor," she said in the same tone that one might use to announce they'd found an elephant waiting for them on the front stoop.

"I do hear that there are quite a few of those walking out and about," Beatrix replied.

"Well, this one says that he's here to talk to you," Violet said, pointing a playful finger at her sister. "You must tell me who he is this instant!"

"Considering I haven't had the chance to see him myself, I couldn't say," Beatrix murmured.

"He's rather tall with a headful of hair poking out in all directions," Violet declared, gesturing upward as she spoke. "But he has the most charming smile, as if he isn't aware of the effect it has."

"It can't be," Beatrix hissed as she shot upward from her chair, banging her shins yet again against the side of the desk.

"It can't be who?" Violet asked, her foot tapping so quickly against the floorboards that the ladies sitting closest to the back door of the shop wondered if a woodpecker had somehow gotten loose in the house.

"Jennings," Beatrix whispered, brushing her hand through her hair and down her dress to put herself in some semblance of order. But the ink that she'd spilled was still fresh on her skin, leaving vibrant blue slashes on her temple and across the front of her blouse.

"You can't mean *the* Jennings," Violet gasped. "The one you spoke of so often in your letters that I started to wonder if he was real or one of those imaginary friends you were always talking about when we were girls?"

"I did not write about him that often," Beatrix hissed, moving to wrap her arms defensively around her rib cage and failing when her elbow caught the edge of a stack of outdated calendars, sending them tumbling to the floor.

"Oh yes, you did," Violet said with a smile. "And now that he's here, I'm going to figure out exactly what has been going on between you two."

"My relationship with Jennings is purely professional," Beatrix insisted, but as soon as the words left her lips, a singed sweetness filled the room, and she knew that Violet could taste the flavor of her lie.

"I'm going to speak with him," Violet declared as she turned away from Beatrix and started to step toward the door that led to the front parlor.

"You will do no such thing!" Beatrix cried as she bolted after her, hoping to avert disaster.

The thought of her sister trapping Jennings in the entryway and demanding he tell her all she wanted to know made her pace quicken, and she managed to catch up with Violet just as she reached the threshold, pulling her back in time to shut the door behind her. The house, knowing that Beatrix had experienced enough distress for one day, clicked the lock so that Violet would have to walk through the busy kitchen to get to the tearoom.

"Traitor!" Beatrix heard Violet cursing at the walls as she wove through the tables of ladies sipping their tea and moved toward the front of the shop, where she could see the top of Jennings' head peeking over the corner that led to the entryway.

As soon as she caught sight of those unruly locks, which Jennings had the habit of running his fingers through whenever a conflict arose in her calendar book, Beatrix felt her breathing slow for the first moment since she'd woken up that morning, only to have it pick up again when his gaze found hers across the room.

"Miss Quigley," Jennings said, beaming from ear to ear as she got closer.

"Jennings," Beatrix replied, feeling a pleasant ache in her cheeks as her own lips turned upward into a smile.

"It's good to see you again," Jennings said as he took a step toward her, the movement causing a curious tingling sensation to bloom at the base of Beatrix's spine.

Beatrix opened her mouth to reply but realized that the shop had become suspiciously quiet.

Turning around, she was horrified to realize that most of their customers had halted their conversations and were staring blatantly at the scene unfolding in the front of the shop. A few of the ladies had even turned their chairs so that they could lean forward in the hopes of overhearing as much as they possibly could.

"I think it's best if we step outside," Beatrix said as she wrapped her hand around Jennings' forearm and pulled him toward the door. "To avoid disturbing the customers."

"Of course, of course," Jennings replied. "I wouldn't want to intrude."

"But you weren't intru—" one of the customers nearest the hostess stand started to call out, only to be cut off when Beatrix slammed the front door closed, the sound of the bells drowning out the rest of her sentence.

"It's quite busy in there, isn't it?" Jennings remarked as they stepped onto the sidewalk.

"Yes, it is," Beatrix said. "My sister Anne expanded the shop while I was away, and it seems that the extra seats she's put in are always filled."

A strong gust of wind blew through the snow-covered street as Beatrix uttered those last words, causing her teeth to chatter.

Noticing the way that Beatrix was beginning to wrap her hands around her waist, Jennings quickly pulled off his coat and draped it around her shoulders before she could refuse. The fabric was worn with rough stitches that were clearly holding everything together by the barest thread. But as Jennings pulled up the collar so that the exposed skin of Beatrix's neck would be shielded from the wind, she couldn't help herself from burrowing a bit deeper into the garment's warmth.

"You mustn't, Jennings," Beatrix insisted. "You'll catch a cold while standing out here without your coat."

"I'll be just fine," Jennings said, his smile widening a fraction as he looked down at her. Beatrix wondered if he was amused by the way the long sleeves seemed to engulf her delicate frame, but it wasn't humor that glinted in his eyes. No, it was something else that she couldn't quite put her finger on.

Before Beatrix could give it any more thought, though, another blast of wind whipped down the street, nearly knocking her off-balance. Instinctively, she slipped her hands into the pockets of the coat to brace herself and was surprised when her fingers hit something wrapped in parchment paper.

"I've brought you a gift," Jennings said when he saw the confused expression flit across Beatrix's face. "It arrived at the office this morning, and I knew you'd be eager to see it."

Curious now, Beatrix pulled the object out and looked down to find the outline of a book covered in brown paper with the address for Donohoe & Company scribbled across the front.

"Open it," Jennings said, clearly eager to watch Beatrix's reaction.

Slowly, she pulled back the paper, exposing the bright green of the cover design, so cheerful that it almost made Beatrix believe the clouds had briefly parted to let in a single glimpse of summer. Then her eyes wandered to the gold title printed above the embossed flowers, and the sight gave her such a shock that she nearly dropped the book onto the sludge of the sidewalk.

"But this isn't meant to be out yet!" Beatrix exclaimed as she ran her fingers along the spine.

During her tour, Beatrix had the fortune of hearing about a new book written by another author who was taking England by storm. She'd been crestfallen when she learned that the story wouldn't be available in America for some months yet, impatient to slip into a tale that she was sure would keep her up well into the evening hours.

But here it was now, resting between her very own hands!

"How did you get a copy of this?" Beatrix asked in amazement as she flipped open the cover and let her eyes take in the watercolor illustration that awaited her there. It depicted a garden, so bursting with hydrangeas and summer flowers that Beatrix almost forgot that her own breath took the shape of clouds whenever she exhaled.

"I may have pulled a few strings with our London branch," Jennings said, clearly delighted. "I hope you like it."

"Like it?" Beatrix echoed in disbelief. "I'm not going to be able to stop myself from reading it cover to cover in a single sitting."

As soon as the words left her lips, though, Beatrix thought of the empty notebook that she'd abandoned in the study, and her excitement shifted, slipping beneath the worries that had whispered in her ear as she tried to write.

Instantly, her shoulders slumped forward, and her gaze darted away from the book and toward those invisible troubles that awaited her.

"Is everything all right?" Jennings asked, seeming to notice that Beatrix was slipping into herself.

He lifted his hand, and for an instant, Beatrix thought she was about to feel his warm palm against her chilled cheek. To her surprise, she felt disappointed when it landed lightly on her upper arm instead.

"This is a wonderful gift," Beatrix said in a rush, hoping to assure him that she wasn't being unappreciative. "It's only that I'm so busy with the next novel. I don't know that I'll have time to start it."

"Don't tell me you've refused yourself the pleasure of reading?" Jennings asked, clearly dumbfounded that someone who loved the written word as much as Beatrix would have taken such extreme measures.

"I'm afraid of getting distracted," Beatrix replied, trying to be as honest as she could without giving any hint that something serious was amiss. "Not when there seems to be so much to do and in such a short amount of time."

Jennings paused for a moment, and in that brief beat of silence, Beatrix worried that he might ask to see what she'd written so far to ensure that everything was on the right path. That he'd realize she hadn't strung together a single sentence and the expression of delight that always flashed across his features when he saw her would twist into cold disapproval.

But to her great relief, that was not what Jennings wanted to know.

"When was the last time you read anything that you didn't write yourself?" he asked, taking a step closer.

"I'm not sure," Beatrix answered, genuinely at a loss for what to say.

Dozens of books were stacked beside the settee in the family parlor, but Beatrix hadn't packed a single one to bring with her on the tour. Had it really been that long since she'd turned a cover with the intention of reading past the first paragraph?

"How can you expect to write if you've forgotten what it's like to experience the simple magic of reading a new story?" Jennings asked with a grin as he wrapped his fingers around the corners of the book, his hands so close to Beatrix's that she could feel their warmth, and pushed it toward her.

"I'm not sure it's a good idea," Beatrix murmured as her thoughts drifted away from the cover beneath her touch and toward the empty notebook once more.

"Reading is always a good idea," Jennings said as he leaned in just a bit closer to wipe away the ink that Beatrix had smudged across her temple.

He was near enough now that she could smell coffee and freshly cut paper. The scent was so familiar that Beatrix nearly stepped forward, to do what, she wasn't entirely certain.

But before she could lift her boot from the pavement, the sound of raised voices filled the street, drawing Beatrix's attention away from Jennings and toward the shop.

Through the foggy glass of the windows, Beatrix could see a vibrant flash of auburn curls darting from one end of the front parlor to the next, and she realized that it wouldn't be long before they were interrupted.

"I must say goodbye," Beatrix sighed, casting an apologetic glance in Jennings' direction as she took a step back. "I think my sisters need me in the shop."

"Of course," Jennings said in understanding, though Beatrix caught the barest whisper of disappointment in his voice, so soft that she wondered if she'd been mistaken. "But please promise me that you'll read the book. I want to see why critics have been making such a fuss, but I won't turn a single page until you've finished the entire thing. Then I'll have someone to talk with about it."

Beatrix was about to say that she couldn't make such a promise with the deadline looming before her. But then she glanced upward at Jennings' crooked smile, and her reply melted away as quickly as the snow on her boots would when she stepped back into the shop.

"I promise," Beatrix said instead, a grin tugging at the corners of her lips.

"I'm very pleased to hear that," Jennings replied as he began to step away, still facing Beatrix as he started to move down the street. "I'll come to call again soon to be sure that you're holding your end of our bargain."

"I look forward to it," Beatrix said, pulling the book closer to her chest as she watched Jennings give her a final nod of the head and turn around the corner.

When he finally disappeared from sight, Beatrix discovered that she'd been holding on to the same breath since the moment Jennings had started to walk away.

Before she could ponder what that meant, though, the sound of the front door being thrown open caused her to jump.

"There you are," Violet declared, her wild eyes flitting up and down the street when she realized that her sister was alone.

"We've just said goodbye," Beatrix said in a rush. "I'm afraid you've missed him."

Violet's brows pinched together in frustration, but when her gaze settled back on Beatrix, surprise flashed across her face, quickly followed by a look of smug satisfaction.

"What?" Beatrix asked, unnerved that Violet suddenly appeared so pleased.

"I've already learned all I need to know," Violet said with a laugh as she turned to step back inside the Crescent Moon.

Beatrix was about to ask her sister what she could possibly mean, but as she reached out to grab Violet's sleeve, she instantly stopped.

Jennings' coat was still hanging about her shoulders, so warm and familiar that Beatrix hadn't even remembered it didn't belong to her.

CHAPTER 9

A Candle
Foreshadows a revelation.

By the time Beatrix stepped back over the threshold of the shop, Anne was so focused on her task in the divination room that she didn't even notice the sound of the bells hitting the front door or the rising voices of their customers, who were full of speculations about why such a charming young man had come to call.

It helped that the house had shifted the room slightly so that its entrance now spilled into the hallway rather than the front parlor. Since the expansion, one too many curious customers had tried to pull at the moss-colored curtain to see what rested behind it, and the walls had to resist the urge to snap the fabric back as a washerwoman does when trying to shoo a muddy dog from a fresh line of linen. Though the divination room was now positioned farther from the heart of the shop, the tinkling of porcelain and gentle hum of tea carts rolling across the wooden floors could still be heard if someone was paying attention.

But Anne's focus was firmly fixed on the shelves, so these everyday rhythms went completely unnoticed.

"Which to choose next ... ," Anne muttered to herself as her gaze drifted along jars packed full of dried petals, stacks of tarot cards, bags of dust, and other tools of her craft.

In the light of the evening fire, the Quigleys had decided that Anne should use her magic to determine their next step. Violet and Beatrix seemed certain in their sister's ability to uncover a sign, their belief in her skill so infectious that Anne found a bit of her confidence returning as she listened to them argue about who would watch over the shop while she got to work the next day.

But the sense of steadiness that she'd felt when tucked away in the family parlor the night before had faded somewhat after sitting alone in the divination room for hours without coming across the barest hint of foresight.

Already, she'd worked her way through several spreads of tarot cards, gazed into the shadows of her grandmother's crystal ball, and cast so many stone runes across the floor that Tabitha, who'd been hiding beneath the table, darted out to chase them, scattering any hope of piecing together the predictions etched in the stones.

"It seems that Mr. Crowley's fate is just as difficult to sort out in death as it was in life," Anne sighed, reaching to knead away the ache in her neck.

She knew, of course, that her friend wasn't to blame. No, as Anne stepped away from the shelf and saw her own worn expression reflected against the surface of the crystal ball, she realized that the trouble rested with her. She was trying to twist her magic into an unnatural position rather than letting it flow effortlessly from within, guiding her toward the answers that waited in the shadows.

As she'd learned over the past year, power wasn't so much about control as it was a willingness to let go and listen.

Releasing a shaky breath, Anne decided that now wasn't the time to slip into old habits. Instead of reaching toward the shelves and pushing herself further, she drifted toward the rocking chair that sat in the corner, just beneath bundles of dried sunflowers that smelled like slumbering sunshine.

Leaning into the curve of the chair, Anne began to rock back and forth, willing her fear for the future to fade away with every creaky swish of the wood. By the time her head began to loll, Tabitha had hopped up to join her, curling into her lap as Anne stroked her inky black coat.

The cat had a habit of slipping away as quickly as she came, but she'd remained close this winter, as she always seemed to do whenever trouble brewed within the walls of the Crescent Moon.

The gentle creak of the rocking chair blended with the sound of Tabitha's purrs, drawing Anne into a state that felt present and far away all at once. Though her eyes were too heavy to open, she could sense a warmth starting to climb up her toes and knew that the house must have struck a match in the hearth, hoping that the crackling of the flames might help her fade into a much-needed rest.

As Anne felt herself slip farther away from the Crescent Moon, she began to smell the aroma of peppermint, black tea, and morning dew.

Her magic was up to something.

Content to let it pull her along where it may, Anne sank deeper into what was beginning to feel like the edge of a vision. Her breathing slowed to the languid pace of places beyond the bounds of time, and she gradually lost touch with the smooth wooden arms of the chair.

And then she was no longer in the shop at all, but standing at a window looking down at a snow-covered street just starting to flicker with the light of gas lamps.

Anne was struck at once by the unusual texture of the vision, which possessed the faded quality of a photograph left too long on a south-facing wall. It seemed that she had fallen back into the past rather than toward the future.

Reading someone's fortune always involved peeking into the past, but since Anne's powers had taken on a life of their own, she'd found herself slipping back in time more and more. Her visions of what came before were sporadic and beyond her control, though. She couldn't conjure them by force of will or direct herself to a specific point in time.

Anne wondered if this was because the past was more difficult to interpret than what rested ahead. For while the future was yet untouched, the past was always tethered to emotions that rippled outward into the present.

Though Anne felt an initial impulse to turn around and see where, exactly, her magic had led her, she knew that doing so might disrupt the vision. And so, she kept her gaze locked toward the street, waiting to see what would happen next.

It wasn't long before she saw the figure of a young boy walking slowly across the road. He was hunched over in a way that suggested his little shoulders were already carrying the weight of too many secrets, and his steps were so slow that it was obvious he was trying to make the short journey as long as possible.

Turning her gaze toward the building on the other side of the street, Anne could understand the boy's reluctance. He was moving closer to one of the most imposing town houses she'd ever seen, a monstrosity of white marble that looked colder than the icy pavement beneath the child's feet. Just one glance at it made Anne shiver, her eyes shifting so quickly away from the striking image that she nearly missed the name carved in the stone just above the front door: Crowley.

Anne's gaze flashed back to the little boy just as a voice rang out from her side of the street. As soon as he turned and the lamplight hit his face, already so firm and suspicious, Anne knew that she had managed to fall into a moment from her friend's childhood.

The shape of another boy, this one about the same size as young Crowley, appeared on the street, and as he moved, Anne caught the barely perceptible glint of something gold hanging about his neck. The newcomer seemed to be asking young Crowley to go with him somewhere, gesturing excitedly toward the house that Anne was peering out from. A look of hope and then reluctance crossed over Crowley's small features as he spoke with the boy, telling Anne all that she couldn't hear. It was as clear as ivy stretching toward the rim of a cup that he wanted to go with his friend but had to return home.

Anne realized that she was watching Philip asking him to come and play. Hadn't Mr. Crowley said that they'd lived across the street from one another as children?

She was beginning to lose sight of the boys now, though, the scene beyond the window obscured by unnaturally large flurries that made her feel as if she was trying to gaze into a snow globe. Perhaps if she lifted the latch on the window and pulled it open, she might be able to hear what they were saying and find a clue that could save them both.

But as soon as Anne clicked the lock at the top of the pane, she heard someone ask, "Who are you?"

The words were spoken in a soft hush that carried the texture of secrets slipping through keyholes. Anne thought the hue of the voice belonged to a woman, but she'd need to look behind her shoulder to be certain. As she tried to move her head to see who was standing behind her, though, Anne discovered that she couldn't turn her neck. Her face was locked forward, as if someone had put their hands on either side of her cheeks and refused to let her go.

Anne's heart began to beat faster as she tried to loosen the invisible hold and turn around, but the more she resisted, the fainter the vision became, until it looked just like a room consumed by the sharp rays of sunrise.

By the time Anne managed to free herself and began to turn around, she could already start to feel the rocking chair beneath her palm and the weight of Tabitha sitting on her lap.

"Who are you?" the voice asked again just before Anne's eyes flew open and she found herself back in the divination room, all traces of the vision gone except the barest echo of that final question.

Anne drew in a deep, steadying breath, releasing it so slowly that Tabitha mistook it for a hiss and nearly jumped off her lap.

"I think the correct question is," Anne finally said once she was certain that her mind and body had returned to the familiar confines of the Crescent Moon. "Who are *you*?"

CHAPTER 10

A Closed Box
Suggests that something
lost might be found.

While Anne was trying her best to hold on to her vision of the past, Violet's attention was focused on staying in the present. Though chasing Beatrix through the house and serving the ladies who lined up at the front of the parlor in the hopes of securing an open table had kept her occupied during the rush of the early afternoon, the crowd in the Crescent Moon was starting to thin as the clock ticked nearer to closing.

It was beginning to feel like the shop was lulling into a late-afternoon nap as the voices of their customers lowered from a vibrant pulse to a steady murmur and the shadows in the corners grew dim enough to consider turning on the gas lamps. It was a moment of the day that Violet would have savored had the memories of her restless night not been waiting to nip as soon as her mind wandered away from the fortunes that peeked out of swirls of ginger, cloves, and citrus.

As long as she was distracted in the shop, the fear that had gripped Violet's heart remained at bay, only flashing forward when she wasn't speaking with a customer or racing from the front parlor to the kitchen, where the scent of vanilla and nutmeg was so strong that it chased away any lingering memories from the night before.

But even Violet couldn't manage to always be moving, and whenever the rhythm of the shop slowed just enough for her feet to stay in the same place for more than a few seconds, she became aware of the guilt that was now always simmering just under the surface, like a pot of caramel that was a second away from burning.

Violet could feel her heart beginning to quicken the longer she stood there, the grooves between her fingers growing clammy as she started to fall into the memories she'd carried with her, slipping away from the comfort of the Crescent Moon though she was still perched behind the hostess stand.

"You seem preoccupied," a familiar voice murmured, snapping Violet's attention away from thoughts tinged with the scent of cold sweat and heartache.

Grateful for the distraction, Violet lifted her gaze and saw Celeste standing before her, wrapped in several layers of woolen garments that were covered in snowflakes from the late-afternoon storm sweeping through the streets.

"I'm sorry, Celeste," Violet replied as she stepped forward and began to help their guest slip out of her coat and scarves. "I'm afraid I found my thoughts wandering."

"Yes," Celeste said slowly, drawing out the word as her gaze came to rest on the lines that fluttered outward from Violet's eyes, betraying her lack of sleep. "I can see that."

"Are you waiting for Katherine?" Violet asked, knowing from the reservation book that this was the time the two of them usually came to the shop together.

"Unfortunately, I've just run into her on the street and learned that she won't be able to join me this afternoon," Celeste sighed. "Something about a new year's blessing that needs to be taken care of as soon as possible."

"I'm sorry to hear that," Violet said, disappointed that she wouldn't get to see her friend's warm smile on a day when it would have been most welcomed. "Shall I sit you in one of the wingback chairs by the hearth, then?"

Celeste's gaze drifted slightly downward, and Violet had to lace her fingers together to keep from shielding the dark half-moons beneath her eyes.

"Why don't you join me instead?" Celeste finally asked, taking Violet by surprise.

Though Anne had written about Celeste in her letters, Violet still felt that she didn't quite know the witch who'd helped the Quigleys accept their diverging paths.

"That sounds delightful," Violet replied. "But I've promised to look over the shop until closing."

"The girls seem to have everything in hand," Celeste said as she gestured toward Franny and Peggy, who were moving confidently between the tables with carts of fresh tea and scones. "And no one seems to need a reading at the moment."

Violet surveyed the parlor and realized that Celeste was correct. All their customers appeared to be deep in conversation, lost in the stories that they were telling one another rather than searching out a Quigley sister to string one together about their own future.

"I could use a cup of tea," Violet sighed, thinking of how it would feel to grasp the hot porcelain between her hands, which were still chilled from dreams that threatened to slip into daytime.

She led Celeste toward an open table nearest the window, where they could watch the sidewalks slowly disappear beneath snowflakes and evening shadows.

At first, Violet was uneasy about the silence that unfolded between them after they settled in their seats and ordered a pot of tea, wondering what meaning undercut Celeste's quiet gestures as she rested her chin atop her clasped hands and gazed out the window.

But then, as one second slipped easily into the next, Violet realized that her companion was merely the type of person who didn't feel the need to fill every quiet moment with chatter. Each word was formed only when she thought it necessary. And though Violet was normally one for speaking so quickly that the sentences she strung together practically flew from her tongue, there was something about Celeste's steady silence that managed to calm the erratic tempo of her pulse.

"How does it feel to return home?" Celeste finally asked after Franny set a piping hot pot of tea on the table and poured them both a cup.

When Violet lifted it to her lips, she smelled mugwort and anise, the same herbs that Clara Quigley had blended whenever she hoped to clear her mind to make space for a vision of the future. It was a tea favored by witches of their sort who practiced divination, and Violet couldn't help but wonder if Celeste ever felt a pang of regret when she took a sip of the blend and remembered what she'd lost.

"Like I'm finally able to breathe again," Violet answered before she could remember to say something that didn't ring so loudly with the truth.

"Does it?" Celeste asked.

Violet was surprised to realize that she wanted to tell Celeste about what had brought her back to the Crescent Moon. Though she hadn't yet found the words to share her troubles with her own sisters, there was something about the witch sitting across from her that made her inclined to say more. Perhaps it was the knowledge that their conversation would well and truly end when Celeste slipped out the door, taking Violet's secrets along with her instead of letting them brew within the house, where they would grow stronger than they already had.

"I thought that after I completed my Task, everything would be so clear," Violet said as she stared away from Celeste and out the window. "But something's happened, and I haven't been able to get my feet back under me. Being here makes me feel steadier somehow."

She expected Celeste to ask the obvious question, to lean forward and inquire about what, exactly, had pushed Violet so far off course that she'd landed right where she started.

But she didn't.

Instead, Celeste merely sat back in her chair and stared straight into Violet's eyes, as if she was trying to decipher something there. Eventually, though, she broke her gaze and looked out the window as she stirred her tea, the silver spoon clinking delicately against the sides of the cup.

"It sounds to me like you've lost something but don't know how to go about the task of recovering it," Celeste finally said.

"Yes," Violet agreed with a nod. "That's exactly right."

"I know what it's like to be in such a position," Celeste murmured, something like the shadow of sorrow flashing across those eyes that once peered into the future but could now only see the present.

Violet remembered what Celeste had looked like that first night she'd wandered into the Crescent Moon, her cheeks so sunken that it seemed as if her missing magic had left a vast hollow at the very center of her being.

"How did you bear it?" Violet asked, her voice barely above a whisper. "Knowing that you'd never get it back again?"

Celeste remained silent for a moment, her eyes drifting away from Violet and toward the table that rested in front of the hearth where she'd first sat with Katherine and Mr. Crowley.

"I discovered something else that I'd thought had been lost," Celeste finally replied. "The spark within myself that made life worth living in the first place."

For a moment, Violet let the taste of mugwort overwhelm her senses as she tried to think of what, exactly, she would need to find to reclaim the fire that had blazed within her, shooting her forward without a single worry of when the flame would burn out. But it was difficult to think of something potent enough to fill the strange emptiness that had made a home in her heart.

Violet set her cup back in its saucer and reached toward the pot to pour Celeste another helping, but before her fingers grasped the handle, she caught a movement out of the corner of her eye.

Glancing upward, she saw a flash of auburn hair and realized that Anne was waving at her from the threshold of the door that led to the back hallway, trying to get her attention without disturbing their remaining customers.

"Excuse me, Celeste," Violet apologized with a note of genuine regret as she placed her cloth napkin on the table. "It seems that Anne needs me."

"Of course," Celeste said, her gaze already returning to the street beyond the window, which was so coated in snow that it was difficult to tell where the fog on the glass ended and the world outside began.

"Is everything all right?" Violet asked Anne once she slipped into the hallway and closed the door behind her. She caught the distinct aroma of peppermint as she said the words, and that, along with the glint of excitement in her sister's eyes, was enough to tell her that something important had happened.

"I need to visit Mr. Crowley's home," Anne announced. "As soon as possible."

Violet's brows pinched together in concern.

"I'm not sure you'll find the warmest welcome in that house," she sighed.

Though the Quigleys had helped uncover Mr. Crowley's Task, his family no doubt associated the sisters with his decision to ignore destiny and pursue his own path. The Crowleys came from a long and distinguished line of necromancers, witches gifted with the ability to speak to the dead, and it had been beyond embarrassing that one of their own had neglected such a significant errand.

"I imagine any resentment they hold will be overshadowed by the prospect of Mr. Crowley's Task tearing a hole in the fabric of Fate," Anne said, lowering her voice so that there was no chance of it slipping between the cracks of the door and into the shop. "I know that they run their business out of their home, and I'm certain that the key to saving Mr. Crowley can only be uncovered if I go there and see what we can learn about his past. There's something waiting in that house, I can sense it. Something that feels lost and lonely."

The word "lost" caused another tingle of recognition to skitter across the back of Violet's neck. It was so strong that she reached a hand up to cover her skin, as if she'd stepped too close to a sparkler and was trying to brush away the heat.

"I'm coming with you, then," Violet said, surprising both herself and Anne, if her sister's raised eyebrows were any indication.

"I'm not sure that's the best idea," Anne replied hesitantly. "I don't want the other members of the Council to learn that I've told you the truth of what's happening until we've tied everything together again."

If this conversation had unfolded the day before, Violet would have merely grown quiet, accepting that her initial impulses couldn't be trusted.

But now she felt the oddest flash of determination. It wasn't strong enough to make her feel like she could dive in headfirst without a second thought like she would have done in the past, but a nearly forgotten flicker of curiosity was starting to spark to life, tempting her to step beyond the threshold of the shop and see what she might find.

"I want to go," she said, her voice firm.

Only a year ago, Violet would have expected Anne to stand her ground and insist that she was being too rash. But something in her sister's expression shifted, the hard set of her jaw loosening the longer she stared at Violet.

"Fine," Anne relented. "But only because there's something I need you to do for me while I'm speaking with the Crowleys."

"Let's go now," Violet insisted, eager to leave before Anne had the chance to change her mind. "Most of the customers have left for the afternoon, and Franny and Peggy can close the shop."

"Very well," Anne replied, though Violet was already walking away from her.

"And be sure to get Bee from her study!" Violet called out as she reached the other end of the hall. "She's coming with us."

"Do you really think—" Anne began, but the hard smack of the door shaking on its hinges as Violet marched into the front parlor snapped off the end of her sentence.

Had she paused for a breath and turned back, though, Violet would have been surprised by what she saw. For Anne wasn't muttering in frustration or rubbing the side of her temple as she always did whenever a new problem arose. No, instead, she was smiling, two dimples appearing on her cheeks as she released a sigh of unexpected relief.

Because for the very first time since Violet had returned to the Crescent Moon, Anne had seen that spark start to light up her eyes again, ever so faint but with enough flicker to suggest that something of her old self was waiting to catch an ember once more.

CHAPTER 11

A Curtain
Indicates that something
important is being hidden.

As the Quigley sisters stood in the center of the street and gazed up at the building towering before them, Anne felt a shiver that had nothing to do with the brutal winter wind raking down her spine.

"It's rather imposing, isn't it?" Beatrix remarked, the words garbled by the sound of her teeth clicking together. They'd managed to catch a cable car that dropped them only a block away from the Crowley family home, but the sun had already started to set for the day, giving way to crisp night air that made the tips of their toes and fingers tingle.

"That's one way to describe it," Violet scoffed as she wrapped her arms around her rib cage and stomped her feet against the ground to keep them from going numb.

After growing up in a home that always felt as if it was pulling them into a warm embrace, the Quigleys couldn't help but wince at the cold austerity of the Crowley manor.

Though the white marble must have cost a fortune to bring to Chicago, the house's stark exterior made those walking along the sidewalk pick up their pace, as if they feared a force beyond their control might reach through the dark curtains that covered all the windows and grab them by the coattails.

In fact, the only artistic flair that could be found along the smooth marble surface was the Roman numeral XIII, which was etched just to the right of the door, where the street number should have been.

"A bit too direct, don't you think?" Violet asked as she gestured toward the inscription, which was the same that rested at the bottom of the death card in the tarot deck.

"Well, they are necromancers, after all," Anne replied, trying to turn the situation in a more promising direction. "And the death card is not always an ill omen, as you know."

In fact, whenever the Quigleys flipped over that particular card, it was usually an indication that one chapter was about to close so that another could be embraced.

But even Anne acknowledged that something about seeing the numbers printed on the stark surface of the white marble made it feel more like a warning than a sign of new beginnings.

"Are you sure that you don't want us to come inside?" Beatrix asked, placing her hand along the crook of Anne's elbow, as if the thought of letting her sister wander through the threshold by herself was too much to bear.

"I'm certain," Anne said, placing her gloved fingers over Beatrix's and giving them a reassuring squeeze. "I'm the Diviner now. There's nothing waiting beyond those doors that I won't be able to handle. And besides, I need you two to do something for me while I'm speaking with the Crowleys."

"What's that?" Violet asked, curious and eager to avoid waiting quietly outside of the house for Anne to return.

"You see that building over there?" Anne asked as she turned them around to face the other side of the street.

They were too far away to see what rested inside, but even across the road, Anne could tell that time had not been kind to the poor building. There had obviously been a shop on the first floor at some point, but the gilded letters painted along the sign that hung above the large windows were chipped away, leaving behind an indecipherable etching of dull lines and curves. And even though a gas lamp sat nearby, everything seemed consumed by shadows, as if the storefront had resigned itself to a life in the darkness decades ago.

"I think that's where Philip used to live," Anne continued. "Why don't you try to learn more about it?"

"Of course," Violet said as she rubbed her hands together, clearly enjoying the promise of a challenge. She was already stepping toward the shadowy structure, eager to uncover its secrets. "Come on, Bee."

Before her sister could protest, Violet grabbed her by the arm and started pulling her away. Beatrix had only just enough time to cast a hesitant expression in Anne's direction before she disappeared from her side, caught by Violet's unrelenting grip.

Anne watched her sisters cross the street and then turned back to the marble monstrosity, wondering what awaited her inside.

When she reached the very top of the stoop, Anne was surprised to find that the front door was entirely black. From the street, she'd thought it was merely obscured by shadows, but Anne could see now that the surface had been painted to create that effect.

She lifted her hand to grasp the brass knocker that was fixed at its center, but before her gloved fingers could touch the smooth metal, an odd sensation made her pause and reach for the handle instead.

At first, she thought it had to do with the fact that the knocker was coated in frost and looked too cold to touch. But then she became aware of a barely perceptible warmth that wrapped around the finger where Mr. Crowley's ring rested and realized her hand was being pulled forward of its own accord, like a magnet that had just found its mate.

And as soon as she heard the muffled click of the ring hitting metal through the cloth of her glove, the door creaked open.

Though Anne wasn't in the habit of waltzing into a witch's home unannounced, the stillness that greeted her when she stepped over the threshold kept her from calling out.

The entire entryway smelled of chrysanthemums and faded fabric, like the fragrance that fills the room when a box that's held a wedding dress is opened for the first time in decades. It wasn't an unpleasant aroma, but it reminded Anne of when a customer seemed to be holding on to a memory too tightly, as if they feared the whole of it might crack if they forgot the exact color and texture of the moment.

Everything was so silent that Anne swore she could hear the beat of her heart echoing against the smooth, dark stone beneath her feet.

Before she could wonder what to do next, a lone flame fluttered to life in the hallway, daring Anne to walk forward. She moved toward it, and another candle a few feet from the first flickered as well, encouraging her to follow the trail that was unfurling in front of her.

Anne took another step and then another, the row of candlewicks catching and growing brighter as she moved closer to a room at the very end of the hall.

When she was only a hair's breadth away from the threshold, Anne sensed a strange noise slipping between the cracks of the door. It sounded like a thousand whispering voices struggling to come together to the same beat of a metronome. The ring on Anne's hand began to vibrate then, and once more, she felt herself reaching for the knob, pulled to it by something beyond her control.

But as the door creaked open and Anne saw what rested within, she forced her feet to stay rooted to the ground, no matter how much Mr. Crowley's ring begged to be brought inside.

The walls were covered from the baseboards to the ceiling with clocks of so many shapes and sizes that Anne doubted she'd be able to say for certain how many there were, even if she stood in the center of the room all evening and tried to count them. Some looked as if they could be pocket watches while others were so large that the walls shook with the force of the pendulums that swayed back and forth beneath their faces.

But their hands ticked at exactly the same moment, filling the space with a steady *click-click-click* that seemed to tug at her thoughts and pull them deeper into the room.

And as the beat grew stronger, so did the whispers.

In the hallway, they'd just been the barest echo beneath the ticking of the clocks, but now they were becoming louder. Anne knew that in a moment the texture of their words would finally take shape, coming together to tell her something that felt urgent, the syllables taking on the texture of desperation and longing.

Anne was torn between a sensation in the back of her mind that insisted now was the time to turn away and a desire to step into the room, where she could better hear what promised to be shared.

But before she could decide which impulse to follow, Anne felt a hand roughly grab her by the shoulder and pull her back into the hallway.

"What in Hecate's name do you think you're doing?" an icy

voice demanded, nearly lost beneath the sound of the door being thrown shut.

Resisting the urge to scream, Anne whirled around and realized with some relief that she hadn't come face-to-face with a ghost. No, as she turned her chin upward, Anne took in the sight of a perfectly real man with shockingly blond hair who looked so angry that she worried his cutting glare might bore a hole straight through her chest.

"The house let me in," Anne said defensively, taking a step back to put her hands on her hips. The brash disapproval that laced the man's tone instantly made her want to straighten her spine and stand as tall as she possibly could. "So you could say that I've already been invited inside."

The stranger's brows rose in surprise at that, and he whirled around as if waiting for the walls to tell him that she was lying. As he turned back to face her, Anne realized with a start that the man's hair wasn't blond at all but perfectly white. She hadn't noticed at first because he couldn't have been more than a few years older than herself, much too young for his hair to settle into that stark color naturally. But then Anne remembered that the type of magic used by necromancers came at a cost: it turned a strand of hair white every time they were able to contact a spirit and give them the voice they needed to speak to the living.

And Anne couldn't see a single lock of hair on this man's head that wasn't a shocking shade of white. She was facing a very powerful witch indeed.

"The *house* let you inside?" he scoffed in disbelief, swinging his arm upward as if reprimanding the wainscoting for some grave misdeed.

When his hand cut through the air, Anne caught the faint fragrance of cypress and myrrh and knew that his magic was pulsing just beneath the surface, waiting to be called upon if needed.

Her own power sparked then, infusing the hallway with notes of black tea and peppermint that should have overpowered the subtle aroma that already lingered there but ended up complementing it somehow.

"My name is Anne Quigley," she said, her tone firm and unwavering as she took back the step that she'd relinquished earlier. "Who, may I ask, are *you*?"

Anne expected the man's eyes to widen in surprise when he learned who she was, but instead, those white brows settled into an even deeper scowl as he crossed his arms over his chest.

"Vincent Crowley," he answered. "The owner of this traitorous house. Excuse my manners, Miss Quigley, but I didn't expect the city's Diviner of all people to wander into my home without so much as knocking on the front door."

The accusation in his voice told Anne that he wasn't apologetic in the least, and it set her teeth on edge.

"As a member of the Council, I don't need permission to step through someone's threshold, as you well know, Mr. Crowley," Anne replied. "Which is entirely beside the point, as your house invited me in. And encouraged me to open this door here, I might add."

"The house should know better," Vincent grumbled, glowering at the walls once more.

"What's the purpose of this room?" Anne asked, her curiosity getting the best of her.

Vincent looked like he wanted to tell Anne that wasn't any of her concern, but he bit his lip, obviously trying to hold back the harsh words that threatened to slip from his tongue, and drew in a breath before answering.

"It's one of the rooms where we help our clients commune with the spirits," Vincent explained reluctantly. "The ticking of the clocks helps us focus our magic and steadies the dead, who have trouble centering themselves long enough to break through the veil."

"I heard voices," Anne said before she could help herself.

"I'm not surprised," Vincent replied, his tone losing its rough edge for a moment as his gaze turned toward the door. "There are many waiting for their chance to be heard, after all."

He sounded so sincere then that Anne nearly forgot he'd looked as if he wanted to shove her out onto the street a moment earlier. In that instant, Vincent's sharp features softened a fraction, and Anne realized with a start that he was rather handsome, if one cared about such a thing.

But before she could linger on that thought for long, the hard angles had settled back into his face, causing her spine to snap back so that she was as straight as a sewing needle.

"I assume that you're a relation of Mr. Capricious Crowley, who passed away some months ago?" Anne asked, though she already knew what the answer would be. The Council kept track of the various networks that knit the magical community together, and as soon as Vincent told her his name, she knew what kind of ties linked him to her old friend.

"He was my uncle," Vincent said, his tone lacking any flicker of warmth. Instead, the word seemed weighed down by a sense of unease, as if just saying it aloud promised trouble.

"And you keep the house?" Anne asked.

"I use it, just like everyone else in the family," Vincent replied. "But ever since my uncle's death, it's not . . ."

Vincent grew silent then, the end of his sentence cut as abruptly as the tail of a satin ribbon.

"You were saying, Mr. Crowley?" Anne asked, raising an eyebrow.

"Nothing at all," he replied defiantly.

A fresh wave of annoyance swept over Anne, making her more determined to get to the heart of the matter.

"Mr. Crowley," Anne began, "I'm here because your uncle chose not to complete his Task, as I expect you well know."

The way Vincent's lips tightened confirmed that he was quite familiar with this fact.

"What you might not have realized, however, is that your uncle was more powerful than he led us to believe," Anne continued. "And that in deciding not to complete his Task, Mr. Crowley has caused a rip in the fabric of destiny."

Anne watched as Vincent's eyes narrowed, but the movement seemed too deliberate to be natural. When she whirled around to face him only a moment ago, she'd seen the way his features twisted in shock at finding a stranger lurking in the hallway, with one brow cocked just the barest touch higher than the other and his eyes so hard that they could have been cut from the marble facade of the house. That flash of surprise was gone now, though, replaced by a sense of resolve. His reaction wasn't what Anne had expected in the least, and she had to stop herself from taking the barest step closer, where she could better decipher the firm lines of his face.

"I'm sure you've heard of a few odd happenings by now," Anne continued, wanting to get a sense of just how many other secrets Vincent might already have tucked away. "They will only worsen unless the Council finds a way to complete Mr. Crowley's Task for him."

At that, she slipped her hand free of her woolen glove, shifting it back and forth so that the grains of the hourglass drifted from one side to the other.

"We must discover who this ring belongs to," Anne said, her eyes fixed on Vincent's face. "As soon as we possibly can, before things become so tangled that other witches cannot complete their own Tasks. To do that, I need your family's help."

Anne waited for Vincent to react, but she was met only with

silence that seemed so charged she could feel it brush against her skin.

And then Vincent abruptly turned his back on her and began to march away, the candles flashing behind him as his footsteps echoed against the walls.

"I must ask you to leave, Miss Quigley," Vincent announced once he reached the front door.

"I beg your pardon?" Anne said, her voice sounding unnaturally loud in the cavernous hallway.

"You won't receive any help here," Vincent replied, his words as still and unmoving as a pair of dates etched on a tombstone.

"But it's in your best interest to see the Task brought to a close," Anne insisted as she strode toward Vincent, anger seeping through the rapidly fracturing cracks of her composure. The irritation that had been simmering just beneath the surface was so potent now that if she touched a metal doorknob with her bare hand, sparks would have snapped from her fingertips. "If it remains unfinished, it will mean no end of trouble for you and your family."

Vincent's shoulders stiffened at that, as if he'd already been aware of the burden that the Crowleys would shoulder when the odd magical unravelings were linked back to them.

But the cutting glint in his eye only grew sharper as he opened the front door and let in the brutal whip of the wind. It grazed Anne's cheek, but the bite of Vincent's next words felt harsher than the unrelenting grasp of winter.

"You must leave," he said, any promise of an explanation fading faster than an ember tossed into the snow.

Anne knew that she should beg him to reconsider, to apologize for her tone and ask that they sit down to start the whole conversation anew. To somehow undo this disastrous first impression as one does when they've skipped a knot in their knitting and pull back the yarn so that they can replace the mess with neat, even rows.

But something about Vincent made Anne want to push herself to the limit, to say things that she'd never dared utter before.

"You will change your mind," she said instead, so firmly that the picture frames started to rattle on the walls. "And when you do, you can find me at the Crescent Moon."

If Anne had lingered for just a moment longer at the threshold, she might have noticed how her words brushed against the whispers that seeped out from the cracks of the door at the end of the hall, saturating the foyer with the sound of longing and unmet intentions waiting for a chance to finally be fulfilled.

CHAPTER 12

A Lighthouse
*Suggests that light will be
found in the darkness.*

While Anne was being pulled toward the ticking of a clock in the Crowleys' home, Beatrix was standing in front of the shop across the street, her face pressed against the cold glass as she attempted to see what rested inside.

The evening shadows had stretched out their tendrils, and the light of the gas lamps reflected against the shop windows in a way that somehow made it more difficult to determine what was on the other side of the glass.

"I'm not sure we're going to be able to find anything," Beatrix sighed as she turned toward Violet, who had been standing farther back on the sidewalk so that she could see the faded gold lettering above the shop.

"The windows are all boarded up from the inside," Violet murmured, as if she hadn't heard Beatrix at all.

"Well, then I'm not sure how much we can do," Beatrix said. "Not when the hour is so late and we can't see anything through the windows."

She threw her hands down in defeat then, the tips of her gloved fingers grazing the glass, just enough to leave a streaky impression against the frost.

But before her hands could lose touch with the window, one of the boards clattered to the floor of the shop.

"What did you do?" Violet asked as Beatrix slowly leaned forward to peer through the crack left by the fallen board.

"Nothing," she insisted. "It must have been loose already."

Once more, Beatrix peeked through the glass, placing her hands on either side of her face to block out the reflections cast by the gas lamps.

At first, it was difficult to make out what rested in the shadows, but after a few moments, those odd stacks and shelves started to take shape.

"It's a bookshop," Beatrix gasped, transfixed by the sight.

"A very dusty one at that," Violet remarked with a sniff, as if the mere sight of what rested inside made her want to sneeze.

As Beatrix squinted to see past the grime on the windows, she realized that Violet was correct. All the piles of books looked like they had toppled over long ago, with no one to come along and line them up in neat stacks again.

If this was indeed a bookshop, no one seemed to have set foot in it for decades.

"It's in a sorry state," Beatrix sighed, pained at the thought of all those books waiting patiently for a reader to come along and pick them up.

Nothing quite captured the sense of loneliness that had recently settled within her own soul better than the shelves of books that rested beyond the glass, filled to the brim with stories that might never be shared. It made her remember what it had felt like that very morning at her writing desk as she tried and failed to put a single word on the page.

"We should find a way inside," Violet announced, instantly

snapping Beatrix's attention away from her own worries and toward the trouble unfolding in the here and now.

"What?" Beatrix asked, the words coming out louder than she'd intended. "You can't possibly mean that."

But Violet was already walking toward the alleyway that separated the shop from its neighbor. It was so thin that she practically needed to turn sideways to fit, but that clearly wasn't enough to stop her.

"Violet!" Beatrix hissed as she begrudgingly followed her sister into the damp shadows.

Beatrix shivered as the snow that had built up in the alley began to seep into her boots and opened her mouth to beg Violet to let them return home, where they could take off their icy socks and warm their toes by the fire.

But before she could say anything at all, she heard the familiar noise of a rusty handle giving way and then the slow creak of a door falling open.

"It's unlocked," Violet declared in disbelief before stepping inside.

Again, Beatrix began to argue that they should go home, but her warning was lost among the sound of something crashing to the ground within the shop, quickly followed by a slew of her sister's most colorful curses.

"Are you all right?!" Beatrix cried as she rushed through the door, her hesitation forgotten in her worry for Violet.

But as soon as she stepped over the threshold, a sudden gust of wind snapped the door closed behind her, engulfing the room in complete darkness.

Startled, Beatrix drew in a gasp, but as she did, a familiar fragrance drifted to the forefront of her attention, instantly pulling her back into one of her fondest memories of the past.

It smelled of aged paper with the barest hints of vanilla, almonds, and the promise of a well-spun story—the same aroma that accompanies the sensation of fading between the pages of a book.

And for the first time in a long while, Beatrix remembered what it had felt like when her only fear was knowing that her fingers would eventually turn the last page.

She drew in another deep breath, trying to capture the fragrance again and the recollections that came along with it. But this time, a heavy undernote of dust and neglect caught in her throat, causing her to cough. As quickly as it had begun, the spell was broken, snapping her away from the enchantment of the past and toward the trouble unfolding in the present.

Beatrix hesitantly reached into the darkness, trying to find purchase as she listened to the sound of books tumbling to the floor crash against Violet's curses.

Eventually, her palm met a wall, and as her fingers trailed along its tattered surface, she stumbled upon what felt like a gas lamp. Though the chances of it working with the shop being in such a state of disrepair seemed slim, something made Beatrix turn the knob anyway, and to her shock, a flame sparked to life, casting a comforting glow over the room.

As her eyes adjusted to the light, the details of the shop started to take shape against the shadows.

Beatrix realized with a start that many of the books had been thrown from the shelves and tossed to the floor, as if someone had knocked everything askew in a fit of fury. The covers were thrown open, and some of the spines had cracked, casting loose pages across the boards and tangling the different stories together in a riot of faded yellow paper and stark black ink.

It pained Beatrix to see so many words left to rot in the dirt and grime. But before she could so much as lean forward and pick up the nearest book from the floor, an unfamiliar voice filled the shop, booming from the direction of the alleyway.

"You've come after all!"

Beatrix's gaze snapped to the open door, where a middle-aged woman stood in the threshold with only a thin shawl to shield her shoulders from the harsh winter winds. She didn't have the flushed cheeks and stiff posture of someone who'd been chilled to the bone, though. No, the woman merely looked as if she'd just stepped out of her home for a moment to grab the evening paper from the porch, the wide smile stretched across her face making her seem even warmer.

Beatrix opened her mouth to ask the stranger what she meant, but before she could utter a word, Violet lifted herself from the mountain of books that she'd fallen into and moved toward the woman, her arm extended in greeting.

"Yes!" Violet said with enthusiasm. "We've come."

As she grasped the woman's hand in her own, Violet turned toward Beatrix and winked.

"What a relief," the woman replied as she moved deeper into the shop, trying to avoid stepping over the upturned book pages but failing to find a clear surface to place her sodden boots. Beatrix winced as she watched clumps of snow melt into the ink of what looked to be a novel, resisting the urge to reach out and save the story from its unfortunate fate. "I was so disappointed when I received your note this morning telling me that you weren't interested in seeing the shop any longer. As you know from my letters, we've only recently inherited it, and my husband and I are eager to find a tenant. The apartment upstairs is in quite a state of disrepair, but the shop could be lovely with a bit of attention."

Beatrix glanced at the upturned shelves and sea of papers set adrift across the floorboards and thought that it was going to require quite a bit of attention indeed to get this place in working order.

"I apologize for the confusion," Violet replied. "My sister found another property that she thought would suit our needs, but as it turns out, someone else came along and claimed it for themselves before we could sign the papers."

"How fortunate," the woman said with a sigh of obvious relief. "I can assure you, if what you're looking for is a bit of peace and quiet, you need not look further than this shop. Come with me, and I'll show you the rest."

Beatrix and Violet trailed behind their unexpected hostess as she moved quickly past the tumble of shelves and toward a door in the back of the room.

"Pardon me," Violet said while the woman pulled out a ring of keys and went about the task of testing them in the lock. "But I've forgotten your name."

"Think nothing of it, dear," she replied. "I know what it's like trying to find a place to rent in this city. No doubt you've been writing to a dozen people all at once. My name is Brigit, Brigit Müller."

The keys tinkled against one another as she continued her search for the one that would unlock the door.

"I apologize," Brigit said with a sigh. "My husband only just inherited this building from his aunt a few months ago, and it's been a trial to figure out which doors each of these keys unlock. I've been trying to find the right match for weeks, but nothing seems to fit."

Just as she uttered that final word, though, the sound of the lock clicking open echoed through the shop, followed by the hiss of another gas lamp.

"Oh, what luck!" Brigit exclaimed as she shuffled them inside the adjoining room.

Something in Beatrix's chest loosened as the light filled the room and her eyes flitted over the different textures that awaited them there. At first, all she could decipher was the arm of a worn leather chair, the gentle curve of a rolltop desk, and the flash of a red carpet. But once most of the shadows had slunk away, the full scene came together, and for a moment, Beatrix forgot to breathe.

"The last person who ran the shop must have used it as their office," Brigit remarked as Beatrix stepped closer to the back wall, where hundreds of books were packed tightly along the towering shelves.

Their spines practically inched forward as her hand hovered within reach, begging her to pull them free and give them a chance to stretch.

"You aren't planning to open the shop, correct?" Brigit suddenly asked, snapping Beatrix's attention away from the stories that were resting within her grasp. "You said in your letters that all you needed was a place to work."

"That's right," Violet replied, her face taking on an expression that Beatrix recognized from their childhood days. It was the same one that appeared whenever her sister was piecing together some sort of plan that would no doubt have them sent to bed without dessert later in the day. "Just a quiet room to focus on the task at hand."

"Wonderful," Brigit said, the word punctuated by a loud clap of her hands. "Just wonderful. I don't mean to rush you, of course, but I only stepped away for a moment to see if you'd changed your mind about coming. We live in a building just down the street, and I left a pot of water to boil on the stove when I saw that someone had lit a lamp in here."

"That's perfectly fine," Violet said with a thoughtful nod that made Beatrix wonder what she was up to. "I believe we've seen all we need to."

"Here's my card," Brigit said as she pulled out a piece of paper with her name and address scribbled across the center. "In case you've misplaced the other one. Please let me know if you're interested in becoming our new tenant."

When Violet turned to tuck the paper in her pocket, though, Beatrix noticed her gaze catch on something carved into the threshold of the office door.

A flash of disbelief crossed her face, quickly followed by excitement. But before Beatrix could straighten her spectacles and lean closer to see what had so captured her sister's attention, Violet was pushing her forward again, obviously eager to catch up with Brigit.

"If you'd like to see it again in the daytime, don't hesitate to ask!" Brigit cried, her words nearly lost beneath the sound of the wind as she opened the door that led toward the alleyway.

"We'll certainly be in touch," Violet replied when the three of them had stepped outside. "Thank you, by the way, for leaving the door open for us."

"Oh!" Brigit said, clearly confused. "I was wondering how you'd managed to get inside. My husband must have forgotten to close everything up properly yesterday when he was showing the place to someone else."

Beatrix turned curiously toward the door, surprised by the sharp pang of reluctance that rose in her chest as she pulled the knob and stepped aside to let Brigit turn the key in the lock.

"Well, in any case, we appreciate you walking through the cold to meet us," Violet said as they all shuffled out of the alleyway.

When they stepped onto the street, the wind hit them so strongly that they had to brace themselves from falling onto the cold pavement.

"It wasn't a bother at all," Brigit said as she reached up to keep her bonnet from flying off the top of her head. "And to think, if I hadn't glanced out the window at just that moment, we might have missed one another entirely."

As Violet turned to say a final goodbye, Beatrix shifted closer to the window, a piercing need to gaze at those mountains of dusty covers growing stronger in her chest.

Though it was now far too dark to see through the glass, Beatrix shuddered as she remembered the sight of all those books tossed haphazardly across the floor, the pages so coated in dust and bent at the corners that she worried the stories beneath were dying alongside the bleeding ink.

Even as Beatrix shook her head and began to move farther away from the storefront, she was still drawn to the thought of all those lost words that would eventually fade from the paper as readers forgot they ever existed in the first place.

Unless someone was able to brush them off before it was too late.

CHAPTER 13

A Cauldron
Hints that unexpected opportunities
could soon emerge.

"Incorrigible," Anne muttered as she stirred her tea in the family parlor, her teeth chattering so hard that the spoon rattled against the side of the cup. "Utterly incorrigible."

Violet wanted to reply, but she was still trying to catch her breath after the trudge back to the Crescent Moon. The three of them had only needed to walk a few blocks, but the wind was merciless, slipping into the gaps of their scarves and causing gooseflesh to pebble along the delicate skin of their necks.

As soon as they'd stepped through the front door of the shop, the house had shivered at the sight of their rosy cheeks and trembling shoulders and lit the stovetop in the kitchen so that they could brew themselves a warm pot of tea.

Now that their damp woolen cloaks were dripping from pegs in the kitchen, the Quigleys were attempting to tuck their chilled toes as close to the fire as they could without having to rise from the comfort of their seats. The house had wrapped the quilts so tightly around their legs that it was impossible to move anyway, leaving the sisters no choice but to sink deeper into the familiar fabric and relish the scent of ginger that rose in steamy tendrils from their cups.

"Was he really so unpleasant?" Violet asked after she took her first sip and felt the spicy sweetness warm her throat.

"He was beyond unpleasant," Anne replied, the words so full of annoyance that the house tried to inch her chair a bit closer to the fire, where some of the iciness in her voice might have a better chance of thawing. "I've never met such a rude man in all my life. And he doesn't seem concerned in the slightest about completing Mr. Crowley's Task."

"But what did he say, exactly?" Beatrix asked, obviously confused that someone could be so coldhearted when it came to matters of their own flesh and blood.

"Nothing. That's precisely the problem," Anne sighed in exasperation. "Only that he wouldn't help."

"But he should want Mr. Crowley's Task to be finished," Beatrix remarked, the furrow between her brow deepening even further. "If the other witches learn that the Crowleys refused to help in such a serious matter, the scandal of it could cast them out of the coven entirely."

"He's keeping secrets," Anne said, her voice growing stern as she hit her spoon roughly around the edge of her cup. "I'm sure of it."

"What do you think they could be?" Violet asked.

"I can't say for certain," Anne replied. "But I'm going to find out."

The determination in their tone made the mirror above the mantle rattle.

"Our Mr. Crowley wasn't accommodating either," Violet reminded her. "But he eventually grew to trust us enough to share the truth. Perhaps it's a family trait and his nephew will follow suit."

"We'll figure out how to save Mr. Crowley and Philip with or without his help," Anne declared so sternly that Tabitha cracked open one eye from her place in the basket of yarn to see what all the fuss was about. "Did you learn anything about the building across the street?"

"It's a bookshop," Beatrix replied in the same reverent tone used when speaking of sacred spaces.

Violet remembered what she'd seen as they followed Brigit out of the back room, though, and rushed forward before Beatrix could say another word.

"I think there's more to be uncovered there," Violet said, a note of excitement creeping into her voice as the passion that had flickered out within her seemed to catch a spark.

"What do you mean?" Anne asked as she leaned closer.

"I saw something carved into the doorframe," Violet explained, her heart beating a bit faster as she thought of the moment her eyes had caught on the wood.

"What was it?" Anne asked, setting her cup and saucer on the end table so that she could lean forward.

"Their names!" Violet answered. "Capricious and Philip. Next to lines that just barely reached my rib cage. They must have been children when they made the marks."

"So there is a connection after all," Anne said with a nod. "You didn't get a chance to see the apartment above the shop, I take it?"

"Not yet," Violet answered. "But I have a feeling that Crowley's nephew isn't the only one keeping secrets. There's something waiting to be found there too, I know it."

"Is there anyone we could speak to who might remember

Philip?" Beatrix asked hopefully. "Someone who can tell us about his life and how long he might have lived in the building?"

"Mr. Crowley never mentioned that he had any family," Anne said with a shake of her head, recalling how her friend had spoken of Philip as if the two of them were the only ones who existed in the refuge they'd managed to create all those years ago. "And it's been so long now that I doubt anyone would remember."

Time, after all, was a strange creature. In the present moment, it might seem like the impressions left behind will last forever, but even memories that are etched in stone wear away with every rainstorm when there is no one left to tend to them.

"We're on the right path," Violet insisted, her voice stronger now. "We just need more time to see what secrets might be lingering in the shop."

As she spoke the words, Violet felt some of the haziness that had clouded her thoughts these past several months start to clear away, lending her a sense of focus that felt as fresh as poking her head into the frosty morning air.

"But how do you plan to get back in?" Beatrix asked. "By the sound of it, the Müllers are determined to let the place as soon as possible, and once someone moves into the building, I doubt we'll be able to return."

Violet grinned then, feeling the same coy smile start to spread across her face that had always appeared when they were children, just before she was about to pull her sisters into a plan that would end with the house in shambles.

"We'll have plenty of time to search through the building," Violet replied. "Because you're going to be the one who rents it."

"Me?!" Beatrix cried, startling the house so much that the kettle in the kitchen shrieked.

"Of course," Violet continued. "Don't you see it solves two of our problems? We need more time in the shop and the apartment upstairs to better understand what might be keeping Philip from moving into the afterlife, and you need somewhere to work."

"I have my study here," Beatrix insisted, panicked now at the thought of being displaced from the familiarity of her old desk, no matter how cramped it had become.

"You can barely sneeze without hitting your head against the wall and cracking the plaster," Violet scoffed. "And you're getting distracted by all the commotion in the tearoom. Or did you think we hadn't noticed?"

Beatrix opened her mouth to protest but snapped it shut again when she couldn't conjure a proper defense.

"It's decided, then," Anne said with a nod as she lifted her cup to take another sip of tea. "Write the Müllers first thing in the morning, Violet, and tell them that we want to rent the shop."

"I certainly will," Violet replied, letting herself fall against the welcoming embrace of the settee now that they seemed one step closer to ensuring Mr. Crowley and Philip remained together.

As Beatrix and Anne continued to discuss the details of their day, Violet let herself sink into the soft murmur of their voices and the sound of the sleet hitting the window.

And for the first time in months, it felt like her dreams were carrying her toward an unexpected twist of Fate that she didn't want to turn away from, one that made her consider what it would be like to stretch beyond the shadows of the past and seek out a brighter future.

CHAPTER 14

A Chair

*Appears before the arrival
of an unexpected visitor.*

When Anne opened the front door the next morning to turn the open sign toward the street, she was surprised to find that the entire storefront was covered in a spectacular sheet of ice. She'd met a bit of resistance when her hand had grasped the knob, but the house stepped in and helped her shove the door open, revealing the strange scene that awaited outside.

Though Chicago certainly saw its fair share of storms, something about the way the ice had settled against the bricks seemed odd. Taking a few steps closer to the Crescent Moon, Anne gazed at the storefront and tried to put her finger on exactly what seemed out of place. And then it struck her, the realization sending a shot of alarm down her spine that made her toes tingle.

Each building along the street looked like it had been covered in buttercream icing and dipped in sugar glaze. Even the icicles, which hung in such profusion from the eaves that it was a wonder their weight hadn't pulled down the entire structure, appeared as if they'd been piped by a careful hand. The frozen coating was much stronger than a gingerbread house, though, and Anne's neighbors were busy trying to break through enough of it to open their own front doors. As they chipped away at the glistening surface with hammers and shovels, their children slid down the road wielding icy shards the size of sabers, laughing at the frozen wonderland that they'd awoken to.

Everything was perfectly straight, molded to the frames like chocolate that had been sprung from a tin. The wind should have whipped the ice to one side, but instead, the buildings looked as pristine as the biscuit villages displayed behind the glass of bakery windows during the holiday season.

Stranger still, Anne hadn't heard the telltale pitter-patter of ice hitting the pane the night before. She'd fallen into a fitful sleep, visions of ticking clocks and hourglasses that never seemed to run out of sand keeping her awake until the house tugged at the corner of her blankets to let her know it was time to embrace the day. She would have certainly heard a storm as fierce as this one, but instead, it seemed like the ice had simply appeared out of thin air . . . as if by magic.

Before Anne could give the problem more thought, however, a pair of women bundled in woolen cloaks and thick knit scarves appeared at her side, asking if the shop had opened yet. When they spoke, perfectly formed impressions of snowflakes appeared in the icy windows of the shop, and Anne knew that they were winter witches who'd been eager to explore the strange sight but now wished to thaw out over a steaming pot of tea.

It wasn't long before more customers stepped over the threshold of the shop, mostly other winter witches who enjoyed sliding across the slick sidewalks and were drawn to the freshly fallen snow, but there were a handful of humans who ventured in as well in search of something sweet to chase away the chill.

Though the Crescent Moon certainly wasn't stretched at the seams, there were just enough visitors to breathe a sense of life into the shop and fill the parlor with the scent of crisp apple turnovers and a blend of velvet oolong that carried the same texture as a warm quilt waiting to be slipped into at the end of a long day. Their laughter, along with the fire crackling in the hearth, warmed the shop to its rafters and melted away the ice that clung to the street-facing window.

By the time Violet and Beatrix stepped into the kitchen, Anne had already realized it would be a slow day and insisted that they use the afternoon to visit the bookshop. If the ice storm was any indication, the effects of Mr. Crowley's unfinished Task were continuing to ripple outward, and the sooner they could piece together what needed to be done, the better.

After helping her sisters into their heavy woolen cloaks in the entryway and warning them to be careful, Anne began to turn back toward her customers, but the sound of bells tinkling against the front door kept her from stepping forward.

For a moment, she thought that Violet or Beatrix had come back to retrieve a missing glove, but then the faint scent of myrrh tickled her nose, instantly snapping her gaze back to the threshold.

"Miss Quigley," Vincent said coolly as he stepped inside and reached toward his hat.

When he removed it, Anne was surprised, once again, by the whiteness of his hair and the way it drew attention to the striking quality of his eyes. Now that they weren't peering at one another through shadows, Anne realized his irises were an unusual shade of amber, almost as rich as the bottle of cognac that she kept because she loved the way it looked beneath the cut glass. Instead of letting her attention linger there, though, Anne turned her gaze away, deciding to focus on the hard lines around Vincent's mouth that reminded her of the way he'd scowled during their last conversation.

"Mr. Crowley," she replied, trying to keep the surprise from her voice.

Though Anne had told him that he would change his mind and seek her out, she hadn't expected her premonition to come to pass so quickly. Now that her days seemed marked by moments she knew would fold neatly into her visions of the future, Anne rarely encountered anything that truly took her off guard.

But the man standing before her had managed to do just that, and Anne wasn't quite sure what to make of the fact that she couldn't predict his each and every move.

It was strange to see him there, dressed head to toe in a perfectly tailored black suit that showed nary a wrinkle, against the cheerful floral wallpaper and the profusion of joyfully patterned coats and shawls that hung along the wall. Though Vincent certainly didn't seem as intimidating as he had in the shadows of the Crowley manor, Anne could feel a subtle tension start to unwind between them while his gaze darted around the room, as if he expected to find a monster tucked somewhere beneath the doilies and embroidered tablecloths.

"I've come to speak with you," Vincent said as he dropped his voice to just above a whisper, the rough timbre of his tone causing the hairs on Anne's arms to rise. "About the matter you brought up after I caught you in my home yesterday."

Instantly, Anne's heart began to beat just a bit faster, and she very nearly lost control of the sharp retort that threatened to whip off the tip of her tongue. But she caught the barb just in time, managing to hold it in by pinching her lips together.

Flustered by the effect that the witch seemed to be having on her but not wanting to show it, Anne returned his nod and clenched her hands, which were hidden in the folds of her skirts.

"If you wouldn't mind following me . . . ," Anne replied stiffly, letting the end of her sentence fade away as she turned and started walking toward the spiral staircase.

She didn't look back but could hear his steady footsteps trailing behind her as she climbed the steps, the firm tread of his shoes entangling with the happy chatter of the customers, who were murmuring in delight as Peggy served them one of Violet's favorite recipes, a ginger molasses cake that would remind anyone who ate it of the first time they'd heard snow crunching beneath their boots.

The Crescent Moon, which had been watching Vincent with curiosity, was confused by the odd tangle of emotions that were radiating from Anne. One glance at the stern set of Anne's mouth was all it took for the house to know that their guest's presence had unsettled her. But the lively tempo of her pulse also reminded it of the moments just before she mastered a particularly challenging spell.

It didn't know whether to prim up the poinsettias to make a strong first impression or pull the cushion away from the chair that Vincent was moving toward so that he'd be inclined to leave earlier than planned.

In the end, though, the house merely twisted the ribbons that dangled from the banister as if wringing its hands together.

"I see that you've changed your mind," Anne said after they settled into their seats at the furthest end of the room, where their voices wouldn't drift down and interrupt the pleasant hum of the parlor.

She'd meant her words to take on the same hue that they did whenever a trying customer came into the shop and she needed to stifle her irritation beneath the strongest sheen of control. But instead of sounding inviting, her voice lost all its smooth edges, replaced by clipped tones that made it clear she hadn't forgotten their unfortunate first encounter.

"You come to the point rather quickly, don't you?" Vincent

replied, the restraint that had laced his voice when he'd stepped through the threshold fading faster than a handprint on a foggy windowpane.

Instead of shifting farther away, though, Vincent clasped his hands together and leaned onto his forearms. If the idea weren't so absurd, Anne would say he seemed relieved they were both pulling away the veneer of propriety that had kept them in check downstairs.

"I don't see that we have any time to waste, given the circumstances," Anne remarked sternly as she gestured toward the stained-glass windows, which were so encrusted with ice that hardly any light could filter through them.

"That's one of the reasons I've come," Vincent said, his eyes remaining fixed on Anne's face instead of shifting to where she pointed out the pane. "It's not just State Street. It seems that the ice has reached nearly every corner of Chicago, if my family is to be believed."

"You've spoken with them?" she asked, hoping they'd had a change of heart now that it was clear what the consequences would be if they continued to ignore the trouble that was brewing.

Anne thought he would answer straightaway, but Vincent drew out the pause, playing with the silence in the same way she sometimes pulled at a skein that was nearly at its end to see how far the yarn might stretch. The brief pause should have given her a chance to breathe, but it somehow seemed to make the unanswered questions that rested between them more tangible, thickening the air and causing some of the frost to melt down the glass of the nearest window.

"Yes," he answered. "But you won't be pleased with their reaction."

"You still don't intend to help, then," she said, her frustration returning so fiercely that the fire in the grate on the first floor flickered out entirely, to the dismay of the winter witches, who'd been drying their boots along its hearthstones.

Surprised by the intensity in her tone, Anne nearly considered apologizing so that Vincent wouldn't rise from his chair and walk out of the shop before she could convince him to change his mind. But when she glanced upward, she saw that he'd remained perfectly still, his amber eyes flashing in the same way Tabitha's did whenever something interesting caught her attention.

"I didn't say that," Vincent murmured carefully, as one does when they're used to weighing the cost of each and every word.

"Then what are your intentions?" Anne inquired, tapping her fingers in a slow and deliberate tempo against the top of the table in the hopes that it would remind her to stay composed.

"After giving the matter more thought, I believe it's in my family's best interest to see that my uncle's Task is completed as soon as possible," he replied. "It won't be long before the rest of the coven realizes that the Crowleys are at the root of the problem. There is our reputation to consider, after all."

"It's strange you didn't come to this conclusion yesterday, when I expressed exactly that," Anne said before she had the chance to keep the clipped words contained.

She expected Vincent's eyes to widen in annoyance at her lack of tact, but instead, his mouth ticked upward into the barest hint of a smile, as if he knew that Anne had lost just a bit of her control and wanted to see how much more of it he could chip away.

"In any case, I'm offering my help now," Vincent said as he leaned forward, seeming to test whether Anne would push her chair back to keep the distance between them.

She managed to stay just where she was, though, mulling over his words while resisting the impulse to pull away.

Though Vincent seemed sincere, the oddest flavor saturated

Anne's senses as what he'd said lingered in the silence between them. It reminded her of a caramel apple that looked perfectly sweet on the outside but was rotten once you bit into the core. The taste always unfurled alongside truths that concealed darker revelations, and once again, Anne wondered what he was hiding.

"Very well," Anne replied as she threaded her fingers together and set them on the table.

The movement drew Vincent's gaze to the ring, and Anne noticed that his attention seemed to linger there a beat longer than she'd expected.

"So, for the time being, I'm at your disposal," Vincent said, his focus shifting from the ring to Anne's eyes. "How would you like to proceed?"

That morning, before Vincent walked into the shop, Anne had still been trying to piece together a plan. She'd thought of all the possible paths to take should he decide to help and, like a lace maker who'd lost control of her pins, had quickly become tangled in the mess of potential consequences.

But something about the way Vincent was staring at her now, as if they were playing a game of chess and he was calculating her next move, made her act without a single hesitation.

"I assume you've already asked your family whether they know anything about the ring," Anne said.

"I have," Vincent replied with a nod. "It's been the sole topic of discussion since we learned the true nature of my uncle's Task, and no one seems to remember anything about it."

It was the answer that Anne had expected. Of course his family would have exhausted all possibilities in an attempt to resolve the matter and avoid the scandal of the whole situation.

Again, she wanted to press him about the reason for his sudden change of heart. If Vincent grasped the severity of the situation, why had he been so insistent about refusing to help her?

But she could tell by the steely glint in his expression that she wouldn't get a firm answer from him and decided to turn their conversation in a more promising direction.

"Am I also correct to assume that you've asked *every* family member?" Anne inquired, raising a copper brow.

"Are you asking if I've tried to speak with someone beyond the veil about the ring, Miss Quigley?" Vincent asked, his tone deepening.

"I am," Anne answered, holding firm though the shadows in the room seemed to stretch just a bit closer, as if enticed by the sound of Vincent's voice.

"My uncle is the only Crowley to leave a Task unfinished," he finally said. "So no one else has remained behind."

"Have you tried to speak with him?" Anne asked, her voice softening a fraction as she wondered if there was a chance of hearing her old friend's voice again.

Since Mr. Crowley had been so careful about ensuring his Task remained unfinished in life, she doubted he would reach out in death, especially to his family, who would be eager to draw everything to a neat close before the rest of the coven noticed what was happening. As her chest began to tighten, though, Anne realized that she still held to the faint hope of seeing him once more.

But then Vincent's eyes hardened, confirming exactly what she'd suspected.

"He won't answer me," he replied simply, the clipped edges of his tone making it clear that she shouldn't ask any further questions on that point.

Anne thought she caught the barest hint of hurt buried beneath Vincent's austerity, a roughness cracking through the steely surface of his voice.

Before she could press any further, he straightened in his

chair and continued on, obviously eager to push their conversation in another direction.

"But that doesn't mean other ghosts haven't remained in the house and seen a thing or two," Vincent said. "Spirits who linger carry so many regrets with them, and they're attracted to witches who might be willing to listen."

Anne remembered the murmurs that had crept through the cracks of the door in the Crowley mansion, the whispers laden with longing and desperation.

"And what have they told you?" Anne asked.

"Nothing that could point me in a clear direction," Vincent sighed. "Ghosts are notoriously difficult to orient. Their sole concern is trying to share something that might give them peace, and they aren't able to grasp questions unless you can ground them."

"And how do you manage that?" Anne inquired.

"We use sensations that might have meant something to them in life," Vincent explained. "The steady ticking of a clock, the scent of smoke, the jolt of surprise when you see yourself in a mirror. Anything that reminds them of what it was like to feel alive. Objects that they might have seen or touched before passing on are the most useful."

"You mean objects like this?" Anne asked as she lifted her hand and let the light hit the gold band once more.

"Yes," Vincent replied simply, though Anne could sense a wealth of meaning in that single word.

"Then we must use the ring," Anne said. "If no one living can give us the answers, our next step is clear."

"I agree," Vincent replied as he rested his upturned palm a few inches away from Anne's fingertips. "If you'll lend it to me for a time, I can see whether it will help steady the spirits."

Anne pulled away then, concealing the ring beneath the table in the same way Mr. Crowley had when she'd insisted on using it to discover his Fate.

"I understand that the type of magic you perform is of a private nature," Anne said as she straightened her spine. "But I would prefer to be there."

Vincent remained still, his forearms resting lazily against the table without the barest hint of concern, but out of the corner of her eye, Anne saw the shadows that had started to creep forward whip their tails in agitation. She should have been alarmed by the sight, but something about it made her want to see just how far they would reach if she continued to stand her ground.

"If time is truly of the essence, Miss Quigley," Vincent murmured, the barest sliver of tightness seeping into his tone, "then it would be best to simply give me the ring. As I've already mentioned, my magic requires a great deal of focus, and I can't afford any distractions if we need to bring this matter to a close as soon as possible."

"I'm surprised to hear that, Mr. Crowley," Anne replied, her words as slow and deliberate as a knife being sharpened against stone. "I would have thought you had enough control over your power not to be bothered by the presence of another witch. But if you don't believe you're strong enough for the task . . ."

She let the tail end of her sentence fade away as a tense silence fell between them, thick enough that the house wondered if it should crack open a window to let out some of the heat. Their magic was so close to the surface now that the customers downstairs started to wonder where the odd aroma of peppermint and cypress was coming from.

Anne watched as the shadows that had been slowly shifting forward abruptly unfurled, covering the windows as if a cloud had suddenly shifted to block the sun. It might have been a trick of the light, but she thought his eyes deepened, too, that striking amber hue melting into something more akin to coals burning at the bottom of a hearth.

But before she could be certain, Vincent turned over his open palm so that it rested against the table, and whatever spell had been coming together instantly faded away, snapping the shadows back into the corners of the parlor.

"Very well," he said in the same detached tone that one might use when asked if they'd prefer a dash of cream in their morning coffee. "Would you be able to stop by the house tomorrow evening? After sunset would be best since the spirits are more attracted to the light of a witching moon."

She nodded, understanding that they'd need to work during the time of night when everything was so still that it felt like magic could be touched beneath the silence. It was a moment brimming over with the promise of the impossible, and though the thought of leaving the warmth of the Crescent Moon after the shop had nestled in for the day made her bones ache, Anne knew she didn't have a choice, not when so much hung in the balance.

"I can see myself out," Vincent announced as he rose from his chair.

Anne couldn't tell if he was trying to save her the trouble of showing him to the door or simply didn't want to be in her presence any longer. Before she could decide, he paused and turned to her.

"There is one last thing," Vincent said just as his boot was about to land on the top step of the spiral staircase.

"Yes?" Anne asked, her breath catching as she waited to hear what he would say next.

"You should call me Vincent," he replied, turning so that his amber eyes met hers. "Since Mr. Crowley already has a certain meaning for you."

He was right, of course. Among their kind, names possessed a distinct texture that carried into conversations. Whenever Anne said "Mr. Crowley," memories of her old friend always managed to seep through, throwing the whole encounter off-balance. The name already belonged to someone else, so much so that she couldn't bring herself to change the inflection to make it better fit the man standing before her.

Anne wasn't sure she wanted to call Vincent by his first name, though. Not when it was becoming abundantly clear that it was best to keep as much distance between them as possible. But she certainly wasn't going to let him know that she was unnerved by this show of familiarity.

"Very well," she relented in the same reserved tone that he had used only moments ago.

Again, a flash of interest flickered in Vincent's amber eyes, but before Anne could think anything of it, he had already turned away.

The house sensed Anne's unease and rekindled the fire in the hearth so that the scent of nutmeg and citrus might chase away her worries.

Releasing a deep sigh once Vincent was out of sight, Anne felt some of the tension melt away from her shoulders as she let her posture loosen for the first time since he stepped into the shop. But the withdrawn breath scattered a pile of sugar that a customer had spilled from her spoon, the grains shifting across the tablecloth as they swirled into a new shape.

The house watched with curiosity as Anne's brows pinched together and she lifted her hand to brush away the sugar, as if destroying the sign might erase the memory of what she'd glimpsed there. But just before her palm touched the grains, the Crescent Moon saw it: the silhouette of a hawk, its talons outstretched and ready to grasp whatever was waiting below.

After so many years of looking over the sisters' shoulders

during readings, the house had learned enough to know what it meant when a hawk appeared on the horizon. In some situations, it suggested that a person had just entered your life who would use their calculating nature to help you reach a much-desired end. But in others, it warned that an enemy was near.

As the bells chimed against the front door and Vincent stepped onto the street, the Crescent Moon wondered which interpretation would prove true.

CHAPTER 15

A Coffeepot
*Represents a desire to settle
into simple pleasures.*

As Beatrix's hand rested on the doorknob, she wondered if the bookshop would feel different under the light of day than it had at night, when the shadows that crept beyond the reach of the gas lamps made it seem like the shelves were teeming with secrets.

She should have been eager to step over the threshold and prove that the strange sense of loneliness she'd felt when walking over the piles of abandoned books had come from somewhere within the depths of her own imagination. But in the moments before she pushed open the door, Beatrix found herself lingering again in the possibility that she'd found a kindred spirit, something else that had once shone bright but now felt lost and bent around the corners.

"Why don't you go inside and get settled?" Beatrix heard Violet say, snapping her away from thoughts tinged with dust and disarray.

Glancing up, Beatrix saw that her sister was standing farther down the alleyway, her fingers flipping through a ring of keys. They flashed against the light as she tried to discern which would unlock another door, the one that led to the abandoned apartment upstairs. Though Brigit had looked surprised when she learned that the Quigleys wanted to rent the rooms above the shop as well, she didn't seem like the type to question a good turn of luck and had happily handed over the keys with instructions to be careful on the rickety staircase.

"I'll see what there is to find upstairs while you get to work," Violet continued, a cry of triumph punctuating the end of her sentence when she managed to find the correct key.

The word "work" sent a ripple of panic down Beatrix's spine, causing her hands to grow clammy beneath her woolen gloves.

She began to slip into the same worries that had consumed her at the writing desk the previous afternoon. But before she could conjure the feeling of dread that always made her stomach drop, the door clicked open at the same moment a strong gust of wind whipped down the alleyway, knocking Beatrix off-balance and nudging her forward.

She didn't remember turning the knob, but as the world within the shop came into focus, Beatrix found herself drawn away from the threshold and toward the sight that awaited her.

The boards that had covered the windows the night before were gone, allowing the faint rays of light that managed to slip through the clouds and snow to filter into the room. The aisles between the shelves were still littered with open books, but the dust drifting up from the pages was now illuminated in such a way that it seemed to sparkle. As if all the possibilities that had remained hidden between the covers of the stories were finally making their way into the world again.

Bewitched by the subtle transformation, Beatrix slowly set

the velvet bag she'd carried with her on a wooden counter just next to the door. She hadn't brought much, only her notebook, a pen and ink, and the novel that Jennings had given her, still wrapped in parchment paper. But as she put the bag down and took a step toward the glittering books, Beatrix couldn't help but think that a heavier weight had been lifted from her shoulders.

How would it feel to lean forward and pull one of the books from the river of stories that spilled between the shelves? When she opened the cover and her eyes settled on the page, would she find that she'd fallen into the middle of a romance? Or the lines of a biography? Or a stanza of a poem? Would the texture of the words cast their own kind of spell, making her heart slow or race to meet the rhythm of the sentences?

Before Beatrix could think to stop herself, she was sinking onto her knees and reaching into the chaos of covers, her fingers dancing along the spines as she decided which to choose.

A tingle of excitement tickled the delicate skin along her collarbones, and for a moment, Beatrix felt just as she had long, long ago when the house revealed an entire trunk of books that it had been hiding until the girls were old enough to read. As her little hands had flitted over the colorful covers, they'd shaken ever so slightly in anticipation.

Even then, Beatrix had known that reading was magic. It transported her to places both within and beyond herself, where the flat words of the page took on a texture that felt more tangible than the boards beneath her feet.

Her hands were trembling now in that exact same way, not out of fear but from the pure rush of possibility. All she had to do was close her fingers around the spine, crack open the cover, and she'd be drawn again into that same sensation that sometimes drifted to the forefront of her memory when she thought about her childhood—the one tinged with the scent of aged paper and the promise of losing herself between the chapters of a book.

The title of a novel caught Beatrix's eye then, its gold foil practically winking at her when she reached forward and pulled it closer. As her fingers touched the spine, the light changed, as it does when a cloud shifts to reveal the sun, and when Beatrix glanced up, her gaze fell on a blue wingback chair sitting at the front of the shop just beneath the window. It was positioned so that the rays poured directly on the worn fabric, and Beatrix instantly envisioned herself leaning back into the soft upholstery and drifting further from her worries.

Beatrix was moving toward the chair now, her fingers running over the letters of the book's title as she shifted away from thoughts of her empty notebook and toward promises that she'd read only one chapter before finally sitting down to work.

But just as she was imagining how it would feel to ease back into the curved spine of the chair and turn the cover, she caught the sound of something trailing across the boards.

Shifting her gaze to the floor, Beatrix noticed that a loose paper was pierced through the heel of her boot.

She crouched down to save it, but when she pulled the page free, it started to crumble beneath her touch, the material damaged beyond repair from the snow that was dripping off her shoes.

She watched the ink bleed, the words blooming until they fell apart in her hand, like petals that hadn't clung strongly enough to the stem.

It was her birthday vision come to pass, a warning of what might happen if she failed to knit together another story.

In an instant, Beatrix's chest was aching from the weight that had settled back into place, and she flung the book down, wincing at the loud thump that it made against the floor.

Though Jennings had tried to convince her otherwise, now wasn't the time to lose herself in stories that had already been written, not when the pages of her own notebook begged to be filled with her familiar scrawl.

Releasing a tight sigh of frustration, Beatrix marched toward the office in the back room, grabbing her bag from the counter along the way, and shut the door behind her with a decided click.

If she had bothered to turn back, she may have noticed that the dust dancing up from the books no longer twinkled, their shimmer fading with every step that Beatrix put between her and the stories that she'd left sitting in the shadows.

CHAPTER 16

A Sunflower
Suggests that something important
will soon come to light.

Brigit had been right to warn Violet about the rickety steps, but there was more to watch out for than a few loose floorboards.

The moment she opened the door and stale tendrils of dust poured into the alley, Violet felt it: years of memories bottled up and ready to be freed once more. Even someone without a hint of magic could have sensed the heavy layers of recollections that clung to the plaster like wallpaper, though most would have stumbled back and shut the door behind them, bewildered by the odd jumble of emotions that seemed to fill the stairwell.

As she pressed her hand to the railing and climbed the steps, Violet could feel the layers of memories pulsing beneath her palm: trinkets of the past that had sunk into the very foundation of the house and refused to fade no matter how thorough the spring cleaning.

And though some of them were dark and lonely, she could

sense happiness there, too, and laughter that had settled into the cracks of the wainscoting, waiting to slip into the empty echoes once more. For though built of brick and mortar, the walls of old houses have a habit of capturing the best moments for safekeeping, soaking them up as quickly as a cake that's been covered in caramel.

But these ripples of joy were buried so far beneath dust and disappointment that Violet doubted anyone else would be able to sense them at all. Perhaps the pleasures of life that lingered beneath all that neglect were more palpable to her because she'd been longing to lose herself in forgotten places.

When she reached the top of the steps, Violet stumbled into a sea of yellowed linen and shadows. What she assumed had once been white sheets were tossed across the shapes of settees and tables, though it was difficult to tell, given that only the barest slivers of light managed to slip through the thick velvet curtains that clung to the windows.

The whole scene looked like the inside of a dollhouse that had seen daydreams come to life but was now left abandoned in the attic as it waited for a new pair of hands to wipe away the spiderwebs stuck in its corners.

Violet wondered if someone would eventually come along and do just that, but Brigit hadn't been too hopeful about the possibility when she'd passed over the keys.

"The chimney's toppling over, and there are so many holes in the floorboards that it's only a matter of time before some poor soul falls clean through," Brigit had said. "It's no wonder the place has been empty for so long."

When asked exactly who had lived in the old apartment, though, Brigit hadn't been able to say very much at all.

They didn't even know their aunt had owned any property until she'd passed away, and the neighborhood had changed so much that no one could say for certain when someone had last occupied the apartment, let alone who.

Sighing, Violet wondered how she was going to learn anything about the people who had once called these rooms their home.

As it was so often the case, she hadn't planned beyond her first bold leap. She realized she'd barreled through the door without a clear direction, and now all she could do was stand as still as the ghostly furniture that hadn't moved in decades.

That subtle turn of thought instantly drew Violet back to the memory of why she'd returned to Chicago in the first place. And quicker than she could snap her fingers, the ember that had started to flicker to life within her soul was overpowered by the icy chill of her nightmares. She could feel it numb the tips of her fingers and toes before creeping across her chest, tightening the bones there until her breaths grew faster and uneven.

After she'd completed her Task, Violet thought that everything else would fall smoothly into place, like a pearl that was being threaded from one end of a ribbon to the other. That once she'd finally managed to find her purpose, there was no chance of ever feeling lost again, not when her destiny had been met and there seemed to be no more twists of Fate to contend with. But here she was, a kite who'd been cut away from its anchor and was fighting to stay on course.

Shuddering, Violet reached out to find some sort of purchase and rested her hand along the mantle's ledge. Her pulse was pounding beneath the thin skin of her temples, so quickly that she worried it would carry her away from the present entirely and toward memories that needed to stay in the past.

Lifting her fingers to her brow, Violet saw that the white fabric of her gloves was now coated in a thick layer of dust. Sighing, she moved to brush it away, but a sudden thought made her pause.

What if she used magic to help uncover a sign?

Since leaving home, Violet hadn't made much use of her powers, preferring to embrace the fantastical sensations of flying across the circus tent. She'd read a few fortunes at the bottom of a cup when asked, but those instances had grown fewer and further between once she started spending most of her time in the ring. And then after the accident, it was as if she was fixed in time, unable to look toward the past or future as she desperately clung to the here and now.

If she was very honest with herself, Violet could admit that she worried her magic had faded the more she neglected it. What if she reached for the threads of foresight and found that she no longer had the strength to pull them toward her? Reading the remnants of their customers' velvet oolong was one matter, a task that came as easy as breathing. But trying to reach beyond the present without someone sitting across from her, their hopes and fears as potent as their perfume, was another challenge entirely.

Anne was the sister who seemed to have inherited their mother's abilities, not Violet, who'd never paid enough attention during their lessons and couldn't seem to channel her efforts in any focused direction. And now that she'd distanced herself from the Crescent Moon, it was becoming difficult to remember the wisdom that their mother had done her best to pass down.

But you're still a Quigley. . . .

The thought flashed through her mind so quickly that she wondered where it had come from. But as Violet turned the words over in her head, she started to believe that they might be true.

Perhaps, if she managed to push aside her own unease of the past and concern for the future, Violet could shift beyond her fears and help Mr. Crowley and Philip so that their destinies could at last be tethered together, the knots holding their bond so tight that nothing would be able to pull them apart. And in doing so, she might just find her own way again.

Glancing back down at the dust that coated her gloves, Violet decided that if she wanted to recover her courage, she'd need to discover parts of herself that she hadn't even known were there.

With deliberate care, Violet pulled off the cloth that covered her hands and then ran her palm against the entire mantle, pulling it from one end to the other so that by the time she lifted it up once more, her skin was covered in dust.

In a single heartbeat, she was lost in the memory of her mother showing her how to read the signs this way when she was a child.

On the first true spring day when it was finally warm enough to throw open the windows, Clara Quigley would wrap an apron around her waist, run her finger over the wainscoting, and blow the dust across the room as one does when making a wish on a dandelion. And in the swirls that fluttered in the rays of light, she'd find not only hints of the future but remnants of the moments that unfolded when they'd been tucked away from the cold and snow.

For like dust, memories have a habit of settling into the darkest corners of our minds unless we make an effort to bring them back into the light.

"Moving forward means remembering what came before," Violet murmured, repeating the same phrase that her mother had always said just before she let out a deep breath and blew the dust from her fingers.

And then she released the sigh that had been welling within her ever since she'd watched Emil slip out of her grasp and let it push the soot from her hand. As the dust flew through the air, the honeysuckle notes of Violet's magic emerged, tangling with the shimmering particles and her thoughts of Philip.

They wove together to create sharp lines that bespoke happiness and fulfillment, stretching so far across the room that Violet could almost hear laughter echoing against the walls. But just when she felt a smile begin to tug at the corner of her mouth, the lines suddenly wobbled before shattering into a thousand tiny pieces. The force of it threw open a door on the other end of the room, and Violet's brow furrowed while she watched the swirls of dust fly away from her and over the threshold, as if pulled toward a window that had suddenly been thrown open.

Violet chased them, but by the time she reached the doorframe, the last of the dust had fallen to the floor, lost in the cracks between the boards.

"Medusa's curls," she cursed, shaking her head in frustration.

The initial signs had been so strong, but Violet hadn't managed to hold on to them long enough to get even the barest hint of a reading. She might be a Quigley, but in that moment, Violet felt like she'd strayed so far from her roots that she had no more power than a child wishing on a birthday candle.

She hit her hand against the doorframe then, hoping to release some of the anger and disappointment that were starting to return. But when the flesh of her palm hit the wood, she felt something unexpected, a divot where there should have been nothing but smooth oak.

Violet turned toward the frame and then slowly lifted her hand to see what rested beneath it. As she pulled her fingers away, she noticed a name embedded in the wood.

May.

Leaning closer, Violet continued to brush the grime away, studying the scrawl to see if it matched the names she'd stumbled across in the shop below.

But there were subtle differences in the letters that told her they'd been etched by another hand. The ones downstairs had been so neat and even, while whoever printed the name here had elongated the "M" so that it towered over the rest of the lines and curves.

It could have belonged to any of the tenants who'd filtered through the apartment over the decades. People always seemed eager to leave their mark on what had felt like home, tucking their initials in grooves and corners in the hopes that the walls, at least, would remember even if those who came after them never learned of the stories that had unfolded on the floors beneath their very feet.

But something that Violet had done her best to push to the side was starting to make its way to the surface of her awareness, impatient to be heard.

It was her intuition telling her that there was more to be uncovered beneath the dust of forgotten dreams.

As of late, Violet had done her best to avoid any flicker of interest that might pull her onto an unexpected path. She worried that her misstep had created a snag in the delicate fabric of her reality and believed the key to keeping everything from unraveling was remaining perfectly still. But as her gaze roamed over the remnants of someone else's past, Violet felt her foot tapping against the boards of its own accord while her mind drifted toward new possibilities that felt as fresh as breathing in the brisk winter air.

There was an answer waiting here, as quiet and unassuming as the cobwebs tucked in the corners, and for the first time in what felt like an eternity, Violet was eager to take a step forward and see what she could discover.

CHAPTER 17

A Fireplace
Symbolizes the need for family, recovery, and rest.

𝓘n the winter months, when the sun never quite seemed to reach through the clouds and touch the sidewalk, the Crescent Moon liked to remind the Quigleys that comfort could still be found in the darkness.

When it noticed the last customer settle back into her chair in a way that hinted she would soon leave to catch the next cable car home, the house let its attention wander to the family parlor. It began to kindle flames in the hearth, tucking sprigs of sage around the logs that would chase away memories of icy toes and fingers. And then, when it could smell the faintest scent of herbs and rich wood, the house went about the task of lighting the wicks of beeswax candles. Every day that the night drew longer, it added another stub to the growing collection until it lost count of how many flames flickered against their brass holders. Then it would pull the curtains back on just one of the windows, revealing the softly falling snow that reminded whoever was sitting in the warmth of the parlor that they could enjoy the simple beauty of winter's touch.

That evening, the Quigley sisters savored the sense of slipping away from their worries as they grasped warm cups between their hands and allowed themselves to remember what it had felt like to draw each and every day to a close in this way—the nights when time itself only seemed to stretch as far as the furthest flicker of the fire's light.

But as pleasant as it was to revisit the past, they knew it wouldn't do to linger there too long. And so, after their cider had cooled just enough to take a first sip, they drew in one last sage-scented breath and went about the task of moving forward.

"We need to make more progress," Anne said as she leaned forward in her chair, feeling her pulse quicken though the house was trying its best to get her to rest into familiar comforts. "The effects of Mr. Crowley's Task are growing stronger with every passing day. It's only a matter of time before everyone starts to notice that things are not as they should be."

Anne remembered the chill that had skittered across the back of her neck when she stepped out of the shop that morning and saw the ice coating the street. It was a wonder that the other witches hadn't realized something had gone horribly wrong.

"I might have uncovered something in the apartment above the bookshop," Violet said as her foot tapped excitedly against the carpet.

"What is it?" Anne pressed, pleased to hear some of the familiar fire in her sister's voice sparking to life.

"Do you remember what we used to do on the first day of spring?" Violet asked. "When we'd run our fingers along the dusty mantle and remind ourselves of the memories we'd made during the winter?"

"Of course," Anne replied, her thoughts already slipping back to what it had felt like to see the dust dancing in the bright light pouring through the open windows.

"Well, I tried my hand at reading the past in the dust of the apartment, and do you know where it led me?" Violet continued. "Straight to a mark on the doorframe, like the ones in the shop below, but the name printed alongside it was May."

Suddenly, Anne remembered the voice that had echoed through her vision as she'd shifted back and forth on the rocking chair, the one that felt like it had crept to the very edge of her consciousness.

"I know it isn't much, but I feel like there's something important about her," Violet insisted. "The memories that led me to the threshold were so joyful and then filled with absolute loss, the same sensation that's slipped through the floorboards and into the bookshop."

"You think she's linked to Philip in some way?" Beatrix asked.

"Yes," Violet replied, her tone steady and certain. "When I blew the soot across the room, I tried to focus my attention on Philip, and the magic led me straight to May."

"I think you're right, Vi," Anne agreed, relieved that they might have found a clue.

"I'll do my best to learn more about how she fits into all this," Violet replied with a nod.

"Did you make any progress, Bee?" Anne asked, her gaze shifting to the other end of the settee.

Beatrix grew still then, her grip on the cup's handle so tight that Anne worried it might crack.

"Everything's just as it was before," Beatrix finally murmured, her eyes hardening as they drifted toward the notebook that sat on the end table.

Anne noticed the stiff set of Beatrix's shoulders ease, though, when Violet touched her arm, a quiet reminder that they already understood what she was struggling to put into words.

"And what of your day, Anne?" Violet asked once Beatrix had taken another sip of her cider.

"Vincent Crowley visited the shop while you two were out," Anne replied, her brows pinching together at the memory. "He's agreed to help.'

"But you told us that he was adamant about staying out of the whole affair!" Beatrix cried in surprise.

"It seems that he's changed his mind," Anne sighed, the words sounding more clipped than she'd intended.

"You aren't convinced, though, are you?" Violet murmured, her brow rising slightly at the uncharacteristic hue of annoyance in her sister's tone.

"No," Anne replied, setting her cup atop the table with enough force to make the house winch. "I'm certain that Vincent has an entirely different reason for offering his assistance."

"And what do you think that is?" Beatrix asked.

"I don't know," Anne grumbled. "But I'm determined to find out. Tomorrow evening, he's going to use his magic to see if we can find any answers about the ring."

"You don't mean . . . ," Violet began, the words fading away as if she couldn't bring herself to say them aloud.

"Yes, we're going to see if one of the ghosts who've taken up residence in the Crowley manor can help us," Anne said before reaching for her cup again, trying to make her tone as steady and unbothered as possible though she could feel her sisters' worried gazes boring into her skin.

"But you've never tried that before," Beatrix whispered, concern lacing her voice. "None of us have."

A shiver of unease crept up Anne's back as she wondered what it would be like to watch Vincent call upon a spirit.

But then she remembered what she'd heard from other witches who'd reached beyond the veil and discovered a sense of closure that they hadn't expected to find in the shadows. They'd spoken of the experience in the same soft tones that most use to describe the sensation of running a hand across cashmere where one expected to find coarse wool.

"I know that the kind of magic the Crowleys possess has a certain reputation, even among our kind," Anne sighed. "But from what I've learned in the past year, it's not as frightening as you might think. Their power is centered on providing comfort to the restless, after all, and peace to those who want so desperately to move forward."

The sisters thought of their own customers, who came to the Crescent Moon for much more than a sweet treat and a glimpse into their future. Every day, they stepped through the threshold searching for signs of hope nestled somewhere in the remnants of their tea leaves. Was the magic that the Crowleys were gifted with so very different from their own?

"I suppose you're right," Beatrix conceded, sighing as she leaned back into the settee. "And with Vincent, we have a much stronger chance of helping Mr. Crowley and Philip remain together as they wished."

Anne followed suit, letting the stiffness in her back fade into the familiar warmth of the candlelight while she and her sisters drifted into thoughts of their old friend, who'd helped them look past their own fears of the unknown and toward a brighter future.

And as they sank deeper into those memories, the Quigleys wondered if, when all was said and done, they'd be able to do the same for him.

CHAPTER 18

A Plow

Represents struggles and
difficult challenges.

*N*othing, Beatrix thought as she tapped her pen against the top of the desk, carried the weight of a blank sheet of paper.

Though most might peer over her shoulder and scoff at such a notion, if they turned to glance at Beatrix's face and saw the worry lines etched there, they would have been able to see that the emptiness of the page was in fact brimming over with hopes and fears.

When words grew on the paper, they pushed these worries to the side, the strength of the story quickly overpowering doubts that could feel as sharp and sudden as the prick of a pin.

But if left to fester, these troubles transformed into something else entirely.

When Beatrix had first stepped over the threshold that morning, the bookshop was just as dusty and disheveled as she'd left it. But as she drew deeper into the front room, Beatrix had detected something beneath the scent of neglect and faded pages: notes of vanilla that hadn't been there the day before. The aroma instantly reminded her of what it felt like to pull an old book off the shelf and breathe in the smell of a well-spun story, tempting her to reach toward the sea of tales littered across the floor. She'd nearly done it, too, her eyes dancing eagerly from one title to the next until the weight of her blank notebook snapped her attention back to the task at hand.

Focus was what she needed, and so Beatrix had marched straight to the office in the back of the shop, pulled out her pen, and imagined that chains were binding her feet to the wooden legs so she wouldn't be tempted to fidget herself into distraction.

But even then, no words came, and as Beatrix had continued to stare at those blank sheets in her notebook, which were normally so tightly packed with sentences that she had to squeeze them along the sides, the ache that had grown along her back from holding herself still gradually shifted to her chest.

Her imagination began to drift then, not toward a tale that could enchant and delight but a different kind of story altogether, one where Beatrix was at the center.

The scenes came to her in flashes, growing in their intensity the longer she allowed them time to feed off her deepest anxieties.

She saw herself standing up from the desk as the day came to a close, having failed to string together even two syllables that were worth keeping. Heart racing, Beatrix envisioned the sight of her empty notebook as the shadows of sunset stretched across the blank pages. That impression was quickly consumed by another, though, one that caused her pulse to pound even harder. She was walking down the street, the snow having given way to spring sunshine that drew attention to her pensive expression and unmarked hands. Beatrix watched in horror as she imagined herself arriving at the front door of Donohoe & Company, where she stood in silence, trying to find the words she'd need to explain that the deadline for the next novel didn't have the barest wish of being met.

These fantasies were sewn from the fabric of Beatrix's wildest fears for the future. And they grew and grew and grew until there wasn't any space left for her characters' voices to be heard through the recesses of her imagination.

But she continued to etch the finer points of each scene in her mind, drawing out the shadows that spilled across the sidewalks and the feeling of dread that unfurled in her chest as her fingers reached for the doorknob of the publishing house.

Beatrix, of course, knew that this wasn't the story she should be bringing to life. But a jolt of alarm struck her to the very core whenever she considered what might happen should these nightmarish thoughts fade and reveal that there weren't any fresh ideas waiting for her in the silence of her mind. And so, instead of turning away from the worst of possibilities, she kept drafting the details of an ending that was quickly taking on a hue of inevitability.

Until a gentle tapping snapped her away from the troubles that could unfold and back to the present, where her senses were instantly captured by the scent of dusty books and the realization that someone was knocking on the door.

Beatrix stumbled up from the chair and moved toward the front of the shop, wondering who might be waiting in the alleyway.

"Jennings," Beatrix gasped in surprise when she pushed open the door and saw him standing in the middle of a snowdrift. "What are you doing here?"

He was wearing another coat now, this one even more patched together than the first had been. Beatrix's cheeks grew warmer as she thought of the coat draped atop the post of her bed and remembered that she hadn't yet sent it back to Donohoe

& Company so that Jennings wouldn't be shivering in the snow. She'd meant to do it only yesterday, but the scent of coffee and freshly cut paper that drifted from the fabric had made her forget why she needed to return it so hastily.

"Mr. Stuart asked me to find you, and when I went to the tearoom, your sister told me that you were working here," Jennings said with a grin that managed to stay fixed despite his chattering teeth.

"It must be rather urgent, then," Beatrix said, pulling at the collar of her blouse to try to keep the icy wind from slipping down her neck.

"Everything always is with Mr. Stuart," Jennings replied with a shake of his head. "He wants to know if it's possible for you to finish your draft a few weeks early."

"Early?" Beatrix said, hoping that the sound of the wind would drown out the panic in her voice.

"He's considering publishing this one serially first," Jennings explained. "To drum up even more excitement, you see. He'd like to show the opening chapters to the papers soon and get the bidding started."

Beatrix's hands were shaking now, so badly that she pulled them to her chest to pretend they'd grown cold.

Again, she was at a complete loss for words, unable to taste the barest whisper of an excuse on her tongue.

"Perhaps we could go inside," Jennings said as his eyes settled on Beatrix's trembling shoulders. "And get you out of this cold."

"No," Beatrix gasped, so quickly that the sound of it echoed against the bricks.

She couldn't let him see her like this, crumbling from within just like all those pages scattered across the dusty floor, the spines that they'd been clinging to having lost the strength they needed to hold everything together.

And what if he saw her notebook splayed across the desk and the white crispness of the paper revealed her secret?

"But it's freezing out here," Jennings insisted, his expression growing more concerned as he watched her lips, which she knew must be turning a light shade of blue.

"I'm sorry, Jennings," Beatrix said as she shook her head and began to step back through the threshold. "But I'm in the middle of a chapter. I really can't afford to be distracted."

His smile faded then, the sight of it causing Beatrix's chest to tighten even worse than it did whenever she stepped onto the street and drew in an unexpected breath of frosty air.

"Very well," he murmured, his boots crunching against the freshly fallen snow as he started to move away from the door. "I'll tell Mr. Stuart that you need more time to think it over."

"Yes," Beatrix murmured, resisting the urge to set aside her worries and let him inside. "Thank you. I'm sorry I can't give him an answer right now."

She wanted to apologize for more than that, but the feelings that were brimming to the surface just wouldn't string into coherent sentences.

"I did bring you something," Jennings said as he reached into the pocket of his coat, his movements more hesitant than they had been the other day when he'd presented her with the book. "But I'm afraid it's rather worse for wear now."

At first, Beatrix was only aware of a flash of red against snow, but then she leaned a bit closer and saw that Jennings was holding a carnation, its petals bent from rubbing against the cloth of his pocket but still vibrant nonetheless.

"It's beautiful," Beatrix whispered as she reached forward to grasp it from Jennings' palm, the tips of her fingers brushing against the thick wool of his gloves.

"Don't ask what I had to do to get it," Jennings replied as he watched her trace the delicate outline of the petals, clearly hoping that the sight of the flower would make her smile, just as it had in the frosty confines of the train car.

And then, before Beatrix could think what to do next, he touched the brim of his hat in a silent goodbye and disappeared, his tattered coattails lost in the heavy snowfall.

As Beatrix lifted the petals to her nose and breathed in the sweet floral scent that should have carried her mind far away from thoughts of winter, she felt a tear slide down her face, the delicate stream freezing against her cheek before it had a chance to fall.

Because the chapter unfolding before her was starting to feel very much like the end.

CHAPTER 19

A Pendulum

*Appears when something is
trying to break free.*

As Anne climbed the front stoop of the Crowley mansion, the speech that she'd been piecing together ever since she'd seen Vincent's dark shadow of a suit slip away from the Crescent Moon kept whirling through her thoughts.

He'd surprised her yesterday in the shop, his shocking white hair and stern expression so out of place among the familiar comforts of the Crescent Moon that she'd been thrown off-kilter from the start of their conversation.

Anne had always been reassured by the fact that no matter the prickly temperament of a customer, she could reach within herself and find the steadiness she needed to keep whatever sharp remarks that bubbled to the surface in check. But when it came to Vincent, all it had taken was one sarcastic lift of a brow for the sharp remarks that normally stayed tucked away to whip off the tip of her tongue.

To make matters even worse, Anne had noticed the gleam of

satisfaction that flashed in his eyes when she'd bitten back instead of remaining indifferent.

But that most certainly wouldn't be the case this time around.

In the moments when she was shifting between readings, Anne had rehearsed exactly what she intended to say to Vincent during their next encounter, repeating the lines over and over again in her head until they took on the exact inflection that would help her feel as unfettered as a doorstop. And then, as she'd gotten ready to rest for the evening, Anne had added on to them as one does when drawing out a map with dozens of alternative directions etched along the various streets and alleyways.

First, she'd greet him in her most civil tone, saying his name as simply as she could so that the texture of the syllables didn't have a chance to taste familiar. After she gave him a moment to reply in kind, Anne would outline her aims for the evening, making it clearer than crystal that she wouldn't be riled again and expected all of her questions to be met with a definite answer. Their conversation wouldn't unfurl as it had yesterday, when each exchange felt like an ember crackling unexpectedly in the stove.

She'd charted every possible barb and comment that might make her as bristly as a boysenberry bush and was determined to keep everything on course, no matter how much Vincent managed to rile her.

As Anne reached toward the brass knocker and tapped it against the wood, she pictured the first turn of their conversation, the sentence that she planned to say so solid on her tongue that she could very nearly feel it.

But when the door swung open and she parted her lips to speak, Anne realized that Vincent wasn't standing there at all. The foyer was just as it had been the other day, empty aside from the fading light of sunset that crept in through the front door and the shadows cast by the candles flickering in the hallway.

The house, it seemed, had decided to let her in of its own accord again.

Anne's brows furrowed as she stepped deeper into the hallway and wondered at the obvious display of hospitality. Strange that the house would let shadows and dust gather in its corners but so eagerly welcome a guest out of the frosty winter streets.

Before she could give that question any more consideration, however, the oddest noise drifted into Anne's awareness.

It sounded like a soft strain of music, the vibrations strange and familiar all at once, as if she'd hummed the tune before and her body remembered the chords though she herself could not recall them.

And before she knew quite what she was doing, Anne had stepped closer to a door in the center of the hallway where she could hear the gentle hum slipping through the cracks along the frame.

As she rested her hand against the knob and started to turn it, though, Anne vaguely remembered that magical temptations aren't always as innocent as they seem, but the pull of the music was much stronger than the ticking clocks had been. It was as if every note tugged at a place deep within her soul, making her feel like she was moving toward something that promised to reveal a hidden part of herself.

She could practically feel the tempo rippling against her skin now, growing stronger the more she thought about turning the knob to see what waited on the other side.

Tilting her head, Anne moved to do just that, but as she started to pull the door open, a hand flashed from behind her and snapped it shut again, causing her to jump in surprise.

The gentle pulse of the melody was instantly overpowered in Anne's awareness by the scent of cypress and myrrh.

"What are you doing?" Vincent's icy voice asked from behind

her, so close to her ear that Anne knew if she whirled around, their faces would be separated by only the barest whisper.

The rough timbre of his tone should have made Anne feel like she'd just been doused in cold water, but instead heat rose to her cheeks as she turned her neck to glare at him.

"Seeing what's on the other side of this door," she answered sharply, all her intentions of remaining civil evaporating the moment she heard him speak.

"Why?" Vincent asked, his question urgent and laced with worry.

"I heard music," Anne answered, startled into confessing the truth by the sudden earnestness of his tone.

Vincent's arm snapped around her waist then, as if she were on the bow of a ship about to be pulled into the sea by a force greater than her own.

"Have you lost your senses?!" Anne cried as he pulled her away from the door and down the hall.

"You shouldn't have been able to hear it," Vincent murmured, though he seemed to be speaking more to himself than to her.

Anne braced her hands against his chest and pushed just as Vincent opened the door to the room where the clocks dangled from the walls. It was the same moment that he loosened his hold, the unexpected release causing Anne to stumble backward.

"What, exactly, is it that I shouldn't have been able to hear?" Anne asked as she regained her footing and ran her hands along the sides of her skirts, trying to brush away the feeling of his hands against her waist.

But Vincent ignored her question again, his full attention riveted on Anne's face. He was staring deeply into her eyes, as a physician does when trying to determine if someone's been injured by a blow to the head. The scowl that had already become a familiar sight was softened by a genuine look of concern that instantly loosened some of the strain in Anne's clenched hands. It was strange, really, how such a simple change transformed his entire face, and for the barest second, she wondered what it would be like to see that stony mask fall away entirely.

After a few moments, he seemed satisfied that no permanent damage had befallen her. But then his expression shifted into something far more alarming: raw curiosity.

"I knew that you were an unusually powerful witch," Vincent said as he took a step closer to Anne. "I wonder . . . "

An insistent voice in the back of Anne's mind told her to move away, but she refused to give Vincent the upper hand and defiantly stood her ground instead, a pleasant prickling sensation skittering across her collarbones as she dug her heels deeper into the floorboards.

"What, exactly?" Anne asked as her magic whipped to the surface and the distinct scent of peppermint and early morning dew saturated the room.

"If you can see more than the future," Vincent said, his reply sending ripples of shock down her spine.

Anne had told no one about her ability to slip back into the past. It was so new that she hadn't wanted to speak to the rest of the Council about it, not when she didn't have full control yet. Though Anne had worked hard to secure her place among the coven since becoming Diviner, she knew that as a witch grew more powerful, so did the consequences of showing the slightest sign of weakness. She couldn't let anyone else know about her abilities until she'd harnessed them, or the coven would grow uneasy, shaken by the thought that the person who'd kept them on course could lose her own way.

"And why would you think that?" Anne asked, trying to keep the surprise out of her voice.

"That music can only be heard by those who've walked beyond

their own pasts," Vincent said slowly, clearly wanting Anne to take in the underlying meaning of every single word.

"You mean . . . ," Anne murmured, her mind drawing toward the obvious conclusion only to skitter away from it as quickly as possible.

"Yes," Vincent replied. "Only the spirits can hear it."

"But your magic is tethered to the past," Anne insisted. "You should be able to hear it too."

"No," Vincent answered with a shake of his head. "My magic is tied to the parts of the past that cling to the present. It isn't the same."

"I'm not a ghost," Anne said in confusion.

"That you most certainly are not," Vincent replied, his hands twitching at his sides as if he were remembering how solid she'd felt beneath his hands only a few moments ago. "But you've found a way to drift back nonetheless."

Anne felt heat rise to her cheeks again, torn between frustration over having her new powers exposed and a strange temptation to reveal the truth to the one person who might be able to help her understand them. Vincent was right, of course. He couldn't see the past in the same way she could, but his magic was intimately woven to spirits who were still tethered there, the echoes of what came before beating at a constant tempo beneath his everyday.

For a moment, Anne let herself consider what it would feel like to have one fewer burden to keep in the shadows. There were so many of them stacking atop her shoulders now that everything she said needed to be weighed with careful deliberation. As irritated as she'd felt during her conversations with Vincent, it had been thrilling in a way to find herself forgetting to keep each word and gesture in check. She wondered how he managed to do that, make her feel fully in the present even when so many of her responsibilities were rooted firmly in worries about the future.

But before Anne could let herself drift away from the sense of prudence that had always steadied her before, she managed to hold herself back.

"What does it matter?" Anne said warily, hoping to bring the conversation to a close instead of driving it forward.

"It matters a great deal," Vincent murmured, softening his voice the barest fraction while making it clear that he refused to shy away from the point. "If you can slip into the past, the spirits will be more attracted to you. They'll see you as a kindred soul."

Anne's thoughts flashed back to the first time she'd entered the house and heard the whispers drifting down the hallway, an undercurrent of longing so strong that it had pulled her forward.

"I'm not like you," Anne insisted. "I can't call on ghosts."

"Of course you can't," Vincent conceded. "But I wonder what would happen if I opened the way."

Abruptly, Vincent took another step and reached toward Anne, closing the distance between them.

At first, she thought he was going to touch her face, but just as her chin jerked away, his fingers landed on the clock pinned to the front of her blouse.

"You wear this every day," Vincent said. "It means something to you."

"I don't see why—" Anne began, her guard starting to rise again as she realized that Vincent had been observing her closely enough to notice such a thing.

But before she could say anything more, Anne sensed that the scent of myrrh was growing stronger.

"What are you doing?" Anne grumbled, repeating the same question he'd asked her only a few minutes before.

They were always doing that, it seemed: making it impossible for the other to know for certain what would happen next.

"Shh," Vincent hissed back, his eyes falling closed as he seemed to concentrate on something beyond what Anne could sense. "Just listen."

Anne huffed as she tried to think of something to say that would end this absurd situation, but then she heard it.

The soft ticking of her own clock, so familiar and reassuring that she couldn't help but feel the tension between her shoulders relax just a fraction. It was the sound that always steadied her when the tearoom was at its busiest, the gentle *click-click-click* a reminder that time always moved forward at a slow and even pace even when it seemed like the seconds were whirling away.

As her attention grasped on to that reassuring thought, the other clocks in the room began to tick to life as well, their hands shifting to the same beat, though it seemed impossible that they could have all been set to the exact time.

And then Anne began to hear the whispers again, the sound as subtle as a breeze brushing against the hillside on a sunny day. She could sense the loneliness still, a heavy weight that made her own heart ache, but there was something else curling at the corners of the noise now. It was the same sound that crept into Violet or Beatrix's voices when they had a secret to reveal, their words laced with excitement and expectation.

Instead of wanting to share the worst of their grief, as Anne had feared, the spirits seemed kindled by curiosity, the feeling that they were about to encounter something new overpowering any desire they had to express their sorrow.

"Can you hear what they're saying?" Vincent asked, causing Anne to jump.

The sensations pressing in on her from all directions were so strong that she'd nearly forgotten he was standing there.

Vincent seemed to realize that he'd startled her and began to take a step back, but Anne surprised them both by grasping his wrist so that he would remain exactly where he stood.

"I hear them whispering," Anne murmured, letting the steady beat of Vincent's pulse orient her as she tried to speak above the eager voices. "But I can't tell exactly what's being said."

Vincent took another step forward then, slow enough that all it would take to keep him back was the slightest pressure of Anne's fingers. But she remained still, letting him draw so close that she could hear him clearly in the chaos of hushed confessions and feel his jaw graze against her curls as he parted his lips to speak.

"And what do you feel?" Vincent asked, the answer that instantly sprang to mind causing a blush to burn Anne's cheeks.

"Longing," Anne answered honestly as she was struck once more by the note of yearning that weighed down each and every whisper.

"Anything else?" Vincent asked, as if he could sense that she was holding something back.

"Curiosity," Anne finally confessed. "And excitement."

"They're memories," Vincent explained, his words coming faster now. Anne recognized the urgency that radiated from his voice. It was the same feeling that emerged whenever an unexpected twist of magic made her believe that she was about to discover something no one else had seen before. "They want to show you how it felt to be alive. The sensations tied to moments that seemed simple but in the end were everything."

Anne's heart was racing so rapidly now that she should have had trouble hearing the clocks, but they continued to click at the very front of her consciousness, each tick making the hairs on her arms stand on end in a way that reminded her of the blood pulsing beneath her skin.

"Start drifting back," Vincent said, his free hand moving to her shoulder, as if he intended to ensure her feet stayed on the ground while her mind faded beyond the current moment.

"No," Anne whispered, understanding exactly what he was telling her to do.

He wanted her to slip away from the present and into the past, but her powers couldn't be harnessed as well whenever she toyed with the boundaries of what she was capable of. In the safe confines of the Crescent Moon, where the scent of cinnamon buns and cardamon laced the edge of every indrawn breath, Anne was willing to test these lines, pushing just a bit further every time to see what would happen.

Letting go now, when the pounding clicks of the clocks and the alluring scent of Vincent's magic were causing her to forget why she wanted to stay in control, was beyond impossible.

Anne's magic seemed to have an entirely different opinion in the matter, though. As soon as it heard Vincent's suggestion, it started tingling against Anne's skin, begging her to let it take the reins.

The house began to shake then as Anne grappled with her power, the gears of the clocks screeching as they rattled against the walls.

"Drift back," Vincent insisted again, louder this time.

The texture of his voice matched the same urgency that undercut her magic, tempting her to let go and discover just how far she could push herself. It was so compelling that she very nearly released the weight of responsibility that she carried, the one that always made her think through each and every action for fear of the consequences. But in the end, she couldn't fall into the moment and forget.

"Enough!" Anne cried out, determined to gain sway over her power once more.

The moment she spoke a pulse of light flashed from her

hands, pushing Vincent away and knocking all the clocks from their pegs. They crashed to the floor and filled the house with the unsettling sound of metal being twisted out of place.

Anne stood at the center of the wreckage, trying to catch her breath as the final *click-click-click* of the clocks faded away.

"You're holding back," Vincent said accusingly as he raked a hand through his hair, causing the straight locks to stick up like spears.

Anne was startled by how much she missed the soft hue that had saturated his tone only a moment ago, but her shock gave way to a sense of relief at the iciness in his voice. It felt like a window had been thrown open in a hot house, letting in a bracing breeze that reminded her to put some space between them.

"That's none of your business," Anne hissed, crossing her arms protectively over her chest.

"Isn't it?" Vincent spat back. "When you've come to my home asking—no, *demanding*—my help? When leaving my uncle's Task unfinished will have an irreparable effect on the coven and it's clear that working together is the only way?"

Anne tried to find a sharp retort, but Vincent's words struck her to the core.

The only thing she could share in her defense was that she couldn't control her powers yet, and that was something she most certainly wouldn't admit. Not when she was the city's Diviner and even the barest hint of vulnerability could have disastrous consequences.

"Why are you holding back?" Vincent repeated, his tone even stronger and more demanding than it had been before.

"I'm *not*," Anne said, but the lie was so obvious that the smell of burnt meringue instantly infused the air between them.

Vincent's frown deepened as he drew in the scent, his eyes growing even colder than they'd been during their first encounter. Anne could practically feel the waves of distrust and suspicion radiating from him as he stepped away from her and surveyed the damaged clocks scattered around the room.

"If you're worried about drifting too far beyond your magic's control, I could anchor you," Vincent said.

That final word instantly caused a spark of alarm to shoot down Anne's spine.

When a witch worried that their powers might lure them away from what made them feel rooted, someone else could offer to ground them. Anne had been told that witches who wanted to be anchored didn't give up any control over their magic. It was more like calling a friend back when they were about to teeter off the edge.

If Anne let Vincent anchor her, though, she'd have to open her mind to him, exposing her inner self in a way that she'd never done before. They'd lace their hands together, and once Anne lowered her defenses enough to let his magic touch hers, the hidden layers of her awareness would be revealed for him to see. Vincent wouldn't know exactly what she was thinking, but he'd feel the pulse of her soul, tying his magic to hers long enough so that she would remember to stay rooted. It was an extraordinarily intimate act, one that would make it impossible for them to keep their distance.

Anne may have instinctually grasped Vincent's wrist when searching for a source of steadiness only a moment ago, but she certainly wasn't willing to consider letting him anchor her, no matter the strange pull she felt toward him.

"We can't try again tonight anyway," he sighed, clearly irritated by Anne's silence. "The spirits will be too unfocused now to draw in."

"It seems the clocks will need to be repaired before we try again," Anne said as she touched one of the gears that had been thrown across the floor with the tip of her boot.

"We won't be using them next time," Vincent said, that thoughtful glint having already returned to his eyes.

"What are we going to use instead?" Anne asked, worried now by the excited edge in his voice.

"I think it's best that you don't know beforehand," Vincent replied. "Since you have a tendency to linger too long on all the possible outcomes."

"You think you know me so well?" Anne retorted, none too pleased that he'd decided to keep her in the dark about the plan that was obviously taking shape in his mind, or that he seemed to have figured her out so quickly.

"Well enough," Vincent said, his gaze snapping back to hers.

They remained that way for what felt like an unbearable amount of time, her piercing blue eyes melting into the amber depths of his, with neither one of them willing to be the first to break the spell.

"I don't trust you," Anne finally said, hoping that it would rattle Vincent enough to look away.

"I'm not surprised," Vincent replied. "How can you when you don't even trust yourself?"

The words stung so deeply that Anne found her hand reaching toward her heart. She stopped it just in time, though, moving to clasp the clock that was still pinned to her blouse, comforted by the familiar way it warmed beneath her touch.

"I'll return tomorrow," Anne said simply before striding away from Vincent and out the door, determined to leave the house before she lost any more of her will or wits.

As she neared the front door, Anne thought she heard her name echoing down the hallway and the sound of footsteps trailing behind her, but she didn't turn around.

Instead, she slammed the door closed on her way over the threshold, determined to forget all the revelations that had managed to spring to light in a house that seemed filled with nothing but shadows.

CHAPTER 20

A Teacup
*Represents the subconscious
rising to the surface.*

When the very last teacup had been left to dry on the linen cloth spread across the countertop, Violet decided that it was time to rest.

She'd insisted on running the shop that day so that Anne could focus on her meeting with Vincent, but by mid-afternoon, the front parlor had been bursting at the seams with customers who'd had enough of staying tucked away at home and braved the sleet for a plate of scones and some much-needed company.

The cloaks hanging in the entryway had been so soaked that the house shuddered at the sight of the water pooling along the baseboards, but once it noticed the laughter that seemed to touch every corner of the shop, it merely sighed and got to work cleaning up the mess when it was certain no one was looking.

Violet, too, had warmed at the sense of cheer that filled the parlor, the laughter and hums of approval so loud she could hardly hear the ice tapping against the windows. She'd been so pleased listening to the steady rhythm of the shop that a bit of her magic slipped into the honey apple cake she was baking, saturating each slice with a hint of enchantment that made everyone who took a bite feel like the chill of the streets had finally thawed from their toes.

Now that everyone had gone for the evening, though, and she was left with nothing but the ache in her feet, Violet's worries were starting to creep in, as sharply as a winter breeze slipping through a crack in the pane.

If it had been any other time of the year, she would have burst through the door, walking so quickly that her fears wouldn't be able to keep pace with her. But winter had a habit of keeping you indoors, where recollections grew so strong that they became impossible to avoid. Perhaps that was why most shied away from the coldest season, not due to the snow and sleet that fell along the sidewalks but because they feared being driven inward.

Shaking her head to untether the thoughts that were beginning to take root, Violet decided to wait for her sisters upstairs, where she could distract herself by untangling skeins of yarn or rearranging Beatrix's books, anything to hold her attention now that the shop was starting to drift into a silent slumber.

After untying her apron and slipping a leftover ginger snap into a cloth napkin, Violet made her way up the steps and opened the door to the family parlor, where the house had already lit a fire in the grate and the snowflakes were falling delicately on the other side of the windowpane. Instantly, the warmth of the scene caused her muscles to loosen, and instead of reaching for the basket of yarn on the floor, Violet was stretching along the cushions of the settee, promising that she'd get to work with the chores she'd given herself after letting her feet rest for just a moment.

But then Tabitha jumped onto her chest, twisting her body in a way that made it clear to Violet she was about to settle in for a nap. Wondering if there was a way to move the cat, Violet started to shift, but before she could so much as twitch, Tabitha was peering at her with those vivid green eyes, warning her to remain still.

Reconciling herself to the fact that she was well and truly trapped, Violet sighed and slipped into the feeling of Tabitha's purrs. The soft vibrations sank into Violet's skin, and before she realized what was happening, her own eyes had drifted closed, lulled by the familiar hum and comforting weight of the cat.

In what could have been hours or the barest blink of an eye, Violet had faded into another scene entirely as the sound of the logs popping in the hearth gradually shifted into the sharper hiss of firecrackers. And when she stretched her toes, it wasn't the worn velvet of the settee that she felt beneath her feet but the rough wooden boards of the platform that sat alongside the circus ring.

Fearing she'd fallen into the same dream once more, Violet braced herself for the worst. But then the song ringing through the tent touched her ears, and her racing heart began to still. It was much slower than it had been before, the hectic high notes replaced now with something more similar to the pitch of a lullaby that had ushered her into soothing fantasies as a child. Her costume, too, was different, the gold spangles replaced with blue satin that made Violet wonder if she would look like a moonbeam when she slipped from one bar to the next.

At the thought of having to jump from the platform, Violet's pulse quickened again, and she took a step back, hoping to distance herself from the edge and the choice that would need to be made there.

Instead of feeling the familiar boards beneath her, though, Violet's foot met open air, and the sensation of her stomach shifting upward just before an unexpected fall caused a scream to build in her throat. But before it could make its way to her lips, a pair of strong arms wrapped around her waist, pulling her into the scent of midnight smoke.

"Are you ready, Wildfire?" she heard Emil's voice rumble against her back, the sound of it laced with excitement.

Violet stared once more at the edge of the platform and instinctively tucked herself deeper into Emil's embrace, where she knew they'd both be safe as long as she stopped moving forward. They would be fine if she just remained still, coating the moment in bronze so that neither of them could be hurt again.

"I can't lose you," she whispered, her words nearly lost among the sound of the murmuring crowd, which seemed to be shifting in expectation.

She wrapped her hands around his shoulders then and pulled him close, burrowing her nose in the crook of his neck and expecting to draw in the aroma that reminded her of watching the logs of a fire burn bright. Violet parted her lips so that when she told Emil she couldn't take another leap of faith, the words would taste more familiar.

But as she breathed inward, an unexpected fragrance came to the surface of her awareness: rosemary, so fresh that it caused her temples to tingle.

It cleansed the refusal from her tongue and made her think of forgiveness and new beginnings. And for one brief moment, Violet wondered what would happen if she loosened her grip on the fears that shackled her to a single defining moment.

Then the scent grew so strong that Violet realized it was coming from somewhere beyond her dream, her eyes snapping open in such a rush that the shapes of sparklers and tent stripes left shadowy impressions against the walls of the parlor when she blinked.

Worried that she may have disturbed Tabitha, Violet glanced

down, only to see that the cat was already awake, her own gaze fixed on the door, as if she were watching someone who had just stepped into the room.

Again, Violet drew in a breath and was met by the distinct fragrance of freshly cut rosemary.

"Who's there?" she asked.

And for the briefest of moments, Violet detected something that she couldn't quite put her finger on. It felt like the weight that fills a room just before someone asks for a favor, the texture of it heavy and laced with earnestness.

But then the scent of rosemary faded as suddenly as it had come, the strange sense of need and longing vanishing along with it.

CHAPTER 21

A Chess Piece
Emerges when a new strategy is needed.

After the last skirt train shifted over the threshold and the sound of the lock clicking into place echoed through the shop, the Crescent Moon had done its best to primp up the kitchen. It was eager to watch the Quigleys wrap their tired fingers around warm porcelain cups and savor the taste of freshly baked apple bread once they all returned home and drifted toward the scent of mulled cider brewing in the cauldron.

But the house's dreams of a quiet winter's night were dashed to pieces when Anne stumbled through the back door and cast her cloak to the floor with a cry of frustration, followed quickly behind by a bewildered-looking Beatrix.

It wasn't long before Anne was snapping the cabinet drawers open and closed, mumbling curses beneath her breath that she realized must have slipped straight up the chimney when a disheveled Violet appeared in the kitchen, her eyes still foggy from sleep.

"What's happened?" Violet asked, a note of desperation slipping into her tone as Anne prepared a pot of tea with so much aggression that she knew there was little doubt of the copper kettle acquiring another dent or two when all was said and done.

"I'm not going back," Anne grumbled as she pried the lid from a metal canister and began scooping out a blend of blue cornflowers and black tea, most of which fell across the tops of her boots instead of the strainer, though she was too focused on her own troubles to bother brushing them away. "That man is impossible to work with. We're better off trying to find where the ring belongs on our own."

"But you're normally so patient," Beatrix remarked, keeping her voice soft and low, as one does when convincing an angry cat to crawl out from beneath the bed. "Even with the customers who demand a table when they don't have a reservation or criticize the daily specials."

"This is much worse than insulting Peggy's bonbons, Bee," Anne scoffed. "Vincent notices too much. It's like he can sense exactly what I'm thinking, and now he's discovered something about me. Something that should have remained a secret."

Violet reached over and took hold of Anne's elbow then, pulling her attention away from the pot of boiling water and toward questions that she knew needed to be answered.

"What sort of secret?" Violet asked, unable to hide her curiosity.

Anne sighed and tossed the strainer against the counter in surrender before sinking into a chair at the table.

"Do you remember when I told you that there aren't any clear lines between the past, present, and future for me anymore?" Anne asked, brushing away some of the curls that had broken loose from her bun earlier in the evening.

"Of course," Beatrix said as she and Violet took their places on the opposite side of the table. "We were talking about our birthday visions, and you said yours must be an echo of what's come before."

"Yes," Anne said with a nod. "But what I didn't tell you is that the glimpses I get from the past are much more than echoes. I can drift backward now into moments and places that I've never encountered before."

Anne watched as Violet and Beatrix widened their eyes and leaned forward, demanding to hear more, though neither uttered a word.

"It's why I think the bookshop and the apartment above it are important," Anne finally explained. "I was searching for an answer to our troubles, and my magic brought me back to the past that unfolded there."

"This is a very rare power," Violet said, and Anne knew she was thinking the same thing as her: Seers get hints of the past from time to time, but only so that they can learn something about the future. "I've never heard of a witch being able to peer into the past in the way you've described."

"I wanted to test it a little at a time," Anne explained, lacing her fingers together as if the movement might help keep her magic in check. "But Vincent realized what I can do and wants me to use my power to better connect with the spirits."

"It could work," Beatrix murmured with a nod, her brows pinching together in the way they did whenever she was considering a potential plot twist.

"But you don't want to," Violet said with a pointed look at Anne's hands, which were clasped so tightly that they looked shockingly white.

"He thinks that I'll need an anchor," Anne said, each word a hiss between her teeth. "And has offered to do it."

"Of course you'll need an anchor," Violet insisted, clearly shocked that her sister had thought otherwise. Anne had proven to be an unusually skillful witch, but her new powers had the potential to run wild without someone to remind her to stay grounded.

"I'm not sure that's true," Anne replied. "I've never had any trouble keeping myself in check before."

The house shuddered as it remembered the feeling of the black ribbons that Anne had used to bind her magic slithering across the floor.

"This isn't the same thing," Beatrix argued, her words fast and insistent. "The power you're describing is much more unpredictable, and your magic will be tempted to stretch you further than it's done before. You could break if you try and do this on your own."

Anne suddenly noticed that the familiar softness of her sister's voice had dimmed under the strain of the day, to the point where each of her words seemed like they were about to buckle. The sound of it instantly changed the texture of the room, the heat of Anne's anger giving way to alarm as her gaze shot from her clasped hands to Beatrix's worn expression.

"I'm not the only one who's at risk of crumbling, it seems," Anne said as she reached forward and grasped Beatrix's hand, her gaze flickering to her sister's face as she noticed for the first time the red trails where tears had frozen to ice against her skin.

"I still haven't been able to think of a single sentence," Beatrix whispered, her voice shaking now. "And Mr. Stuart wants the story even earlier than he did before."

The house wanted to rattle its pots and pans then and push Beatrix toward the nearest wingback chair in the front parlor so that she would finally rest, but Violet acted first.

"You need to stop thinking so much about what you'll write

next," she insisted. "You've grown to view storytelling as something that comes from checking off a neat list of steps instead of remembering what it truly is: magic."

"How can I sit back and do nothing at a moment like this?" Beatrix asked as she shook her head, unconvinced.

"Resting is the best thing you can do when searching for inspiration," Violet argued as Anne nodded in agreement. "How can you expect a tale to come to light if you don't make room for it to grow?"

"Any distractions would be too risky now," Beatrix insisted. "Not when we don't have any time to lose."

Violet's gaze shifted from Beatrix to Anne then, a plan obviously stitching itself together beneath the startling hue of her eyes.

"What if Anne promises to try again with Vincent," Violet said, "so long as you agree to let yourself rest, Bee? You can't keep staring at a blank page in your notebook or you'll go mad."

Anne sighed then, understanding what Violet was up to.

They would both need to take a risk, Anne pushing beyond her boundaries to see how far she could go and Beatrix falling back to discover if what she'd lost could be reclaimed.

Neither would step away, so long as it meant leading their sister down the right path.

"Then it's settled," Violet said happily as she shifted away from the table and toward the cauldron bubbling in the hearth, where the scent of mulled cider had grown stronger beneath the current of their conversation.

At Violet's declaration, the strain that had seeped into the floorboards began to ease and notes of cloves and apples saturated the kitchen as the Quigleys sipped from their mugs and thought of the days ahead.

They could still feel something tightening within their own

chests, but tucked in the warmth of the kitchen with the curtains drawn against the night, the sisters thought it was merely their own worries tangling together.

The house let its awareness shift beyond the front door, though, and instantly recognized the sensation for what it was: a sign that things were continuing to slip out of place beyond the safe confines of the Crescent Moon.

CHAPTER 22

Snowdrops

Appear when hope is about to be found after a period of difficulty.

When Beatrix stepped into the bookshop the next morning, she was struck by the icy chill that crept into the gaps between her knit scarf, making her shiver.

Startled that the room seemed colder than the streets, Beatrix walked swiftly toward the front windows, worried that the frigid temperatures may have deepened a crack in the pane that she hadn't realized was there.

But everything was sealed shut, and when she moved her hand along the edges of the glass, Beatrix didn't so much as feel a soft breeze.

Wondering where the source of the trouble was, Beatrix's gaze flitted about the shop, her eyes catching every now and again on details that must have slipped her notice before.

It may have been because the sky was cloudier than it had been yesterday, but she could have sworn that there were more shadows creeping inward from the corners of the room. And she thought there had been books stacked neat as pins along the top of the shelves, their covers facing outward, as if to tempt passing hands to pull them closer. But now, they were scattered across the floor, their spines cracked down the middle and splayed on the dirty boards.

As Beatrix strolled from one shelf to the next, finally taking a moment to focus beyond the confines of her own thoughts, she began to notice something else beneath the veil of neglect that seemed to cover every inch of the shop.

Though coated in dust, the shelves were crafted with care, as if they'd been built with the intention of having them last several lifetimes. And when she ran her gloved finger along the peeling wallpaper, Beatrix realized that the colors beneath the grime must have once been vibrant. Her touch left behind trails of green, blue, and pink, remnants of hand-painted floral buds that would have looked beautiful against the warm walnut of the shelves.

Before the boards were nailed to the windows and the sign out front started to fade, someone had loved this room and the books within it, that much was clear.

But now the shop felt like it was grieving, a sense of loneliness and loss of hope having settled into the wainscoting and cracks in the plaster.

The weight of it brushed against Beatrix's shoulders, reminding her of what it had felt like to sit at the desk for hours the day before, only to walk away without having put a single word on the page.

Is this what she would become, the dusty memory of a story that had touched someone's soul but couldn't quite be remembered?

Suddenly, Beatrix heard the familiar sound of a book slipping from the shelf, and instinctively, her hands reached forward to grasp whatever was about to fall to the floor.

With a start, she looked down and saw that she was holding a battered blue book. Turning it over, Beatrix noticed that the spine was held together by the barest threads, and the cloth was worn about the corners in the way it always is after being held too many times.

Before Beatrix could think of what she was doing, her fingers were lifting the cover and flipping through the pages. It was a collection of fairy tales, she realized, so similar to the one that she and her sisters had read as young girls that it felt like the years were falling away with every chapter she turned.

Once she reached the middle of the book, Beatrix noticed that one of the pages had been roughly bent at the corner, as if someone had marked their favorite story so often that the fold was about to rip apart. A simple sketch of a raven was perched just beneath the chapter number, peering at Beatrix with a knowing expression that suggested the creature had something to say.

Skimming the first lines, Beatrix realized that it was a tale she'd read before, one about a sister whose brothers had been cursed to turn into a flock of birds.

Wondering why the book's owner had been so interested in this particular tale, Beatrix shook her head and flipped to the very last page, knowing that a familiar phrase awaited her there.

But, to her confusion, *The End* had been crossed through with pen and ink.

And beneath that, Beatrix saw that a new message had been added. . . .

A good story has no end.

When Beatrix's eyes drifted over the words, a sudden sensation of relief poured into her veins, melting the ice that had started to grip her heart long before the first snowfall. And as she read the sentence again and again, the pain fell away like chunks of sleet exposed to morning sunshine.

How would it feel to fill the silence with words that weren't her own? Let the story beneath her fingertips pull her away from the present and toward possibilities that made her remember what it felt like to seek out a sense of wonder?

Instead of setting the book back on the shelf, Beatrix found herself wandering toward the wingback chair at the front of the shop, where the sun was now spilling through the glass so that the black ink was practically shimmering beneath the light.

It wasn't long before the feeling of the cushions disappeared entirely and her thoughts had traveled far, far away from the shop, the troubles that had held her tight fading as she gradually returned to the girl who'd spent entire afternoons between the pages of a book in the attic.

Lost in the rhythm of the words, Beatrix didn't even notice when the tattered wallpaper behind her started to piece itself together or the way some of the dust that had settled along the surface of the windows seemed to vanish of its own accord, chasing away the shadows between the shelves.

She wasn't even aware of the barely perceptible curve that was just beginning to appear in the groove between her thumb and forefinger: the barest hint of a letter rising up along the lines of her skin.

CHAPTER 23

A Violin

*Appears just before hidden
emotions rise to the surface.*

Before Anne turned the corner that would lead her to the Crowley manor, she paused on the sidewalk and let the snow drifting down in sheets gather along the curve of her shoulders. Anne's magic seemed to sense her hesitation and grew stronger, warming the tips of her fingers and toes in the places they'd grown numb during her walk from the shop. It reminded her of when she'd bound herself to keep her power from unraveling, how the spark that had been lit aflame couldn't be contained by the threads, no matter how often she tied the knots.

Anne hadn't realized just how tightly she'd still been holding on to her magic since the day she'd let those black ribbons slither to the floor. It had felt so surreal, the rush of potential and an opening of a whole new world, that she'd failed to notice she was only allowing herself to become untethered a single inch at a time.

There was so much more she was responsible for now, and

Anne couldn't risk the consequences if she lost control, even if it meant holding back a part of herself that longed to burst free. She'd intended to unfurl her power slowly so that any trouble could be quickly managed, as one does when gently pulling a string of yarn from the center of its skein to avoid creating any snags.

But she didn't have a choice now, it seemed.

Drawing in a frosty breath that heightened her awareness, Anne could feel a sense of loneliness rippling beneath her resolve. She always needed to present a version of herself to the coven that was as untouchable as the tip of a pin. And though Anne could share all the emotions that simmered beneath that steady surface with her sisters, she knew they'd never be able to fully realize what she was experiencing. Just as she could hear Violet explain what it felt like to fly across the circus tent or listen to Beatrix describe the satisfaction of tacking a period at the end of a well-crafted sentence and fail to grasp the depth of meaning that these sensations held for them.

As Anne was starting to realize, there are some things that can only be understood by those who need no words at all.

But she'd already lingered long enough in the present moment, where hidden truths have the best chance of coming to light, and needed to return her focus to the demands of the future.

Sighing, Anne opened her eyes once more and marched toward the manor, her pace becoming more determined with every step.

As her hand reached toward the knocker, the door started to creep open, but this time, instead of the empty corridor, Anne was met by the sight of Vincent's stern face.

They stared at one another silently for a moment, the bitterness of their last parting still as fresh as it had been the night before.

But then Anne began to shiver, and the hard lines of Vincent's face softened the barest fraction before he shifted backward, opening the door wider in invitation. When she took that first step over the threshold, Anne saw some of the stiffness in his shoulders ease, as if he was relieved to have her back despite the strain that still lingered between them.

"You knew I was here?" Anne asked as she instinctively began to tug off her heavy woolen coat.

It wasn't until she reached the third button that Anne realized the house was warmer than it had been before, the sharp edge of the cold having faded enough from the air that the entryway didn't feel nearly as brisk as the street.

"I was watching from the window," Vincent explained. "The house has gotten into the habit of letting you in unannounced, and I don't want you to wander into any of the rooms without me."

Anne wondered if that was because he didn't trust her or the house itself. But then a curious thought struck her.

"Is that not something it normally does?" Anne asked as she watched the candles that lined the hallway slowly flicker to life. "Let people in when it knows you'd rather the door stay shut?"

Vincent's mouth tightened as he reached forward to take Anne's coat and hang it on a peg near the door.

"No," he admitted. "It has been unruly as of late."

Anne wanted to ask who else it had let in without his permission, but before she could so much as part her lips, Vincent began to speak again, his face turned away from her as he stepped forward to close the door.

"I wasn't certain that you'd come," he said, the familiar stiffness of his tone giving way to a hushed murmur that changed the texture of his voice, smoothing it out in a way that Anne hadn't expected.

"I wasn't certain either," Anne whispered, the truth slipping out before she could craft a more careful reply, one that wouldn't reveal just how much she'd wavered.

Vincent grew still, and for a moment, Anne wondered if she'd made a mistake in letting him glimpse some of the vulnerability she'd tried to tuck away on the street. But then he clicked the door shut and nodded, turning to face her with an expression of silent understanding.

In that moment, some of the uneasiness lifted between them, and Anne could have sworn the shadows flickering against the walls grew gentler as well, the harsh lick of the candlelight seemingly dancing to a less harried rhythm.

"Come this way," Vincent said as he gestured for her to follow him.

As they made their way down the hall, Anne realized that Vincent was keeping his pace even with hers so that they were walking side by side. Before, one of them had always pushed forward, but now they were closer, so much so that her hand nearly brushed his.

The hasty tempo of Anne's pulse gradually slowed as she listened to their footsteps echo against the walls. But when Vincent came to a sudden stop in front of the same door that he'd pulled her from the day before, her heart started to beat to a faster rhythm, one that matched the music drifting from the gaps around the threshold.

"Surely you aren't thinking of bringing me in there?" Anne asked as she dug her heels into the floor, trying to resist the urge to lean closer so that she could better hear the chords vibrating through the soles of her shoes.

"That depends," Vincent replied as he turned around and stared down at Anne, leaning against the doorframe and crossing his arms loosely over his chest.

Evidentially, he expected whatever argument that was about to unfold between them to take some time.

"On what?" Anne asked, her brow creasing as she tried to focus on Vincent over the music that was already pulling at her chest.

"Whether you're willing to see how powerful you really are," he said. "To communicate with the spirits, we must call them here and convince them to stay. It's one thing to draw them close enough to hear the whispers, but in order to get them to share anything concrete, we'll need to offer something more substantive to grasp on to."

"I'm not sure I understand," Anne admitted.

"People often associate ghosts with fear and sorrow, but those aren't the things that they cling to," Vincent explained. "It's happiness, suspense, curiosity, wonder, and warmth that the spirits are always searching for. They're drawn to it like moths to a flame, though there are moments where their grasp for lost things can be too tight."

Anne thought of the memories that she believed were worth returning to and nodded.

"In order to draw them closer, we re-create the same sensations that they remember from life," Vincent continued. "But we normally have a better idea of who, exactly, needs to be called upon. This time, we'll have to convince the spirits to share their memories with you, and in those glimpses, see who might know something about the ring. When they sense what you can do, the spirits will want to pull you into moments that feel familiar."

"You think that if I start drifting into the past, they'll guide me in the right direction?" Anne asked, wanting to be certain that she understood.

"It would be like meeting them in the middle," Vincent said with a nod. "It normally takes weeks to draw out a particular ghost, let alone get them to express anything concrete through a shared sensation. But with your help, it will be different. Once the spirits appear and begin to share memories linked to a particular sensation, you'll think about the ring, and they'll pull you toward recollections that strike a chord with them."

Anne could tell from the firm set of Vincent's jaw and calculating glint in his eyes that he didn't have a single hesitation about her abilities, as if it was a surety that her power was strong enough to accomplish such a task.

With a shock, she realized that her magic was already starting to rise to the surface, lured by the excitement rippling beneath Vincent's suggestion.

"What are we going to do to draw them out?" Anne asked, her eyes flashing toward the door as she wondered what rested behind it.

Vincent must have noticed the note of interest that had woven itself into Anne's voice because a smile was starting to creep into the corners of his mouth, the sight of it causing a sudden jolt of expectation to shoot down her spine. It felt just like she'd looked up from the cards she'd been dealt and known from a single unspoken look at her partner that they had a winning hand.

"Let me show you," Vincent answered as he pulled the door open and ushered Anne inside.

After seeing hundreds of clocks dangling from the walls in the other room, Anne had expected to find just as much clutter in this one as well.

But the entire space, from the black marble stone of the floor to the towering white ceiling, was empty.

Despite the fact that the walls were bare and there wasn't a stitch of furniture, the room somehow felt full, as if the very air tingled with something that couldn't quite be seen.

And then Anne noticed it, a closed silver box small enough that she could have held it in both hands sitting atop the mantle of an unlit fireplace.

The tune dancing just beneath Anne's consciousness was spilling from it, growing stronger and stronger with every step she took.

"It's a music box," she murmured in comprehension as she glimpsed the cylinder catching against the delicate metallic teeth through the intricate cutwork along the lid.

"It's much more than that," Vincent whispered from behind her shoulder. "It's a heartsong."

Anne nearly gasped then, catching her breath just before it had a chance to slip from her lips for fear the sound might disrupt the melody.

A heartsong was an extraordinarily rare magical artifact, forged from the hopes and dreams of a witch whose power rested in the strains of music. Each person who happened across one would hear something different, a score that matched the pace of their deepest fears and desires to a perfect pitch. They were crafted to draw out fantasies that had grown silent, tempting those who heard the notes to discover pieces of themselves that were buried beneath the weight of their reality.

Though Anne knew that such things existed, she'd only heard of them in the confines of fairy tales.

"Where did you find one?" Anne asked in surprise, her gaze still fixed on the gears turning within the box.

"My family acquired it long ago," Vincent answered. "From a witch who made one specifically for our purposes. Heartsongs are usually crafted to help guide the living, but this one draws out the deepest longings of those who aren't tethered to the present, pulling them back to moments when all seems possible. That's why only the spirits can hear it."

"And me," Anne said to herself, so softly that she was certain Vincent wouldn't hear her.

"And you," Vincent replied before reaching forward to lift the lid, causing the strains of music to grow even stronger.

The shocking familiarity that danced from each and every note made gooseflesh rise along Anne's forearms. It seemed strange to think that the sound pouring from the music box had rippled beneath the everyday rhythm of the Crowleys' lives for generations without being truly heard by any of them.

"What should I do now?" Anne asked, already entranced by the sense of possibility that beat beneath the rhythm.

"Close your eyes and listen," Vincent instructed as he turned her gently to face him. "Once you think the tune is strong enough, start to drift backward and see if the spirits have anything to share. They'll be drawn by the way the music makes you feel and want to show you moments when they experienced the same thing. It will seem like they are pulling you back in time."

"You said before that they sometimes grasp too tightly," Anne said, trying to keep a sliver of fear from slipping into her voice.

"There shouldn't be many of them to contend with," Vincent said. "Ghosts are solitary creatures, so coaxing them out takes time. And if you let me anchor you, I'll be sure you don't get too drawn into their memories."

He lifted his hands then and turned his palms upward in silent expectation.

Though Anne still hadn't yet decided to accept Vincent's help, she found herself reaching for him, drawn to the memory of how it had felt to grasp his wrist amidst the sound of clicking clocks and hushed whispers. Even if she had no plans to open her mind to him, what harm was there in letting the warmth of his skin make her feel more grounded in the present?

When her hands came to rest on his, Vincent turned his palms and wove their fingers together, instantly making Anne feel like he was drawing her closer though neither had taken a single step forward.

"Just listen," Vincent whispered, the gentle hue of his tone encouraging Anne to let her lids grow heavy.

She did just that, allowing the darkness to heighten the song that felt just as if it were slipping beneath her own skin.

At first the melody reminded her of the steady ticking of her own clock, a faint beat that encouraged her shoulders to ease and the tightness in her chest to drift away with every exhaled breath.

But then a stronger strain that felt just like the slow pull of a bow against strings entered the score, tugging at the hopes that she'd buried deep within herself. It reminded her of hidden desires tinged with the heavy texture of danger and the promise of discovery: the pieces of herself that didn't quite fit the picture she wished to present to the rest of the world but were always pulsing there beneath the surface of each and every intention.

Her magic felt the shift and danced along with the music, drawn to the way it was making Anne feel more and more alive. If she opened her eyes, Anne wondered if she would see the glow of it flickering beneath the dark cotton of her sleeves.

As she let her powers awaken, Anne could sense the presence of Vincent's magic. The strength of it vibrated through their clasped hands and seemed to sink into her bones. She could feel him starting to open his awareness to her, the texture of the spells he was crafting growing so tangible that it felt like she could touch them.

"Drift back," she heard Vincent murmur, though his voice was more distant than it had been before, as if he were speaking to her through a current of water.

With a final release of breath, Anne did as he instructed, eager now to see what would happen if she let herself go, just this once.

And as she slipped away from the present moment, sensations that vibrated to the same rhythm of her heartsong began to strum to life, brushing against her skin as they pulled her deeper and deeper into the past.

She heard the tinkling of glass and an echo of laughter, so

rich that Anne could very nearly taste champagne touch the tip of her tongue.

The bittersweet flavor faded as her vocal cords began to vibrate, as if she were singing, though no note escaped her lips.

And then the overwhelming scent of roses and twilight-touched soil filled her nose, chased by the nervous anticipation that comes whenever you fear no one will ask you for a dance.

The memories came so quickly that Anne was starting to feel like she was peering through a spinning kaleidoscope as she gazed back into the past. The vibrant texture of a taffeta ball gown caught in the corner of her inner gaze before her attention shifted to the polished gleam of a cello and then a crisp white collar that covered a man's neck.

Distantly, Anne thought she heard something rumbling beneath all these sensations. It sounded almost like a muffled voice calling through a closed door, and the deep timbre of it warmed the tips of Anne's fingers. But she was too swept away by the feeling of each scent, taste, and touch to concentrate long enough and make any sense of it, turning a lock in her mind so that she wouldn't be tempted to pull her attention away from the past.

And then she saw it: a brief flash of a gold signet ring as she watched a woman's hand shoot within sight, only to be lost among a whirl of marble when she was pulled into a memory of someone looking down at the floor as they flew from one partner to the next.

She had to drift further back. It was the only way....

"Anne."

The word was saturated with warning and cut through her growing need to stretch the boundaries of her magic, but it wasn't strong enough to draw her focus away from the feel of a hand pressing against her lower back as she was pulled closer into a waltz.

She thought of the flash of gold again, and in the next instant, she was clasping a woman's hand in her own, their fingers brushing for the barest instant as they flew down a line of dancers, just long enough for Anne to see the ring once more.

When she glanced up, Anne was shocked to find that the woman standing across from her was leaning forward, so close that she could smell the white roses tucked in the ribbon covering her hair. And when Anne managed to focus on her face, she realized with a start that the laughing eyes staring back at her didn't match. One was a rather ordinary brown, while the other looked as if it had been carved from a sapphire.

The woman's lips parted, and Anne leaned forward, eager to hear what she was about to share, but she felt someone grab her gently by the arm then, urging her to move forward in the dance.

She tried to shake the hand away, but the pressure suddenly shifted to her shoulders, turning rough and insistent, as if someone was shaking her as hard as they could.

"Anne!"

Anne's eyes flew open then, and she was startled to find Vincent's face drawn deep with worry instead of the strange eyes that had peered at her through the past only a second ago.

"Why did you stop me?" Anne asked as she gasped for breath.

She tried to snap her spine straighter, but for some reason, her body felt as if it didn't know how to steady itself, and she ended up tipping over.

Vincent instantly shot forward, pulling Anne against his chest to keep her from hitting the unforgiving marble floor.

"To save you!" he cried in exasperation. "I've never seen so many ghosts in one place before, and you just let them keep coming."

"I saw the ring!" Anne said excitedly. "A woman was wearing it. She had the most unusual eyes, one brown and the other blue."

She felt Vincent's hold tighten then as he tried to keep her in the present moment.

"I have to go back. Let me go back!" Anne insisted.

"No," Vincent said firmly.

"But I can learn more," Anne said, pushing herself away from Vincent now that she felt her feet were her own again. "It was right there."

"You might see the ring again, but whether you'll be able to return is another question entirely," Vincent hissed. "You wouldn't let me anchor you."

"I didn't think it was necessary," Anne said. "I can control my own power."

"Not from what I saw," Vincent scoffed. "You may be able to traipse into the future without any worry whatsoever, but the past is different. It's laced with deep emotions that ripple outward into our own time. You can't predict where the memories will pull you, and sometimes, they're so alluring that you forget why you'd want to return to the present at all. There's a reason people want to linger in the past instead of looking toward the future."

Now that some of the haziness was starting to thin, Anne noticed the way Vincent's hands were shaking and realized that he must have truly believed he was about to lose her, that he had sensed her drifting further and further away and been terrified there was nothing he could do to stop it.

Guilt poured through Anne's veins, so hot that it drew all speech from her tongue.

"For someone who holds the fate of an entire city in her hands, you've acted recklessly," Vincent said, the crackling heat in his tone instantly smothering the apology that Anne was just about to offer.

"Why should I let you anchor me?" Anne asked, infuriated that the same person who'd kept her from falling to the ground only moments ago had now struck her to the core. "I don't know anything about you."

"You know enough to understand I'm capable of keeping you safe," Vincent spat back. "Or are you questioning my power again?"

"It's not your magic that I'm worried about," Anne said, stepping forward so that their faces were only the barest breath apart. "It's you."

Was it a trick of the light, or did Anne see a glimmer of panic flash across Vincent's face then?

Before she could be certain, the rich amber hue of his eyes became noticeably darker.

"I'm determined to uncover the history of the ring," he said, his voice rough with frustration. "You know that."

"What I know is that you're keeping secrets," Anne hissed back. "There is more to this story than you're letting on. Or did you think I wouldn't notice all the shadows creeping about the corners of this house?"

The candlelight that had been filtering into the room abruptly flickered out then, as if the hallways hadn't liked being brought into the conversation.

Though she couldn't see him any longer, Anne could feel the warmth of Vincent's heavy breaths against her cheek. Now that they were standing in complete darkness, they seemed nearer to each other than they had been only a moment ago when the light of the candles had seeped into the room.

She expected him to step back, but Vincent surprised her by shifting even closer. Though he didn't touch her, Anne could feel his magic pulsing to life beneath his skin, causing the hairs along her neck to vibrate as he drew his mouth nearer the groove beneath her ear.

Anne didn't know what he was about to do, but just as she had when entangled in the memories of the spirits, she found herself wanting to slip into dangerous places where not knowing what would happen next made the tips of her fingers tingle.

She heard his lips part then and felt the words brush against the soft skin of her ear before they came together in her thoughts.

"Perhaps. But I'm not the only one keeping secrets, am I?"

CHAPTER 24

A Lamp
Suggests that hidden
truths will come to light.

*I*n the evening hours, when the fires had been flickering so long in the grate that the walls were warmed to their rafters, the Crescent Moon always nodded off to sleep. Though made from brick and mortar, the house was a place of magic, and so it needed time to dream. After it felt that restless breaths had grown steady, it slipped into an easy slumber, where it could thread together fantasies of its own design and imagine what could be crafted beyond the bounds of reality.

And as its thoughts drew inward, a stillness settled across the creaking floorboards. When the Quigleys were just girls, they'd sometimes wake in the night and tiptoe as quietly as they could out of their bedrooms. Like sleepwalkers, they'd shift in the darkness, awed by the strange sense of calm that seemed tangible enough to touch. And if the weight of the day kept them from being able to slip into their own dreams, they would sink to the floor of the hallway, lean against the wainscoting, and let the familiar silence lull them away from troubles left in the daylight. When they listened carefully enough, the rumble of the house's flights of fancy could be heard beneath the quiet, the barest echoes of its imagination causing the baseboards to vibrate beneath their touch.

Though it had been decades since Violet had last sunk to the floor to better sense the house's fantasies, she found herself doing just that now.

As she'd slipped between the sheets of her bed, Violet had tried to think more about the name that was etched into the woodwork of the apartment. Her thoughts had drifted to different possibilities, but her magic depended on instinct to lead her in the proper direction. And just as it tried to tug her toward a potential insight, Violet would hesitate and lose her grip on the fragile thread of an idea.

The more she'd wondered who May could have been, the more tangible Violet's sense of loss became, drawing her toward dreams that smelled of firecrackers and sawdust.

And just as the smoky fragrance had grown more potent and Violet feared she wouldn't be able to stop herself from drifting back toward mistakes that couldn't be forgotten, the sharp scent of rosemary had snapped her awake again. She'd only been aware of the strange aroma for a second, but it was enough to steer her away from the worst of her past and toward fantasies tinged with the texture of fresh choices.

But rather than close her eyes again and see what she'd find there, Violet had stayed awake wondering which was worse: the certainty of a mistake that she'd already made or the possibility of taking another wrong turn in the future.

Violet hadn't wanted to fall back asleep then, and so she'd slipped from her room and snuck downstairs, trying her best to avoid the squeakiest boards so that she wouldn't wake her sisters.

And when she'd made her way to the kitchen, where the soft outline of cinnamon buns rising beneath sheets of white linen instantly eased the tension in her shoulders, Violet sank to the floorboards and listened to the even rhythm of the house as she did her best to avoid drifting into slumber.

Her eyes were just beginning to fall again when she heard a door creak open and saw a shadowy figure reach toward the lantern sitting atop the table.

"Anne?" Violet whispered as the light of the flame came to life and she saw the familiar outline of her sister's face. "I thought you were already asleep upstairs."

She'd heard Beatrix tiptoe by her open door hours ago and had assumed that Anne had slipped in shortly after.

But as Violet rose from the floor and stepped closer, she noticed that Anne's cloak was still draped around her shoulders, the blue wool littered with fresh snowflakes that glimmered in the lantern light.

"Have you only just returned?" Violet asked in surprise.

"I needed to clear my head," Anne replied as she warmed her fingers against the glass of the lantern. "So I took the long way home."

Violet settled into the chair beside her, lifting the legs so that they wouldn't screech against the floor.

"I feel like we're girls again," Anne said, a faint smile tugging at the corners of her lips. "Whispering so that the house won't catch us trying to sneak biscuits from the tin after bedtime."

"Those are happy times to return to, aren't they?" Violet replied, letting her thoughts stray back to when just a few steps in the darkness had felt like a true journey indeed.

Anne grew quiet then, and Violet knew that her sister hadn't been able to drift as easily into the past as she had, not when so much rested on her shoulders in the here and now.

"Has something happened, Anne?" Violet asked softly as she tried to read between the worry lines that were stretched across her sister's brow.

For a moment, Anne pinched her lips a bit tighter, and Violet thought she was tucking a bit deeper into herself, afraid to share the burden of her secrets.

But then, her face softened, and Violet was relieved to hear the soft exhalation of a sigh that suggested she had decided to share more.

"Things didn't go quite according to plan this evening," Anne said, folding her hands atop the table so that the gold ring glimmered in the lantern light.

"Were you not able to let go?" Violet asked.

"Just the opposite," Anne replied. "I let go so much that the memories of the ghosts nearly swept me away."

"Oh, Anne," Violet sighed, nearly buckling forward at the realization that her sister could have been lost. "But you promised."

"I know," Anne said, turning her gaze downward. "I just couldn't let him anchor me in the end."

"But why?" Violet asked. "I know you don't trust him entirely, but do you really think he would let the spirits hurt you?"

"I just couldn't," Anne said, the words breaking into tiny pieces as they left her tongue. "He would keep me safe, but I can't afford to let anyone that close. I'm the Diviner. I shouldn't need anyone else's help. I have to be strong enough to stand on my own and keep everything tethered together."

Violet watched as Anne's features tightened, a sure sign that she was battling against a need to give way to her vulnerability and let the tears of frustration building within her spring free.

"I'm so afraid," Anne said, her voice shaking now. "So afraid that I'll make a mistake, and it won't be just me who suffers this time."

Instantly, Violet thought of her own mistakes, the ones so horrible that she hadn't even been able to tell her sisters. But, again, that subtle scent of rosemary drifted into her awareness, just enough to make her temples tingle, and before Violet could even think of hesitating, she spoke.

"But doesn't that show you're on the right path?" Violet asked as she laced her fingers through Anne's. "After all, we only fear losing the things that are worth keeping."

As Violet's words lingered in the silence of the kitchen, the truth of what she'd said grew stronger and stronger, just like the jars of vanilla bean essence that rested on the shelves next to the tea tins.

It was obvious to every witch who walked through the threshold of the Crescent Moon that Anne did care, not just about her sisters or the shop any longer but the entire city. Like the map that Violet sometimes saw out of the corner of her eye in the hallway mirrors and guessed rested in the Council's meeting room, the boundaries of the Quigleys' home had gradually extended, encompassing people and places that were now tied to Anne's very being. Violet knew that her sister's uncertainty hadn't grown from a fear of weakness but the possibility that she'd lose what she'd grown to love.

As she gazed at the worry lines around Anne's eyes, though, Violet couldn't help but wish that her sister could lean on someone just as powerful as she was so that the weight of all she held dear didn't seem so heavy.

"Let Vincent anchor you," Violet said, the words growing from a place deep within herself that insisted the witch could be trusted to keep Anne safe. "So that you'll remember to stay rooted to the home within yourself."

"When did you become so wise?" Anne asked as she wiped away the tears slipping from the corners of her eyes.

"I believe it was somewhere between New Orleans and Tallahassee," Violet laughed, happy to see that glint of amusement spark in her sister's eyes once more. Just looking at it made her hopeful that the light within her own soul might flicker to life again one day.

"Well, while we're here, we might as well have a cup of tea," Anne said as she rose from the table and moved toward the stove, eager now to shift into familiar comforts that would ease away the strain of the day. "As long as we keep quiet."

The house had already woken, though, pulled from its dreams by the tears that had laced Anne's confession. Years of tending to the sisters when they woke from nightmares had made it impossible not to stir when the first notes of their distress brushed against the walls.

But, like the Quigleys, it was learning that sometimes the best thing you can do for those you love is simply remind them that they are not alone. So it sent a gentle breath against the linen cloth dangling from a rung next to the stove, brushing it against Anne's cheek in a way that would feel just like butterfly kisses. And once it was certain that her tears had given way to laughter, the house withdrew a sigh of relief and drifted back to a place where all was possible.

CHAPTER 25

A Bookcase

Indicates that long-awaited desires will
be met through devotion and patience.

When Beatrix stepped into the bookshop the next morning, something made her pause at the threshold. It wasn't the sensation of icy fingers skittering across her spine or the knot in her chest that seemed to tighten every time she thought of the deadline.

No, the instant she turned away from the wind that lashed down the alleyway and toward the earthy aroma of old books, Beatrix felt like the weight that had become a familiar presence against her shoulders was starting to lift.

It had been so long since the tension in her neck had loosened that it took Beatrix a moment to recognize the feeling of being at ease. She paused, her hand still wrapped around the doorknob, and braced herself for the tightness in her chest to return, but when she drew in a shaky breath, the fragrance of the bookshop grew stronger and more complex, pulling her attention away from her fear of the future and toward the rich memories of the past quicker than she could have snapped her fingers.

Before she could think to stop herself, her body remembered the sensations that always accompanied an afternoon of reading—the way it felt to run a thumb along a book's spine in anticipation of turning the next page, how a twist of the plot could cause her heart to stop and then race forward, the tingles that skittered along the sides of her neck when it became clear how all the threads of the story would weave themselves together in the end. And in that moment, it seemed that her worst worries would remain behind in the street, like a pair of snowy boots that were too damp to be brought into the house.

As Beatrix's attention shifted from her inner world to the shelves, she wondered if some of the changes that she felt were starting to cast a rosier hue across the shop as well.

Though she hadn't touched the windows, the glass seemed clearer, as if someone had come along in the night and wiped away the layers of dust and grime that had stretched the dark shadows from the corners of the room. Now the snow falling from the other side of the pane seemed softer and full of wonder instead of something to turn away from with a shiver. It made Beatrix want to stand by the glass and slip quietly into a daydream laced with the magic of winter, just as she used to do as a young girl when their mother said it was too cold to wander out of the house.

And the chill that had made Beatrix turn up the collar of her coat when she'd stepped into the shop before had faded away as well, replaced by a sense of warmth that tempted her to remove her heavy woolen cloak and sit down in the worn wingback chair until the feeling returned to her thawing toes and fingers.

She thought about the book that Jennings had given her. It was waiting there as well. After she'd finished the fairy-tale collection, her hands had instinctively reached for another story, and she'd found the novel resting within her grasp on the floor next to the chair.

Now its open covers were draped across the arm to mark her spot, though Beatrix could have sworn that she'd left it on the shelf for safekeeping when she finally pulled herself away from its pages the night before. The sight of it caused Beatrix's fingers to twitch and made her want to settle into the velvet embrace of the chair and lose herself in the story once more.

As Beatrix lifted her hands to do just that, she caught the scent of bergamot and citrus drifting from the back office, where it mixed with the musty sweetness of old books.

Curious, Beatrix followed the familiar fragrance until she was standing in threshold of the back office, where she saw a kettle resting atop the small woodstove with a chipped cup waiting on the end table just beside it.

A smile tugged at Beatrix's lips as she realized that Brigit must have tidied things up in the shop that morning and left her a cup of tea.

But how had she known this blend was Beatrix's favorite, the one she reached for on the shelf in the kitchen of the Crescent Moon whenever the weight of the day had been too heavy?

Before Beatrix could dwell on that thought, though, she heard a soft tapping that was quickly followed by the sound of the door to the alleyway creaking open.

"Hello?" she heard Jennings call out.

His voice chased away the lingering numbness in Beatrix's toes and made her heart beat just a bit faster.

"Jennings?" Beatrix replied as she moved away from the back office and into the shop, where her visitor stood in the middle of the room, surveying the explosion of books across the floor as if he was unsure where to step without staining the yellow pages with the heel of his boot. "What are you doing here?"

"Another request from Mr. Stuart, I'm afraid," he said, patting the leather satchel strapped across his chest, where piles of papers were no doubt waiting for her careful consideration. "You haven't signed the paperwork approving the final version of your last manuscript, and he wants it today so that we can start the printing process."

"Of course," Beatrix said, pulling nervously at the chain of her spectacles. "I don't suppose anything has changed since I last looked at it?"

The initial rush of excitement of hearing Jennings' voice was giving way to something else as she thought of their last encounter and worried about what he must think of her. Beatrix's shoulders stiffened, bracing for the hint of frostiness that would lace his tone as he remembered the way she'd thrown him out into the worst of winter.

But, to her surprise, the only hints of coldness in Jennings' appearance were the snowflakes that fell from the brim of his hat as he lifted it from his head and began to pull a pile of papers from his satchel.

"Not a single comma," Jennings assured her as he flipped through the pages to find the place where Beatrix would need to add her signature. "I made sure of it."

Beatrix heard the protectiveness in Jennings' voice, a smile pulling at her lips as she took the pen from his outstretched hand and moved to the counter, where he'd set the papers for her to look through.

She turned her gaze toward the lines of the document, but her attention remained fixed on the sound of Jennings' footsteps as he wandered between the shelves.

"I haven't gotten the chance to fix things up yet," Beatrix said, embarrassed now that she hadn't taken the time to pick the poor books up from the floor.

"No, it looks like you've been doing something far more important," Jennings replied, his tone laced with kind amusement.

Beatrix looked up then and saw him bending over the worn wingback chair to grab the novel perched along the arm.

For the barest instant, Beatrix felt her pulse race with embarrassment and shame, but then she saw the excitement dancing in Jennings' eyes, and the tight breath that she'd been holding on to slipped from her lips, carrying away the heaviest of her worries.

"I had hoped that you'd start this," Jennings said as he turned the cover over and let his fingers run against the rough-cut pages. "How are you liking it so far?"

"It's wonderful," Beatrix answered, her thoughts already racing back to the chapter that she'd dog-eared in her memory. "I feel just like I'm slipping into a warm summer day whenever I read it."

"Well, I can't wait until it's my turn," Jennings said. "Then we can talk about it together."

The word "together" made the skin above Beatrix's collarbones tingle in the most pleasant way, just as it did whenever she stepped out the front door after hearing rain pattering against the window all day and realized that the sun was finally shining.

"Though I'll be sure not to bother you until you're ready," Jennings added, seeming to mistake Beatrix's silence for hesitation. "I know you're busy with the next book at the moment. But once you've gotten through the first draft, perhaps we could find a spare afternoon to discuss the story."

The weight that Beatrix thought had been left out in the cold returned then, so sharp that she had to keep herself from gasping. But just when she felt the tension start to sink into her shoulders, the scent of bergamot grew stronger, pulling her attention back to the shop and far enough away from her worries that she was able to speak.

"Of course," Beatrix managed to say as she hastily scribbled her name on the page.

Jennings appeared to sense the change in her spirits, his eyes flicking to her face in concern as he packed the papers back in the satchel and pulled his scarf a bit tighter around his neck.

"I'd better be off, then," he said, his lips stretching into a smile that didn't quite reach his eyes. "Or Mr. Stuart won't be pleased."

"I'd offer you some tea before you leave, but I'm afraid I only have one cup," Beatrix said, worried that Jennings had misread her reaction and that she'd managed to leave him with yet another poor impression.

"I would have enjoyed that," Jennings replied with a nod. "But perhaps it's for the best, what with Mr. Stuart waiting for me back at the office."

"Yes," Beatrix murmured as she followed him to the door. "I suppose you're right."

"Just let me know if you need anything," Jennings said as he opened the door and began to walk into the alleyway, lingering long enough in the threshold to make Beatrix wonder if he intended to say something more. "And enjoy the rest of the book."

As he turned and walked into the snow, Beatrix found herself wanting to call out and ask him to stay. But instead, she shut the door with deliberate slowness and followed the scent of bergamot and citrus back inside, needing to taste the rich, familiar flavor more than ever.

But as she stepped into the office and turned toward the stove, something stopped Beatrix in her tracks.

It was the sight of two matching teacups resting beside one another next to the kettle.

CHAPTER 26

A Tree

Represents family.

*H*ours later, when the gas lamps along the sidewalks were just beginning to flicker to life, Violet felt her thoughts begin to slow for the first time all day. Their customers had flocked to the Crescent Moon, gathering outside and tapping on the windows before she had a chance to turn the open sign to face the street. When Violet had finally managed to unlock the door, they'd spilled into the entryway in a river of silk brocade and velvet, rushing as quickly as their snow-clad boots would let them toward the tables closest to the hearth. And once they bit into the brandy snaps that had only just cooled, the rich flavor of brown sugar and secrets had unfurled on their tongues, so strong they couldn't keep from leaning across the table and sharing a bit of news that sparked an eruption of conversation.

Though Anne tried to step in to lend a hand, Violet had pushed her back again and told the house to keep her away from the shop so that she could rest before her meeting with Vincent later that evening. Though Anne seemed to believe that she could pull from her magic like a bottomless well, Violet understood that she'd need to muster all she could for the task ahead.

But that left her to tend to the waves of ladies who swooped into the shop, and by the time shadows began to creep across the glass panes of the windows, she was growing weary of the ache in her feet and the frustration that had started to return the more she let her mind drift back to questions that remained unanswered.

She wasn't like Anne, whose inner clarity grew stronger as she went through the motions of moving about the shop. No, Violet needed a different kind of rhythm, one led by whims that whipped her in surprising directions.

If she paused long enough while shifting between tables, Violet could hear it: the same tempo that had led her to the circus over a year ago beating ever so gently beneath her skin. But instead of leaning into the sensation, she had done her best to push it further away from her awareness. The music reminded her of mistakes now instead of possibilities waiting to be grasped.

Glancing around the room for hope of a distraction, Violet spotted a familiar figure standing in the entryway, draped in layers of woolen twill.

"Celeste," Violet said as she stepped across the parlor to greet their unexpected guest. "You've come again on your own?"

"I'm afraid so," Celeste replied with a shrug as she freed herself from the heavy weight of her cloak. "Katherine has been called away for the afternoon, but I still need a cup of tea. It's been so cold out there, and I can't seem to chase away the chill."

"I think that you'll find we've got just the remedy for that," Violet said with a grin as she led her toward the table nearest the front window. "Anne couldn't keep herself from brewing a special blend this morning."

"Oh?" Celeste asked, raising one brow as she settled into

her seat and began to tug off her gloves. The wind had been so sharp that the tips of her fingers were bright red from the cold, though they'd been covered by a fine layer of leather. "And what does it do?"

"I'm not exactly sure," Violet replied as she sank into her own chair and leaned back, stretching out the soreness in her calves. "I haven't had a chance to sit for a single moment since we opened the shop."

But she'd seen the faces of the customers who ordered the blend and knew that Anne had worked her magic yet again. The creases in their foreheads had instantly relaxed when they'd taken their first taste, and their eyes glimmered with a faraway look that told Violet each sip carried them further away from the shop and toward something worth remembering.

"For someone who's been running about all day, you seem rather restless," Celeste remarked, her gaze flitting to Violet's hands, which were tapping against the red tablecloth, causing the fabric to wrinkle.

"I suppose I am," Violet sighed, not bothering to deny what was so apparent from the tempo of her feet and fingers. "I'm having a bit of trouble piecing something important together."

The memory of the name carved into the doorframe of the apartment flashed through her thoughts then. To move forward, Violet had to discover how May fit into the puzzle of the past, but she was uncertain where to turn.

A year ago, she would have simply let her impulses whip her along where they may, but she couldn't give herself permission to be so reckless again, even when her very pulse seemed to beg her to let go once more.

"Are you?" Celeste murmured, clearly surprised. "I wonder why when you've always seemed so trusting of your instincts. As if you knew exactly what to do before even realizing it."

"My instincts haven't served me well as of late," Violet answered with a shake of her head, just as Franny appeared with a pot of piping hot tea.

"Sometimes the hardest person to forgive is ourselves," Celeste said with a knowing nod, her words mingling with the sound of the tea pouring into the porcelain as she lifted the pot and began to fill their cups. "Our mistakes have a habit of staining our souls, even when they should have washed out long ago."

"All I want is to forget," Violet replied, wrapping her fingers around the smooth sides of the porcelain and drawing it closer.

"But you can't forget," Celeste insisted. "Not when moving forward means finding the best of yourself to take along. Even with a fresh start, you can't leave everything behind."

Violet wondered if what Celeste said was true, if the parts of herself that she'd tried to shake loose could be embraced again, but before she could follow that thought, the scent of the tea tickled her nose and began pulling her in another direction entirely.

As she touched her lips to the cup's rim and took her first sip, she could sense the texture of Anne's magic washing over her, the threads of it coaxing Violet from her doubts and toward something coated in nostalgia: a moment that the aroma of vanilla and cloves was coaxing from the depths of her memory.

By the time the undernotes of nutmeg and cinnamon hit the back of her tongue, the tightness in her chest had all but disappeared, leaving her free to enjoy the sensation of slipping into the past. Her toes tingled, as if they'd just skittered across the hot stones of the hearth, and she could smell the fragrance of freshly cut pine, the same aroma that had saturated the family parlor whenever their father dragged in a tree to celebrate the longest night of the year. And her ears rang with the faint echoes of youthful laughter and the tinkling of delicate glass decorations that rattled as she and her sisters tried to push one another to the side so that they could have their heights marked along the doorframe of the parlor and see how tall they'd grown. Violet could nearly feel the grip of their hands against her forearm and waist, tugging her this way and that to ensure she wasn't standing on her tiptoes as they pressed a pencil just above her head.

She had been drawn back to her warmest memory of winter, the sensations of that moment sinking into her skin long enough for her to remember those few seconds with striking clarity.

But mixed among the smell of pine and citrus was something that didn't belong, the same rich scent of rosemary that had laced her birthday vision and appeared in her dream. It drew her just enough into the present for her mind to wander toward other thresholds where she'd seen similar marks along the frames. And before Violet could think to shy away from her intuition again, a realization struck her and took hold.

Her feet stilled as she worked to catch the pieces and put them together before her fear of making a misstep could stifle her racing thoughts.

Hadn't she done the same with Anne and Beatrix? Marked the doorframe to leave some kind of proof that they were shifting away from childhood with every added inch of height?

"May," Violet murmured as she sank back into her chair.

"What was that?" Celeste asked, startling Violet so much that she nearly jumped from her seat.

"Nothing," Violet replied quickly. "Nothing at all."

But as she remembered the symbols that emerged from the dust, Violet became certain that the joy and grief lingering in the apartment were connected to Philip and what he was still clinging to, even after all this time. . . .

A sister.

CHAPTER 27

A Hand Mirror
Symbolizes the need for looking inward.

Just as the spicy notes of nutmeg and cinnamon were pulling Violet back into her warmest memory of winter, Anne was fighting through the icy gusts of wind that whipped through the streets.

Though she'd managed to fall asleep after she and Violet parted the evening before, ill omens had been creeping to the surface of her awareness since the moment she'd awoken to a flock of birds fluttering near the windowsill.

Threads so tangled that they hadn't a hope of being undone slithered among the flames that flickered in the grate. A teacup fell to the floor, cracking so that the handle broke away from the base. And worst of all was the sensation that her sleeves were slipping down her forearms, though the buttons were clasped tightly around her wrists.

When she'd seen the first of these signs that morning, Anne's thoughts instantly flew to her troubles with Vincent. But as the hours slipped by and she'd brushed against the lines of Fate that each witch carried with them into the shop, Anne recognized the omens for what they were: warnings that the threads of destiny were continuing to untether.

She'd spent the rest of the afternoon locked in the divination room, struggling to find a means of uncovering a solution on her own before sunset, when she'd need to leave the Crescent Moon and return to Vincent.

But the shadows that flickered across the crystal ball refused to weave into a coherent impression, and all the leaves at the bottom of her cup washed away when she turned the rim atop the saucer, seemingly pushing Anne down a path she wasn't certain she wanted to follow.

Even as she climbed the frosty steps of the marble manor, Anne was trying to map her way through the different directions she'd charted for herself, searching out a route that would help her avoid what she knew was the most obvious destination.

She intended to linger before the door and take just a few more minutes to search out a final sign, but as soon as her boot grazed the threshold, the lock clicked open, and the soft caress of warmth drifting from the foyer brushed against her cheek, inviting her to step inside.

"You've let me in again, have you?" Anne remarked as she took in the vivid glow of the candles that lined the hallway. They seemed stronger than they had before, chasing away some of the shadows that spilled from the corners and casting the dark marble of the floors in a more welcoming hue.

"It seems so," Vincent's voice echoed as he stepped into view and held the door wider in silent invitation.

Anne blushed, embarrassed to have been caught speaking to the house, but then she noticed the dark circles beneath Vincent's eyes and her attention shifted from her worries to the ones so clearly impressed across his face.

As she began to slip out of her coat, she noticed that Vincent's jacket and trousers were rumpled, as if he'd slept in them during the night before and hadn't quite found the time to change into something fresh. The white locks of his hair, normally so meticulously brushed into place, were tousled as well, softening the hard edges that always made him seem so severe.

She found herself wanting to reach a hand upward to push aside a strand that had fallen across Vincent's brow, and before Anne was aware of it, her hand lifted to do just that. But she caught herself at the very last moment, her fingers shooting toward her own face instead to brush away a curl that had sprung out of her bun and into her eyes.

"What room will you be showing me tonight?" Anne asked quickly, hoping to push her thoughts in another direction.

Instead of an answer, though, she was met with silence.

Gazing upward, Anne was surprised to find Vincent carefully reading her expression, his eyes lingering on the tired lines that she'd seen in her own reflection as she gazed in the looking glass that morning.

"I'm not certain that we'll be going into any of them," Vincent sighed, his gaze shifting slightly so that he was staring directly into the depths of Anne's eyes.

"Whyever not?" Anne asked, knocked off course yet again.

"Because you won't trust me to keep you grounded," Vincent answered. "And I'm not willing to let you drift so far away that you might be lost entirely."

The old instinct to shield herself against his accusations rose to the surface, causing a tightness in her chest that felt just like a plate of armor. But as she stared back at Vincent, she was surprised to find that instead of fire, his eyes were filled with nothing but resolve.

"You won't call on the spirits if I don't let you anchor me," Anne murmured in understanding.

"I can't help if you won't let me," Vincent replied. "You can drift into the past, and I can ground you in the present when the memories become too great a temptation. Our magic will create a balance that keeps you tethered to the here and now, but you refuse to lean on my powers."

Anne remained quiet, uncertain of what to say.

"You think that I won't keep you safe," Vincent said.

"It isn't that." Anne insisted, more alarmed than she thought capable by the sliver of hurt that had crept into Vincent's voice.

"Then what is it?" Vincent asked.

"I've never done that before," Anne confessed quietly. "Let someone else anchor my magic."

Vincent frowned in confusion.

"How is that possible?" he asked. "Didn't your mother ground you when you were coming into your power?"

"She never needed to," Anne murmured. "When I was a child, I was always the one who held myself back when it came to testing my magic. And then after my powers started to grow stronger and I became Diviner, I couldn't afford to let anyone see what I was capable of."

Realization dawned in Vincent's expression.

"You're worried that I'll try to control your magic," he said. "That anchoring you will give me some kind of power over it."

"I know that's not how it works," she said. "That you'd only be reminding my magic of what I want when it reaches far enough to do me harm. But even still, I can't bring myself to . . ."

Struggling to find the words that would explain what was holding her back, Anne sighed and ran a hand through her curls, causing a few more tendrils to fall from their pins. How could she tell Vincent that it wasn't just the worry of not knowing what would happen if she let him anchor her? No, what made Anne's heart race in alarm was the growing awareness that she *wanted* to show him facets of herself that she hadn't shared with anyone else because he of all people might understand the desires and fears that lurked there.

Just as Anne was about to turn away, though, she felt the warmth of Vincent's palm brush her cheek as he pushed a lock of her hair back into place.

"Let me help you," Vincent murmured, his hand still laced through her curls, cradling her temple as if he hoped she would lean into his touch. "So that you can safely see how far you can go."

It was on the tip of Anne's tongue to refuse, to say that if she couldn't depend on her own will to keep her magic in check, then it shouldn't be given free rein in any circumstance.

But then she looked upward and caught sight of the circles beneath Vincent's eyes again, the stark half-moons that told her he, too, was losing sleep over a potential future that was fast becoming a certainty.

She may not know all his secrets, but one thing, at least, was certain.

They both wanted the same thing in the end: to uncover the history of the ring and tuck away loose ends.

"I'll let you," Anne finally managed to say. "I'll let you anchor me."

A tension that had been hovering in the hallway eased then, so much so that Anne could hear the floorboards and wainscoting creak.

"Are you certain?" Vincent asked, the furrow between his brows growing deeper. "You won't change your mind and slip away again?"

"Yes," Anne said.

Vincent sighed, and some of the strain that Anne had noticed was pulling his shoulder blades together began to loosen.

"Then let's begin," he said, extending his free hand in invitation for Anne to follow him down the hall.

Anne didn't know what she expected to find when Vincent stopped in front of a door that was a few steps away from the one where she could still hear the heartsong slipping through the cracks of the threshold. But as he turned the knob and she saw what awaited her on the other side, her breath caught in surprise.

Instead of clocks, the walls of the room were covered in gilded mirrors, some clear as crystal and others tarnished along the corners or cracked so that the flames licking from the fireplace seemed to scatter across the surface. Even the floor was littered with them, the quick flashes of light that twisted against the curves and cracks of the glass leaving only the barest of paths to step along.

Anne felt as if she'd fallen into a chandelier, catching only the barest fraction of her expression as her gaze flitted from one glimmer of glass to the next.

"What do we need to do?" Anne asked, startled by the strangely unfamiliar perspective that each shard managed to cast back.

"The spirits will be attracted by the feeling of catching yourself unexpectedly in a mirror," Vincent explained as he led them toward the center of the room, his gaze fixed on the edge of Anne's skirt train, as if he was worried she might need help keeping it from snagging on the frames.

"You'll need to linger in that sensation to call them in," Vincent continued. "Then think of the ring as you drift back, just as you did before."

Anne remembered how compelled she'd been to go deeper and deeper into the past, the memories so visceral that they'd felt even more alive than the ones she was experiencing in the present.

"When you sense yourself drifting away, reach for my magic," Vincent said, as if he could tell what direction Anne's thoughts had turned. "And I will ground you."

But that was precisely what Anne had always struggled with the most: accepting that she needed help from a source beyond herself.

As she slowly lifted her own hands and rested them in the warmth of Vincent's, though, Anne started to feel her hesitation fade away, replaced by the distinct aroma of peppermint and early morning dew entangling in notes of myrrh and freshly cut cypress. She could sense Vincent's magic brushing against hers now, and instead of pulling away, she leaned into it, encouraging her power to weave into his. Once the final thread was tethered, Anne felt as if her entire body had been dipped in gold, the strands of her magic glowing so brightly that she knew it was time to finally let go.

"Drift back when you're ready," Vincent whispered as he laced his fingers through hers and held them tight. "And see what you can find."

Anne released a shaky sigh then and focused on the sensations that would help her sink into the moment unfolding before her: the way the firelight refracted along the cracks of the mirrors, the shockingly pleasant infusion of their magic, and the warmth of Vincent's power as it anchored her.

Anne's attention shifted outward then, and she became aware of another impression creeping along the edge of her consciousness. At first, the spirits were merely whispers, softer than the ones that had slipped between the ticking of the clocks, but then she started to see silhouettes taking shape in the corners of the glass, the textures of clothes and hair growing more vibrant with every exhaled breath.

Before Anne let herself be consumed by the memories that the ghosts were so carefully crafting together, she pulled lightly at the threads of her magic, testing to see whether they were tethered to something that would remind her of the beauty of the present.

And when she did, she caught the barest glimpse of Vincent's own power, a force that felt as grounded as a tree whose roots had remained fixed to the soil through centuries of thunderstorms.

"I've got you," she heard Vincent say as his magic brushed

against hers, soft enough to remind Anne that she was still in control.

She grasped his hands tighter, pulling him forward so that she could lay her forehead against his chest if the weight of the recollections became too great. For a moment, Anne feared he might step away, but then she felt his chin come to a gentle rest atop her head, tucking her even closer.

And then, when she felt cradled by Vincent and his power, Anne let go of the hold she'd been keeping on her magic and drifted back into a sea of sensation.

She felt the soft fur of a shawl slinking down her shoulder.

Wind whipping through her hair as she ran closer to something worth racing toward.

A tingling along the skin beneath her ears just before a crescendo.

The hot sting of bourbon sliding down her throat.

These memories didn't belong to her, but Anne found herself sinking deeper and deeper into them anyway, lured by emotions that were yearning to be touched, tasted, and heard.

"Don't get lost," she heard Vincent murmur as he tightened his hold on her hands, reminding her that she was a creature of the present, not an echo of the past.

The urge to fade into the memories was still tempting, though. At the same moment she was savoring the first drops of honeysuckle in early summer, Anne was enfolded into the bittersweet sensation of a final embrace. She didn't know whether to laugh or cry at the beauty of all the wonders that made up a lifetime, and so she remained still as they brushed against her body.

But then Vincent's magic touched hers again, as gentle as a finger tapping lightly on her shoulder, and she remembered what needed to be done.

With great effort, Anne turned away from the sensations that the spirits were trying to share and offered one of her own: the warmth of the gold ring as it drew in the heat of her and Vincent's clasped hands.

In what felt like an instant, the ghosts latched on to the sensation, eager to show Anne moments of their own lives that were linked to the one in the present.

And among the feeling of pearls being draped across her neck and the flashes of wedding bands passing between hands, Anne saw her again, the woman with the mismatched eyes from the night she'd fallen under the spell of the heartsong.

But Anne was peering through a keyhole now instead of standing across from her at a ball, watching as she stood and reached for a wrinkled hand rising above a pile of quilts atop the mattress.

With a shock, Anne realized that the woman's hair was completely white, from the roots to the tips of the curls that swayed against the small of her back, just like Vincent's. Before, it had been hidden beneath ribbons and roses, but now Anne could see the startling hue.

And then Anne's attention was gripped by the quick flash of gold as the person in the bed placed the ring in the woman's upturned palm and whispered a single word that carried through the keyhole.

Legacy.

In the rough texture of the vowels and consonants, Anne was pulled even deeper into the past, the ring growing at the center of her vision as it was handed from one palm to the next and the next and the next.

She suddenly felt Vincent's magic tugging at her own, a reminder not to drift too far into recollections, and in the instant his power touched hers, Anne snapped away from the past and toward the future, as abruptly as a string that had been holding too much weight.

As she shifted into what was yet to come, Anne was consumed by the scent of myrrh and magic, her gaze coming to rest on a single image: Vincent grasping the ring from a hand touched by time and slipping it onto his own finger.

Her eyes flew open then, startled to find the face she'd seen in her inner vision so close to her own now, the lines and grooves of it etched with concern and curiosity.

"What did you find?" Vincent asked, the rapid beat of his pulse reverberating against Anne's skin as he waited to hear what she would say.

But instead of giving him an answer, Anne pulled away abruptly, releasing his hands and taking a step back so that she could put some distance between them.

The movement broke the bond tethering their magic together as well, causing it to snap back so painfully that Anne gasped and reached for her chest.

"I don't know," she finally replied as she caught her breath.

The different threads of what she'd seen, heard, and touched were coming together now, though, as quickly as a spider weaving a web. As she took all the pieces that had been reflected in the mirrors and placed them alongside one another, she saw the answer, so simple and improbable all at once.

"I don't know," Anne murmured again, but the words this time were laced with the distinct burnt sweetness that exposed them for what they were.

A sinking sensation gripped Anne's stomach as she watched all the softness in Vincent's face start to harden.

"You don't know, or you won't tell me?" Vincent asked, his voice cutting through the thick silence of the room.

Anne turned away from him then, but his narrowed eyes were reflected in every shard of glass scattered across the walls and floor, making it impossible to escape them.

"I need some time to put it all together," she said as she raked a hand through her curls. "I have to be sure of what it all means first."

"You won't let me help you even now," Vincent sighed, "when you've already seen what we can do if we let one another in?"

Anne paused, but as his question echoed through the room, she blinked and saw the edge of a hawk's wing flutter from one mirror to the next, leaving feathers across the glass that looked so real she nearly leaned forward to pick the closest one up.

She whirled toward Vincent, the suspicion that had slipped into the back of her mind rising to the surface again, so strong and unexpected that she could feel the blood rushing to her cheeks.

"Perhaps. But I'm not the only one keeping secrets, am I?" she said, using the exact words he'd uttered the evening before, when the space between them had been thick with suspicion.

It was clear that their uneasy truce had shattered and they'd already settled back into their familiar stern grooves, as unmoving as the script etched in tombstone.

The echo of a memory drifted forth from the past then, this one from Anne's own recollections instead of the careful crafting of the spirits.

I don't trust you.

And as quickly as Anne could have snapped her fingers, she felt the weight of her responsibility settling across her shoulders. A burden so precious that it had to be carried alone for fear of being stolen.

Before she could let her words or silence reveal anything more, Anne turned away and ran from the room, not bothering to follow the thin trail that would have led her safely to the door and shattering one of the gilded mirrors in her haste.

The last thing she heard before she flew onto the street was Vincent calling her name and the sound of glass cracking beneath her boots.

CHAPTER 28

A Mouse

*Suggests that someone is keeping an
object that doesn't belong to them.*

By the time Anne, Violet, and Beatrix wandered up the steps to the third floor of the Crescent Moon in the hopes of easing the tension of the day, the house still hadn't lit the candles in the family parlor.

When the Quigleys stepped through the threshold of the room, they nearly spilled their mugs of hot chocolate across the carpet as they stumbled about in the haze of the hearth's embers. And it wasn't until Violet found a spare box of matches hidden in the depths of the end table that they were able to recover their footing.

"Something has the poor house rattled," Beatrix murmured after they managed to strike enough candles aflame to settle into their spots around the hearth.

As Violet sank down beside her, she patted the arm of the settee, as one might a dog frightened by the rumble of thunder. She soon realized that the house wasn't the only one in need of consolation, though.

Anne sighed and set her cup on the end table with a soft thud in the way she always did whenever she needed to let go of whatever weight she could.

"Secrets," Anne finally said after Violet turned a questioning glance in her direction. "The house sensed secrets slipping back into the cracks and is worried what might come of them."

"Whose secrets?" Beatrix asked, leaning forward so quickly that her own cup nearly toppled to the floor before she could catch it.

"My own, I'm afraid," Anne confessed, turning away to gaze at the flames that were just starting to flicker to life in the grate.

"You discovered something, then," Violet said, the lick of excitement in her voice fading as she noticed the strained set of Anne's mouth.

"I did," Anne sighed. "When I let him anchor me, I was able to slip back into the past. I caught a clear vision of the ring, and then that link snapped me toward the future."

Violet noticed that Anne hadn't said Vincent's name, as if the sound of it was too difficult to utter aloud.

"And what did you see?" Violet pressed, shifting forward so that she wouldn't miss a single word.

"The ring is an heirloom," Anne said as one does when they've finally clicked the last piece of a puzzle into its proper place. "I saw it being passed to a woman with the same white hair as all the Crowleys, and then as I drifted further back, I realized that it's been in their family for generations. Perhaps even centuries."

"But how is that possible?" Violet gasped. "Philip was the one who wore the ring. And if it belongs to the Crowleys, why haven't any of them laid claim to it?"

Objects passed down through a line of witches were protected with fierce devotion because they often carried enchantments, giving them a type of power that grew even stronger with time. It seemed impossible that Mr. Crowley's family wouldn't have seized on it the instant he died if it was in fact an heirloom instead of letting it be given to Anne as he had instructed.

"You said that you caught a glimpse of the ring's future," Beatrix murmured. "Did you see who the rightful owner is?"

"Yes," Anne said, drawing out the word so that it sounded like the hushed clip of a whisper. "It's Vincent."

The sisters became so still that they could hear the snowflakes hitting the glass pane of the window and the whip of the wind rattling the sign on the street.

"Are you certain?" Violet asked as she reached forward and grabbed one of Anne's hands in her own. They felt icier than the sidewalks along the road, except for the finger that held the ring, which was warm to the touch.

"It belongs to him," Anne said with a shaky nod. "I saw him as clear as crystal in the vision."

"But wouldn't he have known that already?" Beatrix asked, her brow furrowing in confusion.

"Not necessarily," Violet stepped in. "Sometimes, people hide the things that carry the most meaning so no one else will try to lay claim to them. And then, when there isn't anyone left to share the story, it slips away from the object entirely."

"What do you mean, Vi?" Beatrix asked, her brow furrowing.

"Perhaps Mr. Crowley hid the meaning of the ring so that no one in his family would try to take it from him," Violet replied. "What better way to ensure his Task remained incomplete than to hide the history of the ring? If he's the only one who knew its story, the tale would be lost once he passed on."

Again, Violet's thoughts drifted to the apartment above the bookshop, where she'd felt forgotten stories rippling from the abandoned furniture and picture frames. But before she could drift too far from the parlor, the sound of Beatrix's voice pulled her attention back to the here and now.

"What did Vincent say when you told him?" Beatrix asked as she turned toward Anne.

But Anne's gaze was still fixed on the flames in the grate, as if she was afraid of what her sisters might read in the stern set of her face.

"I didn't tell him," Anne finally said, her confession causing frost to gather along the sills of the windows.

"But we can't keep this from him, Anne!" Beatrix cried. "The Crowleys should know about the ring. The absence of the heirloom could be having a horrible effect on them, especially if they aren't aware of what's causing it. Has Vincent mentioned anything about his family?"

Anne began to shake her head, but she suddenly grew still, an expression of dawning realization starting to spread across her features.

"Something isn't right about their house," she murmured. "I don't know what it is, but there are too many shadows lurking in the corners."

"Then you must tell him," Beatrix insisted.

"Vincent is also keeping secrets," Anne replied, lifting her chin in the same way she had as a child when her sisters tried to change her mind. "I don't trust him not to take the ring once he learns the truth. And then Mr. Crowley and Philip will be separated again. We need to discover what's keeping Philip from moving forward before we complete Mr. Crowley's Task."

Violet watched as Anne drew back into her chair, a sense of weariness settling across her shoulders that revealed some of the weight she carried.

"We may be getting closer in that respect," Violet interjected. "You remember the mark I found on the doorframe in the apartment? The one with 'May' etched into the wood? I think she was Philip's sister."

"A sister?" Anne murmured. "But Mr. Crowley never mentioned a sister."

"May was Philip's sister," Violet repeated, her voice growing stronger. "I can't explain it, but I'm certain. I feel it as strongly as the beat of my own pulse."

Violet waited with bated breath to see how her sisters would respond. A year ago, she knew that Anne would have simply dismissed her, preferring to depend on signs that revealed themselves to her and her alone. And although Beatrix's thoughts were always entangled in fairy tales, she possessed a levelheadedness that had kept her from following Violet's wildest flights of fancy.

As she glanced between her sisters, though, Violet was relieved to find excitement flickering in their eyes instead of the skepticism that she'd expected.

"Yes, it is possible," Anne said as she sat against the back of her chair with a thoughtful expression.

"But if Philip did have a sister, how can we find her?" Beatrix asked. "She could be anywhere, and who's to say that the reason he hasn't passed on is because she's a ghost herself?"

"If we brought Vincent to the apartment, he'd be able to tell us if she's still alive, wouldn't he?" Violet asked, an idea taking root in her mind.

Anne's mouth tightened, evidentially understanding the direction Violet's thoughts had turned.

Some witches who practiced death magic had the ability to pick up an object that someone else had given the barest touch and say with certainty whether they were still alive or not. Though she wasn't sure if Vincent possessed this skill, Violet knew from Anne's stories that he was powerful.

"I don't know that he'll be so obliging once he discovers what I've been keeping from him," Anne said hesitantly.

"As you've already told us, Anne, we don't have much time," Beatrix said. "The fabric that holds all our magic together is unraveling. If we want to keep everything together and have a hope of saving Philip and Mr. Crowley, we're going to need all the help we can get."

"He's stubborn," Anne sighed. "And determined to finish Mr. Crowley's Task."

"So is someone else we know," Violet murmured as she stared pointedly at Anne.

"You can't mean me," Anne scoffed.

"That is exactly who I mean," Violet replied. "If anyone can convince him that this is a Task worth waiting to complete, it's you."

"Do you really feel he's so unbending, Anne?" Beatrix asked softly.

Anne's shoulders pinched together in the way they always did when she was about to grasp even tighter to her opinion, and Violet prepared to make her case once more, but then something flickered across her sister's eyes, dulling the hard glint there.

"Whenever he speaks about the spirits, it's as if he's truly lived their joys and fears," she whispered. "I can see the sympathy so clearly etched across his face. It makes me wonder. . . ."

Anne paused then, letting the unspoken words linger in the silence, but her sisters understood their meaning nonetheless.

Would his sympathy for wandering souls be enough to overcome his desire for the ring?

"I'll do my best," Anne finally relented. "Though I can't say that I'm looking forward to our conversation."

"You should go to the apartment to see what you can find," Violet suggested. "And bring Vincent with you to help. Memories are lingering there, so potent that you can feel the weight of them whenever you draw a breath. Together you may be able to uncover something that I haven't been able to see."

"Perhaps," Anne repeated, though she didn't sound as certain as Violet had.

"And while you're dealing with Vincent, I'm going to have a talk with our landlady," Violet added. "Now that we have a name, she may be able to tell us a thing or two."

Though Brigit hadn't seemed to know anything about the history of the building, a sudden urge to ask her again was prickling at the corners of Violet's awareness, so potent that it made her temples tingle. She would trust herself this time, following her impulses instead of burying them beneath the weight of the worst possibilities.

Anne nodded in agreement as she leaned forward to let the rich notes of cocoa and hazelnuts chase away the worst of the day's worries.

But just as she touched the warm porcelain to her lips, something on the other side of the window made her grow still.

"What is it?" Violet asked as she watched her sister's face fall.

Instead of answering, though, Anne rose from her chair and moved toward the glass pane, pushing aside the curtains so that her sisters could see through the window.

"Medusa's curls," Violet cursed when she turned around and saw what awaited them there.

The snowflakes that had been drifting to the sidewalk only moments before were now shifting in the opposite direction, like stars on strings that were being slowly lifted by a puppeteer who realized too late that they weren't meant to be in the scene.

"Our time is running out," Anne whispered, her declaration fogging the glass as she gazed out the window and wondered how long they had before the threads of Fate were so frayed that they wouldn't have a hope of weaving them back together.

CHAPTER 29

A Spider
Appears just before a time of creativity.

As Beatrix walked along the sidewalk the next morning, she scanned the streets, searching for anything else that might have shifted in the night.

The woolen figures shuffling beside her had their heads pointed firmly to the ground, the heat of their breath coming in clouds that rose from beneath their hoods and hats. Their heels were tapping quickly against the stones, as if they believed moving at a faster pace might give them a chance of overtaking the icy whip of the wind. Though the people who called Chicago home were more than willing to cast a smile at those who passed by in the warmth of summer, the frigid grip of winter kept them from noticing anything beyond their tightly clasped hands.

As Beatrix turned her own face upward and straightened her shoulders to get a full view of the street, she couldn't help but feel grateful that the unrelenting edge of a particularly cold day had caused everyone's attention to move inward.

Though nothing was out of place enough to cause anyone to

halt in their tracks, a few unusual details emerged for those who lingered long enough in one spot: faint light pouring out of a third-story window in the way it only does in the pitch-darkness of night, reflections in shop-front windows that didn't quite match the silhouettes of the people shuffling by, and curbsides that felt like they were five inches taller than they actually were, causing an unexpected sinking feeling in the stomach of anyone who had the misfortune of stepping down too quickly.

Worse still was the odd sensation that something important had been left behind.

At first, Beatrix believed this uneasiness was brewing from within, but the longer she walked, the more she suspected that the other people on the street were plagued by a similar feeling. She kept bumping into women who stopped abruptly on the sidewalk to peer into their reticules with concerned expressions that pinched their eyebrows too tightly together. And the men kept patting the breasts of their coat pockets and playing with the rims of their hats, as if deliberating whether or not to turn back around.

Something felt like it was sliding slowly off-kilter, enough that people kept reaching for their pocket watches and pearl drop earrings to ensure that they were still in place. And though most pushed aside this odd apprehension, attributing it to nothing more than the short days and cold weather, Beatrix knew better.

When she saw the chipped paint of the bookshop's storefront from beneath the rim of her hood, Beatrix peered up at the sign and wondered, not for the first time that morning, whether she was making the right choice. How could she justify settling into the wingback chair beside the shelves for yet another afternoon when so much hung in the balance?

She'd started to express as much at the breakfast table, only to have her worries cut to the quick by Violet and Anne, who'd thrown a woolen cloak across her shoulders and shoved her out into the street faster than Beatrix could draw in a breath to protest.

"We need a good turn of Fate," Anne had said as she threw a knit scarf out the door. "And she's best found when you least expect her."

Beatrix shook her head as she stomped her boots on the sidewalk and remembered the sense of certainty that flashed in Anne's eyes whenever they spoke of the bookshop.

In those moments, Anne reminded Beatrix so much of their mother: assured and certain once she got a clear look at a sign and knew what the outcome would be. And though Beatrix wasn't sure she was helping in the least, whenever she said as much, Anne would merely remind her of the scent of aged paper that she'd sensed in her vision, as if that alone was enough to draw their conversation to a close.

Beatrix trusted Anne's instincts, of course, but that didn't keep her concerns at bay. Now more than ever, she worried that in closing herself away in stories that drew her from the present, she'd miss something important and ruin any hope of helping untangle the knots that seemed to only grow tighter the more they pulled at them.

She felt an icy trickle down the side of her cheek then and realized that her doubts had managed to pour over, taking the shape of tears that were freezing against her skin.

By the time Beatrix walked down the alleyway and slid the key into the door, it felt like she was ensnared body and soul by the most lonesome parts of winter: shoulders grown stiff from hunching too long against the biting wind, greetings cut short for fear of the cold, toes and fingers that never seemed to thaw.

As soon as she stepped over the threshold of the shop and drew in her first breath, though, the tightness in Beatrix's chest flickered out as quickly as the wick of a candle. Startled, she stood in the doorway, wondering why the sense of dread that had consumed her only moments ago had suddenly faded, but then, as her thoughts began to still, certain details slipped slowly into her awareness, becoming more potent the longer she focused on them.

The scent of bergamot and citrus saturated the shop as it had yesterday, but new notes emerged as well, the fragrance of beeswax polish and fresh air. It was the same smell that filled the Crescent Moon the mornings after it decided to throw open a window to let out the worst of the dust and dread bottled up during the winter months. And beneath that arose the barest hint of newly cut paper, vanilla, and ink just barely dried on the page. It was a startling contrast to how the shop had smelled the first evening that Beatrix and Violet had stumbled through the threshold, the muskiness that arises from painted windowpanes and neglect all but lost beneath aromas that loosened the knots in Beatrix's soul before she had a chance to notice what was happening.

Shrugging out of her coat, Beatrix held her breath as she gazed from one corner of the room to the next.

Had the floral buds painted along the wallpaper always looked like they were just about to bloom, the barest hint of pink petals tucked beneath lush green leaves? Why was it less of a chore to find a place to step without hitting the corner of a book with the toe of her boot? She could nearly see the intricate pattern of the rug beneath now, the rich red texture showcasing the shining walnut shelves, which had somehow shaken themselves free of dust sometime during the night except for a few patches in the farthest corners.

And, most curious of all, how was it that Beatrix was starting to feel like she could finally rest, as if all the troubles brewing within her would simply vanish the moment she sat in the wingback chair with a warm cup of tea and lost herself in the final chapters of a story that she hadn't realized just how much she needed?

"You don't have to hide from me any longer," Beatrix whispered as she rested a hand against the side of one of the empty shelves.

Her declaration was met with silence, but she sensed the texture of the air shift, as if someone was holding an indrawn breath.

"I've finally realized what you are," Beatrix continued, louder now, as if she was having a conversation with a person on the other side of the room. "And I dare say you've figured out that I'm not exactly normal myself."

Again, Beatrix was met with nothing but silence, and as one moment slipped into the next, she started to wonder if she was merely being foolish, wishing for magic where there was only dust and disappointment.

Feeling an ache return to her chest just above her heart, Beatrix leaned her forehead against the bookshelf.

"I've felt empty without stories, too, you know," she murmured. "And so, so lonely for the joy of turning the page and not knowing where it will take me."

She sensed it then, a slight vibration beneath her boots and the subtle sound of pages brushing against one another.

"But it's time that we both embraced who we are, don't you think?" Beatrix asked. "So that we can remember why life is worth taking a chance on, even when it feels like you've lost your way."

The light filtering through the windows grew stronger then, the colors of the woodwork and book spines growing more vibrant as the sun's rays stretched across the floor.

"What's a writer who's forgotten the simple beauty of a book?" Beatrix said. "And what's a bookshop who's lost its readers? We're searching for the same thing, you and I."

The shop suddenly grew still, the air thickening in a way that made the emotions clinging to the walls more tangible. She could feel them now, the frustration and grief that coated every inch of the shop, ensuring that not even the barest shred of joy could slip in from the world outside.

But then, Beatrix sensed the walls expand and contract, the loose pages flying about the room as if someone had released a deep, long-held breath. In what felt like the blink of an eye, all the books snapped back onto the shelves, flying so quickly from one end of the shop to the next that it was a wonder they didn't collide and burst into confetti.

The shop had awoken at last, eager to shake away the anger and hurt it had felt after decades of neglect and absorb the satisfaction that radiated from readers whenever they stumbled across a promising story.

Beatrix clasped her hands together and lifted them beneath her chin as she took in the shining book spines and scent of leather, wondering if there could be anything in the entire world more magical than an enchanted bookshop.

As the light hit her fingers, though, she was shocked to find that the shelves weren't the only thing to have changed.

Just beneath the skin, Beatrix could make out the faintest swirls of letters. They were still scattered, too far apart to make any words, but there nonetheless.

"I think I'm starting to dust myself off too," Beatrix said with a laugh, the sound a bit rough from the sense of relief that shook her to the core.

The barest thread of an idea for a story began to tug at the back of her mind then, and if she held herself still enough, Beatrix could hear the faint murmur of a character's voice just starting to take shape. It wasn't a sensation that she could easily craft into words, this feeling that the promise of a story was dangling precariously on the edge between imagination and awareness. But she was certain that if she reached for the thread too quickly and pulled at it in desperation, the entire tapestry it was tethered to might unravel, leaving her even more frustrated than before.

In that moment, the shop, which had always known precisely what balm Beatrix needed to soothe the wounds that no one else could see, nudged her toward the wingback chair, the nails in the floorboards lifting just enough to snag the train of her skirt and point her in the proper direction.

"I know," Beatrix relented, letting the seed of her next story rest a bit longer so that it could grow firmer roots. "The time isn't right yet."

But as she sank into the velvet upholstery of the chair and turned to the page she'd marked the other evening, Beatrix knew with certainty that it wouldn't be long before she finally turned a different kind of chapter, one strung from the fabric of good fortune and the magic she'd been waiting so long to remember once again.

CHAPTER 30

A Closed Hand

Predicts an argument.

As Anne stood on the front stoop of the Crowley manor, she wondered about the cost of keeping things from the places they belonged.

Though the chill of the street was sharp enough to make the hairs of her eyelashes stand on end, the ring wrapped around her finger was warm, as if it had been left on the windowsill during the brightest day of summer. It had begun to feel that way the moment Anne turned the corner, and with every step she took toward the door, a tingling sensation pricked at the delicate skin beneath the gold.

There was no mistaking where the ring belonged, but as Anne lingered in front of the house, she struggled with the potential consequences of telling Vincent the truth. She wanted so desperately to believe that he would listen to her, but as she lifted the knocker, she could only think about the way he'd looked when she'd lied to him, all the warmth in his expression chilled to the bone.

By the time the door creaked open, Anne had nearly convinced herself that keeping the truth from Vincent was the wisest choice, that she didn't need his help to piece everything together.

But the moment he appeared in the threshold and his amber eyes met hers, the ring flashed to life again, so fiercely that she knew her skin was reddening under the heat, and in that instant, Anne made her choice.

"I don't want to keep secrets any longer," she said, her words as stark as the snow that still coated the street.

She watched as Vincent's brows pulled together, his suspicion so potent that Anne didn't know whether to take a step back or move nearer, closing the distance between them where no more half-truths could hide.

"So you are keeping secrets," Vincent said, the final syllable causing gooseflesh to skitter across her skin.

"We both have," Anne answered as she lifted her chin. "But secrets won't save us. Not when there's so little time left."

"Then that's what you want?" Vincent asked in the same tone she was beginning to recognize as the one he always used when weighing a cost. "An exchange?"

"What I want is to make you understand," Anne replied, her tone softening then as she thought of what was at stake.

Vincent stiffened, and for a moment, Anne wondered if he was going to close the door and shatter all the possibilities she'd let herself imagine.

But as he stared down at her, something in his expression shifted ever so slightly.

"Then try," Vincent finally said. "Try to make me understand."

Anne blinked in surprise, wondering if she'd misheard, but then the ticking of her clock reminded her there wasn't a moment left to waste.

"I need your help first," Anne said. "If you're willing to come with me."

In answer, Vincent reached for his coat without hesitation and stepped onto the stoop, closing the door behind him.

"We aren't going far," Anne said as she followed Violet's directions and began moving toward the door in the alleyway across the street that would lead them to the apartment.

They didn't speak again until she lifted the key from the pocket of her skirts and began to slip it into the lock.

"Is it true that you can know whether someone is alive or dead simply by touching something they've held?" Anne asked, watching Vincent's reflection in the surface of the dusty window of the door.

"It's true," Vincent replied, unable to hide the curiosity that flittered across his face.

"Follow me, then," Anne said as she turned the knob and led them up the steps.

As the stairwell filled with the creaks that their boots made on the boards, Anne couldn't help but remember what Violet had told them about the memories that saturated the apartment. With every step, she could feel the weight and texture of them bearing down on her. Some caused the skin just beneath her ear to tingle like it always did when she heard laughter ringing in the front parlor of the shop, and as her palm grazed the smooth wood of the railing, it practically vibrated with the sense of satisfaction its occupants had felt as they left the troubles of the outside world at the door and eased into the warm comfort of home.

But there were the echoes of other moments resting there as well, remnants of loss and longing so potent that they nearly took Anne's breath away.

"Philip lived here," she whispered once they reached the parlor, afraid that if she spoke too loudly, what they were searching for might skitter away.

"I know," Vincent replied, though the words were softer than Anne had expected them to be, as if he'd glanced through the icy panes of the windows in his own house and wondered what, exactly, had drawn his uncle to the other side of the street so long ago.

Nodding, Anne silently led him toward the threshold on the other side of the room, where Violet had told her she'd find the marking along the frame.

"Can you tell me what you sense from this?" Anne asked, her fingers hovering above the name etched in the wood.

Vincent's eyes met hers then, and Anne saw questions flash across them as clearly as if he'd spoken them aloud. She could already feel her spine straighten as she prepared herself to answer each one, persuading him to continue. But he surprised her again, turning to face the doorframe without a single comment and gently resting his palm on top of the carving.

Anne should have turned away, given him a moment as he began to work his magic. Before, she'd closed her eyes whenever he'd started to thread his spells together, trying to draw herself into the sounds and textures of the moment. But now, she was facing him and could see the way his features changed as he focused on weaving together an enchantment, the hard cut of his jawline relaxing and his lips parting as he murmured silent words meant to pull secrets from the very foundation of the house.

Eventually, though, the fragrance of cypress and myrrh faded, and Anne noticed the tension returning to Vincent's shoulders, the blades pinching even closer together than they had before.

"What is it?" Anne asked, taking a step back, though what she wanted to do was place a hand on his forearm to keep him from pulling further away from her.

"The girl who touched this doorframe," Vincent murmured, his voice tight. "Who was she?"

Anne's heart began to quicken, but it was too late to turn back from the path she'd already started down.

"Philip's sister," Anne answered.

Vincent's mouth tightened, and Anne knew he didn't need to be able to read the future to know where their conversation was heading.

"I thought you were focused on trying to discover where the ring belongs," he murmured. "But it seems your attention has been pulled elsewhere."

Anne bristled at the silent accusation in his tone: that she'd neglected her duties as Diviner when the fate of the city rested so squarely on her shoulders.

"I already know where the ring belongs," Anne announced, the strength of her words causing the picture frames along the walls to rattle on their hooks, scattering even more dust atop the baseboards.

Vincent stilled, staring back at Anne with such intensity that his own power caused the shadows in the corner of the room to stretch until they toyed at the heels of their boots.

"You know where the ring belongs," he repeated. "And you haven't thought to tell me."

"I only realized yesterday," Anne explained.

"Who does it belong to?" Vincent asked, taking the barest step closer.

Anne drew in a deep breath then, needing to remind herself that she was making the right choice.

"You," she whispered. "It belongs to you."

Vincent's eyes widened, but then a spark of recognition flittered across his face, as if he'd been given an answer that confirmed a sneaking suspicion.

"You already knew," Anne said as a sinking sensation gripped her stomach and threatened to pull her under.

Vincent was silent for a moment, but eventually, something in his expression broke, and the stiffness in his shoulders seemed to loosen.

"The possibility had crossed my mind," he admitted before releasing a heavy sigh. "Ever since my uncle's passing, the house hasn't let anyone inside but me. I get the sense that it's unsettled, holding its breath until something shifts into the proper place."

That revelation startled Anne. Homes, especially those of a magical nature, enjoyed company.

"It let me in," Anne countered, but then she glanced down at her gloved hands where the outline of the ring pressed against the fabric and understood what Vincent had already suspected.

The house had recognized the ring and welcomed her inside in the hopes that it might be returned.

"That's what you think the ring's power is, then?" Anne asked. "It gives the wearer control of the house?"

Vincent shifted his gaze, pressing a hand to his temple in a way that told Anne he was trying to decide how much of the truth to share with her. She could sense that there were still secrets lurking beneath the surface of their conversation, keeping them from moving forward.

"It's more than that," Vincent finally relented, his voice rawer now, more urgent. "Much more."

"Tell me," Anne said.

"The Crowley magic is fading," Vincent replied, the confession rough.

"I don't understand," Anne said. "Your family is one of the most powerful in the coven."

"It started when my uncle died," Vincent explained. "After his passing, it felt like something cracked in the foundation of our magic."

He paused then, clearly trying to find the words to describe something that must have felt so visceral and abstract all at once.

"We've always been able to do so much more than other witches of our sort," he continued. "The spirits gravitate toward us like moths to a flame, in need of soothing. But ever since my uncle died, we have to call to them, and they don't always answer. No one understands why. It's as if something slipped out of place that day, and the further it drifts, the more we lose."

"Then why didn't you want to help me?" Anne asked, more confused than ever as she remembered just how eager Vincent had been to get her to leave the house during their first meeting. "Didn't you think there was a chance all of this was tied to your uncle's Task?"

"I thought the ring was cursed," Vincent admitted, raking a hand through his hair in frustration. "No one in the family had ever seen the band before my uncle started wearing it. Then I went to his grave and saw the blackthorn, and I knew that he'd hidden his power so that he could be with Philip. When I asked my family when they first remembered seeing my uncle with the ring, I realized it was around the time Philip had died. I thought he'd found a hex witch to enchant the band so it would draw away his abilities so he could be with Philip in the end and that when he'd passed, the curse latched on to us, drawn by the same kind of power that he'd asked it to dampen. Why else would it have an hourglass etched on its surface? It's the symbol of our death magic. I was convinced the ring must be attracted to our power, draining it from us once my uncle was no longer here to provide what it needed."

As Anne glanced down at the hourglass carved into the ring, her mind went to another sign, the entwined snakes that she'd seen imprinted on the windowpane just before a flash of a man's coat sleeve caught her attention.

"It was you that day," she murmured as a jolt of realization settled into her bones. "You were outside the shop. That's why you didn't look surprised when I told you my name that first night at the manor."

"I needed to learn more about the ring," Vincent said, lifting his hands in a way that told Anne he was trying to make her understand. "After I moved into the manor, I started to hear the sound of sand shifting against glass, and when I followed the noise, it led me to the ring . . . and you. I hoped that you might give it to me when you learned just how dangerous it was to us."

Vincent said the word "dangerous" in the same tone that a gardener might use when talking about a sprig of English ivy that needed to be burned at the roots to keep it from spreading.

"You wanted to destroy it," Anne whispered, gooseflesh rippling across her skin as she realized what Vincent's intention had been from the beginning.

"I had no choice," Vincent said, taking a step closer. "My family's magic was slipping away, and all signs pointed to the ring."

Anne's thoughts swirled as she listened to what he was saying. She could understand why Vincent suspected the ring was cursed after learning just how much his uncle had been willing to sacrifice to be with Philip. But he still hadn't explained why he'd been so adamant about refusing to help her when she first appeared at the manor.

Anne must have furrowed her brow while trying to put all the pieces together because Vincent began to speak again, this time with an urgency that suggested he feared she may come to the wrong conclusion before he had a chance to reveal the truth.

"I knew that my uncle had left his Task unfinished because of Philip," Vincent explained. "But I didn't know what, exactly, that entailed. He never told us what you'd revealed in your session with him, remaining tight-lipped about it until the very end. Imagine how I felt when you showed up in the manor and told me that you were intent on giving away the very thing that I needed to save my family's magic."

Anne remembered how he had looked that afternoon in the house, his panic and frustration barely contained beneath a stony mask.

"You seemed so certain that the Task was to give the ring to someone else," Vincent continued. "But the idea of a curse made me consider another possibility: that my uncle's Task was to destroy the band so no one else could be harmed by it. That perhaps where it belonged wasn't with a person but nowhere at all. I knew that if I told you the truth then and there, you'd ensure I never came close to the ring again. And so I did the only thing I could: refuse to help you."

Anne wondered, if that was indeed the case, though, what had changed? Why had he appeared at the Crescent Moon the next day offering his help?

A gasp escaped her lips as the final piece clicked into place.

"You didn't want to help me after all," Anne murmured, stepping back to keep the distance between them. "You just wanted to see how much you could learn about the ring through me, and before I could give it to someone else, you planned to snatch it away."

"But I changed my mind!" Vincent insisted. "When I pulled you into the clock room and felt your powers stirring, some of my old abilities started to awaken. They'd begun to fade, making it nearly impossible to so much as hear a spirit's whisper. But suddenly, their voices were clear again, even stronger than they had been before. I was still intent on destroying the ring, but I wanted to help you along a bit more to understand why my magic was flickering to life again. And then, on the night I showed you the heartsong, I realized that I was mistaken about the ring being cursed."

"Why?" Anne demanded, trying to remember the details of that night to find an answer.

"You told me about a woman with eyes that didn't match, the one who wore the ring in the vision that the spirits pulled you into," Vincent replied. "That description matched my grandmother. She was one of the most powerful witches my family has ever known, so I realized that the ring couldn't have been cursed. And that it had been with us before my uncle was even born."

"You realized it was an heirloom," Anne whispered.

"Yes," Vincent said with a nod of his head. "And that the ring might be the source of our power instead of something that drew it away. Whenever you came to the house, bringing the band along with you, it seemed to come to life again, and so did my own magic. And since the doors only opened for me and no one else in the family, I began to suspect where the ring might belong."

"But you didn't tell me," Anne replied as she clenched her hands and tucked them into the folds of her dress, where it felt like the ring was protected. "You must have still been planning to take it away."

"No," Vincent insisted, surprising Anne by reaching out to rest his hand against her temple, in the same way he did that night he'd led her into the mirror room and asked her to trust him. "That isn't why I kept the truth from you."

"Then why?" Anne asked in disbelief. "What could you possibly care about more than completing your uncle's Task and saving your family's magic?"

Vincent glanced down at the ring then, and an unmistakable expression of raw longing settled across his features. His attention lingered there for only a moment, though, before traveling upward to rest on Anne. As their gazes met, she realized with a start that the desire burning beneath those amber eyes had only intensified.

"I wanted you to stay," he confessed, the words so low and rough that Anne could feel them brush against her skin. "And put the pieces together for yourself so that you wouldn't learn I had planned to betray you."

"I would have understood," Anne murmured, but she could taste the bittersweet flavor of a lie unfurling along the back of her tongue before she'd even had the chance to finish the sentence.

"It was safer to let you make the connection yourself," Vincent said with a shake of his head. "And then, once the ring was back in its place and you could be sure the city was safe, I was going to tell you everything."

Anne could sense the underlying meaning of what Vincent had said, as intensely as she had felt his magic sinking into her veins when she'd let him anchor her. But just as she was about to lean into the warmth of his hand, he drew it away from her face and began to speak again.

"Yesterday, when you let me anchor you, I was certain that you'd see the truth and give me the ring," Vincent said, his voice growing harder as he took a step back, as if he needed to put some distance between them to stay on course. "But you didn't, even though I could sense you found something in those memories that pointed you in the right direction."

"I did see something," Anne admitted, startled by how much she missed the feel of his fingers entangled in her curls. "Your grandmother being given the ring. And all those before her who'd received it, and finally . . ."

"Finally?" Vincent whispered, pressing her forward.

"You," Anne said. "I saw someone passing the ring on to you."

"Then why didn't you give it to me and finish the Task?" Vincent asked, his voice so low and laced with confusion that the sound of it made her wince.

Anne thought of Vincent's position and what it would be like to realize that her entire family was losing their magic, the skills that generations of Quigleys had worked to perfect and pass down fading into dust, though her ancestors had tended to the ends of the spells as gently as one might care for quilts that had an entire spool's worth of histories stitched into their worn fabric. Just imagining the possibility made her shiver, and she understood why Vincent wanted so desperately to put things to rights. When she considered what she would have done in Vincent's place, Anne realized that she'd already forgiven him for deceiving her.

But there were still Mr. Crowley and Philip's destinies to consider. As startling as Vincent's revelation was, Anne hadn't forgotten what had brought her there in the first place: a desire to ensure that their threads of Fate would never be severed.

"I'm going to save Philip," Anne finally confessed. "So that when we finish your uncle's Task, they can be together."

She waited for Vincent's reaction, the texture of the silence thickening between them with every outdrawn breath.

"Anne," he finally sighed. "Philip's spirit has been lingering for too long now."

"No," Anne insisted, throwing her hands upward, as if the simple gesture would have the strength to hold back his doubts. "He can be saved. If we learn what is keeping him here, we can set him free."

She marched over to the doorframe then and ran her fingers over the inscription carved into the woodwork.

"Is she alive?" Anne whispered as she turned back to face Vincent.

"Yes," Vincent replied. "But do you even know where to find her?"

"Not yet," Anne answered.

Vincent rubbed a hand against his temple, as if he could hear the conviction in those two words and knew that Anne would never relent.

"Can't you wait for the ring until we save Philip?" Anne asked. "We're getting so close. I can sense it. If we find May, I know that we can help them both."

"At what cost?" Vincent asked, his voice hardening again. "If we wait any longer, the whole of Michigan Avenue could sink into the lake. And who's to say my family's magic won't disappear entirely? Are you willing to risk the fate of everyone to save them?"

"I want to try," Anne answered.

"You are making a dangerous choice," Vincent murmured. "As the city's Diviner, you know where your duty lies."

Anne felt her cheeks redden in anger then, and before she knew it, she was marching toward him, ripping the fabric from her fingers and flashing the ring inches from his face. The closer it got to him, the warmer the gold became, until she wondered if it was going to singe her skin.

Anne should have been shocked by her reaction, but she knew that this eruption had been smoldering within her since that first night at the manor when she'd whirled around and found herself facing Vincent.

He always seemed to do this to her, draw the deepest parts of herself from the shadows and transform them into something that fueled her fire.

"Then take it!" Anne cried. "Take the ring off my hand if you want and finish your uncle's Task, but I certainly won't be the one to curse him to an eternity apart from the one person he ever truly loved. Not until I've tried everything in my power to find another way."

She watched as Vincent's eyes latched on to the ring and

imagined what it would feel like when he grasped the flesh of her wrist and pulled the band from her finger.

But as the moment drew on, the tension that filled the room started to ebb, leaving behind the stark sound of their breathing and the overpowering scent of peppermint and myrrh infusing the parlor, signaling that their magic was ready to be unleashed at any second.

And then Vincent turned away from her, breaking the spell so abruptly that Anne nearly gasped.

Before she could fully register what had happened, the sharp slap of the door shook the apartment.

He'd left her behind with the ring exactly where it had been before.

Why was it, then, that Anne felt like everything had changed?

CHAPTER 31

A Triangle
Appears just before an unexpected meeting.

Violet didn't bother clutching her hood as she marched down the street, her eyes darting from the card clutched between her bare fingers and the numbers etched along the sides of the brick buildings, which were half-obscured by snow.

Though most would have drawn the velvet ribbons tighter to shield the delicate skin along their cheeks and nose, Violet was beyond caring about the cold and hadn't even noticed that her curls had fallen from her bun and were now whipping furiously in the wind. She was entirely focused on finding the address printed on the bottom of Brigit's calling card, the determination that had been kindling within her warming the tips of her toes and melting away any remnants of winter's chill.

By the time she found the matching number aside a charming red row house, Violet was practically vibrating from anticipation, her foot tapping relentlessly against the icy stoop as she lifted her hand to knock on the front door.

Her knuckles didn't even have a chance to hit the wood, though, before the door creaked open, revealing the landlady, who was so bundled up that it was a wonder she was able to move at all.

"Dear me!" the poor woman cried as she glanced up and saw her unexpected visitor. "Miss Quigley, you must excuse me. I had no idea you were standing here in the cold!"

"You've nothing to apologize for," Violet assured her, trying to speak slowly though all she wanted to do was rush forward. "I've only just arrived."

"All the same," Brigit said in a fluster. "And here I am just about to step out to run an errand."

"Oh, I'm sorry to have come at an inconvenient moment," Violet replied, her foot already lifting to fall back on the step.

Perhaps her intuition hadn't been something to follow without question after all.

"Actually," the older woman said, a note of excitement sparking in her tone, "you've come at just the right time."

A tingling sensation skittered from the base of Violet's spine to the bottom of her neck then.

"You see, a family acquaintance stopped by unexpectedly this morning to pay her respects. She was a close friend of my husband's late aunt and only just heard the news," Brigit continued.

"A family acquaintance," Violet echoed as the rhythm of her heart began to beat to a quicker pace.

"In fact, she might be the person you should speak with if you want to know more about the history of your building," Brigit said as she looped her scarf around her neck. "She just told me that she lived there as a young girl. That's how she got to know my husband's aunt, whose father rented out the apartment at the time."

It can't be, Violet thought to herself.

"What's her name?" Violet asked, her voice shaking as she spoke, though her teeth weren't chattering from the cold.

"Mrs. Margaret Hall, but she was little May Schultz when she lived in the apartment," Brigit answered. "I imagine she has all the answers you've been searching for."

"I believe so," Violet replied as the corners of her lips began to lift into the start of a smile.

"She's sitting in the parlor if you'd like to speak with her yourself," Brigit said, gesturing to a room down the hall. "I'm just going to pop out to the bakery so that I have something to offer her with tea. I'll only be a minute."

"If it's not an imposition," Violet murmured, trying to keep her wavering voice steady.

Brigit must have mistaken Violet's anticipation for a shiver, though, because she quickly ushered her inside, mumbling about warming her bones next to the fire and helping herself to a cup of tea as she began to step down the stoop.

When the front door snapped closed, Violet could hear the crackling of logs in the hearth and the subtle rustling of stiff brocade skirts from the direction that Brigit had nudged her toward. And then she noticed a now-familiar scent drifting down the hallway: the aroma of freshly cut rosemary.

It beckoned her forward, tingling her temples as she took a step and then another until she was nearly turning the corner into the parlor. Something was waiting for her there that had been trying to weave its way into her dreams.

When Violet paused at the threshold, she felt just as she always did when hovering on the edge of the circus platform, lingering in a space where all was possible and wondering if she was going to find her courage in time to take a bold leap.

But as she drew in another breath laced with rosemary, Violet knew with certainty that she needed to step beyond the moment and act.

Turning the corner, she marched into the parlor, only to stop short when she saw an elderly woman sitting by the hearth, her gaze already fixed on Violet as if she'd been expecting her all along.

They continued to stare at each other, the scent of rosemary that Violet had noticed in the hallway intensifying, though she realized now that it wasn't coming from the woman. It seemed to be drifting from the empty seat beside her, as if someone else were sitting in the matching wingback chair that faced the fireplace, the heady notes of their perfume growing stronger from the warmth.

And then Violet caught the scent of chrysanthemums, more subtle than the rosemary, but present nonetheless. And she finally understood.

"They're here," she said before she could help herself, though the words were entangled in a gasp and should have been too rough for anyone to understand.

But the face of the woman sitting in front of her instantly pinched together before falling apart, like she'd been prepared to go on the defense only to let herself shatter.

"I had wondered if anyone would ever come," May finally said, grasping her handkerchief in the way that Violet did when she needed something to cling to.

"Who have you been waiting for?" Violet asked, confused by her reaction.

"One of your kind," May replied. "Just like Crowley."

"You know what I am?" Violet asked, shocked.

"After you've seen magic, you always keep your eyes open for it," May replied. "I used to catch Crowley casting spells for Philip when they thought I wasn't looking. Just the barest wonders, but

I could never turn away. I suppose I've been searching for a hint of enchantment ever since."

Her eyes took on a misty hue then, as if she'd made a habit of falling back into the past, where memories built on sand felt truer than the ground beneath her feet.

"And you practically twinkle with it," May finally continued, her gaze focusing on Violet once more.

Instinctively reaching for her cloak to pull it tighter, Violet was startled to find that the heavy cloth was missing. Brigit must have taken it off to hang on one of the pegs near the door when she wasn't paying attention, and with all the excitement, her magic was shining just a bit brighter than it should have been.

"Crowley was the same at first," May said with a nod of recognition as she watched Violet's hand shift toward her chest. "Reaching to see if his coat was hanging about his shoulders. Though, as the years passed, he became more forgetful. Or perhaps it was because he loved Philip, and you can't love fully when you're worried about clinging to a mask."

"You knew him?" Violet asked as she stepped closer.

"Of course," May said with a smile. "How could I not when he was over so often? Though the older he and my brother became, the more they drew themselves into a world of their own making. Or maybe I was moving outward. Even after all this time, it's difficult to know for certain."

A sadness crept into May's voice then, saturating the nostalgic softness that had been there only moments before and causing her shoulders to curve inward.

"Though it seems that they're both with me now," May said with a slight smile as she glanced at the chair next to her, but there was a weight to her words that made them sound more like a confession. "Just like they were before."

The scent of rosemary and chrysanthemums grew so strong

then that the air became thick and heady, causing moist rivulets to form on Violet's brow. It suddenly seemed as if the room was fuller than it had been before, and she knew for certain then that they were not alone.

"You're what's keeping him here," Violet said, noting the way May's gaze always seemed to return to the wingback chair, like she was making sure that something was still there.

May paused, her shoulders tightening as if she was trying to find a way to protect her secrets, but then she shuddered, all the strength that remained in her body crumbling beneath stark truths.

"Please don't think ill of me," May pleaded, her grasp tightening around her handkerchief as tears began to form in the corners of her eyes.

The sight of them made Violet remember all the sorrows that had poured from her cheeks and onto the pillow whenever her dreams pulled her toward memories of things that might be lost.

"How could I?" Violet answered. "When I'm a sister myself."

There was a world of meaning in that word: "sister." It bespoke ties of love and longing that were so entangled nothing could sever them, not even death.

"We never said goodbye," May said with a deep sigh that suggested she was grateful to finally have someone who could listen to her story. "The last time I saw my brother, we had a horrible argument. I was a young woman then, you see, and had accepted the proposal of a man who was developing quite the reputation in the mercantile business. Philip didn't approve."

"Why not?" Violet asked.

"Because we weren't in love," May explained. "He was everything else I thought I wanted, and I willed myself to believe that it would grow between us eventually, but Philip thought differently.

How could he not when he already knew what it felt like to find someone who made waking up every morning worthwhile?"

She released another shaky breath then.

"Philip did always have a habit of being right in the end," May murmured, the words laced with a lifetime's worth of disappointment. "But I thought I knew better at the time, and the last words I spoke to him were the worst I've ever uttered. I woke the next morning regretting them to my core, but when I went to ask for forgiveness . . . a terrible accident had taken place . . . and he was no longer with us. Something broke inside me then, letting in a well of emptiness that I couldn't fill."

Violet remembered the stifling fear that had gripped her when she thought that she and her sisters would be separated, a numbing terror that had kept her from moving forward. And she understood why the woman sitting before her seemed to be living so fervently in the past.

"The lonelier I grew, the more I wished that my brother were still here, and I remembered a hushed conversation where Crowley told him that ghosts aren't made from anger but love. They remain when the people they've left behind can't seem to let them go," May continued. "And so I clung on. And through all the disappointments, he's been beside me."

"You knew he was there," Violet said, startled by the revelation. She wasn't admonishing May, was merely shocked that she'd been able to find a way to keep her brother with her. "You did it on purpose."

"How could I not?" May sighed. "When I never got the chance to let him go in the first place?"

"But you have it now," Violet said. "You can set them both free."

May blinked again, lifting her glove to her cheek and staining the lily-white fabric with tears.

"How can I do that, knowing I'll be alone?" May asked, her voice so fragile that Violet could hear it cracking into a thousand tiny pieces.

The rosemary notes grew stronger then, and Violet watched as May reached toward her shoulder, as if someone had placed a comforting hand there.

Violet recognized the wealth of longing in that single gesture and struggled to find the words she needed to convince May to let Philip go. If she were asked to cut the only remaining thread that tethered her to Anne or Beatrix, would she have the will to do it?

But then Violet remembered the intricate tapestry that held them all together, the one that tied May to not only Philip and Mr. Crowley but all those souls who wandered about the city in search of the steady comfort of knowing they were moving closer to where they belonged.

She couldn't turn back now.

"Things are shifting out of place," Violet murmured as she stepped in front of May and placed her own hand where the woman had been reaching. "I think you may have sensed it."

May looked startled when Violet's hand clutched her own, as if she'd been so used to grasping at a memory that the feel of flesh and blood beneath her fingers was a shock. But then her gaze turned upward, and Violet saw understanding there.

"Yes," May replied. "I noticed after Crowley returned to us. He'd once told Philip that there are consequences among your people when you leave something important undone, and I suspected that might be the case with him."

"He refused to move forward so that he could be with Philip," Violet explained. "But in doing so, he's caused a disruption, one that can't be mended unless we help him. We know what needs to be done, but if we take that step and Philip isn't ready to go along with him, they will be separated again, perhaps forever. They've been lingering so long in between that the only way to be certain they'll find one another on the other side is if we can make it so they leave together."

An icy chill consumed the room then, so cold that the fragrant notes faded entirely and Violet and May's breath turned into foggy clouds before their faces.

"Why should I be made to choose?" May gasped, crossing her arms over her chest as if the movement would keep her from shattering. "Is their love so much more important than the one that my brother and I share?"

"Of course not," Violet answered. "Love isn't something that can be measured and weighed like coins on a scale. This isn't about deciding which is more important. It's about trying to bring peace to the dead so that the living can go on."

"But what about my peace?" May cried. "How can I go on when this is all that I have left?"

Violet tried to wrap a comforting arm around May, but she pushed her aside.

"Please don't ask it of me," May whispered, her gaze turning away from Violet and toward the empty armchair once more.

"But . . . ," Violet began, only to stop when May cut her off.

"Please," she said again, her tone as cold and icy as the frost that now clung to the windowpanes.

Violet's mind instantly began to spin faster than a top, grasping at all the things she could say to try to convince the woman sitting before her that she was making the wrong choice.

But the rigid set of May's jaw and the way she kept her gaze turned away told Violet that their conversation had come to an abrupt end.

"Won't you talk with me again?" Violet asked. "Brigit can tell you where to find me."

But May remained silent, her attention already drifting away from the chill of the present and back toward the familiar comfort of the past.

Violet nodded then and began to move toward the entryway, sensing that she didn't have a chance of reaching May. Not in that moment.

But as she stepped over the threshold of the parlor, she felt something strange: the sensation of two pairs of hands coming to rest on her own shoulders. It wasn't a firm grip that would have caused her to jump back in alarm, but rather the barest pressure, not unlike what May must have felt when Violet placed her own hand on her shoulder. And then she smelled it again: the aroma of chrysanthemums and fresh rosemary.

"I won't give up," Violet said, though her words weren't meant for May or even herself. "I promise."

And with that, she slipped out of the house and onto the street, where the air wasn't so thick with memories that had been kept from the sunshine for fear of fading.

CHAPTER 32

A Kettle

*Indicates a need for healing and
the search for inner peace.*

Though the thick layers of their woolen coats should have kept them warm enough, the Quigley sisters couldn't stop shivering as they wandered back to the Crescent Moon. They'd gathered in front of the bookshop just before sunset and linked their arms together to ground themselves against the brutal push of the wind. But though they'd managed to fight against the snow and sleet to return home, more than ever, they felt frozen in place, having been given all the pieces they needed to complete the puzzle but unable to draw the picture together.

"It's an impossible position," Anne murmured as the three of them settled into the warmth of the parlor, desperate to find some sense of familiarity among all the revelations that had come to light that day. "To give up the comfort of her brother's presence after all this time could break her."

"Yes," Violet sighed. "I could tell from the way she spoke that he's helped soothe the worst of her disappointments. If left to face them on her own, I fear she'll crumble."

"But if she refuses to help, the world will fall apart around her anyway," Beatrix said from her side of the settee.

Anne leaned forward then and clutched her head between her palms, hoping that the pressure of her hands would push her thoughts in the direction they needed to go to save everyone in time.

"You know I can't let that happen, Bee," she finally murmured, tears starting to press into the corners of her eyes as her thoughts turned to the inevitable conclusion. "I have to protect the city, even if that means finishing Mr. Crowley's Task before Philip can move on. The threads of Fate must be tethered before it's too late."

The house could see that Anne was shaking now and tried to tuck her tighter in an embrace of calico quilts, but she was too lost to notice.

"But we're getting so close," Violet insisted as she and Beatrix shifted so they were each perched on either side of her chair. "Everything's bound to come together in the end. I can feel it."

"You can't know that," Anne replied, her voice so rough and full of despair that it didn't sound like it belonged to her. "It feels as if I can't see past the next second, let alone what might unfold in the coming weeks. I keep reaching for what rests ahead in the hopes of finding another sign, but nothing comes."

"We believe in you," Beatrix said, placing her hand atop Anne's knee. "You are our sister and the city's Diviner."

But Anne's worries had pulled her so far from the comfort of the parlor that she didn't even hear what Beatrix had said.

"He was right," Anne whispered.

"Who was right?" Violet asked, her brow creasing at the sudden shift in conversation.

"I don't trust myself," Anne finally confessed, the words unfurling a bitter flavor on her tongue. "It's as if I'm frozen in place, afraid that each step I take could lead toward disaster."

Violet sat up straighter then and clutched Beatrix and Anne's hands in her own.

"Do you remember what she used to tell us?" Violet asked, not even needing to say Clara's name for her sisters to understand who was on her mind. "When the snow and sleet had fallen for so many weeks that we were begging her to tell us when spring would return?"

Anne shook her head, as if she were about to tell Violet that they didn't have time to return to the past when the future was so uncertain.

"Do you remember?" Violet asked again, her hold growing even tighter.

"Winter serves a purpose," Anne said, the words bringing back a rush of memories.

"It slows us down enough to take stock of ourselves," Beatrix continued. "And remember all the things from our past that we should carry forward."

"The season of waiting and realization," Violet murmured. "That's what she always called it. When we felt trapped and thought the answer was something to be found outside ourselves, she told us to pause and search for the power within that would bring us rest."

"I feel like I've used all my power already," Anne said with a shake of her head. "That there's nothing left to find."

"There's always something left to find," Beatrix said as she lifted her hands and let the light of the fire flicker against the curves and consonants that looked as if they would soon emerge from beneath the grooves between her knuckles. "If you remember to listen for it."

"You just need to trust yourself again," Violet added. "As you've told us before, magic knows the difference between love and duty. Let it show you the way instead of stifling it with self-doubt, and all will be well again."

"The stakes are so much higher than they were before," Anne whispered.

"They are," Violet said, leaning forward so that she could stare Anne straight in the eye. "But you've grown stronger too."

Anne was still holding on to her breath, uncertain if she could believe what she'd just heard: that she was powerful enough to make the right choice.

"Trust yourself," Violet whispered. "That's all you need to do."

Anne closed her eyes then, using the darkness to draw deeper into her awareness, where her magic was stirring. Focusing on the warmth of her sisters' hands, she allowed her attention to drift away from all the worries that had stifled her and let other sensations drift inward, the firm grasp of Violet's fingers a reminder of all the love anchoring her to home.

The now-familiar scent of rosemary and the rich aroma of aged paper grew so strong that she could taste it, and beyond that she could hear the ticking of her own clock. The metallic strikes grew so loud that Anne couldn't even hear her own breath any longer, and for a moment, she wondered if they'd all slipped away from the house entirely and into another place where everything could be depended on to unfold at just the right time.

And then Anne's eyes snapped open, so suddenly that the house whipped back the curtains, revealing the snow falling outside the windows.

"What is it?" Violet asked hurriedly.

"You were right," Anne said, the words nearly lost in a sigh of utter relief. "Everything is already set on its course. We just need to wait for the final piece to fall into place on its own."

"What's the final piece?" Beatrix asked.

"I'm not sure," Anne said. "But my magic is telling me that we've done all we can to ensure it happens, and just when it needs to."

"Are you certain?" Violet asked.

"I am," Anne answered with a nod. "More certain than I've been in quite a long time."

The sense of assurance that laced her words sank into the shadowy corners of the house, warming the places that had grown colder the longer the Quigleys had let their doubts fester.

"Then we will wait," Violet said as she let her head fall against Anne's shoulder, shifting slightly so that Beatrix could do the same from her side of the wingback chair.

The three of them remained like that as the logs continued to snap in the grate. And while they listened to the crackles in the hearth and their own steady breaths, they did just as Clara Quigley had told them: rest and rediscover the home within themselves.

CHAPTER 33

A Table

*Signifies that someone will
soon give their support.*

The following afternoon, a stillness settled over the Crescent Moon, so potent and calming that the customers noticed it as soon as their boots passed over the threshold.

It wasn't a silence that caused their chests to tighten in expectation or their shoulder blades to draw back in alarm.

No, as the ladies began to slip out of their coats and unravel their scarves, they were reminded of what it felt like to wake before dawn and sit in the quiet of a place between night and day, when for a few strange moments, they were both intensely aware and at ease all at once, suspended beyond their regrets of the past or worries over the future.

And as they wrapped their icy fingers around warm porcelain cups and drew in the rich fragrance of their tea, the women in the shop didn't feel the need to speak at all. They were content to simply be and settle into the sensation of waiting, though it wasn't clear to them what, exactly, this pause was building toward.

By the time Anne would have needed to begin reading the signs at the bottom of her customers' cups by candlelight, no one seemed to want a glimpse of their fortune at all, content to merely close their eyes, lean a bit more deeply against the back of their chairs, and listen to the sound of tinkling porcelain and crackling logs.

Anne, too, was surprised to find that it felt like she'd loosened the strings of her corset and could finally take a deep breath. Now, instead of reminding her that time was slipping away, the steady clicking of her clock seemed to reassure Anne that everything would fall into place at just the right moment. It was a strange sensation, being unburdened of the self-doubt that had weighed down each and every decision, but as Anne paused to take in the sight of the shop, she had to admit that it was a feeling she hoped would linger.

Drawing in a cinnamon-tinted breath, Anne leaned against the wainscoting and let her own eyes fall closed, taking note of the shapes that danced beneath her lids. Rocking chairs, wheels, and violets shifted into view, reassuring her that a turn of fate was just around the corner. All she needed to do was wait and trust her ability to read the signs.

Gradually, though, Anne became aware that the ring around her finger was getting warmer, as if she'd rested it for too long against the bar of the oven door. And just when she opened her eyes to glance down at her hand, she heard the barest creaking of the garden gate. The house had managed to wake itself just in time to announce that they had an unexpected visitor.

By the time a knock carried into the parlor from the back door, Anne was already stepping into the kitchen, the sudden aroma of myrrh hinting at who was waiting outside.

Vincent's amber eyes met hers as she opened the door, and again, she felt the ring flash with a sudden jolt of recognition that seemed to sink into her veins and skitter up the flesh of her forearms.

For a moment, the pair stood at the threshold, not so much searching for the words they wanted to say as they were carefully reading each other's faces.

"May I come inside?" Vincent finally asked.

Though his tone was firm and steady, Anne noticed that he clutched his hat just a fraction tighter while waiting for her answer, as if unsure of how she might respond.

Anne stood in silence for a moment and then slowly opened the door further.

The pots and pans rattled as Vincent stepped over the threshold and set down his hat, the house trying its best to clear the worst of the crumbs off its counters and primp itself up for this unexpected visitor who made Anne's heart race.

"Would you like some tea?" Anne asked as she glanced about the room, making sure that they had the kitchen to themselves.

At first, Vincent remained silent, and Anne found her cheeks reddening in embarrassment for asking such a question. After the way their last conversation had ended, it seemed ridiculous somehow to be offering him refreshments.

But just as she opened her mouth to sigh and turn away from the kettle boiling on the stovetop, Vincent finally spoke.

"I would," he said. "If it's not too much trouble."

Anne glanced up in surprise before quickly turning away to face the wall of tea tins and jars stuffed to the brim with leaves.

"What kind would you prefer?" she asked slowly, wondering what he might say.

"Whichever you think suits me best," Vincent replied. "You're the expert, after all."

Nodding, Anne gestured for him to sit at the table while she considered the rows of tins.

Eventually, her fingers grasped a plain black canister with gold edging along the trim. She carried it over to the boiling water before pulling a well-worn teapot off the countertop along with a pair of matching cups.

When she finally sat down at the table across from Vincent and placed the pot of tea between them, she could tell by the subtle furrow between his brows that he was curious.

"We need to wait for the tea to brew," Anne warned him. "Only a few minutes, but the timing needs to be just right."

"I see," Vincent said with a nod, though from the way he was eyeing the handle of the pot, Anne could tell that he'd rather go ahead and fill his cup.

Again, a silence enveloped the room that was different from the pleasant stillness of the parlor. It was full of expectation and the sting of their last exchange, the words that they'd cast at one another so potent that it felt like they were being spoken aloud once more.

"Have you come to take it?" Anne asked as she tapped the gold band softly against the top of the table.

Vincent's attention slid to her hand then, his eyes glinting in the way they always did when something caught his interest.

But then his gaze shifted from the band to Anne's face, though the sharp intensity in his expression remained, as if he were still looking at something he wanted.

To Anne's surprise, she didn't feel the impulse to shift back in her seat. Instead, she found herself doing the opposite, leaning forward so that they were drawn closer together instead of farther apart.

"Do you truly believe that you can save everyone if we wait?" Vincent asked.

Anne considered him for a moment, taking note of the firm set of his jaw and the way he seemed to be reading her face, as if every flicker of her lashes and shift of her lips carried a wealth of meaning.

"More than ever," Anne answered. "Everything is on the right course. We only need for the pieces to come together."

The silence that filled the kitchen was saturated with the worst and best possibilities, and the house couldn't help but wring its hands alongside Anne as they waited to see what would happen next.

"Then I will wait," Vincent said, easing away the tension that rested between him and Anne and leaving behind only the scent of the brewing tea. "Until you decide to give me the ring yourself."

"Why?" Anne asked, confused by his sudden change of heart. "When there's so much at stake for you?"

Vincent glanced away from her then to stare at his own hands as he leaned back in his chair, but it wasn't long before his eyes returned to hers.

"Our magic is different," he said. "Mine is centered on drawing out the past to provide comfort in the present. Yours is linked to the future. In this case, it seems that you are the one who should know which path to take."

He paused for a moment then, and to Anne, it seemed as if he was deciding whether to say something more.

"And my uncle deserves peace," Vincent finally murmured. "I don't want to be the reason he and Philip are separated in the end either."

Anne wondered if he was trying to deceive her somehow, pretending that he had conceded with the intention of turning the cards in his favor. But then she noticed the shadows and fine wrinkles around his eyes, telltale signs that he'd had too little sleep. And in those lines, Anne read the signs of regret. They were the same as the ones that she'd seen reflected in her mirror that morning when she thought of the harsh words they'd spoken the day before.

"You trust me, then?" Anne asked.

Though Anne tried to tell herself that it didn't matter what Vincent said, she couldn't help but notice that a knot seemed to be building beneath her breastbone as she waited for him to answer.

"I do," Vincent said with a nod. "I've seen your selflessness, Anne. Even when it came to embracing your own power, you never lost sight of your purpose. If you say that everything will come together as it needs to, then I believe you."

Anne felt the tension in her chest ease, replaced by a warm sensation she couldn't quite place. It made the tips of her toes tingle, but she quickly pushed the feeling aside, hoping that she could snuff it out before a blush rose to her cheeks.

"Well, then," she finally managed to murmur as she pretended to brush aside crumbs from the pristine tabletop.

"You concede to nothing, do you?" Vincent said as a ghost of a smile began to work its way into the corners of his mouth. "Even when it comes to a compliment."

"Not often," Anne admitted with a cautious grin. "I've been told on more than one occasion that I have quite the stubborn streak."

"The same has been said of me," Vincent replied, his words instantly rekindling the not-unpleasant prickling feeling in her toes.

"It's ready now," Anne said as she focused on pouring the tea into their cups, releasing a rich, smoky aroma that infused the kitchen as the steam spilled from the spout.

"What is it?" he asked, obviously drawn to the fragrance and curious about what it would taste like.

"It's not a common blend," Anne explained. "Dark oolong

mixed with assam and puerh. It has a bold, smoky taste that can't be balanced out, no matter how many spoonfuls of sugar you pour into the cup. The flavor is too strong for some."

"Is it unpleasant for you as well?" Vincent asked.

In response, Anne lifted her own cup and took a sip.

"It took some time," Anne replied. "But I've found that the flavor has grown on me."

The house felt something shift between them then. It was a subtle change that reminded it of the way the nails in the wainscoting sometimes loosened during the height of summer, when the heat forced the boards to give way.

Vincent's hand moved forward, and Anne expected him to reach for his tea so that he could taste the notes that she'd just described. But instead of grasping the handle and drawing it to his mouth, his fingers laced through Anne's, pulling her closer until his lips were brushing against hers.

It felt just as if she'd fallen into a memory again, one filled with heat and life and longing, but this time, another kind of spell was threading its way between them.

And for once, Anne was more than willing to let go and see where the enchantment carried her.

CHAPTER 34

A Raven

*Symbolizes foresight, prophecy,
and connection with the spirits.*

Before the house had lit the fire in the grate or heard Vincent grasp the handle of the garden gate, Beatrix was sitting in the bookshop with her finger perched on the top-right corner of a novel.

There was only one page left in the story, and once she pulled it back to reveal the final lines, everything would be brought to a close.

Though she had a strong sense of how the book would end, Beatrix lingered with her thumb along the back cover, in slight disbelief that she'd have to say goodbye to the characters, who had become more alive with each paragraph.

Leaning her head against the smooth velvet of the wingback chair, she closed her eyes and imagined how the last words of the story were going to make her feel. Would they cause her chest to rumble with quiet laughter? Her hands to grip the binding a bit tighter? A tear that she hadn't realized was building to slip down her cheek? There was a wealth of possibility in just a few short sentences, but she knew every scenario would leave her feeling more at home in her soul than she had before her eyes met the first line.

Just as the tip of her finger started to dip beneath the corner of the page, though, Beatrix heard something—the gentle creaking of the front door.

Startled, she gazed over the top of her book and watched as an elderly woman bundled in layers of heavy black wool and satin stepped into the shop, her shoulders hunched against the merciless whip of the early evening winds.

As she pulled back the hood of her cloak and began to peer about the shop, Beatrix couldn't help but think that she looked lost, her eyes unfocused and slowly shifting from one corner of the room to the next. But then, something else entirely began to settle into her expression. It was the same look that had crossed over Beatrix's own face the moment she'd returned to the Crescent Moon, an almost childlike wonder that she'd somehow managed to trick time and slip so thoroughly back into a cherished memory.

"It's the same," Beatrix heard the woman whisper to herself. "Just the same."

A book that Beatrix hadn't realized was resting on the arm of the chair toppled to the floor as she shifted, the slight thump instantly drawing her visitor's attention.

"Oh," the stranger gasped, her eyes widening in surprise. "I'm so sorry. I didn't know anyone was here."

The woman turned her back to Beatrix then, her hand reaching for the doorknob, the hasty movement conveying a deep sense of embarrassment.

"Please, don't go," Beatrix said as she rose from her chair and pushed her spectacles higher up her nose. "Are you looking for something in particular?"

The question took Beatrix herself by surprise. She hadn't ever considered opening the front door and selling the books that rested along the shelves. Her thoughts only went so far as the next chapter of the story she was reading, but the words had come before she knew what was being said.

The woman shook her head, and her mouth was already forming the telltale shape of a "no." But then her gaze landed on the book that had fallen beside the chair, the one that Beatrix hadn't remembered putting there, and her eyes widened in recognition.

"What's that?" she asked, her voice softening as she took the smallest step away from the door.

Beatrix turned to where she was looking and leaned down to grab the book. The light pouring in from the windows was fainter now, but she could just make out the blue cover.

"It's a fairy-tale collection," Beatrix replied with a grin. "One that's been well loved, by the look of the pages."

The woman drew closer still then, as if she wanted to reach out and touch the cover but couldn't quite bring herself to do so.

"Would you like to see it?" Beatrix asked as she extended the book toward her guest.

The woman glanced back at the cover, clearly warring with herself. But eventually, she nodded and shifted forward, grasping the spine with a shaking hand.

Beatrix watched as she ran the tips of her fingers over the book, obviously enjoying what it felt like to touch the cloth binding and smooth gilded letters of the title.

But instead of turning to the first page, as most readers would, the woman reached for a spot in the very center of the book and flipped it open, as one does when they've read a story so many times that their hands remember where to find the best part.

"You've read it before," Beatrix murmured in wonder. "This book was yours."

The woman's gaze was still locked on the page that she'd turned to, but she nodded silently.

"You must be May," Beatrix murmured gently, finally drawing the pieces together.

"I had forgotten this," May replied in disbelief, as if she hadn't heard Beatrix at all. She was entirely absorbed in the book now, the feel of the pages against her thumbs and scent of aged paper drawing her away from the present and into the past. "My brother used to make me tell him the stories aloud when he was teaching me how to read. He said that everything I needed to learn could be found in fairy tales."

"Is he the one who left the note?" Beatrix asked, gesturing toward the very back of the book where the text had been crossed through.

"Yes," May murmured, her gaze still fixed on the words beneath her fingertips. "He was always saying that . . . *a good story has no end.*"

Beatrix knew that she should have pressed May then, begged her to help them so that everyone could meet a happy fate.

But in that moment, all she saw was a reader slipping into the familiar comfort of a beloved story, and she didn't have it in her to disturb that kind of magic.

"Was this your favorite?" Beatrix asked with a smile as she stepped beside May and looked down at the page.

As she expected, it was the tale that had been dog-eared so many times that the corner at the top was nearly falling away, the one about the sister whose brothers turned into ravens.

"It was," May whispered. "I haven't given it a thought since I was a child, but now it seems as if I could recite it word for word."

"The stories closest to our hearts have that effect," Beatrix agreed with a nod of understanding. "We may forget them, but they always find their way back to us."

"Whenever I read it to Philip, I'd tell him that I was going to be like the girl in the tale one day," May said, her voice rough with the tears that she was holding at bay. "That if he ever needed me to, I would walk across the whole world to save him."

Beatrix remained silent, sensing somehow that she needed to let May wander down the path she'd stumbled onto instead of pushing her in a particular direction.

"This was Philip's shop, you know," May said as she looked about the shelves. "He opened it after our parents passed the mercantile store on to him. Said he wanted to fill it with what people really needed: stories that would help them discover what was worth living for."

She took in a deep breath then, the barest start of a smile pulling at the corner of her lips as she sank into the scent of polished wood shelves, aged paper, and leather-bound books and let the aroma carry her back.

"After he died, I couldn't bring myself to step foot in here," May continued. "And when I finally wanted to return, I heard it was dusty and broken. I didn't know if I could face it then either."

"It seems to have come alive again," Beatrix said as she ran her hand across the shelf and took in the sight of the shop alongside May.

It had struck a few lamps, and now shadows were dancing playfully across the edges of the books, as if tempting them to wander with their hands trailing along the spines until they felt like they'd found just the right one.

"I didn't think it was possible," May murmured, her eyes turning toward Beatrix then. "You're like her, aren't you?"

Beatrix's brow creased in confusion.

"The woman who came to see me yesterday," May explained. "The one who told me that I needed to stop holding on to Philip. She looked just like you."

"We are sisters," Beatrix said with a nod, understanding now.

"Tell me," May said as she stared down at the open book. "Would you let her go? Even if you weren't certain you'd see each other again."

Beatrix paused, trying her best to find the words to describe something that seemed inexplicable.

"I'm like you," she finally answered. "I'd walk the whole world for my sister if she needed me to save her. Even if it meant losing her in the end."

The tears that May had been holding back slid down her cheeks then, and suddenly, the scent of rosemary began to rise alongside the aroma of stories waiting to be read.

"I believe you're right," May said after she wiped away the worst of her tears. "We are the same."

Beatrix stepped forward and grasped May's hand in her own, and when their fingers met over the pages of the book, the words that had been lingering just beneath Beatrix's awareness sprang to life, unfurling a story that needed to be told.

And as the voices of her characters grew stronger, sentences spilled out across the groves of her fingers and palms until the entire surface of her hands was impressed with the threads of her next novel.

Then, as she watched May's eyes widen and felt the rumblings of another story come to life beneath her skin, Beatrix felt the distinct sensation of warm oil pouring down the crown of her skull and sinking deep within her bones. It was so strong that she had to lean against the nearest bookshelf for support, worried that her legs were going to give out beneath her.

Suddenly, she remembered Violet describing the same sensation when the three of them had stood in the circus ring after her first performance, just after she completed her Task.

Could it be?

"Maybe there's still a bit of magic left to discover after all," May whispered as she gazed in wonder at Beatrix's hands, just as a child does when they first turn their head up toward the night sky and see the stars.

"There certainly is," Beatrix said as she faced May and smiled. "For all of us."

CHAPTER 35

A Ring

Represents hope, unity, and completion.

Just as Anne and Vincent were reaching the bottoms of their cups in the kitchen of the Crescent Moon, the bells tethered to the door began to rattle, as if the house was shaking in anticipation.

"Is something wrong?" Vincent asked as his gaze darted around the room before settling on Anne.

"No," Anne replied as she rose from her chair and rested her palms against the smooth oak of the table, listening to what the house was trying to tell them. "I think it's just the opposite."

"Someone's coming!" Violet cried as she barreled into the kitchen with such force that the house had to cling to the decorative porcelain plates hanging on the walls to keep them from shattering. "The bells on the front door are jingling even though no one's turned the handle."

Violet took in another breath then to continue speaking, but the words on her tongue seemed to vanish when she turned and saw Vincent sitting at the table, his gaze still darting about the room, but always returning to Anne.

Before Anne had a chance to explain why Vincent Crowley of all people was sitting in the middle of their kitchen, though, the soft murmur of two voices drew everyone's attention to the back door.

As the sound drew closer, the ticking of Anne's watch became louder and louder until it could have been mistaken for the grandfather clock whose chimes had enough strength to echo through the whole house. And then, just as the smaller hand hit twelve, the door opened, revealing Beatrix and May's hooded figures in the threshold.

"I told you that everyone would be waiting," Beatrix said to May as they turned back the hoods of their cloaks and brushed away the snowflakes that clung to their shoulders.

May's stance was rigid at first, the bones of her spine and neck still stiff with cold and a lingering sense of indecision.

But as she tapped the heels of her boots against the well-worn rag rug and took in the sight of the teapots displayed across the shelves, each so colorful and distinct in its own way that she couldn't help choosing her favorite, the stern set of her shoulders began to loosen.

"It feels just like coming home again," May whispered as her eyes continued to catch on all the details of the room.

Eventually, though, her gaze left the comforting clutter stacked along the cabinets and settled on Violet.

"I've remembered something important," May said as she took a careful step toward her.

"And what is that?" Violet asked.

"What it truly means to be a sister," May replied as she reached for her shoulder, just as she had the day before when it looked like she was trying to grasp a hand that had settled there. "I'm here to save him. To let him go his own way so they can finally be at peace."

The fragrance of warm cinnamon bread and citrus scones was overpowered then by the scent of rosemary and chrysanthemums, and the Quigley sisters knew that they had just welcomed two more guests.

"You don't know how much this means," Anne said as she stepped forward and grasped May's free hand in her own. "For all of us."

"I think I'm beginning to understand," May replied with a nod as she gave Anne's palm a gentle squeeze.

When her fingers brushed against the ring, though, May grew still, and her eyes shot downward.

"It can't be," May murmured as she lifted Anne's hand and drew it closer to get a better view of the hourglass etching. "This is Philip's ring."

"You recognize it?" Anne asked, surprised.

"Of course," May answered as she ran her thumb along the smooth surface, the familiarity of the gesture hinting that she'd done the same thing many times before. "He wore it on a chain around his neck when we were children, but when he grew big enough, he never took it off his left hand. I've always wondered where it went after he passed."

The room felt thick with memories as May continued to gaze at the ring.

"Philip used to tell me a story that he'd made up about it when I was a young girl," she continued. "After we'd read through the fairy-tale book so many times that the pages seemed like they were going to give way from the spine."

"What kind of story?" Anne asked.

May paused then and closed her eyes, distancing herself from the current moment so that she could better draw out a tale that had been tucked in the very back of her mind, waiting for just the right moment to emerge again.

"I'm sure I won't be able to tell it quite like him," May said hesitantly.

"That's the way it's meant to be," Beatrix reassured her. "Stories are living things, after all, just like people."

The candles in the kitchen flickered strangely then as the house leaned in to listen alongside the others. And as May's memory of the tale grew stronger, so did the shadows cast along the walls, the light dimming when the Crescent Moon closed its eyes so it could better imagine the story that was about to unfold.

"Once upon a time," May began, the familiar words carrying a kind of magic all of their own, "there was a family who had the power to speak to those who had passed on. They brought comfort to the living and the dead, tying up ends that still needed to be trimmed or tightened."

Anne heard Vincent take a step closer then, drawn to May's words like a moth to a flame. He was standing so close to her now that Anne was tempted to lean back so that her shoulders would graze his chest.

"One day, they were called upon by a witch who no one else would help," May continued. "She'd lost something close to her heart, and darkness had seeped into the gaps left behind. Her grief had made her a bitter creature, and she was met only with fear and repulsion from those she stumbled across. The family gave her peace so that she could find a new purpose: helping others recover the things that seemed to have slipped away. And in return, the witch gifted them a ring."

May smiled then, as if speaking the story aloud again was helping her find something that she thought had been lost as well.

"It was no ordinary ring, of course," May said, her voice taking on a more confident hue as she drifted deeper into the tale. "The witch had enchanted it so that the family's magic would grow stronger the longer her gift was in their possession. But as it always is with fairy tales, there was an important instruction. The ring would only work if passed down to the person who'd been born with the most power and the greatest willingness to share it. They would be the ring's keeper and ensure its history remained a secret. For even the best of families will begin to bicker over an heirloom, and then the witch's magic would destroy the very thing it wanted to reward. The person who wore the ring would reveal the truth only when they passed it on to its next keeper."

The ring grew warm then, and May's eyes widened as she seemed to notice the change.

Carefully, Anne removed it from her hand and gently placed it in May's palm.

"Did Philip say how the ring's keeper knew who to pass it on to?" Anne asked as May ran the tip of her finger along the gold.

"It would let them know by growing warmer beneath their touch," she answered in wonder, confirming Anne's suspicions.

May grew silent then, and the flames dancing atop the candlewicks became a bit brighter, signaling that her story had drawn to a close.

"What do I need to do now?" she asked. "To let him go?"

Everyone's gaze settled on Anne then, waiting expectantly for her to guide them toward what needed to happen next.

But instead of stepping forward, Anne did something that she knew would surprise them all. She moved to the side so that May and Vincent were standing in full view of each other.

"Oh," May murmured as she let her attention shift to Vincent for the first time since she stepped over the threshold. "You look so much like him."

Vincent nodded, understanding that she was talking about his uncle.

"I think . . . ," May began as she glanced from the ring to Vincent. "This belongs to you."

She stretched out her hand then, the band resting in the center of her palm.

Vincent stared down at the gift that was being offered to him, but instead of taking it from May, he reached forward with both hands and wrapped her fingers around the ring.

"Let me help you first," Vincent said. "So that they can both move on together."

"Can you do that?" May asked, her voice wavering again. "So that I don't have to let him go all on my own?"

"Yes," Vincent replied softly. "I can help you."

May released a shaky sigh and then put her free hand atop Vincent's.

"I'm ready," she said. "What do I need to do?"

"Tell him goodbye," Vincent replied in a tone that suggested there was a wealth of meaning beneath that simple answer.

And as the scent of cypress and myrrh started to fill the room, wrapping May in a comforting hold that drew out the best memories of her brother, the Quigleys started to feel recollections coming to life that weren't their own.

Laughter that echoed against the walls of a staircase. The soft rumble of a young man's voice as he read from a book. Someone's arms pulling them into an embrace that felt like home. And though these echoes of the past didn't belong to the Quigleys, they made the sisters feel just as they had when they'd held hands a year ago and tucked away all the memories that would tether them to one another when they were apart.

"Goodbye," May finally whispered, and though tears were streaming down her cheeks, she was smiling.

As she spoke, May slipped the ring onto Vincent's finger, and the scent of rosemary and chrysanthemums grew so strong that the neighbors sat up in their settees and wondered if spring had somehow made an early arrival.

But the fragrance soon began to slip from the kitchen and out of the house entirely, wrapping May in one last embrace before fading from the present.

"He's gone now," May said as she opened her eyes and gazed about the room, her expression finally settled into one of peace and acceptance.

"They both are," Vincent added in answer to the Quigleys' silent question. "They've moved on together."

"Does that mean Mr. Crowley's Task is finished?" Anne asked cautiously.

Vincent held up the ring then, and she noticed that for once, the grains of sand etched along the surface were sitting perfectly still, as if the hourglass had finally come to rest too.

The sight of it was all the answer the Quigleys needed.

"Are you all right?" Beatrix asked as she looped a hand through the crook of May's elbow.

"I think so," May replied with a nod as she pulled Beatrix a bit closer. "I don't feel as alone as I thought I would."

Anne watched as the shadows that May and Beatrix's bodies cast against the wall shifted ever so slightly in the candlelight. Their silhouettes resembled two daffodils swaying in the wind, and they instantly made her think of long-awaited dreams finally coming to fruition.

"You won't feel alone again," Anne said, her tone as firm as when she was reading a sign at the bottom of a cup.

May gazed up at her, skeptical at first, but the longer she stared into Anne's eyes, the more her hesitation gave way to hope.

"You know," May murmured as a smile returned to her face and she wiped away her tears, "I think I believe you."

CHAPTER 36

An Opened Cage
Emerges when dreams are
about to take flight.

By the time the lingering notes of rosemary and chrysanthemums had faded from the kitchen, the Quigleys were settled in the family parlor enjoying the peaceful glow of the candlelight. The moment that a spark struck in the grate, cedar and citrus had infused the room, kindling a sense of warmth that went beyond toasty fingers and toes. As the house watched the sisters tuck themselves beneath quilts softened by slumber and took in the sight of their hands wrapped around hot porcelain, it breathed out a long-held sigh of satisfaction and drifted into the delights of an evening undisturbed by the clicking of a clock.

For what felt like the first time since they'd all returned home, the silence that enveloped the room wasn't teeming with unspoken worries. The sense that something had been left behind or forgotten was gone now, snapped away the instant that Vincent had slipped on the ring, leaving behind only the crackle of the logs and the gentle sound of the wind brushing against the windows.

It wasn't until Violet's foot began to tap against the rug, the steady *thump-thump-thump* eclipsing the gentler noises in the room, that the house remembered some things were still waiting to be put to rights.

"Do you think that they are truly gone?" Violet asked suddenly, breaking the easy quiet that her sisters had fallen into.

Though she kept her eyes fixed on the flames in the grate, Violet could feel Anne and Beatrix's gazes shift toward her.

"Philip and Mr. Crowley?" Anne asked.

Violet nodded then, still turned away from her sisters.

"Yes," Anne replied, sounding surprised by the question. "They have well and truly passed on."

"What's wrong, Vi?" Beatrix asked, leaning toward her sister to place a gentle hand on her shoulder. "Aren't you pleased?"

"Of course I am," Violet said.

"Then what's troubling you?" Anne asked.

The texture of the room shifted, as if a space in the comfortable silence was starting to open to make room for another revelation.

"I think he was trying to show me something," Violet whispered.

"Mr. Crowley?" Beatrix asked, her brows furrowing in confusion.

"No," Violet answered. "Philip. The scent of rosemary started to slip into my dreams, pulling me away from the worst of possibilities and toward something else. But now that he's gone, I'm afraid I'll never quite know what he was trying to show me."

"What kind of dreams were these?" Anne asked, her question slow and steady, as if she knew the answer would finally reveal what had brought her sister back to the Crescent Moon.

"Nightmares," Violet said, the word rough and breathless. "Of a mistake that I made."

"What kind of mistake?" Beatrix asked.

Violet paused then, worried that sharing the memory would give it even more life than it already had.

But then she smelled peppermint and sandalwood, the familiar notes drawing her away from the worst of possibilities and toward the present moment.

"I made Emil leap into an act we weren't ready for," Violet finally confessed. "And when the time came for me to catch him ... I couldn't."

Anne and Beatrix leaned forward then and grasped Violet's hands in their own, surprise and sympathy etched into every gesture.

"He's fine," Violet continued, wanting to reassure her sisters. "He's recovering and eager to perform together again in the spring."

"But you aren't so certain," Beatrix said, her thoughts obviously trailing back to the way Violet's feet had grown unnaturally still against the floorboards when she'd first returned to the shop, as if she had commanded them to conceal her desire for movement.

"How can I be when I keep reliving the moment his hand slipped farther and farther away from mine?" Violet replied. "It's all I've dreamed of for months."

Distracted by Violet's confession, the house loosened its hold on the windowpane, letting in an icy breeze that instantly sank into the sisters' skin and caused them to shiver.

"But what does this have to do with Philip?" Anne asked as she shook away the chill.

"My dream started to change," Violet explained. "I wasn't reliving the past anymore. But I don't think I was seeing the future either. It was like a lucid dream, where I had a choice in what was going to unfold."

"And what choice did you make?" Beatrix asked.

"I was going to tell Emil that I couldn't perform," Violet replied. "But when I opened my mouth to say the words, the scent of rosemary became so potent that I woke up."

Her sisters sat in silence for a moment, seemingly trying to decipher the meaning of what Violet had just said.

"Do you think it's a vision?" Violet finally found the courage to ask, turning to Anne with a pensive expression. "Am I starting to be able to see my own future?"

Anne considered her for a moment, pausing long enough to make Violet's heart begin to race, but then she leaned forward and grasped her hand.

"I think it's something much more significant," Anne answered.

"What's that?" Violet asked.

"What you *want* from the future," Anne said. "Fantasy can be even more powerful than fortune. Possibility begins in our imagination, after all. And when we start to envision what could unfold, we give it a magic all its own. Philip must have tried to stop you from giving power to a choice that he thought you might regret. After watching May linger for so long in the mistakes of the past, it's likely he couldn't let you meet the same fate."

"But I don't know what I want," Violet said, her voice breaking. "Not when my instincts have already led me toward disaster."

"If you don't give yourself the chance to fantasize about the best of what's to come, how can you expect to recover what's been buried beneath your pain?" Anne murmured.

"I'm not certain that what I've lost is worth keeping," Violet sighed.

"Oh, Vi," Beatrix said as she laced her fingers through Anne's free hand so that the three of them formed an unending link. "Of course it is."

They sat for a moment there, threaded into a single braid as they had been before, savoring the sensation all the more because they knew it was only that . . . a moment. Eventually, they'd have to let one another go again so that they could continue their journeys down the paths that had parted for them.

But for now, they were simply the Quigley sisters once more.

"Let yourself dream of the best to come, Violet," Anne whispered, her tone taking on the same hue as when she was gazing over tea leaves or tarot cards. "And by the morning, you'll find what has been lost."

And in less time than it took for the next ember to crackle in the hearth, Violet decided to do just that.

Let herself fall into fantasies that could become the fabric of her reality.

❄

Later that night, as Violet slipped between the warm sheets and drew in a breath laced with lavender, she wondered if what Anne had said was true—that by sunrise, she'd recover what had been lost.

Releasing a shaky sigh, Violet closed her eyes, expecting to toss and turn for so long that her shoulders would grow stiff and there'd be no hope of rest.

But, to her surprise, the moment she grew still on the pillow, she found herself drifting into that place between the here and now and dusty dreams beyond the firm grasp of time.

With each softening breath, Violet felt as if she was drawing on an unfamiliar power that sank into the tips of her toes like liquid gold and pushed aside the stony emptiness that she worried might never crack.

It wasn't long until she felt strangely full and weightless all at once, losing touch with the worn sheets beneath her body and shifting into another place entirely, one that was tinged with candlelight and the soft murmur of a crowd.

In what could have been an eternity or a blink of an eye, Violet was standing on the wooden platform, the hem of the same blue satin dress from her last dream kissing the tops of her bare feet.

She could see the gold halo of the performers below, the light of their sparklers and ribbons set aflame, tempting her forward. Instead of feeling repulsed by the effect, though, Violet found herself taking the barest step toward the edge, a moth drawn to the sheer beauty of the glow.

And then the fragrance of midnight smoke slipped into her awareness, and she knew what she would hear next.

"Are you ready, Wildfire?" Emil's voice rumbled against her back as his hands traced the gentle curves of her shoulders.

Violet thought of what her sisters had said about the power that came from fantasizing about what you wanted your own future to look like. About learning from your mistakes instead of being ensnared by them. And in that moment, Violet let go of the guilt and fear that had bound her and grasped on to what she knew was worth keeping: a thirst for life and unexpected turns of Fate.

"Yes," she said, the tail end of her answer dancing in the wind as she leapt toward the edge, picturing exactly how she wanted the scene to unfurl.

In what could have been an eternity or a blink of an eye, Violet was throwing herself from the top of the platform and into a performance. She heard the satin fabric of her dress flitter through the air as she flew from one bar to the next, the gasps and appreciative claps of the crowd entangling with the beat of her own heart. The sound of it made Violet feel at home again, a smile working its way into the corners of her mouth as the flash of sparklers and turn of a ballerina's skirt reminded her of how she must look to the spectators, a shot of light that couldn't be stopped.

As her hands grasped what she knew to be the final bar, Violet felt a sudden pulse of worry start to slip down her spine, as it always did when she reached this part of her dream. But then she remembered that this wasn't the past any longer but her deepest desire for the future, and she shook away the fears lapping at her dangling ankles, feeling them slip from her skin just like ribbons that had loosened and were now drifting toward the sawdust.

"Wildfire," she heard Emil call to her, his voice carrying above the roar of the crowd.

Violet glanced up and saw that Emil was moving toward her, his body flying from one bar to the next until he was only a swing away, his hand outstretched as he sought to close the distance between them.

Before Violet gave herself a chance to fear the worst, she stretched her arms as far as they would go, her heart beating so hard in her chest that she thought her bones were going to break beneath the pressure.

But instead of grasping at air, as they always had before, Violet's fingers wrapped around Emil's wrist, giving him just the help he needed to grab hold of the bar.

When she could be certain that he was dangling there beside her and not crashing toward the ground, Violet turned to face Emil. He was gazing at her with the same mischievous smile that he had that first night he'd found her in the crowd and given her a taste of what it might be like to feel at home within herself.

And in that instant, Violet was no longer lost.

How could she when it was so clear where she wanted to be?

"Wildfire..."

Though Emil's body was pressed against hers, the sound of his voice felt far away, as if it was coming from somewhere outside the boundaries of her dream.

She moved closer, wondering if his words would sound clearer that way, but as she shifted, a rattling noise began to ripple the red and white stripes of the tent.

Violet's eyes flew open then, and she saw that the frames along the walls were shaking in the way they always did when the house was trying to wake her.

When she turned over, Violet realized that the window had been thrown open, the curtains covered in a fine layer of snow.

"Wildfire . . ."

The word whipped into the bedroom on the edge of the midnight wind, but instead of chilling Violet's skin, it warmed her to the bone.

Not bothering to throw her dressing gown about her shoulders or shove her feet into the slippers that the house was trying to nudge her way, Violet sprang from the bed, racing through the hallway and down the stairs in such a rush that the banisters began to shake for fear she'd slip and fall before she could reach the first floor.

But Violet couldn't be slowed, and before the railing could so much as bend forward a few inches to make it easier for her to grasp, she was already flinging open the front door, knowing with absolute certainty who would be waiting there to meet her.

Emil stood just beyond the threshold, his black curls sprinkled with snow.

Before the bitter cut of the wind could slip past the open door, Violet had pulled him close, needing to feel the touch of his skin to be certain that they weren't in her dream any longer.

"I know you wanted me to come in the spring," Emil said as Violet rested her face against him, one of her cheeks exposed to the harsh night chill and the other warmed by the rumble of his chest. "But I couldn't wait any longer."

He wrapped his arms tight around her then and shuddered, and Violet knew in an instant that it wasn't from the cold, but rather from the sheer relief of being able to pull her close again.

"This is exactly what I wanted," Violet answered, tucking herself deeper into Emil's embrace.

And as they stood there in the faint light of a crescent moon, Violet thought about the future and smiled.

CHAPTER 37

A Pen

Appears when a new chapter
is about to be written.

Though the wind was blowing so hard the next morning that it rattled all the windows of the bookshop, Beatrix failed to notice anything but the sound of her pen scratching against the page.

She'd slipped away from the Crescent Moon late in the night, wandering back toward the bookshop, where the thread of her new story had begun to weave its way into the very center of her thoughts. Scenes were starting to unfold in her imagination as quickly as a kettle that had finally decided to boil over, the texture of her characters' voices and rhythm of the tale somehow becoming more real than the ground beneath her boots.

As Beatrix had walked along the shadows of the street, she'd gradually let herself fade into the tale, each footstep a new line and every turn of a corner a shift in the plot.

By the time she'd stepped through the threshold of the bookshop, Beatrix hadn't even remembered to shut the door behind her or throw aside her snow-covered cloak, so lost was she in the words that were unfurling, ready to be printed on paper.

The bookshop, of course, had taken one glance at the hazy look in Beatrix's eyes and recognized it for what it was—the enchantment of falling thoroughly into a story.

The walls had shaken in absolute delight, guiding Beatrix this way and that, until she'd settled on the wingback chair in the corner of the room with a towering stack of blank pages and a cup of tea that never seemed to grow cold.

As she'd scribbled, the shop had grown warmer, too, the musky scent of old books giving way to the aroma of fresh paper and burning beeswax candles.

And many hours later, when the light had grown bright from sunrise and then started to dim again, the floorboards around Beatrix's feet were so covered in pages packed to the very edge with her scrawl that she couldn't see the hem of her skirts any longer.

So consumed was she by the sheer delight of finding herself again between paragraphs and periods that Beatrix almost didn't notice the sound of the front door creaking open.

It wasn't until the shop allowed some of the harsh bite of the wind to nip at her heels that Beatrix thought to look up from her work and discover that someone had joined her.

More than one pair of hands had grasped the handle of the bookshop that day, lured by the bright covers that were now displayed in the window and the promise of an hour or so's refuge from the winter cold, but the door had remained firmly shut to all who stood at the threshold . . . except this latest visitor.

"Jennings!" Beatrix gasped in surprise, scattering the pages that she'd been balancing against her knees.

Her spectacles, which were perched on the very edge of her nose, flew off as well, landing with a soft click on the floor.

"I'm interrupting you, aren't I?" Jennings asked with a shy

smile as he took in the sight of her practically buried beneath sheets of paper and a small mountain of teacups.

"Not at all," Beatrix said in a rush as she sprang from the chair and stepped toward him, brushing her hands over her hair and quickly realizing that her curls must have broken free of her chignon. "What a fright I must seem."

"You look wonderful," Jennings said as he lifted a hand to her cheek and began to wipe away one of the spots of ink that she'd managed to smear across her face. "Just the way you always do."

"I'm writing my next book, Jennings!" Beatrix cried, brimming over with excitement as she gestured toward the sea of papers scattered across the floor. "It's practically pouring out of me now."

"I can see that," Jennings replied with a grin, but his gaze remained fixed on her face.

"I wasn't going to tell you, but I'd been having trouble figuring out what to write next," Beatrix confessed.

"I know," Jennings said simply.

"You know?" Beatrix gasped. "What do you mean, you know?"

"You aren't the first writer to have a bit of trouble working through a new story," Jennings answered. "And you certainly won't be the last."

"But you didn't say anything," Beatrix said. "You didn't tell Mr. Stuart that he should be worried."

"There was never a doubt in my mind that you'd find your way again," Jennings replied, leaning closer to wipe another ink stain from the tip of Beatrix's nose. "Never a single doubt."

Beatrix watched as a lock of his brown hair fell against his forehead, and before she could think to stop herself, she pushed it back into place, forgetting that her hands were entirely bare and that the words impressed along her skin were pulsing with the thrill of her new story.

Jennings captured them between his own calloused palms,

staring at the words inscribed along her flesh with such intensity that Beatrix knew he was inspecting each and every syllable.

Shocked that she'd been so careless, Beatrix started to pull her hands away, but Jennings held them fast with a gentle pressure, not so much forcing her to remain still as extending an invitation to share a secret.

Beatrix did try to take a step back, just enough to catch her breath, but the shop didn't let her. It snagged the hem of her dress against one of the loose nails so that she couldn't help but remain where she was, standing in front of Jennings.

"I've been hiding something else as well," Beatrix whispered. "Something that I'm not quite sure I can explain."

Her gaze flickered across Jennings' face searching for a sign of disbelief or confusion, but all she saw there was the barest spark of something starting to kindle in his eyes. If she didn't know any better, Beatrix might have called it realization.

"I wanted to tell you," Beatrix continued to say. "I almost did a hundred times. But I've never been able to find the right words. I don't know if I can, even now."

"Beatrix," Jennings said, his voice laced with the same steady kindness that always made her erratic heart beat to a more restful rhythm. "I know this might seem like a strange thing to tell an author, but some things just can't be expressed in words. Perhaps it would be easier if you showed me."

Beatrix hesitated, knowing that whatever she decided to do next was going to throw her down one of two paths. It was the same crossroads her mother must have faced so long ago, when she'd fallen in love and had to decide which trail to follow. The first was laden with secrets left untold and distance that couldn't be closed, but it was familiar and safe, a route that many witches of her kind had stepped along. The other was more uncertain. There was a chance it could lead her toward distrust and wariness, severed ties that couldn't be stitched back together.

But it wasn't the dangers that Beatrix thought of while her hands rested in the warmth of Jennings' grasp.

It was the memory of how she held her breath every time her eyes searched for his in a crowded room. The sound of their laughter entangling in the train car. The list she was always adding to in her mind, of things that she'd need to tell Jennings because they were sure to make him smile.

It was, quite simply, happiness.

And with that thought in mind, Beatrix closed her eyes and let the full force of her magic flicker to life, the strains of her story glowing so bright that she knew they were illuminating the words inscribed across her hands.

She stood in silence for a few moments, terrified of opening her eyes and seeing Jennings' kind features twisted into horror.

But before she could see if her deepest worries had come to life, Jennings' hands were no longer cradling her fingers but wrapped in her curls, pulling her closer until his lips were on hers.

And in an instant, Beatrix was losing herself in another story altogether. One that felt just like coming home.

They would have remained there, entangled in one another as their daydreams slipped into reality, but the bookshop, which had always been a fan of a good romance, couldn't contain its excitement.

The pink buds painted on the wallpaper suddenly bloomed, the petals coming to life and fluttering to the floorboards. And some of the books along the shelves exploded, scattering so many delicate strips of confetti that anyone glancing through the windows might have thought the snow was starting to fall through the roof.

Once Beatrix managed to collect herself enough to understand what was going on, she turned to Jennings, her lips parting to plead with him to stay and not run straight out the door and onto the street.

But, once again, he surprised her.

"An enchanted bookshop!" he laughed in the same wondrous tone that someone might if they'd found themselves stepping straight into one of their favorite fantasies. "I can't think of anything more perfect."

He paused then and stared down at Beatrix, his arms still wrapped around her waist with strips of torn book pages falling from his hair.

"Except for you," he added with a smile that made Beatrix's heart melt.

And as she reached up to pull his lips back to hers, Beatrix couldn't help but think that Philip had been right.

A good story has no end.

CHAPTER 38

A Cardinal

*Emerges alongside a message from
someone who has passed on.*

Snowflakes caught in the curves of Anne's curls as she gazed at the blackthorn that had taken root in Mr. Crowley's grave.

She should have been unnerved by the sight of the thick tangle of thorns that rose from the soil and twisted upward despite the heavy weight of the ice and unrelenting pull of the wind.

But as she reached a hand toward the branches, the magic that had latched on to the soil pulsed against her skin, and all she could think about was how striking the thorns looked against the stark white of the snow. They reminded her that even the slightest seed of hope can sprout in the direst of conditions. She could nearly feel the power radiating from the roots through the soles of her shoes, a silent murmur that somehow managed to cut through the cold and warm the tips of her toes.

As Anne closed her eyes to listen to the gentle hum, she began to realize that the sound of snow crunching beneath someone's footsteps was drawing closer and closer.

By the time she thought to turn, she could smell the scent

of myrrh and had already guessed who she would see standing beside her. She would know him anywhere.

"I didn't expect to find you here," Vincent said as he stopped at the foot of the grave, just close enough that Anne could have brushed the tips of her fingers against his sleeve if she tried.

"Neither did I," Anne replied, some of the cold in her fingers thawing as she leaned closer to Vincent and tucked a hand through the crook of his arm. "But I woke up this morning and found the outline of a coat on the rim of my cup."

"And what does that mean?" Vincent asked.

"Sadness brought on by parting with someone you love," Anne explained as she turned back to the blackthorn bush. "I suppose that I still needed to say one last goodbye."

They stood at the foot of the grave and watched the branches brush against one another in the wind, more so finding their footing in the silence than slipping away from the present moment.

"Have you come to do the same?" Anne finally asked after the wind died down a bit and the branches became still again.

"I'm not sure why I'm here," Vincent admitted. "Everything's been put to rights. The house has opened its doors to my family again, and our power is startling to trickle back. I can hear the spirits whispering now even when I don't call for them, their voices growing clearer and more hopeful with every passing moment."

"But you aren't quite settled yet," Anne said, more a comment than a question.

"No," Vincent replied. "I'm not."

Anne glanced at him out of the corner of her eye, trying to read the firm set of his jaw and lines of his face for a sign of what he might be thinking.

He was staring straight down at the blackthorn bush, trying to peer between the branches to see the stone that had been buried beneath, his expression as hard as the granite that Mr. Crowley's name was etched upon.

"I don't think he meant to keep the ring away from your family forever," Anne said, assuming that Vincent might still be clinging to some resentment over his uncle's choice to leave his Task undone. "He wasn't trying to punish you."

Vincent turned to face Anne then, one of his brows lifting ever so slightly.

"What?" Anne asked, confused.

"Nothing," Vincent said. "It's only that I thought you might have realized."

"What are you talking about?" Anne asked, shifting so that they were facing each other now.

"I don't think my uncle intended to hide the ring away at all," Vincent continued. "Otherwise, why would he have picked you of all people to leave it to?"

"I'm not sure what you mean," Anne admitted.

"He could have left the ring to anyone. Or better yet, tossed it in the gutter where it didn't have a hope of being picked up ever again. But he didn't. He left it to you," Vincent said.

"I still don't see . . . ," Anne murmured.

"If my uncle didn't want the ring returned, why would he have given it to the one witch who'd be able to figure out how to fit all the pieces together at just the right moment?" Vincent asked.

Stunned, Anne shifted her gaze back to the blackthorn bush, wondering if what Vincent said could be true. Had Mr. Crowley left her the ring because he knew that she'd discover where it belonged?

"I think he knew that the journey to finishing his Task would help put all of us on the right course," Vincent murmured as his gaze shifted away from the tombstone, the tension in his expression softening the barest whisper as his eyes came to rest on Anne's face.

"That in trying to tie together the loose threads, we'd find pieces of ourselves that we didn't know were missing in the first place."

"Then why are you here?" Anne asked curiously. "If you feel so strongly that your uncle wanted you to be happy in the end, what are you still searching for?"

Vincent looked as if he was going to draw back into himself then. The icy mask that had become a familiar sight was already starting to stiffen his features. But before it could reach his eyes, something gave way, and he released a deep sigh.

"When someone comes to us searching for help, the trouble isn't often tied to anything they did to the person who's passed on," Vincent explained. "What keeps them from feeling at rest are the actions that they neglected to take. Arguments and broken promises: those are things that you can hope someone forgave knowing what your true feelings were. It's what you leave unsaid that lingers on and makes you wonder."

"Wonder what?" Anne whispered.

"If they knew they were loved," Vincent whispered. "That they weren't alone."

"He must have known how you felt," Anne insisted.

"I'm not so sure," Vincent said, his mouth tightening as he reached a hand toward the branches. "He held himself apart, and I never asked why. Never tried to understand what he was trying to protect beneath all those thorns that kept everyone at bay. Perhaps, if I had . . . but now I'll never know. It's the words I failed to say, you see, that haunt me still. I tried speaking to him after he passed, but even in death, he would not let me any closer."

"You can't keep carrying that kind of burden," Anne murmured. "It will gnaw at you from within until there's nothing left but a shell."

"I know," Vincent said, drawing his hand even closer to the grave. "But that doesn't stop me from wondering."

The moment Vincent's fingertips touched the bush, though,

his thumb nicked the edge of one of the thorns, breaking the skin and causing a few drops of blood to drip onto the branches.

Before Anne was aware of what she was doing, she stepped toward Vincent and reached for his hand. She held it in her own, assessing the wound and reaching into her reticule for a handkerchief to press against it, but before she could retrieve the cloth, her attention was drawn back to the blackthorn, which was starting to shift of its own accord.

At first, Anne thought the wind must be rustling the branches, but she didn't feel a chill whipping against her cheeks. Then, ever so slowly, plump green buds began to grow along the bare branches, softening the sharpness of the thorns before bursting into thousands of delicate white flowers. They looked startlingly beautiful beneath the falling snow, all the hard edges having given way to something far more inviting.

Vincent's hand gripped Anne's as he gazed at the flowers, as if he needed some sense of purchase while taking in the sight that had unfolded before them.

For blackthorn that grew on a grave of a witch bloomed only when someone they loved pricked their fingers against one of its thorns.

"He left you a sign after all," Anne whispered.

"I suppose you're right," Vincent said as he continued to gaze at the buds that were still unfurling, his steely expression having softened at the sight. "As you so often are."

Anne placed her other hand atop Vincent's and leaned against his shoulder as they took in the sight unfurling before them.

Soon, she'd need to return to the chaos of the tearoom, where whispers of new troubles would come to her attention as quickly as steam pouring from the top of a spout.

But for now, she was content to merely savor the scent of flowers blooming in the snow and the comfort of knowing that there are two things in this world stronger than death: stories and love.

CHAPTER 39

Flowers
Symbolize new beginnings.

The Quigley sisters knew it was the first true day of spring the morning they awoke to the scent of beeswax and found their best lace tablecloth missing from the linen closet.

The house always shooed them out into the garden when it decided that the change in the seasons was here to stay, expecting them to enjoy their tea and scones out in the sunshine while it threw open the windows and shook away the dust that had gathered in the corners during the winter.

By suppertime, the floors would glisten as brightly as a looking glass, and all the cinnamon sticks and cedar in the front parlor would have disappeared, replaced by vases brimming over with lilac.

And the day after, when the first customer stepped over the threshold, they would draw in the fresh scent of new beginnings and stand a bit straighter, the weight of long winter evenings quickly fading as daydreams about warm summer afternoons started to take shape.

But before then, the sisters were expected to stay out of the way and simply enjoy the sensation of watching the world wake once again.

"Some things never change, do they?" Violet murmured to Anne as she stepped out of the kitchen and took in the sight of the garden, which was so bursting with daffodils, tulips, and azaleas of the richest pinks and purples that it seemed she'd never be able to look through anything but a pair of rose-colored glasses.

"The most important things never do," Anne replied as she joined Violet in the doorway and wrapped a hand around her waist, giving her a soft tug as they breathed in the singular scent of spring.

Violet turned toward Anne and smiled, her eyes as bright as they had been when Anne first saw her flying across the circus tent.

She and Emil had returned to the ring only a week ago, but Anne could already tell that Violet's heart was beating to that familiar tempo again. The doubt that had so weighed on her sister no longer had any hope of keeping her grounded. On the opening night of the circus's run in Chicago, she'd flown from one bar to the next as if she'd been born with a set of wings and had made a home in the sky.

"Where do we want these?" Emil asked, his voice laced with excitement as he walked into the garden with a croquet set, the wooden sticks worn about the handles from so many years of lively competition in the summer sunshine.

"Anywhere will do," Anne replied as she walked toward the lace-covered table, where Vincent was waiting to hand her a steaming cup that smelled of green tea and elderflowers. "I'm sure it won't be long before we start to play."

His clothes were still a striking shade of black, but all the hard edges that had once marked Vincent's face seemed to have melted along with the snow.

When Emil and Violet turned their backs, trying to determine where to place the posts for their game, he pulled Anne close and whispered something that carried the texture of a shared secret, his lips grazing her ear as he spoke.

"You'll have to keep an eye on her," Beatrix chimed from where she was standing near the gate, her eyes locked on the alleyway that turned onto the street. "Anne's not beneath kicking someone else's ball an inch or two out of the way when no one is looking."

"I most certainly would do nothing of the kind," Anne huffed, trying her best to hide the smile that was tugging at the corners of her mouth. "What are you doing standing over there, anyway?"

"I've invited a guest," Beatrix said, her cheeks growing just pink enough for Anne to guess who might make an appearance.

Though Beatrix had been shy about bringing Jennings around at first, thinking that it would be best to introduce him to a world where magic beat at its core in small steps, once the house learned that he'd been told the truth, it wouldn't let the man out of its sight.

Violet might be marked for a life of movement, but the Crescent Moon was still hopeful that Beatrix could be drawn closer again.

It believed that dazzling Jennings with the magical comforts of home and hearth could be the key to convincing Beatrix to stay, and every time he came to visit, he'd end up lingering hours longer than he'd intended, transfixed by dancing teacups and rooms that seemed to appear from the depths of someone's daydreams.

"Here he comes now!" Violet cried as she leaned forward to better hear the footsteps echoing against the cobblestones. "And it sounds like he's brought someone with him."

A moment later, Jennings appeared at the gate, his hand tucked politely in the crook of May's arm.

She'd abandoned her heavy, dark satin for a lavender linen blouse and straw hat lined with fresh peonies, and the change reminded Anne just how much lighter she looked since that evening in the kitchen months before.

"Isn't this lovely?" she said, her voice as wonderstruck as a child's as she let Jennings help her through the gate and into the splendor of the garden. "Like something from a fairy tale."

"I'm so glad you could come," Beatrix said as she stepped forward and squeezed one of May's hands.

The two of them had become fast friends, drawn together by their shared love of stories and a strong cup of tea.

"Have you finished it?" May asked, a glimmer of anticipation flitting across her eyes as she waited to hear what Beatrix might say.

Beatrix had thrown herself into the new book project, writing from the early hours of the morning until she fell asleep, oftentimes in the worn wingback chair with her hands still gripping the pen. It seemed like the story's characters were pushing her to introduce them to the world as quickly as possible, and she'd lost herself in all the best ways while helping them do just that.

May had been the one to stop by the bookshop every day to ensure that Beatrix was taking a moment to drink a cup of tea and stretch her weary back. And more often than not, she would find herself losing track of time as she sat in another chair that had appeared in the front of the shop, quickly falling into the even rhythm of a story that she'd never read before. The two would sit in companionable silence, the noise that Beatrix's pen made as it scratched into the paper entangling with the sound of turning pages as May moved from one chapter to the next. And before they knew it, the bells of the front door were chiming as Jennings came to pay a visit after the doors of Donohoe & Company had closed for the day.

Of course, it had been too much of a temptation for May to not peek at Beatrix's new novel, and now it was all she could think about. The characters had even started to slip into her dreams, their story unfolding in vivid detail while she slept, only to disappear when the sun started to emerge between the cracks in the curtains and she'd failed to reach the end.

"I have," Beatrix answered with a grin. "I finished the final chapter just last night and can't wait for you to read it."

"It's absolutely wonderful," Jennings chimed in, full of enthusiasm. "The best she's written yet."

"You've read it already, have you?" Violet asked coyly, seemingly unsurprised that Jennings had been by Beatrix's side when she finished the novel in the early hours of the morning.

A blush as red as the begonias flashed across Beatrix's cheeks, and Jennings shifted nervously from one foot to the other, though they couldn't quite keep the smiles from their eyes.

"I have something to share as well," May said as she pulled a piece of paper from her purse and handed it to Beatrix.

"I don't understand," Beatrix murmured as she read what was printed there. "It's the deed to the bookshop."

May waited in silent expectation as Beatrix's eyes came to rest on the final line of the document, where her own name was printed.

"It's mine?" Beatrix whispered.

"It's yours," May said. "If you'll have it. Brigit and her husband were only too willing to sell the building when I made my offer. They are both quite eager to move to warmer climates, it seems."

"But why?" Beatrix asked.

"Because it's what Philip would have wanted," May answered. "To bring the shop and its readers to life again."

"You want me to reopen it," Beatrix said, a note of understanding drifting into her tone.

"I know it's a lot for me to ask," May replied, a trace of hesitation creeping into her voice. "Running the shop might seem like too much to balance with your writing."

"I'll be there to help," Jennings chimed in as he took a step forward before turning to face Beatrix. "That is, if you'll have me."

They all caught the underlying meaning of Jennings' words, even the house, which stilled the pleasant breeze that had been playing at the edge of the lace tablecloth so that it wouldn't miss a single moment of what would come next.

"I'd like that, John," Beatrix finally said as she took his hand in her own. "I'd like that very much indeed."

The house, which was thrilled to its very rafters that Beatrix would have something more solid than childhood memories to root her to the city, had to resist the urge to fling open its shutters and bang all the pots and pans in the kitchen. But it couldn't keep from loosening some of the flower petals so that they caught in Beatrix's curls and the brim of Jennings' hat.

"Cheers to the happy couple!" Violet exclaimed as she lifted her teacup in the air.

But before she could lower it and take another sip, Anne pulled away from Vincent to grasp the handle, peering over the rim.

"What is it?" Violet asked as she let Anne take the cup, clearly frightened by her surprised expression.

Anne's gaze flitted from the rim to Violet and back as she tried to piece everything together, but then a wide smile settled across her face.

"My birthday vision," Anne said. "It wasn't of the past at all."

"You mean the girl's laughter?" Violet asked. "But if it wasn't a memory, what could it be? And how do my tea leaves fit into it?"

"Look here," Anne said as she pointed to a sign at the top of the cup, not so close that it would happen in an instant but far enough away from the bottom to hint that something important was waiting in the not-too-distant future. "Four magpies perched just beneath the handle."

Anne waited for Violet to remember what the sign meant.

One magpie warned of bad luck.

Two hinted at good fortune.

Three flew to the rim just before a wedding.

And four...

"A birth," Violet whispered as her eyes widened in realization.

She caught Emil's gaze over the rim of the cup, clearly wondering whether he understood the significance of what she'd said. But he was already grinning from ear to ear, as if he'd just been told a wish was about to come true.

"It seems that the world's about to meet another Quigley witch," Anne said as she and Beatrix drew closer to Violet.

When they pressed their heads together, the sound of childish laughter rang through their thoughts, an echo of all the best of the past carrying on into the future.

Acknowledgments

I've always wanted to write a story with an enchanted bookshop. When I was younger, I'd close my eyes when I first crossed the thresholds of these storefronts so that the scent of stories was more potent: the aroma of aged paper with a hint of vanilla pulling me to places beyond reasonable possibility. And since then, books and the walls that shelter them have only grown more magical.

In many ways, I hope this book expresses just how much I love and appreciate all the people involved in the process of making a story come alive. From the editors, agents, designers, and publicity teams who see a spark of something special and put all their work into fanning it to life to the readers who decide to pick up a book and welcome it into their world. I'm especially grateful, of course, to all the booksellers who've not only fostered my love of the written word from the very beginning but have also made my wildest dreams comes true during my debut year as an author. I've been truly honored by your enthusiasm for my stories and will be forever grateful for the hint of wonder that you bring to the lives of those who walk into your shops.

I'd like to extend a special thanks, as always, to my editor, Elizabeth Hitti, who once again helped me take the first draft of this manuscript and make it something truly magical. My agent and literary fairy godmother, Adria Goetz, has also been the strongest foundation of support during my first year as a full-time author, and I'm extraordinarily lucky to have her at my side. And then, of course, there's the whole Atria team who made my launch nothing short of a daydream. A very special thanks here to Dayna Johnson, Holly Rice-Baturin, Morgan Pager, James Iacobelli, Jim Tierney, Annette Pagliaro Sweeney, Kyoko Watanabe, Barbara Wild, Lacee Burr, and Nicole Bond.

I would also like to express my gratitude to my family, whose support has made this transition into writing fiction possible. My parents, siblings, and friends have displayed such enthusiasm for my stories, and it means the world to have them cheering me on. Finally, I'd like to thank my husband, Sebastián, for encouraging me to follow my dreams, especially the ones that seem impossible.

About the Author

Stacy Sivinski is the nationally bestselling author of *The Crescent Moon Tearoom*. She holds a PhD in English from the University of Notre Dame with a specialty in sensory studies and nineteenth-century women's writing. In her fiction, Stacy focuses on themes of sisterhood, self-discovery, and magic.

ATRIA BOOKS, an imprint of Simon & Schuster, fosters an open environment where ideas flourish, bestselling authors soar to new heights, and tomorrow's finest voices are discovered and nurtured. Since its launch in 2002, Atria has published hundreds of bestsellers and extraordinary books, which would not have been possible without the invaluable support and expertise of its team and publishing partners. Thank you to the Atria Books colleagues who collaborated on *The Witching Moon Manor*, as well as to the hundreds of professionals in the Simon & Schuster advertising, audio, communications, design, ebook, finance, human resources, legal, marketing, operations, production, sales, supply chain, subsidiary rights, and warehouse departments who help Atria bring great books to light.

Editorial
Elizabeth Hitti

Jacket Design
James Iacobelli
Jim Tierney
Emma Van Deun

Marketing
Dayna Johnson
Morgan Pager

Managing Editorial
Lacee Burr
Paige Lytle
Shelby Pumphrey

Production
Vanessa Silverio
Annette Pagliaro Sweeney
Yvonne Taylor
Janet Robbins Rosenberg

Publicity
Holly Rice-Baturin

Publishing Office
Suzanne Donahue
Abby Velasco

Subsidiary Rights
Nicole Bond
Rebecca Justiniano
Sara Bowne